Imperial Conflict

Imperial Conflict

Le Québécois series—Part III

A NOVEL

DORIS PROVENCHER FAUCHER

ARTENAY PRESS

Copyright © 2006 by Doris P. Faucher

Cover photo © National Maritime Museum, London.
Pocock, Nicholas. *The Battle of Quiberon Bay,* 1812.

ARTENAY PRESS
P.O. Box 664, Biddeford ME 04005

http://home.maine.rr.com/artenayp/
artenayp@maine.rr.com

Library of Congress Control Number: 2006909250

ISBN-13: 978-0-9679112-0-5
ISBN-10: 0-9679112-0-6

Manufactured in the United States of America.

First edition: October 2006

This book is dedicated to my husband, our immediate and extended family, our many old and new friends and acquaintances who often unexpectedly provided valuable historical and genealogical information.
Their generous support often guided me through a labyrinth of research in my efforts to connect the genealogical to the historical records.

One

Champlain, autumn 1715

Louis and Simonne rushed out to greet his older sisters and brother-in-law with a flurry of hugs and smiles and exclamations. They hadn't seen each other in several years; not since Madeleine and Aubin had moved their family to Longueil where he became a butcher and sold animal hides. Marguerite and Antoine had moved to Île Dupas to be closer to his fur-trader contacts in Montréal and to their daughter Renée's children.

Madeleine was dressed in mourning. She seemed quieter than usual but as strong-willed as they had always known her to be. Simonne immediately approached and hugged her in sympathy. "We were so sorry to hear about Aubin. This must be a difficult time for you—a time to be with family. Come right in and make yourself comfortable. How was your journey?"

Louis ushered them into the house. "We were so happy to receive your letter, Antoine! So glad you could come for the wedding!"

Louis' sons saw to the horses and brought in the luggage while their guests huddled by the warmth of the fire.

The couple's children joined the adults and the youngest were introduced to their aunts and uncle. After the initial exchange of greetings, the older daughters slipped into the kitchen to prepare a special dinner for their guests.

"You must have stopped somewhere last night. How were your accommodations?" Louis asked.

Marguerite smiled her mother's smile and told him: "We visited with close friends in Louiseville who put us up for the night. Our fur robes kept us warm enough along the way."

Antoine added: "Ice hasn't formed on the rivers yet. We traveled by *chaloupe* to the landing at the cape where we rented the calèche. The roads were dry and passable and river crossings manageable by bridge or ferry. The ferrymen assured us that our return trip should go just as well."

Louis turned toward his oldest sister. "I wish we could have been there for you, Madeleine. Is there anything we can do for you? Have you considered moving back to this area?"

She seemed to wake from reverie. "I appreciate your concern, Louis, but our children live nearby. We've remained a close-knit family since moving to Saint-François-du-Lac. Aubin had finally found work in Longueil that paid him well. The children have been providing our grain and vegetables for quite some time. Thanks to *Maman*'s spinning wheel and loom, I've always been able to produce enough linen and other homespun cloth for them. We continue to help each other."

"That must keep you very busy!" Simonne remarked.

"I don't mind that at all. I've always enjoyed working with fiber and cloth. Our four youngest still live at home, and several grandchildren live nearby. My days are as full now as they've ever been."

"I can understand why you'd want to stay close to them," Louis acknowledged, "but don't hesitate to let us know if you need anything." His wife nodded in agreement.

"Thank you for that, both of you, but there's no need for you to worry about me. I do plan to keep in touch with the rest of the family from now on. I hardly recognized your children when they came in just now. It made me realize how quickly time slips by— Now tell us about the wedding arrangements. Jeanne must be so excited!"

Simonne replied: "We've known the Carpentier family for years; Médard is a fine young man. They'll be living nearby in Champlain, you know."

"That's good. There aren't many of us left on the cape, are there? How are our two brothers doing?" Marguerite asked Louis.

"Sébastien continues to accept new concessions across the river," he replied. "Once he clears and develops a new lot, he sells it at a profit and moves on to more virgin areas. He seems to be working his way westward along the south shore. On the other hand, François continues to raise his family on his original lot, but he bought a second piece of land in Bécancour a few years back. They both continue to work well with each other."

Marguerite noticed his frown. "Is anything wrong?"

"When Bishop Saint-Vallier decreed that we must build a new stone church here at the cape, François reacted quite strongly against it. He decided that it's unfair to expect the settlers on the south shore to support such a project while they need a church of their own and the bishop won't grant them permission to build it."

"Why would he prevent them from building their own church?" Antoine asked.

"As *marguillier*, I'm caught in the middle of all this. We've informed Monseigneur that the population growth in this area has shifted to the south shore, that only eleven local families are left to contribute to the support of this parish."

This surprised their guests.

"But he's greatly impressed with our Confraternity of the Rosary which is one of the oldest such devotions in Canada. Last year, he personally inspected all the churches in the Trois Rivières region and was convinced that our old wooden chapel was falling apart and disrespectful toward Our Lady of the Rosary. He remarked that because of the great shortage of priests in Nouvelle France, worship of the settlers across the river will be dependent on this parish for quite some time whether or not they eventually have their own church."

Madeleine protested. "We were all married in that wooden church, our children were baptized, *Maman* and Papa were buried there. It seems a shame to see it go!"

Louis agreed and explained to Antoine: "Papa helped to move the original wooden chapel from fief Sainte-Marie and rebuild it on its present site shortly after he arrived from France.

"How does the bishop expect you to pay for all this?" Antoine asked.

"He'll personally contribute funds to the project and raise donations from former parishioners who have moved toward Montréal and Québec. He also expects that the habitants and tradesmen on both sides of the river will voluntarily contribute their time and labor during the construction."

"This sounds like a major undertaking. Is there enough stone and firewood here at the cape?"

"We'll have to gather what we can and collect the rest from across the river."

Simonne added: "François wasn't alone in resisting the bishop's decree; most of the settlers on the south shore were of the same mind. They insisted that the cape parishioners pledge to support them in the construction of their own church once this one is completed."

"That seems fair enough," said Antoine.

Louis nodded in agreement. "The argument continued until Intendant Bégon ordered a joint parish meeting last June to settle the matter. The people on this side of the river finally gave in to their demands."

"Then the matter was resolved?"

Louis smiled. "Would you believe that François and René Leblanc still refuse to pay their tithes?"

Once the laughter subsided, Marguerite observed: "Those two grew up next door to each other and they're still sticking together!"

Louis shrugged his shoulders.

Simonne asked Marguerite: "How are your grandchildren?"

"They seem to be doing well. Renée was a good mother in the short time she had with them; that seems to have had a lasting effect. Of course, their lives have greatly changed since her death. Did you know that their father remarried nine months later?"

"No, we didn't."

"With four very young children all born within three years, it was quite a burden for him no matter how much we tried to help — his business takes up so much of his time.

"His second wife is a lovely young woman close to Renée's age, perhaps a little younger. She's been very accepting of our presence. Our two young daughters have been very good with the children."

Louis interjected: "How are your sons doing?"

"They're old enough to fend for themselves," Antoine replied. "The two oldest have their own land now and live nearby. We're close enough to each other so that we often team up to work in the fields."

They continued to reminisce over a brandy and a hot meal until Madeleine's eyes begin to close despite her best efforts. They soon retired for the night in anticipation of the work that lay ahead of them the following morning. Their stepbrother Baptiste Massé would need their help in preparing the old homestead for the wedding reception.

Baptiste and their three youngest sisters welcomed their arrival. They all agreed that the midday reception and banquet should be held in this house, but since it was not large enough to accommodate all of the expected guests, they decided to set up the barn for the music and dance. This required that they straighten out and clean that area which normally provided work and storage space for a variety of farm equipment and provisions. Baptiste recommended that they provide benches along the walls for their guests, a chore that would keep the men busy for the rest of the day.

While the women prepared to bake batches of bread and tarts for the buffet, their daughters moved unneeded furniture and equipment from the downstairs area to temporary storage in the loft.

Louis came by later that morning to deliver some table linen, serving dishes, bottles of wine and casks of cider. He walked over to the barn where he found the men in one of its deeper corners, puzzling over four heavy wooden pieces of equipment that had been stored, covered, and obviously forgotten over the years. He quickly recognized these as sections of the ropewalk equipment that his father had used when he and his brothers were still young children.

Antoine was amazed. "Are you saying that Bastien actually made his own rope?"

Louis nodded. "Not only for his own use, but also for the local stores. Papa offered shelter to an elderly Norman sailor who had served as ropemaker on the ship that brought him to Nouvelle France. René Le Cordier could no longer sail and would have been stranded in Québec had they not decided to make and sell rope to the local merchants. Rope and cable were rarely available in the colony at that time."

This reminder about the ropewalk reawakened Louis' cherished memories of his youth. He later found his original bow and arrows. He tested the bow, its string snapped apart. The stone-tipped arrows were still sound, but their bindings to the shafts had rotted, and their feather strips had fallen away.

As legal guardian of the bride, Louis had come by to pick up Jeanne and take her home with him for the notarized reading and signing of her marriage contract with Médard Carpentier. The groom's family would witness the event, as would Louis' children, his son-in-law Pierre Picard, and his lifelong friend François Rochereau.

The document that notary Normandin read that afternoon was typical of such formal civil agreements. It noted the time and place of the reading, named all those who were present, and in this case identified the widowed father of the groom, and the deceased parents and guardian of the bride. It related the financial arrangements agreed to by the couple regarding the merging of their worldly goods, the division of their common estate should one predecease the other, and it committed them to marry within the Catholic Church as soon as possible. The groom pledged to his wife a *douaire préfix* of 500 livres and a *douaire préciput* of 300 livres should she survive him. Her guardian Louis formally released Jeanne's family inheritance which amounted to 110 livres in French currency, but was necessarily presented to the couple in the colonial equivalent 170 livres of card money. Louis also officially released control over Jeanne's personal and real property including a portion of land that she had inherited following her mother's death.

The couple's acceptance of the contract was signed by several of the witnesses: Médard's father, Louis as the bride's guardian, his daughter Angélique, his son-in-law Pierre Picard, and François Rochereau.

Family and friends filled the old wooden church of Sainte-Marie-Madeleine that following morning as Abbé Paul Vachon united the couple in Christian matrimony and celebrated their nuptial Mass. Louis and Simonne both knew how proud his father Bastien and her mother Catherine would have been to witness their oldest daughter's wedding ceremony.

The bride wore a *coiffe flottante* over her hair, one of natural homespun and fine linen edged with lace that Simonne had tatted and sewn together for her. The groom's hair was tied back with a ribbon bow. He was dressed in matching brown serge breeches, waistcoat and frock coat, a ruffled linen shirt, clocked silk stockings and leather buckled shoes.

Wedding guests followed the couple back to the reception and presented a variety of gifts, the most notable of which included copper candelabra and oil lamps, pewter cups and dishes from the groom's relatives. Jeanne's sisters gave their family's more traditional bed and table linen of homemade cloth and needlework. Louis and Simonne gave them a carving set, kitchen utensils, and pewter flatware. Her brother François presented a handmade wooden chest on which he had reproduced their father's periwinkle carving. Another brother Sébastien and sister Anne gave the couple a woolen blanket that they had purchased, and a quilt that she had pieced together for them. Jeanne immediately placed these into the chest and hugged her brothers and sisters.

The buffet consisted of ham, turkey, fish, and root vegetable dishes; pork, fruit, and maple sugar tarts; fresh baked bread and home-churned butter; wine, beer, eau-de-vie, and cider.

The younger people moved toward the lively cadence set by fiddle, spoons, recorder, and jaw harp that emanated from the barn. The ladies remained in the house awhile and discussed the bride's trousseau, the gifts, and their own children.

Antoine managed some time alone with François. "I understand that there's to be a new church built here at the cape," he began.

His youngest brother-in-law and former neighbor broke into a smile. "So you've heard. What have you been told so far?"

"That it's to be a larger, more permanent structure built of stone and that the settlers of Bécancour and Dutort continue to resist having to contribute to it."

"You know what it's like to raise a young family at Bécancour—how hazardous and major an undertaking it is to cross the river with women and young children. Most of us continue to attend Mass and receive the sacraments at the Abenaki mission and at the small chapel at Nicolet."

"That small chapel was built five years ago just as we prepared to move to Sorel. Is it still a small log structure?"

François nodded and added: "With thatched roof and built on the riverside. It has four roughly-hewn wooden benches on both sides of the center aisle, each of which is long enough to seat four people. The *Récollet* priests from Trois Rivières continue to serve the community as a mission ever since the peace treaty was signed in Montréal. We've voluntarily supported their work ever since."

Antoine sympathized. He understood a father's concern for his children's spiritual development but surely never at the risk of their personal safety.

"What did you people on the south shore hope to achieve by resisting the bishop's decree?"

"We simply insisted that once the new stone church was built with our help, the parishioners of Cap-de-la-Madeleine should in turn assist us in building an adequate church to meet our needs on the south shore."

"That seems reasonable enough," Antoine agreed.

"But the pastor and bishop insist that we must continue to pay our tithes to support the parish of Sainte-Marie-Madeleine after we have provided volunteer labor and materials to their building project here at the cape."

Antoine frowned and asked François about his family and his crops.

Louis and Sébastien joined them and once they had all caught up on family news, Louis asked Antoine: "How are the people of Sorel reacting to the loss of *Acadie*?"

"Those of us who arrived from France sailed close to that area before entering the Saint Lawrence River. We realize that England now controls our only access route to France, but the Canadian-born settlers have no idea how threatening that could prove to be. What I'm most concerned about, Louis, is that our half-year access to shipping to and from France could be in jeopardy. That would certainly leave us at the mercy of the English."

"I've heard reports that France is building a great fort on Cap-Breton to protect us against that threat."

"Let's hope it does."

Pierre Picard had joined them by now, and so had their sons who rarely had the opportunity to participate in such a serious discussion.

Louis' son Jean-Baptiste asked Antoine: "You've made many voyages out west *mon oncle*. How did you get started?"

"Shortly after I arrived in Nouvelle France, I happened to do business with a fur merchant. My first job for him was to cut and deliver eight hundred wide boards cut to a specific length. He paid me with merchandise worth 320 livres and that allowed me to buy my first parcel of land. I set myself up on two arpents frontage in Bécancour and that's where I first met your grandfather and your Aunt Marguerite."

"Did you voyage *aux pays d'en haut* for that merchant?" Sébastien's Jean-Baptiste asked.

"No, but he recommended me as a domestic to Jean Le Moyne, another fur merchant who was *seigneur de Sainte-Marie*, and I apprenticed with his voyageurs."

"Papa told us that his first voyage was with Nicolas Perrot," said Louis' son.

"Yes, your papa was very fortunate to train under a master voyageur."

"What is it like, to live and travel in the forest for a whole year?" asked another nephew.

"It's certainly not as comfortable as being at home, especially at night when it's cold or rainy." Louis replied, and Antoine nodded in agreement. "The work is often very hard, but there's a certain sense of freedom that makes up for that." He hesitated as he tried to recall how his own father had described the experience. "The scenery is beautiful and constantly changes as you travel deeper into the forest. Your *pépère* told us that it allows you to enjoy land, water, and sky just as God created them."

Louis' younger son, Joseph, asked him: "Why did you want to go?"

"When your mother and I decided to marry, it was the quickest and surest way for me to raise the means to establish a home for us. Besides that, my papa had traveled overland to Hudson Bay when I was just a child; I always remembered what a profound experience it had been for him."

"And of course, Joseph, your own papa was also trained by an Algonquin chief who was highly respected among the western natives," Antoine added. "Your papa already understood their native language."

Louis added: "I've tried to share those skills with you during our camping and hunting trips into the forest."

"Have you ever missed voyaging?" asked his oldest son.

"Rarely," Louis smiled. "Only at times like this when I'm reminded of what it was like. Otherwise, I've been perfectly happy to stay home with my family and watch you grow into young men who obviously yearn to do the things Antoine and I have done."

His son-in-law Pierre Picard spoke up. "My sister recently married a fur merchant in Montréal, and he's looking for next year's voyageurs. Is anyone interested in applying?"

Louis and Antoine quickly looked at each other. Louis had a lively look in his eyes; Antoine, who was older, did not.

"Can you tell us more about him?" Louis asked.

"His name is Louis Ducharme and he's been quite active."

Louis scanned the room to locate his wife and saw her looking his way. His cheeks colored slightly; he felt that she must have sensed what was on his mind.

She made her way over to him and asked: "What are you men discussing?"

Her son Jean-Baptiste blurted out: "Papa may be thinking of voyaging again!"

Two

Médard and Jeanne prepared to leave the reception by mid-afternoon. His family had already loaded the couple's gifts and the bride's property into a wagon, and were ready to deliver these to their new home in Champlain. The remaining guests gradually said their goodbyes and left before dusk. Those who were to cross the river boarded a shallop that Louis had hired for their safe return home. Antoine's sons and Louis' brothers were among them.

Louis and his house guests stayed awhile and discussed the day's events with Baptiste and their younger sisters as they helped straighten out the old farmhouse and barn.

Simonne worked alongside her daughter Angélique and asked: "Did you young people enjoy the dance?"

"It was such lively music, *Maman*! Baptiste took turns with all of us, but especially with Geneviève Leblanc."

"I'm glad that there was someone there to teach you."

"I think that of all of us, Baptiste had the best time. It gave us so much pleasure to hear him laughing; he's always so serious."

"I'm relieved to hear that. I know how nervous he was about having to host the reception."

The men worked with Baptiste in the barn, Louis all the while silently hoping to discover other forgotten treasures of his youth.

"Are you seriously tempted to voyage again?" Antoine asked.

"Only if I could share the experience with our young men so that they can eventually pass it along to their younger brothers and cousins as they grow older."

"That would indeed be worthwhile, but I assure you that I'm not the least bit tempted to take it up again. You're younger than I am, and more fit for it."

"Perhaps not for long. If I'm ever going to travel again, I'd better do it now while I still can."

"You're right of course—Within a few years our oldest boys will be looking for their own land, to marry and raise their own families. They most likely will have to buy—concessions aren't as easily available now as they were for us."

"Not only was I fortunate enough to learn from Red Dawn, Papa, and Nicolas Perrot but you and I also learned a lot during our militia campaigns."

"Yes, and our sons might never have that experience—How do you plan to go about this? Will Simonne approve?"

"I don't know, nor do I know who would take advantage of the opportunity. I must discuss this with Nicolas Perrot before I reach a decision; he may know what conditions are like out west and whether or not it's still safe to travel there."

"Your son Jean certainly seemed interested."

"Yes he is, and he's old enough to be thinking of marriage."

"How old were you during your first voyage to Michillimackinac?"

"Barely old enough to be in the militia—but Papa thought I was too young to join Governor La Barre's campaign against the Senecas."

"He was right."

"Our Louis would also be old enough, but I don't know if he'd want to do this."

Antoine considered his own offspring. "Our Antoine is twenty-seven and unmarried. "He's been out traveling by canoe with me on overnight trips—he might want to go. I think he'd be of great help to you. Would you take him?"

"I'd be glad to, if this works out—François' and Sébastien's oldest are too young to go with us, but what about Madeleine's François?"

"Not much older than your Joseph—She may not be able to spare him right now."

"Maybe not, but I still think I should discuss it with her."

"Those boys will need more training. How do you propose to accomplish that?"

"I'd start within a week by traveling several days at a time with them this autumn, winter, and spring. They'd certainly need to equip themselves and learn to cook their own meals in the wilderness."

"And gain physical strength for portaging. You sound as though you've already made up your mind."

Louis shook his head. "I won't until after I've talked it over with Simonne and Monsieur Perrot."

Late that afternoon, Simonne joined him in their main room and found him studying the Iroquois peace pipe his father had picked up during the Carignan campaign. He held the small collection of Hudson Bay sea shells in one hand as he turned towards her. These mementos of his father had been on their mantel for as long as she could remember, yet she had never known him to examine them this closely. His eyes showed an obvious yearning to return to the forest. She had last seen that expression after his mother's death, when he had decided to sign up as voyageur to Michillimackinac. The income from that single voyage had provided a comfortable life for their family.

She came to him and said: "I understand that this is something you feel you must do for our sons. I'll miss all of you, but I understand, and if Joseph stays home with me, I know we can manage while you're gone."

They discussed it at length with their guests that evening.

"Madeleine could certainly use the extra income if her son chooses to go with you," Marguerite told them.

Madeleine listened quietly. Since Aubin's death, François had become the man of the house. She wondered how she could manage without her nineteen-year-old son. But then she realized that her older sons-in-law and her younger boy would willingly see to her family's needs.

"How do you feel about this, Madeleine?" Louis asked.

"My first thoughts were of Aubin's three very disappointing voyages. He had such great hopes of success and failed in all of them. It took years for us to pay off our debts."

Marguerite reassuringly took her hand. "I believe that our boys are old enough to make their own decisions. It would be worth their while if they were half as successful as Antoine and Louis were."

Madeleine agreed with her. She trusted Louis' judgement and skills. "I'll speak to François as soon as I return home, but it must be his decision." She turned to Antoine. "Will you prepare him for this voyage if he decides to go?"

"Certainly!" Antoine replied. "He could train alongside my sons. Louis and I will work out a list of required equipment and a training plan. I'd be happy to provide whatever François would need."

Antoine put off their departure until they had thoroughly considered all aspects of this venture.

Louis visited Perrot that following afternoon, knowing that river ice would soon begin to form and make it impossible to travel to the south shore for at least another six weeks.

Sébastien and François had told him that Perrot lived in poverty. Louis brought him a fresh supply of paper, quill pens and ink. Now in his seventies, the explorer's eyes were beginning to fail him, yet he conscientiously continued to write his memoirs to satisfy Intendant Bégon's request.

Madame Perrot met Louis at the door and ushered him into the back room where her husband did his writing in a quiet area. He was deep into this task when Louis hailed him in Algonquin.

Perrot looked up quickly, apparently delighted by his former protégé's visit. Louis was startled by the change in his mentor's appearance; Nicolas Perrot was no longer the commanding figure, no longer stood straight and tall. His hair had thinned and turned white.

They continued to exchange the customary formal native greetings. "I rarely have the pleasure to hear and speak that beautiful language—It's been a long time!" Perrot admitted.

He was pleasantly surprised by Louis' gift. "Just what I need! I was about to run out of paper."

They talked about the past and Perrot showed him his writings.

Louis skimmed through some of it and saw that he related his experiences as they had happened, in plain style, without pretense or embellishment.

"There's been a gradual change in the French government's attitude toward our problems in Nouvelle France," Perrot explained. "Intendant Bégon hopes that my report might persuade the court to provide better support for our western alliances. I sense that they've been seriously neglected."

Louis asked: "Do you still receive direct news from your western friends?"

Perrot nodded. "The English are beginning to recruit the Iroquois to collect the western furs. The Five Nations are already stirring up war along our western frontier and drawing away our trading partners with cheaper trade goods from Albany.

"I've heard that *les Renards* (Fox) are on the warpath. They're enlisting allies against the Illinois who are constantly under attack by their enemies from the east, north, west, and south: the Iroquois, Foxes, Sauks, Kickapoos, Mascoutens, Sioux, and Chickasaws. Our friends are gradually losing their land and their population. It saddens me that we've done so little to help them.

"The English might gain control of the French trading routes on the Fox and Wisconsin rivers and disrupt trade throughout the upper Mississippi region unless France decides to stop them. They know as well as we do that our trade and military alliances with the western nations support and protect our claims to those western and southern lands. The French ministry has only recently revived part of our beaver trade by establishing king's posts at forts Frontenac, Niagara, and Detroit."

His words had a sobering effect on Louis. Ever since the French cession of Acadia and Newfoundland, the great majority of the people of Nouvelle France had focused their concern on the vulnerability of the Saint Lawrence River settlements.

"How has this affected Michillimackinac?" he asked.

"Native fur deliveries to that post have decreased but are still flowing. I've heard that Governor Vaudreuil has managed to persuade the minister to restore the twenty-five fur trading licenses."

"Is the Michillimackinac area well-protected?"

"The troubles haven't reached that far north. Hostilities have mostly flared up against the Illinois tribe, Baie-Verte, and Détroit which blocks English access to fur trade in the northern lakes region."

Louis told him of his tentative plans.

"I envy you," Perrot said. "None of my seven sons have any desire to voyage, perhaps because I've spent so much time away from home."

"Do you have any regrets?" Louis asked his friend.

"I only regret my failure to provide a better life for my family. I tried so hard and lost more than I ever gained." He paused. "I'm tired now of all the losses, and all the debt. My only reward for so many years of government service has been a lifetime appointment as captain of the local militia."

Louis thought that there must be more to this story, and waited patiently for the rest.

Perrot studied the younger man's face, looked into his eyes, and decided to go on. "I've been hounded by my merchant creditors ever since the 1701 treaty negotiations in Montréal. The government never reimbursed me for all the expenses I personally paid for during my negotiations with the western tribes. I finally stopped pleading with government officials and sought justice through the courts against Monsieur Monseignat—He served as Secretary under Governor Frontenac and continues to control government finances in Nouvelle France. He knew how much the government owed me but refused to pay me. A year later, the Sovereign Council judged in his favor and I was ordered to pay court expenses, which I could not afford.

"In 1701, my wife inherited 2,000 livres from her aunt who died in France. We immediately sought advice from our pastor who recommended that she apply to be legally free of my debts. Once this was done, the pastor offered to travel to France to claim the inheritance in her name—It had been temporarily held for safekeeping by a missionary priest. Our pastor returned with the money but refused to turn it over to my wife unless she agreed to grant him half of it as a commission for his trouble. We submitted the matter to the Sovereign Council of Québec and it was resolved in our favor just two months ago. The pastor was ordered to pay my wife the total amount in colonial money. This immediately led one of my creditors to file claim on her inheritance before the Sovereign Council and this new lien is still pending."

"Surely, they must have granted you a pension for your many years of service!"

"I applied to the French Minister for a pension and was refused. Since then, I've had no relief from debt. My only income is the small pension I earn as captain and commandant of the local seignorial militia."

Perrot did not seem bitter, but he was sad for his family. His wife had lived and raised their eleven children alone during his long absences.

Louis struggled to control his outrage. He considered the forty years Perrot had spent on government missions to pacify and secure alliances among the western nations. The natives had called him "the man with the iron legs" because of his constant travel back and forth across enormous distances in faithful obedience to official orders dating back to Intendant Talon and most recently to Governor Callières. The royally appointed French officials in Québec had never formally acknowledged the enormous effort and sacrifice this man had made to protect Nouvelle France and its control over the western fur trade. Many of those who had benefitted from his talents and dedication had either died or returned to France. Later government officials faced a different set of challenges and had no clearer concept of the distances he had repeatedly traveled for the benefit of the colony.

The old voyageur continued to describe the Fox wars and the location of hostilities, assuring Louis that the traditional route to Michillimackinac was safe for travel because it was farther north and east than the problem area. He reported that Montréal was hungry for furs. The glut in French warehouses had eventually rotted and spoiled, and much of the current supply was being diverted or smuggled to Albany by the Fox, the Iroquois, and many of the Canadian coureurs-de-bois.

Perrot gave Louis a memento of his own travels, and used one sheet of paper to write a recommendation for him as an experienced voyageur.

Three

L ouis had already considered how he might organize the venture by the time he reached home. He and Antoine discussed the makeup of the crew, and agreed that those who were most likely willing and strong enough to join the voyage would be Louis' Jean and Louis *fils*, Antoine's Étienne and Antoine *fils*. Sébastien's, François', and Catherine's sons were obviously too young to participate. Madeleine had already told them that her son François Maudoux would most likely wish to participate, thus providing their fifth potential engagé.

They drew up the list of items each crewman must carry in his knapsack: a tin cup, a plate, and a spoon; a small whetstone, a small drawknife, fishing line and hooks, an emergency supply of pemmican, cornmeal, and herbal medicines. Each man would require soft moccasins to wear in the canoe and a rugged pair for portaging, sturdy breeches and leggings, an extra shirt, and a blanket roll; a long knife, a hatchet, a musket, powder and shot.

Antoine offered to provide proper clothing and equipment for his nephew François Maudoux and for his two sons. He would train them to set up camp and prepare a hot meal on the trail, to track the rapids and portage past them, and he would attempt to teach them the basic Algonquin language he had learned during his own voyages.

Since he lived closer to Montréal, Antoine also offered to propose the project to merchant Ducharme. He advised Louis to have his son-in-law Pierre Picard write a notarized letter of introduction that he could present on Louis' behalf.

Madeleine and Marguerite volunteered to provide their mother's recipe and instructions for the preparation of pemmican. Simonne's' daughter Angélique wrote these down for distribution to the rest of the family.

"It's best made with lean, dried deer meat, any dried fruit or berries, and rendered fat from bone marrow," said Marguerite.

Her older sister added: "*Maman* showed us how to use two washed stones to grind the dried meat almost to a powder. We repeat this with the dried fruit and berries, but with a lighter touch."

"We use four measures of the meat, three measures of the fruit and berries, and two of warm rendered fat from the deer's bone marrow," Marguerite explained.

"How large a measure?" asked Angélique.

"I always use a pint, but you can use a large drinking cup," Marguerite explained, and added: "Then I crush whatever sweet nuts I might have and add them to the other ingredients."

Madeleine continued: "I mix these all by hand in a large bowl. If I'm lucky enough to have honey, I add a bit of it for sweetness."

"How do you package it?" Angélique asked.

"I divide the entire batch into four equal portions, double-bag each of these in a leather pack and seal the stitched seams with tallow," Marguerite replied. "*Maman* taught us to flatten the packs to fit one at a time in the knapsack. The mixture will last for months on the trail if it's kept dry and out of the sun—even years if it's kept cool in the food cellar. It actually improves with age."

Simonne had learned a similar recipe from her mother. "Where and when did you two first make this?" she asked.

"About a year after Antoine and I were married," Marguerite recalled, "before Madeleine's and my first babies had learned to walk. Antoine and Aubin were called as militiamen to join Governor La Barre's campaign against the Senecas. We were so frightened by our husbands going off to war—I understand now that this was our parents' way to help us overcome our feelings of helplessness. *Maman* had learned to make this trail food shortly after she first arrived from France, while she lived and worked in the Jesuit manor."

Madeleine added: "I've made it several times over the years, especially when drought or war threatened food shortages. *Maman* and Papa taught us to always keep an emergency supply for the bad times, and I always did."

Marguerite nodded. "So did I."

And so had Simonne.

The men decided to meet together with Pierre Picard; Louis prepared to accompany them as far as Trois Rivières. If Pierre agreed to write the letter, Antoine would deliver it to Montréal and relay his own personal impressions of the merchant to Louis.

Before they left, Simonne and Louis handed one large package to Madeleine and another to Marguerite.

"These are packets of wool fleece that were sheared and processed from the sheep I inherited from my father," Simonne explained. "I no longer spin and weave, but it's our pleasure to share these with both of you."

Marguerite held back momentarily. "But what about our youngest sisters, Simonne? Don't they still work your mother's wheel and loom?"

Louis reassured them. "There's more than enough for all of you because our sheep have multiplied over the past few years."

The two women gratefully hugged them and promised that they would try to visit more often.

Louis rode horseback alongside Antoine's calèche as he traveled back to Trois Rivières. He visited with his daughter Madeleine and learned more from her husband Pierre Picard regarding Louis Ducharme's method of operation in the fur trade.

One week later, Louis received a letter from Antoine informing him that he had met with Ducharme and had shown him both recommendations. The merchant was interested in their proposal. Antoine also told him that he had been impressed with the merchant and had already begun to equip his two sons and François Maudoux according to their mutual agreement.

Both men tested and trained their charges before the rivers froze. They fitted each candidate with a leather *portageur* headband and explained that the natives often used birch bark to support the trumpline against the forehead, softening it over the heat of campfire embers, shaping it to the carrier's head, and setting it aside to dry. Either type could be padded with a handful of moss.

They demonstrated how each pack was tied with leather straps, then swung over the shoulders to rest on the *portageur's* back. The first ninety-pound bundle was suspended to rest across the top of the buttocks, the second to rest above the first. A third was sometimes slipped neatly over the head to lie against the middle of the load. They told their trainees that the average weight would amount to 180–200 livres, but that the most experienced and strongest voyageurs might carry much more.

Forty-eight-year old Louis led his sons on trial voyages up the Saint-Maurice River, on overnight and weekend trips. He judged that the water would continue to flow freely through the rapids for a few more weeks before it froze. They learned to set up the evening *campément* on a pine-sheltered riverbank, and set up the campfire to prepare *le souper*. They practiced making *banique*, a nutritious native bread that their grandfather Bastien had learned to bake over the campfire coals while on his way to Hudson Bay.

Louis made them take turns carrying the canoe past the rapids and warned them that the pressure of the crossbar of the canoe resting on the carrier's lower neck and shoulders tended to rub and irritate the flesh over a period of months. This often generated a cartilaginous growth over the lower nape of the neck. Louis taught them how to avoid this by crossing paddles tied only by the blades to the front cross-bar of the canoe. The canoe was then lifted onto the carrier, leaving his hands free, but it was kept in place on his shoulders by the portage harness. The ends of the paddles then exerted pressure only on the shoulder muscles instead of the end of the collar bone, and resulted in a more comfortable carry. He demonstrated how this method allowed quick release in dangerous situations.

Louis packed a weight-load comparable to the amount of cargo their canoe would carry, offering them the experience of distributing it evenly and safely inside the canoe. They learned to load and unload, embark and disembark a fully loaded canoe while keeping it afloat.

They practiced lifting cargo onto their backs to portage between *posées,* the third-of-a-mile stages set during transfer of all cargo between navigable waterways. Louis told them that Perrot had once described a forty-five-mile portage beyond Michillimackinac that required one hundred twenty-two such stages. Each stage often required several repeat trips for complete transfer of cargo and canoe before going on to the next *posée*.

They learned to perform *décharges* and *cordelles*, but the water soon became too cold for them to practice these against the shallow currents. They turned to practicing the use of long poles against swift currents and minor rapids while tracking upriver in a zigzag course to avoid underwater obstacles.

The three of them worked up to paddling seventy miles in one day, and Louis' call to light up their pipes was the only respite they could claim from paddling. At about every four miles, they would enjoy *une pipe* upon hearing their father call *Allumez!* This allowed them to lay back and relax their backs and arms against the thwarts of the canoe or its cargo, to smoke and tell each other stories and jokes during the quarter-hour break.

Their training excursions ended with the first snowfall. They turned to preparing their equipment and provisions for the spring journey, and practicing daily carries to develop upper body strength. Simonne finally became aware of what Louis' voyaging had been like and was all the more surprised that he was willing to return to it.

1716

Recollect Father Simon Dupont recorded the christening and Christian burial of an unnamed female infant born to Michel Perrot and Jeanne Baudry on January 12th, thus officially opening the parish registry of Bécancour.

Six days later, twenty-nine-year old Baptiste Massé married sixteen-year old Geneviève Leblanc who had grown up next door to Bastien's original concession. Madeleine and Marguerite were unable to attend, but Sébastien, François, and other family members easily crossed the ice bridge to Cap-de-la-Madeleine by horse and open-sleigh.

Following the wedding reception, Louis and Simonne invited their two youngest sisters to visit for a week.

In mid-March, Louis and his sons traveled by horse and sleigh to Île Dupas where they joined Antoine's trainees and proceeded together to Montréal. They were all present during the negotiations of the terms of their contract and the signing of their final agreement with Louis Ducharme.

This was Louis' first visit to the frontier city since he and his father had witnessed the signing of the peace treaty in 1701. The community had greatly expanded since then with more houses, shops and warehouses, many outside the city walls. He noticed a new type of wooden construction among the older stone and half-timbered structures, and he especially admired those that were covered with whitewashed stucco. Ducharme's combined office and home was located in such a building and Louis could barely detect the proportions of the square-hewn horizontal timbers that formed the outer walls because their interior surfaces were plastered and whitewashed.

He found the merchant to be personable, honest, and willing to accommodate their needs. He and Antoine examined and discussed the traditional three-man, and the newer five-man canoes. Although they were impressed with the workmanship and cargo capacity of the longer craft, they both felt that two separate standard canoes would be more practical for this crew. Louis realized that such a choice would limit their load and earnings, but his primary concern was to safely provide experience for these young men.

Louis told Ducharme that they would require two three-man canoes, and that they would be ready to leave immediately after the spring runoff. In working out the details of the agreement, Louis was hired as voyageur-foreman and the others signed on as engagés. His previous experience qualified him to lead the group and conduct the actual trading at the distant post, therefore he was entitled to three times the wage of the engagés.

Ducharme promised that he would provide the canoes, equipment and food provisions, and informed them that by their signatures and marks on the contract, they were now eligible to collect one-third of their wages. He would provide each man with one blanket, one trade shirt, one pair of breeches, two handkerchiefs, and several pounds of carrot tobacco (carrot-shaped twists of one-pound tobacco). The merchant informed them that until they reached Michillimackinac, their daily food rations for each man would be one quart of dried peas, one to two ounces of bacon, two bags each of wheat flour and cornmeal for their communal bread. He would provide each man one keg of eau-de-vie for the entire five-month journey. their supplies and equipment would be ready by the first week of May.

Before they left, Louis asked Ducharme about the new wooden structures, and how living in such a house compared with that of occupying the traditional wooden style.

The merchant replied that such a house was easier to heat in the winter and seemed cooler in the summer. He showed him through the front section of the ground floor he had reserved for his office and stockroom, and the family living-space that occupied the back section of the first and the entire second floor.

When they left the merchant's office, Louis happened to meet his long-time friend and fellow voyageur François Vaudry who lived nearby at Pointe-aux-Trembles. François was in Montréal to negotiate a contract for his last voyage west with his four younger brothers: Jacques, Louis, Étienne, and Joseph, all of whom were experienced voyageurs. They shared the noontime meal at a local auberge during which the Vaudrys updated Louis and Antoine on changes along the traditional Ottawa route to Michillimackinac. François knew merchant Ducharme and spoke highly of him.

The two groups agreed to travel together and made plans to meet in Montréal in mid-May.

On April 2, 1716, Intendant Bégon issued an ordinance forbidding anyone, regardless of class or occupation, to travel under any pretext to Fort Orange (Albany), *Manhatte* (Manhattan), Boston or any other English ports or trading posts without written permission from the governor-general of Nouvelle France. He warned that anyone caught trading furs with the English colonies would be fined 2,000 livres for the first offense, and suffer corporal punishment for any further infraction. It was imperative that the Canadians and their native allies not turn to trading with the English; such activity had begun to erode the colony's major source of income and shift the loyalty of western natives toward the English provinces.

The sun's rays grew warmer in early April, weakening the ice bridges across the Canadian rivers. From the west, the flooded upper Saint Lawrence River carried the snowmelt-overflow from the Great Lakes and merged near Montréal with the flooded waters of the Ottawa River.

Surging currents in the deepest parts of these rivers eroded the ice from beneath and created unseen but dangerously weaker sections that could give way under normal winter traffic. The rising spring runoff created pressure against the thicker ice cover downriver, first near Montréal, then northeast on Lac Saint-Pierre, and finally against the winter bridge between Cap-de-la-Madeleine and Bécancour. Southern, and later northern, tributaries of the lake and lower Saint Lawrence flooded the low-lying riverbanks of the Saint Lawrence River valley.

The people of Nouvelle France anticipated the seasonal *débâcle*, the sudden and dramatic effects of which would not be seen nor heard until after mid-April. This phenomenon would first appear on the Richelieu, Yamaska, Saint-François, Nicolet, and Bécancour rivers flowing in from the south; then on the Assomption, Maskinongé, Loup, Saint-Maurice, and Batiscan rivers from the north.

One afternoon, thunderous sounds echoed throughout the length of the Saint Lawrence River valley as great sections of the river's ice broke up, collided and jammed against each other, temporarily flooding its banks. A mere week later, its water ran free and clear.

On April 27th, Intendant Bégon ruled that parishioners François Ducharme and René Leblanc of Bécancour and Dutort must immediately pay their church tithes to Abbé Paul Vachon, pastor of the parish of Sainte-Marie-Madeleine in Cap-de-la-Madeleine.

This ended their protest against having to pay a church tithe toward the construction of the the new church. The project finally got underway with the full support of the settlers living on the south shore. All stone collected the fields that May would be delivered to the proposed building site and piled near the timbers the local habitants had collected and delivered that winter.

Four

Joseph was nineteen years old when his older brothers Jean and Louis prepared to leave with their father Louis. He had been a willing student of writing and arithmetic and had closely observed his father's management of the family properties. Louis now empowered him as overseer of his farms in Champlain by making it clear to all his engagés that he had fully authorized Joseph to represent him while he was away.

Maple sap ceased to flow freely as maple tree buds burgeoned. The weather had warmed. Snow cover had melted. The soil had dried and farmers prepared their fields for the spring sowing. The three voyageurs said their goodbyes and left for Île Dupas early one morning in May. Antoine stored Louis' canoe in his barn and took the group by horse and wagon to Montréal.

Merchants, voyageurs, and natives crowded the streets of the frontier community. Carts moved trade goods and canoes beyond the Lachine rapids in preparation for their delivery to the entrepôts of forts Frontenac, Michillimackinac, Sault Sainte-Marie, or Detroit.

Louis' crew stood by and watched as many of the voyageur-traders protested against, but accepted the 33% interest rate the local merchants charged on credit granted for trade goods purchases. Louis and Antoine explained to their engagés that self-financing was not the best arrangement for any voyageur; they both knew that it had been Aubin's and Nicolas Perrot's usual practice.

Most of the men who prepared to leave wore trade shirts and sashes, breeches, leggings, moccasins, and knit caps over hair kept long and loose to protect against the clouds of mosquitoes and black flies they would encounter in the forest. They carried long sheathed knives and hatchets tucked under their sashes and each man carried his own backpack, musket, powder and shot.

François Vaudry and his brothers were already waiting for them. They shared dinner together at the local pub and talked about the upcoming voyage. The auberge was filled with last-minute revelers; Antoine remarked that some would carouse all night and be in poor shape to leave the following day.

"Let that be a lesson to you *mes gars*," he pointed out. "Eau-de-vie can soothe a voyageur at the end of a long day of paddling and portaging, but it can also affect his ability to perform his work if it's abused."

Louis could tell that they were all thinking of the keg of brandy each had been allotted for the trip. He told them: "That keg is worth seventy times more in furs at Michillimackinac than it is here in Montréal. Think of it!"

Jean did a rapid calculation and his eyes brightened. "Then I can afford to drink tea!"

Once the laughter died down, Louis added: "I suggest that we open and share one keg at a time. Whatever kegs are left over can be traded and their value in furs be shared by all of us. I for one will be purchasing tea for the trip, but I'll also have one drink of eau-de-vie at the end of the day. I know that it will help me sleep in spite of the nightly swarms of *maringouins* that we'll encounter."

The two groups met again at dawn, had their *petit déjeuner,* claimed their brand new birch-bark canoes, and checked their cargo against the list merchant Ducharme had given them. Louis' party carefully inspected their own equipment. Both canoes measured twenty feet long by two feet wide at the center thwart; they found an ample supply of repair materials tucked neatly into the bow. Such a craft could accommodate four men and 900 livres of cargo, or three men and 1000 livres of cargo.

Louis' charges unanimously selected Antoine Cottenoire *fils* to steer the second canoe. His brother Étienne and cousin Louis *fils* would travel with him. François Maudoux and Jean would travel with Louis *père*.

The Vaudry brothers had chosen the newer, longer, and wider five-man canoe that could carry 3000 livres of cargo but required two or three men to portage overland. None of them had ever used this type of craft, but all were experienced voyageurs and looked forward to the challenge.

While both groups loaded their supplies at the departure point beyond the Lachine Rapids, the three crew leaders agreed that it should take about two and a half months to reach Michillimackinac and that the route was well-marked all along the way. They planned to travel up the Ottawa River to the Olmstead cutoff which led to Lac-des-Allumettes, and then move upstream on the Mattawa River to Lac Nipissing. They would cross that body of water, paddle down the French River to Georgian Bay, the northernmost section of Lake Huron, then follow a string of islands leading westward to the strait of Michillimackinac.

Antoine *père* bade them farewell as they embarked and moved upriver to join a large brigade of voyageurs who might not all be heading for Michillimackinac. According to custom, they stopped at Sainte-Anne's church where they dropped their coins in a small collection box, crossed themselves, and said a prayer asking their patron saint's blessing and protection during their upcoming journey.

Half of the brigade that left that morning headed southwest to enter the upper Saint Lawrence and move upriver toward Fort Frontenac on eastern Lake Ontario. Some would travel farther southwest across that lake to make their way overland through the Niagara Portage to reach and cross Lake Erie which would allow them to move farther west to the Detroit trading post.

After leaving Lachine, Louis and Vaudry's group moved northwest to enter the Ottawa River which would eventually lead them toward northern Lake Huron. They would then part company with the voyageurs who would trade their goods at Sault Sainte-Marie which was located north of Michillimackinac and served as the entrepôt for the far western posts that could be reached through Lake Superior.

Louis' crew had paddled and portaged sixty miles before their two leaders called for their first *campément*. The sun was just above the horizon, and they hoped to get a fire started before the pesky mosquitoes appeared.

The veterans were as weary as the beginners when they began to unload the canoes and set up the campsite. They scavenged dry wood from the surrounding forest and dug a fire hole large enough to hold two eight-gallon kettles. They filled these with water and brought that to a boil before adding six quarts of dry peas to each container, at least one quart per man. When the peas began to burst, Louis and François Vaudry added their crew's daily ration of bacon.

Louis set up another kettle of boiling water, and opened a pack of pemmican and a sack of flour. The younger men watched as he chopped a sizable portion of pemmican with his hatchet. He explained that this *rubbaboo* would be their supper.

The Vaudrys prepared to do the same. They laughed and hollered over: "It's a *ragoût!*"

Louis added a flour paste to the boiling water, pouring it in gradually and stirring steadily to thicken the mixture. He added the pemmican and stirred this in until it melted and added its fat to the flour soup. In less than half an hour they feasted on this food, and later smoked their pipes, sipped their eau-de-vie, and battled the swarms of mosquitoes at the end of a long, eventful day. Louis, Antoine *fils*, and Vaudry set up several smoky campfires on the edge of their campsite in an attempt to keep the blood-thirsty insects at bay.

François Maudoux had been quiet most of the day. That evening, Louis told him: "Your papa owned a flageolet—Did he ever play for you?"

A smile warmed the young man's face. He reached under his shirt and pulled out the small flute. "He taught me how," he proudly replied.

Louis examined the instrument. "Would you play for us?"

The sweet sounds of medieval troubadour songs echoed through the forest that night and every night thereafter.

They buried the kettles in the hot coals, and covered the fire hole to maintain the pea and bacon mixture at a simmer throughout the night while they slept on a thick layer of fir and spruce branches under their overturned canoes.

The two crew leaders awoke before daylight and immediately uncovered the cooking pots. They lifted them out of the hole and added several chunks of *banique* that Jean and François had baked the previous evening. By the time the others had reloaded the canoes and cleaned up the campsite, the mixture of peas, bacon, and biscuits had thickened to fill the containers. They ladled this into their tin bowls to eat with their spoons as they planned their day, and finished off with a smoke.

They cooled the kettles in the river's running stream while they cleaned their dishes. When the food had cooled enough, they lifted the partially-filled containers into the canoes to provide a cold midday meal. They started out at dawn as Louis advised the new voyageurs to watch for berries, game, bird's eggs, fish, turtle, muskrat, or honey to add to their meals. He kept his bow and arrows close by, hoping that he might find a rabbit or a beaver's tail.

Cap-de-la-Madeleine, June 1716

The first ship to arrive in Québec carried Governor-General Vaudreuil who had spent the past two years in France consulting with officials in Versailles concerning their post-treaty colonial policies in North America.

The following Sunday civil announcements informed the population that King Louis XIV had died and that his five-year old great-grandson Louis XV had succeeded him under the regency of Philippe II duc d'Orléans.

Vaudreuil immediately began to reform the colonial administration to better cope with the colony's rapid growth. He also officially declared the reinstatement of the twenty-five Canadian fur-trading licenses that Louis XIV had canceled in 1696. His early inspection of the wooden Montréal fortifications convinced him that a stone wall with flanking bastions must be constructed to surround the town.

Acadia

Shortly after the signing of the Treaty of Utrecht, Louis XIV had ordered the construction of a naval facility to safeguard the entrance to the Saint Lawrence River, one that would be large enough and strong enough to harbor and service the French Atlantic fleet. The governor announced that the king's court planned to construct a great fortress and naval port on the island of Cap-Breton which they had renamed Île Royale.

Evacuees from Newfoundland and other ceded territories had already arrived to develop the site, but the Acadiens resisted

French prodding that they leave their fertile farms and start anew on the barren land of Cap-Breton. The English had granted them freedom of worship and the *Acadiens*, who greatly outnumbered their new masters and were their major source of provisions, had successfully negotiated an exception to the oath of allegiance they were required to make to the British Crown. They had gained the privilege of remaining neutral on their ancestral lands.

Europe

The most recent war between France and England had drained the treasuries of both nations. Several previous governmental attempts had failed to reverse this chronic shortage of hard currency in France. Scottish émigré John Law recommended the substitution of paper *billets-de-banque* for the country's coinage which was now in short supply. Regent Philippe II favored this bold idea on a trial basis.

Cap-de-la-Madeleine

Once weather and ground conditions allowed, volunteer laborers cleared the church construction site on a sandy hillock that sloped on three sides toward the cape's small winding Favrel River.

The local habitants dug the foundations of the new church while deliveries of fieldstone, lumber, and limestone continued to arrive from both sides of the river. Nearby, the master-mason directed the construction of a cylindrical lime kiln that would be open at the top and fired by wood at the bottom. Other volunteers dug trenches to accommodate the slaking of quicklime and the subsequent mixing of lime mortar that the masons required for their construction of the stone walls. They lined these trenches with wooden boards.

Several workers volunteered to process the limestone under the supervision of the master mason. Throughout that hot, dry summer, they pounded the stone into smaller pieces with sledgehammers, loaded it through the top of the oven, and heated it for three days to burn into quicklime.

In late July, *Grand Voyer* Pierre Robineau, with the help of Militia Captain Saint-Pierre of Cap-de-la-Madeleine, lined up the road through the village of Champlain, widened it to 12 feet and extended it to 1° leagues in length. He planned to bridge over a

stream and construct a sturdy span over Rivière-aux-Ânes capable
of supporting the weight of farm-wagons. The way was marked
across the savannah, through a grove of beech trees, and behind
the *pays brûlé* to rejoin and follow the old road which they would
straighten as it passed through the center of a forest clearing
belonging to Louis Provencher *fils*. It would then rejoin the present
road on the cape.

By mid-August, the mason determined that he had enough
caustic lime and directed his workers to slake it by carefully adding
it in measured amounts to water that now filled the sandy-
bottomed trench. The laborers wore protective clothing over all
skin areas because of the intense chemical reaction that occurred
when quicklime reacted with water. To ensure even slaking, they
thoroughly mixed the hot mixture into a muddy consistency.

They continued to stir it twice a day for four days, then several
times a week for a month, allowing about one inch of water to
stand over the lime. The mixture gradually cooled, rendering it to
a pasty consistency, and it finally thickened into a non-caustic
putty. By the end of September, they covered the pit with boards
and insulated it with a thick layer of dirt, leaving the mixture to
rest undisturbed according to the mason's instructions.

Parish records showed payment of 41 livres to mason Michel
Crevier dit Bellerive for having crushed and burnt the lime. Young
Arsonneau received 20 livres for slaking it with the help of Lafleur,
Granbois and others who were also paid for their efforts.

Lac Nippising

The voyageurs would encounter fifty rapids during their voyage
from Montréal to Michillimackinac. These unnavigable river
sections would require them to completely unload their fragile
canoes while holding them afloat in the water, then lift rather
than drag them ashore. They would then portage canoe and cargo
overland to quieter water or to their next campsite.

During their ascent of the Ottawa and Mattawa rivers, Louis
and François Vaudry dealt with eighteen portage sites and as many
other white-water areas that required a partial *décharge*. At each
of these more shallow rapids, the Canadiens partially unloaded
and portaged a portion of their load, leaving others among their
crew to move the lightened canoe by poling and hauling with rope

or cable against the current. This maneuver often required the engagés to push and pull the watercraft while struggling in waist- or shoulder-deep water.

They celebrated upon reaching the north bay of Lac Nipissing where Louis announced that the most demanding part of their voyage had come to an end. Their route would now carry them across this lake, down the French River, across Georgian Bay to northern Lake Huron and west toward their final destination.

Louis explained to his sons and nephews that they were about to experience their first *traverse*. He and the Vaudrys warned them that treacherous windstorms could come up unexpectedly to endanger the canoeists whenever they crossed large bodies of water. Louis told them that during his journey home across Lake Champlain during the Carignan campaign, his own father had experienced such an event when strong headwinds had surprised his brigade. Several canoes had overturned and eight French soldiers had drowned as a result.

François added: "A sudden heavy rainstorm can also make you lose sight of the shore and of what lies ahead; it can ruin the cargo, and even sink a canoe. It's always wise to wait these out on land under shelter and hopefully near a fire."

A great number of white crosses stood at the lake's outlet into the French River. These marked the graves of French travelers, voyageurs and coureurs who had been unexpectedly attacked, robbed, and killed by Iroquois ambushes in this area. Each man removed his cap and prayed in his own way for these poor souls who had been buried in the wilderness so far away from home.

Louis told them that they would descend through a series of island-dotted lakes, many of which were connected by white-water rapids and falls. His young apprentices looked forward to their first experience at shooting the rapids with a valuable load of cargo. They camped beyond this burial site and prepared to travel downriver the following morning.

The Vaudrys led the way in the larger canoe. Antoine, Louis *fils*, and Étienne Cottenoire kept a safe distance behind them in one of the standard canoes. Louis *père* followed last with his son Jean and nephew François Maudoux, thus allowing him to keep watch over Antoine's descent, and he was quite pleased with their performance.

They passed swiftly and safely through the white water and had much to celebrate and talk about that evening while they sat around the campfire. Louis observed that Jean and Antoine Cottenoire had grown more confident in their performance. Antoine as bowman of the second canoe had demonstrated the alertness required to detect by sight and sound the underwater rocks that could suddenly appear within two feet of their vulnerable birch bark canoe; he reacted quickly with coolness, strength, and agility with his long paddle to avoid them. His brother Étienne had also reacted as a keen observer from the stern; as helmsman, his own long paddle instantly matched Antoine's every move, thus effectively lending more power to each controlled maneuver. Louis had felt the effectiveness of Jean's strokes as they navigated their own canoe through the rapids. Louis *fils* and young François Maudoux had watched for obstacles and sat ready to bail out any water that managed to collect in the bottom of the canoes.

They enjoyed a much-needed rest once they reached the French River outlet into Georgian Bay.

Five

Early August 1716

The Huron and Ottawa villages just north of the Jesuit mission of Saint-Ignace had occupied Michillimackinac since 1634, when their original inhabitants had sought refuge from the Iroquois massacres of their earlier mission villages in Huronia. The first French trading post and fort had been built in 1690 on the shore of Lake Huron near the entrance to the strait. An Ojibwa village lay farther north. To the south was Fort De Buade which was surrounded by Canadian and Métis villages.

Crowds of merchants, native traders, voyageurs, and coureurs wandered about both inside and outside the fort. Louis and François Vaudry cautioned their engagés to keep watch over their cargo while they negotiated their trade. The engagés set up camp together along the shore and guarded their canoes and trade goods while Louis, Jean, and François Vaudry scouted the town.

Louis found a much greater military presence than when he had last been here with François Perrot and Grey Cloud. French soldiers had recently completed construction of a second French fort on the south shore of what was now called the Strait of Mackinac and named it Fort Michillimackinac. Commandant Louvigny had just arrived from Québec with a force of eight hundred French troops and they were preparing to travel west across northern Lake Michigan to wage a punitive campaign against the warring *Renards* who were located less than forty miles north of Green Bay.

Louis sought out Louis Ducharme's trading clerk who had accumulated a substantial supply of quality winter furs and was prepared to exchange these for his employer's trade goods. Louis' crew also had three full kegs of eau-de-vie to trade, in spite of his holding back a reserve for their return trip. Their trade negotiation would last several days.

Louis noticed a greater number of western voyageurs exchanging fur pelts for French goods at this post. These *hivernants* spent most of their lives in the western country and rarely returned to Montréal. He learned that many of them would later exchange their fresh supply of trade goods with native tribes who lived in the lower Wisconsin and Illinois countries west and south of Lake Michigan. Others would head for the region of Lake Superior, a more difficult route through the portage of Sault-Sainte-Marie, to enter the largest and westernmost of the Great Lakes.

One evening by the campfire, Louis asked his friend François if he had ever seen one of the new wooden houses being built.

"Do you mean *pièces-sur-pièces*?"

"Maybe—They're built of large square-hewn horizontal logs. There are quite a few of them in Montréal."

François nodded. "That's it all right."

"They look expensive, but sturdy."

"They're meant to last for generations as long as they're well-maintained. Any master-carpenter can build them."

Jean and his brother had also noticed the unusual structures. "Are you thinking of building a new house?" Jean asked his father.

"I've never had the experience of building one," he replied. "I was away on a voyage when my father and brothers built his second house. Our present home came with the land when I bought it. It's definitely as old as *Pépère*'s older house and doesn't keep in the heat as it once did. Your *Maman* has been cold these last two winters."

Louis *fils* asked: "Do you think Monsieur Pallié could help us build one?"

"I don't know, but it would certainly be a learning experience for us if he could."

He turned to François. "What's the usual arrangement?"

His friend responded: "You hire a contractor to set up the plan, and he teaches you to cut and hew the tenons and mortices that fit the timbers of the frame together. Because this type of joint is used throughout the assembly, it's said that the structure lasts longer—its members shrink and expand as a single unit according to changes in the weather. This style of construction also allows you to build a larger house as you must have noticed in Louis Ducharme's office and home."

"I had thought of building with stone but there's so little to be found nearby and I've heard many complain that stone houses are cold in the winter."

"These are said to be warmer in winter and cooler in the summer."

"I'll speak to Pallié when we get back to the cape," Louis decided. He could see that his sons welcomed the possibility.

They picked up fresh provisions for their return journey, including a supply of dry native corn rather than peas. Among the furs they received for delivery to Montréal were bison pelts from the Great Plains. The clerk told them that the fleece from these animals was currently very much in demand in Europe.

Louis' crew and the Vaudrys looked forward to a return trip that would be of shorter duration, mostly downstream. They would likely run as many as fifteen rapids on the Mattawa and Ottawa rivers. The young trainees obviously looked forward to it.

The more experienced among them spent the next few days strengthening the shells of their canoes with the rolls of yellow birch bark, *wattape* (fine spruce roots), and pine gum resin that Louis Ducharme had provided. They had used these regularly to patch their canoes, but now they needed the shells to be extra strong and waterproof because of the additional stresses they would face from the swift-flowing turbulence of those two rivers.

Both groups loaded and launched their canoes from Fort Michilimackinac at dawn one early August morning. They traveled a distance of three *pipes* before mooring offshore for breakfast, bracing their long poles from gunwale to beach.

The return trip led them up the French River, across the height of land to Lac Nipissing, and north across this body of water to reach North Bay. At that point, Louis switched positions with Jean, allowing him to experience the role of bowman as they shot the Mattawa rapids. He did so well that he remained at that position during their descent of the Ottawa River while they sped down the series of rapids they had struggled against on their way west.

Louis, his sons and nephews delivered their cargo of furs to Louis Ducharme in early October 1716, collected their wages and made their way home from Montréal. They parted company with the Cottenoire brothers on Île Dupas, and delivered François Maudoux to Saint-François-du-Lac where the young man proudly presented his earnings to his mother.

Louis told Marguerite, Antoine and Madeleine that they had reason to be proud of their sons and gave a brief accounting of the voyage to both families, leaving the young but newly experienced voyageurs to fill in the details.

Upon his arrival in Cap-de-la-Madeleine, Louis was surprised by the amount of progress the community had achieved toward the construction of the new church. Master-mason Lafond reported that a sufficient supply of fieldstone had been collected, the church cellar and drainage ditches had been dug, and an ample supply of lime was slaking in the covered pit. The stone was now ready to be roughened throughout the winter so that its surfaces would bond with the lime mortar. Much of the lumber had been hewn. Everything would be ready for an early start the following spring.

Simonne and her daughters greeted them warmly. Louis was especially relieved to be home. His wife quickly recognized how much Jean and Louis had matured during their voyage. They gladly answered all of their brothers' questions while their parents managed a few moments alone.

"Did it go well?" she asked.

"Even better than I'd expected. The boys adapted easily and enthusiastically, but I think Jean enjoyed it much more than Louis did. I think Louis will be a good farmer," he added with a smile.

"How about you?"

"I doubt that I'll ever voyage again."

She was startled by his certain admission. Simonne had always known that journeying through the woods had always had a hold on him, even as they had grown up together.

He added: "It's no longer as easy for me as it once was. I'm confident that these young men will share their experience with their younger brothers.

"How did things work out for you here?" he asked

"I know you'll be pleased with Joseph's management skills. I'm confident that he could run this farm if you ever decided to retire."

He held her close and kissed her. "That won't be for a while yet, but I'm happy to hear it—I missed you so much."

Her eyes grew moist. "And so did I—I'm so relieved to know that you won't go away like this again."

They rejoined the group. Everyone had enough stories to tell to last them through the winter.

Louis made up another small packet of writing paper, quill pens and ink the following morning and invited his two oldest sons to accompany him to Nicolas Perrot's home. "Now that you're experienced voyageurs," he explained, "you might enjoy being in the company of a master fur trader and linguist who spent most of his life dealing with the western natives. Monsieur Perrot is a very special man."

Jean and Louis had often heard of the explorer and looked forward to the meeting.

Perrot greeted them warmly, having already heard of their recent return from Michillimackinac. He took Louis' hand and admitted: "I was hoping you'd come back to visit me."

Louis introduced his sons, telling Perrot that they had just completed their first voyage and he was pleased with their performance.

"Did you enjoy it enough to travel again?" he asked them.

Jean quickly replied that he would, but young Louis hesitated.

Perrot eyed him kindly and said: "I'm glad to hear that you were willing to try it. I'm sure that the experience will help you appreciate the comforts you have at home—Nouvelle France is always in need of good habitants."

"And what about you, young man?" he asked the older son.

With a full grin on his face, Jean replied: "I'll definitely go back!"

Perrot turned to their father and exchanged a subtle acknowledgement that this one certainly had voyageur blood running through his veins.

"So tell me all about it! Were you surprised by any of what you saw?"

Louis gave his oldest son a nod of encouragement.

"The size of that fort, so deep in the wilderness," he replied, "and that so many men are willing to spend their lives moving trade goods even deeper into the forest."

"I'm sure they must be trading even farther west than I ever did…"

"How far did you trade?" Jean asked.

"Past Michillimackinac and deep into Baie-Verte which extends into the farther side of *Lac des Illinois* (Lake Michigan)."

Louis reported: "French soldiers have built a new fort with stronger fortifications and a larger garrison at Michillimackinac. We saw increased troop movements toward the west, and more *Troupes de la Marine* than voyageurs at the fort."

Perrot thought about this. "France is finally strengthening its defenses at the key portages to our major fur trading areas."

Louis told him that *hivernants* and Métis now serviced that trade between Michillimackinac and Baie-Verte. "Some spoke of new traffic heading south through another mighty river that reaches to what they call the Spanish gulf. They spoke of a land where it never snows and the rivers never freeze, where a French port is open year-round."

Perrot immediately recognized La Salle's discovery and claim over the Louisiana Territory. "I've been told that many *Canadiens* have begun to settle in that new land. Now that we've lost control over our only access to the great ocean to the east, we certainly can't afford to lose access to the southern gulf."

"How far is it to the gulf, Monsieur Perrot?" Jean asked.

"I've been told that it's again more than twice the distance traveled from Montréal to Michillimackinac."

Young Louis' eyes widened. "Then it must be a year-long voyage?"

"Once you've traveled down the length of *Lac des Illinois*, you portage across a height of land to rivers that flow to the south. It's much easier to travel to the gulf than to work your way back, but there are several French forts and trading posts along the way where you can pick up provisions and rest."

Jean quietly considered this new information.

"Michel Arsonneau inherited a plantation in Louisiana a while ago," Louis reminded them, "and moved his entire family down there at one time. I wonder if he still travels there."

The old voyageur shrugged his shoulders. "From what I hear, the Louisiana colony is still struggling to survive—it's become isolated and neglected since King Louis died.

"Shortly after you left, Governor Vaudreuil returned from France. He announced that we have a five-year old dauphin, and that the new regent has begun to build a mighty fortress on an island beyond Acadia which will serve as a French naval base, entrepôt, and fishing port. They call it Louisbourg."

"That certainly sounds promising for the future safety of Nouvelle France."

Perrot continued: "During my recent visit to the Bécancour mission, I learned that the Abenakis are deeply concerned about the rapid expansion of English settlement on their traditional tribal lands of Norridgewock. *Père* Râle has served that mission since well before the Montréal treaty with the Iroquois. They've told me that the priest counsels them not to sell their land and birthright. Yet every once in a while a tribal chief gets drunk on English rum and scratches his totem sign onto a piece of paper that he can't read."

"Did the treaty give up their land to the English?"

"Our officials deny it. It was never ours to give away—Our missionaries and our Métis have lived on their tribal land by invitation of the Abenakis. The native understanding of land ownership is very different from ours and that of the English. *Les bostonnais* don't seem to understand or honor that."

"Papa once told me that the eastern Abenaki territory can be directly accessed by canoe from the Saint Lawrence River valley or by ship from the eastern sea." Louis recalled.

"That's true and that access can be both a convenience and a danger. The overland journey is very difficult and *Père* Râle's mission is much closer to *les bostonnais* than it is to Québec."

A few days later, Louis resumed his responsibilities as *marguillier* and consulted with master-carpenter Pallié who was now framing the church windows.

"Have you ever built *pièces-sur-pièces*?" he asked.

"I've built a few," the carpenter admitted. "Are you thinking of building a new home?"

"It's time to replace the old one and I greatly admired those new houses in Montréal."

"I'd be happy to do that for you but I'm fully committed with the church for at least one more year."

"Can you tell me what such a contract would require?"

"You must first decide how large a structure you want to build. The contractor will then provide a sketch and a list of lumber that must be hewn to specifications. The lumber would be prepared during the winter and be ready for joining in late spring or early summer, once the owner and his helpers have dug the cellar and built the masonry foundation. Your sons could help you with that. Then you'd all help the carpenter assemble the rest of the house frame."

"And what about filling in the walls and roof?"

"The owner can choose to do that himself or hire the carpenter to do it. In either case, you and your sons would be involved because the sills and plate beams are quite heavy to lift and maneuver when aligning the posts."

"Can you recommend someone?"

"I know that François Dufault has built several of these upriver and in Trois Rivières."

Louis thanked him for his advice and was now prepared to discuss this project with Simonne and his sons.

His wife welcomed the idea. Jean, Joseph, and Louis *fils* were just as enthusiastic. Louis realized that Jean would most likely voyage again, and he decided that if he were to take on this project, he should do so now. Conscious of the fact that their children had already grown into adolescence and adulthood, Louis and Simonne planned to build a larger home. He contacted François Dufault while Jean was still with them to help and learn new skills.

The contract was much as Pallié had described. Louis felt certain that he and his sons could manage to saw and hew the timber and assist with the assembly. Dufault furnished a diagram of the house to ensure that they all shared the same concept, and provided a list of all the lumber that must be shaped to his specifications.

Louis felt a bit overwhelmed at first when the contractor explained that all horizontal *pièces* and upright timbers must be hewed square to eight inches thick, with tenons cut at both ends. The horizontal tenons would be two-inches wide and extend three inches long to fit into the vertical grooves formed along the entire length of each upright post. The uprights would be spaced five feet apart and their four-inch end-tenons fitted into mortices that Dufault would cut into the sill and plate beams; these joints would then be pegged securely with trunnels.

The project would require cedar for the sills and roof, hemlock for the remaining frame, and pine for flooring and all walls.

Dufault agreed to provide a longer center-post for each end of the building to support the ridge pole, and agreed to personally install the ceiling and floor joists. With their help, he would assemble the roof frame by laying trusses from plate to ridge pole and joining them together with braces, purlins, and in this case, diagonal wind braces called *croix de Saint-André*. His second payment would then come due.

Louis, Simonne and their sons attended the contract signing for the family project. Both parties signed the document. Louis made the first of his three payments and toasted the occasion with a freshly opened bottle of Calvados shared by all attending adults.

The actual construction would begin in early summer, once the cellar walls were ready to receive the weight of the sills, and all their lumber cut, trimmed, and lined up for assembly.

In accordance with their agreement, the carpenter helped them get started on the project by marking which trees to fell for the sills, girders, plates, and trunnels. He also showed Louis and his sons how to identify suitable straight-grained trees for the rest of the lumber.

Six

1717

On January 13th, Intendant Bégon and the Sovereign Council of Québec addressed a petition to Regent Philippe II duc d'Orléans, reminding the French government that valuable sources of iron had been identified and assayed in Trois Rivières and Baie Saint-Paul in 1687. They requested that a mining engineer and soldier-laborers be sent to Nouvelle France to finally begin exploitation of this colonial resource.

On Friday, January 18th, Bastien and Catherine Guillet's second daughter, Marie-Catherine signed a marriage contract with Pierre Bourbeau-Verville in her family home in Cap-de-la-Madeleine.

Pierre pledged his bride a *douaire précis* of 800 livres, and a *douaire preciput* of 300 livres to be claimed before family division of his estate should she survive him. In his role as guardian, her brother Louis declared Catherine's ownership of a parcel of land measuring 60 *pieds de terre* (1/3 arpent) frontage by 40 arpents deep that she had inherited through her mother's estate.

Père Vachon blessed the couple's exchange of vows the following morning in the old church of Sainte-Madeleine. Family friends including the Barettes, the Leblancs and the Arsonneaus gathered at the old family homestead for the reception; brothers and sisters of the bride and groom had traveled over the ice bridge from the south shore, allowing Louis the opportunity to catch up on family news. By now, most of Bastien's grandchildren ranged in age from early adolescence to early adulthood.

Louis, Sébastien, François and Antoine Cottenoire watched with keen interest as their younger sons and their cousins gleaned information from those who had recently returned from Michillimackinac. The new voyageurs smoked their pipes and proudly related their experiences.

Simonne's sister, Catherine Massé, shared the news that the Bécancour mission had become overcrowded during the previous autumn. "Many Abenaki converts are leaving their ancestral lands because *les bostonnais* are rapidly populating that area with farms, forts, and villages."

Louis was reminded of Nicolas Perrot's concern that English settlement was moving closer to Nouvelle France.

"The Jesuit fathers are very concerned for the safety of the Norridgewock mission. *Père* Râle has ministered that mission for more than a generation. He fears that if the Abenakis fail to resist the English claims and sale of any of their land, they'll soon be completely driven away."

"You've met *Père* Râle, haven't you?" Louis asked.

Catherine nodded. "*Père* Râle has always been strongly devoted to the Abenakis and they to him. He led the Norridgewocks to establish refuge in Bécancour about ten years ago, shortly after my husband died. He asked me to donate part of my land for the expansion of the mission. François Bigot, Nicolas Leblanc, and I all did and the natives have been good neighbors."

Massachusetts officials continued to claim that the Treaty of Utrecht had given them jurisdiction over the Abenaki land. They had always considered it to be a major part of their frontier province of Maine. Meanwhile, the French persisted in their own claim that they had only ceded control over the Acadian peninsula. They had never occupied the Abenaki land, but had been invited to establish a Catholic mission for them.

Champlain

During the early winter months, Louis and his sons had felled trees and hewn lumber alongside Michel Arsonneau *père* who had told them of the deed to a Louisiana land grant that he had inherited from his Parisian grandfather twelve years earlier.

They resumed that conversation during the wedding reception and were joined by their old friend Laurent Barette, a voyageur and fur trader who had journeyed more than once to the southern gulf. He told Michel: "It took a lot of courage for you to travel down the Mississippi with your young family."

Arsonneau shrugged his shoulders and explained: "I had been warned that I'd lose title to the land if I didn't claim it within a year. I originally planned to make the voyage with my oldest son but my wife insisted that we all travel together. Later on, I realized that she feared I might never make it back home. As it turned out," he added sadly, "she was the one who stayed behind."

Louis explained to Laurent that the family had already begun their descent of the Mississippi River and were more than halfway to Louisiana when they learned that Michel's wife was pregnant.

"The journey became difficult for her," Michel continued. "We slowed down to accommodate her needs but she died during childbirth shortly after we reached our land grant in Bonnet Carré Bend. I had to bury her there—so far away from home." Even now, he turned his face away as his eyes filled with tears.

"That must have been very difficult for you and the children— How long did you stay?" asked Laurent.

"I had to stay and work the land until baby Louis was old enough and strong enough to travel upriver. I traded for food and tools and hired a wet nurse for the newborn. Our only daughter was thirteen years old when her mother died yet she managed to take care of the baby and prepare our meals while my three boys and I cleared the land and built a shelter."

"What was Louisiana like at that time?" Louis asked.

"Uncivilized—We struggled to build a small cabin and palisades. *Les sauvages* attacked the outer settlements. Typhus arrived on ships from Havana. King Louis XIV was fighting another war in Europe so that France provided only the very basic necessities and offered little support. There were times when I wondered if we'd ever make it back home to Canada."

"The trip back is always more difficult," Laurent agreed.

"Why is that?" Jean asked.

"The Mississippi flows smoothly and gently at times, but the major rivers that flow into it set up great currents that speed your descent. These slow you down as you work your way upriver. Some very shallow areas make travel difficult during the late summer months and early autumn."

"Is land as freely available to new settlers in Louisiana as it was here when our fathers first arrived?" Louis asked.

"I think so—at least it was when I was there. My son Michel and I went hunting farther upriver on the opposite shore, and found great numbers of wildlife. Since there were no other settlers in the area, I was able to claim another 250 square arpents of land by building a small hunting cabin and planting two rows of oak trees to mark the place. Michel's messages tell me that our claim still stands. He and his brothers often hunt and fish there.

"They report that French colonial officials don't support Canadian attempts to develop Louisiana's resources. That's not unusual; I had the same experience during my family's short stay there. Most of the original settlers were from Nouvelle France. Many of them have given up their efforts and returned north during the last few years. They've brought me news from my sons and complained that they could no longer afford to live there."

"How long did you stay with your children?" Laurent asked.

"Three years after my wife's death. Once I'd firmly established my claims to *l'Allée-des-Chênes* and to the Arsonneau Plantation in Bonnet Carré, I decided that I would turn them over to our sons when they got to be old enough to run them. Meanwhile, I leased both properties to trustworthy Canadiens and moved my family back to Batiscan."

"Will you ever go back?"

"I doubt it. Michel, Louis, and Alexis are doing very well on their own. They have the youthful energy and ambition to develop the land and they share the profits. Michel may be coming home soon. He complained in his last message that there are no marriageable women available in Louisiana at this time."

Pierre Picard and Antoine Cottenoire both agreed that he should be able to find a willing bride in Montréal where so many families were involved in voyaging for the fur trade.

By mid-afternoon, as the sun accelerated its descent toward the west, many of the guests offered their best wishes to the young couple and prepared to leave. The bride's and groom's relatives and friends loaded the couple's gifts and belongings onto their oxen-sledges and prepared to move these across the ice-covered river to their new home in Bécancour.

Work toward the church construction continued in local barns throughout the winter. Master-carpenter Pallié assigned, and his assistant Louis Champoux dit Jolicoeur supervised the local volunteers who hewed lumber according to well-marked specs. Louis and his sons hauled timber to various sites and hewed their share of the church lumber, but they also managed to provide building materials for their own upcoming summer construction.

While the south-shore habitants continued their deliveries of fieldstone and timber to the building site over the Saint Lawrence River ice bridge, Sébastien and François stopped by to visit their older brother. They examined his house-sketch, and were intrigued by this new mode of construction.

Master-mason Lafond worked on the preliminary shaping of the angled stones for the arched doorway of the church, and supervised his assistants who roughly cut and dressed the fieldstone in preparation for the first application of lime mortar. Since lime mortar dried slowly and was particularly vulnerable to the effects of frost and rain, the actual construction of the stone walls would be limited to the five warmest and driest months of the year, from mid-May through mid-October. Otherwise, the long Canadian winters and the heavy spring and November rains would weaken the masonry during its long curing period.

France

John Law's *Banque Générale* had so successfully regulated its paper currency that the interest rate had fallen to $4^{1}/_{2}\%$ while the note issue had risen to 60 million livres. The Scotsman's policies had sufficiently restored confidence in the country's economy so that the regent decreed in early April that the bank's notes would be accepted in payment of taxes. New branches of this bank were enthusiastically opened in Lyons, Rochelle, Tours, Amiens, and Orléans.

Nouvelle France, 1718

Shortly after the spring débâcle of the Saint Lawrence River, the population of the district of Trois Rivières learned through Sunday civil announcements that *Sieur* Pierre Boucher, the first Canadian colonist to become ennobled by King Louis XIV, had died in Boucherville at the age of ninety-five.

Louis, Sébastien and François related to their children and grandchildren how this legendary figure had helped Bastien and Marguerite establish themselves in Cap-de-la-Madeleine, how he had saved not only Trois Rivières but all of Nouvelle France from the Iroquois threat in the early 1650s, and again fifteen years later by persuading the King Louis XIV to send his best French military officers and regiment of *Troupes de Terre* to subdue the Five Nations. Louis also told them that their grandmother Marguerite had sailed three months across the eastern sea with *Sieur* Boucher to marry Bastien and establish their family's presence in Nouvelle France.

Cap-de-la-Madeleine

The habitants of Bécancour and Dutort resumed their deliveries of construction materials to the cape by shallop as soon as river currents returned to normal.

Temperatures grew warm enough in late April so that Lafond could test several samples of lime mortar and putty. He did this by adding different proportions of clean sharp sand to the quicklime and mixing it with water. Sand was easily available at the cape and grit could be taken from the nearby riverbeds. Drying times varied in length with each sample.

The masons finally accepted one of the mixtures, added a small amount of fine stove ash to make it easier to work with. They soon began to build the church basement's foundation walls that would enclose the parish community's winter burial site. Drainage ditches and canals had already been dug to carry rain water away from the foundation and into the Favrel River.

At the same time, Simonne's brother-in-law, mason Michel Crevier-Bellerive provided the materials and assisted Louis and his sons in the construction of their own cellar walls, basement partitions, and two fireplace foundations for their new house.

Québec

Church and civil authorities faced an increase in social problems. Canadian women and daughters could not safely walk in public without a male escort. Bishop Saint-Vallier complained to French authorities that the quality of immigrants arriving in Nouvelle France had declined due to the poor screening of emigrant candidates by French authorities. Indentures were no longer offered and subsidized. French officials had been emptying their prisons of inmates convicted of lesser crimes. Some of these new arrivals took advantage of this opportunity to reform their lives; others refused to work and threatened peace and security within the Canadian communities.

Le Conseil supérieur received the French regent's reply to its request concerning the mining and exploitation of iron ore in Trois Rivières and Baie Saint-Paul. Duc d'Orléans reiterated that continental France had more than enough iron to supply the Canadians. He reminded the governor's council that colonies existed to meet the needs of the mother country. Therefore the economy of Nouvelle France must not compete with that of France.

The regent's close association with Scotsman John Law's efforts to revive the French economy was barely beginning to bear fruit. France had already committed itself to building the fortress of Louisbourg on Cap Breton, an expensive project that Louis XIV had proposed to compensate for his loss of Acadia through the Treaty of Utrecht.

Cap-de-la-Madeleine

Guillaume Beaudry dit Desbuttes, royal gunsmith and silversmith of Trois Rivières, engraved and delivered a lead commemorative plate to the pastor of Cap-de-la-Madeleine. The parish *marguilliers*, including Louis *père*, officially laid this and the cornerstone of their new church on June 17, 1717.

They recorded payment of 1000 livres to master-mason Lafond who directed and supervised the construction of the stone walls throughout that summer and early autumn. He also completed the final shaping and fitting of the stones that formed the arched doorway of the church.

Although the masonry assistants and apprentices volunteered their efforts, parish records reveal that they received butter, milk, pork, bacon, and eau-de-vie from the local habitants. Their work required that they rinse each stone free of dust and wet it with limewater. They painted a slurry of diluted mortar on all joint surfaces and allowed it to permeate the surface. Once this had lost its shine, they applied a half-inch layer of mortar and allowed that to cure until it became leather-hard but still damp, then added an additional layer twelve- to twenty-four hours later.

Carpenter Pallié and his assistants built wooden scaffolding which provided easy access to the rising wall for the masons. This structure also offered a supporting framework for the layers of wet burlap and waterproof canvas that protected the curing mortar joints against drying wind and anticipated heavy autumn rain.

Champlain

All framing lumber and most of the fill-in logs for Louis' new house had been hewn square with the chisel-edged broad axe, their end-tenons shaped with mallet and chisel, and mortises cut in with *le bec-d'âne*. Carpenter Dufault checked the individual pieces and determined that they were indeed ready for the final assembly of the house-frame.

The five men secured the cedar sills to the foundation walls, overlapped the beams at each corner and pegged these joints securely with slightly oversized trunnels. The rest of the frame above the sill would be of hemlock. They inserted the tenons of the ten-foot upright posts into their individual sill-mortices, including those that formed the door- and window-openings, and pegged these firmly together. With their help, Dufault temporarily braced the longer posts he had provided for each end-wall. These were also grooved lengthwise on opposing sides to receive the tenons of the horizontal *pièces*, but they would reach higher to support the ridge pole.

With occasional minor adjustments, the end-tenons of the five-foot-long horizontal *pièces* were then inserted into and slid down the two-inch-wide by three-inch-deep vertical grooves of the adjacent upright posts. Dufault sealed the spaces between the *pièces* with lime plaster.

They eventually set about their heaviest and more difficult task of lifting the plate beams and fitting the upper tenons of the uprights into their proper mortices. This proved to be an awkward procedure requiring the use of cable and pulley, and much shifting of the heavy plates to fit everything together. Once this was accomplished, they overlapped the plate ends and pegged them together at the corners in the same manner as in the sills, thus finally securing and squaring the walls. These plates would now serve as a base for the roof trusses that would extend diagonally up to the ridge pole.

Dufault undertook his responsibility for framing the roof, but needed help in pulling up the lumber with cable and pulley. He and Louis' three oldest sons joined the trusses with longitudinal braces and purlins, and added diagonal braces to provide additional support against the strong Canadian winter winds, heavy snow and ice loads.

Upon completion of the outer walls, roof framing, floor and ceiling joists in early July, Dufault delivered several cartloads of well-seasoned pine boards from local sawyer Michel Arsonneau. so that Louis and his sons could finish the floors and interior partitions. When these materials were delivered, the carpenter received his second payment. His remaining commitments were to cover the roof and furnish the doors, windows, and shutters to enclose the house before winter.

Cap-de-la-Madeleine

The masonry workers labored at the church site under a blazing sun throughout a serious summer drought. Such weather threatened the proper curing of the mortar joints; Pallié applied extra measures to maintain optimal conditions.

Farmers on the cape worked harder than usual as they strived to irrigate their parched fields and gardens. Entire families gathered water from the Saint Lawrence River and carried it to their shallow irrigation canals. The problem was more acute on the north shore where the riverbank was elevated and its sandy soil was more directly exposed to the heat of the sun.

Norridgewock, summer 1717

The new Governor of Massachusetts Samuel Shute called a peace council with the Abenaki chiefs of mainland Acadia on August 9th. Chief Wowurna of Norridgewock acted as spokesman for twenty Abenaki leaders who met with the governor in Georgetown on Arrowsic Island, at the outlet of the Kennebec River. The governor offered his hand in peace to each of the chiefs and promised them justice if any Englishman should wrong them. He told the natives that they and the English were subjects of the great, good, and wise King George whose religion they should embrace since his was the only true one, and he offered them an English Bible and Christian instruction under the tutelage of Calvinist Minister Joseph Baxter.

The following day, the leading chief of the Norridgewocks addressed the governor and as he did so, Shute repeatedly interrupted him with questions and remarks. The chief asked that he be allowed to speak, but Shute continued to interrupt, speaking directly to the interpreter rather than to the spokesman. The governor insisted on their obedience to the English king and warned that they had no choice in the matter.

Both speakers spoke possessively of his land.

Chief Wowurna declared that there would be peace between them if the English limited their settlements to the west side of the lower Kennebec River up to the ruins of an old English mill. He insisted that the English forts must be removed from their ancestral land.

Shute told him bluntly that he, as the English king's representative, would build a fort for each new settlement if he chose to.

The Abenakis retreated to their temporary encampment to consult with Father Râle. Some of the chiefs returned to the council that evening with a letter from the Jesuit missionary informing the governor that his French colonial counterpart had been assured by the King of France that there was no mention of Abenaki land in the Treaty of Utrecht.

Governor Shute was outraged.

When they learned that the English were preparing to sail back to Boston the following morning, the Abenakis sent messengers to apologize for their rudeness, requested another meeting, and promised to choose a different spokesman to represent them. Governor Shute accepted their apology and agreed to resume their discussions.

The new native representative spoke of a desire for peace with the English. He stated that his people had agreed that the English should feel free to extend their settlements as far as they had formerly done, but no more. In a more conciliatory mood, Shute promised them new trading posts, a gunsmith to repair their muskets, and their choice of a new interpreter.

The twenty chiefs and elders accepted the English governor's words in good faith and made their marks on a new peace agreement which they could not read.

Champlain

By late summer, Michel Crevier-Bellerive returned to Louis' construction site to build the two stone fireplaces and extend their chimneys three and a half feet above the roof line, with flues ten inches wide and inside surfaces fully plastered as required by law.

He also provided and installed a small kitchen sink of smooth dressed stone, and a mantel and molding of the same quality above and around the opening of the fireplace hearth in the principal downstairs room.

Carpenter Dufault covered the roof frame with the help of Louis' sons by nailing two layers of boards to the joists and rafters. The base layer consisted of butted boards and was covered with *planches chevauchées*.

The house was completely enclosed before the autumn harvest.

Cap de-la-Madeleine

After the completion of the September grain harvest, Pallié and his assistants began construction of a temporary wooden roof and outside walls to protect the new church masonry against November rains and winter frosts. The master-carpenter planned to spend the winter months producing and fitting casement windows and wooden shutters for the chapel and sacristy.

Seven

Late spring, 1718

The first ship arrivals brought welcome news to the people of Nouvelle France that work had begun in earnest on Île Royale (Cap Breton). Local militia captains reported that construction of a great fortress was well underway in Louisbourg. France planned to arm its fortifications with over 100 cannons and mortars, and a garrison of 700 soldiers to protect a magnificent village of 1,000 French residents. Louisbourg was to become a self-sufficient colony and a major base for the French Atlantic fleet. The Canadian settlers who had feared English control over their only access to the eastern sea were somewhat reassured by the news.

Although colonial card money had been in use since its introduction by Intendant De Meulles in 1685, the French government had repeatedly failed to redeem the notes in full. Now that John Law had officially gained control over French government and colonial finances, he called in all of the card money at 50% of its face value, removed export duties of 25% on beaver furs and moose hides, abolished the 25% premium on French currency in the colony, and minted new copper coins for colonial use setting their value equal to those of France.

In Cap-de-la-Madeleine, workmen tore away the temporary wooden wall that had protected the church masonry from autumn and winter weather. The lime mortar had cured to the mason's satisfaction but he chose to leave the temporary roof in place.

On May 26ᵗʰ, the parish paid 55 livres to *Sieur* Antoine Bouton for a special lead ornament, a *coq-gaulois* (French-rooster) he had fashioned to be set atop the future church steeple.

Michel Crevier returned to Louis' construction site in Champlain, to apply a roughcast coating of plaster of lime mixed with coarse clean gravel to seal the outside wall surfaces from the Canadian weather. He plastered the interior surfaces of the outside walls with *crépi*, a mixture of finer sand, lime and water that provided a smoother texture. Louis and his sons would whitewash both coatings before the family moved in. The inside partitions were of smooth untreated pine boards.

Louis and Simonne settled into their larger and brighter new home early that summer. Their three unmarried daughters and four unmarried sons were delighted with their new bedrooms. Simonne and the girls were particularly happy with the new kitchen sink that drained directly outdoors in the summer, but would empty into a small water-tight wooden barrel that the men could empty daily during the winter.

Sébastien continued to raise his family in Bécancour, gradually working his way farther westward, clearing and developing new concessions upriver toward Nicolet. *Sieur* de Tonnancour granted him a concession in late June. This lot in fief Roctaillade measured 10-arpents frontage on the Saint Lawrence by 20 deep, bordering the seignory of Nicolet on the southwest and that of *Sieur* Godefroy on the northeast. The seigneur reserved ownership of all oak, pine and cedar timber except for such lumber as Sébastien would require for the construction of his own buildings. This contract granted him hunting and fishing rights.

Louis received a letter from Antoine announcing that he and Marguerite had decided that winter to settle permanently on Île Dupas. They had already bought new land on the island near Sorel. Their daughter Renée's four children had grown to ages ten through thirteen while their son-in-law and his second wife had added four more children to the family during their six years of marriage.

In mid-July, Michel Arsonneau *fils* arrived from Nouvelle Orléans with exotic non-perishable southern produce, some of which he had set aside as gifts for his family and friends: indigo for dye and ink, rice, cotton, pecans, and southern tobacco.

He reported to his father that during his absence, Louis was in charge of *l'Allée des Chênes* and Alexis was overseeing operations in Bonnet Carré.

"Will they be able to manage on their own?" his father asked.

"They have plenty of help. The six black slaves from Saint-Domingue are strong and healthy now. They're good workers, loyal and conscientious because they know that they'll regain their freedom one day."

"Are conditions improving in the colony?"

His son shook his head. "Everyone knows that Crozat's *Compagnie de l'Occident* and Governor Cadillac have always cheated the French merchants who ship supplies to the colony and have overcharged the settlers who bought them.

"Cadillac has repeatedly antagonized Lieutenant-Governor Bienville and the most productive *Canadiens* by his strict control and manipulation of commerce. Two years ago, he insisted that French authorities recall *Sieur* Bienville to France—it was rumored that Bienville had refused to marry Cadillac's daughter. Many of the *Canadiens* have returned to Nouvelle France, others have emigrated to the Spanish territories, so the Louisiana economy has been greatly weakened by chronic shortages of laborers and skilled tradesmen. I'd guess that the population is now down to about four hundred settlers.

"The regent finally recalled Cadillac. As for Crozat, he and his shareholders had heavily invested in their search for gold but he never found any. He finally gave up his monopoly after only five years."

His father sighed deeply, but Michel *fils* reassured him that the situation had improved recently because the new *Compagnie des Indes* had already invigorated the development and expansion of French activities in the area.

In order to finance the heavy investment it needed, Law's company had been granted monopolies over tobacco and Canadian beaver, and exclusive rights to the Guinea slave trade in the West Indies and Louisiana. The terms of the agreement stipulated that the new company must deliver six thousand settlers and three thousand black slaves within twenty-five years.

"Just before I left Louisiana," Michel continued, "I learned that *Sieur* Bienville had been reappointed governor-general. Workers were preparing to build his home just 30 *lieues* north of the gulf and about one-day's travel downriver from Bonnet Carré, on land the regent granted for the future capital of Louisiana. Some say that the proposed settlement will be named 'Nouvelle Orléans' in honor of the regent. French engineers and laborers will soon arrive to drain the land, design and install barracks and fortifications on the site. A royal engineer is designing the city plan."

Michel's and Louis' families talked a while in the churchyard after Sunday Mass, then moved on to Louis' new home. Jean and Michel *fils* had grown up together but had not seen each other in a long time.

"How was your return voyage?" Jean asked.

"No more difficult than usual."

"What brings you back this time?"

"Papa promised me that I'd have better luck finding a bride here than in Louisiana," he answered with a chuckle.

Jean told him of his brother-in-law's connection with Montréal fur merchant Louis Ducharme and that he, his brother and father had voyaged for Ducharme to Michillimackinac.

Michel gave him a brief description of the 2500-mile route to the southern gulf, the differences in climate, flora and fauna. He stressed the many advantages of settling that far south by explaining that the rivers never froze near the Gulf of Mexico and that settlers rarely needed fuel for their fireplaces except for cooking purposes.

Jean was surprised to hear that much of the land required initial draining, that yearly spring flooding of the Mississippi River greatly fertilized the soil, and that crops grew nearly year-round.

Michel talked about the black slaves that Crozat had imported from the French island of Saint-Domingue and explained that they could tolerate working in the heat better than could the Canadians. With his father's approval, he looked forward to acquiring several new slaves who were scheduled to arrive directly from Africa the following year.

France

That summer, the *Compagnie des Indes* took over the Canadian beaver-fur monopoly. It apportioned 72% of this revenue to France, 14% to Canadian merchants and voyageurs; 9% to spread throughout the colony, and 5% to cover colonial government expenses.

John Law's restructuring of the colonial money had generated its own problems. Since there was never enough of the new copper coinage to meet the population's needs, illegal trade with the English colonies resurged as a source of hard currency. Five habitants from the Trois Rivières region were summoned before the judge for having traded in Albany without the governor-general's permission. Their penalties did little to discourage others from doing the same.

On Aug 2nd, France, the Austrian Emperor, Great Britain and the Dutch Republic formed the Quadruple Alliance against Spain's attempts to regain by force the European land its king had ceded through the Treaty of Utrecht. For over a year, Spanish Prime Minister Cardinal Alberoni had pursued an ambitious foreign policy aimed at regaining territory in Italy, and at claiming the French throne for King Philip V, Louis XIV's grandson.

Nouvelle France

Bishop Saint-Vallier addressed his flock and the French colonial ministry, protesting against the increase in public excess and brutality in the colony which he blamed on the arrival of large numbers of non-Canadian officers and soldiers who lived adulterous lives and shunned the Mass and sacraments. He chastised the third of all young Canadian males who avoided marriage and farming to enter the forest as young coureurs-de-bois, thus leaving the colony with a surplus of 2,000–3,000 young unmarried women.

He again criticized French colonial authorities for the marked decline in the quality of immigrants and complained that lack of screening and unregulated immigration had increased lawlessness in the Canadian cities and towns. The bishop cautioned the men of Nouvelle France to accompany their wives, daughters, and sisters whenever they left the security of their homes.

Louis *père*, his son-in-law Pierre Picard, and Antoine Cottenoire had communicated with Louis Ducharme regarding young Michel's search for a suitable wife. Ducharme invited Michel *fils* to Montréal as his house-guest, Picard escorted and introduced him to the merchant's family.

Madeleine Dionet dit Lafleur's husband had died unexpectedly in January of that year. Although she and former Carignan soldier René Deniger had been married eight years, the young widow had remained childless and therefore was his sole heir. She lived alone on her husband's estate in Chambly.

Her mother and younger sister Charlotte were present when Madeleine greeted Ducharme who was a longtime friend of their family. All three women were graciously receptive toward the young man whom the merchant personally introduced. They quickly noticed and admired his dark hair and dark intelligent eyes, his apparent ease and courteous manner.

Michel saw Madeleine as a petite, energetic, self-confident and personable young woman, who appeared to be in full control of her comfortable home and farm. She was understandably cautious during their initial meeting.

They were well-chaperoned, yet they managed to exchange much personal information. He learned that she was the daughter of a soldier and voyageur; that her mother was widowed. She told him that her younger brother had recently voyaged to Kaskaskia on the Mississippi River, so he described that large settlement and its relative distance from Montréal compared to what he must travel to reach the Arsonneau Plantation.

She learned that he had voyaged several times to the southern gulf starting at age eleven, and that he held title to a sizable southern plantation. They were both very much at ease by the end of their first meeting.

When Madame Dionet invited Michel to a second visit with the family at her home nearer Montréal, Pierre Picard returned to Trois Rivières while Michel stayed on as Louis Ducharme's guest.

The Dionet family home was spacious and comfortable. Michel arrived to find that Charlotte's husband Joseph Chevaudier was also present. Madeleine introduced her brother-in-law who had recently returned from a voyage out west. The conversation flowed easily as Charlotte served refreshments on behalf of her mother. Joseph and all three women were fascinated by Michel's tales of southern Louisiana and of the several major trading posts and forts encountered along the Mississippi river banks.

Michel and Madeleine were allowed some time alone at the end of this meeting.

"You have a lovely family," he told her. "They're very comfortable to be with. I was surprised to learn that so many of your relatives have voyaged."

She smiled at that. "Charlotte and I have always envied the men in our family, you know. We women are so restricted in what we're allowed to do. I've often dreamed of voyaging through the wilderness by canoe."

He thought of his mother. "Such travel and camping out at night in all kinds of weather can be physically demanding."

"But the sights that you see must be unforgettable."

"Yes, that does make up for it," he added earnestly. "Is there a chance that you might accept my proposal?" he asked as he looked deeply into her hazel eyes.

She hesitated, but her eyes sparkled as she finally admitted: "I'm seriously considering it."

His face brightened and he unconsciously tightened his hold on her hand.

Their third meeting also took place in Madame Dionet's home in Varennes. She was present when they agreed to marry and they worked out the major details of the marriage contract together. Madeleine would retain control of her inheritance from her first husband's estate. Michel offered her a *douaire précis* of 500 livres and a *douaire préciput* of 300 livres. They discussed arrangements for the wedding and reception, then her mother left them alone for some time and sat with her embroidery in the adjoining room, discreetly leaving the door slightly open behind her.

Michel Arsonneau *fils* married Jeanne-Madeleine Dionet dit Lafleur on September 5, 1718 in the old parish church of Notre-Dame in Montréal. This historical building had been originally constructed in 1672 according to the Jesuit style with transept, semi-circular choir, and single bell tower. Sulpician Superior Dollier de Casson had aligned it with *rue* Notre-Dame according to his original city plan. Its structure had been expanded in 1708 due to the rapid growth of its parish.

Louis, Simonne, and Jean attended the wedding, offering the two men an opportunity to introduce Simonne to the largest city, port, and church she had ever seen.

Rather than spend the winter in Michillimackinac before continuing on to Louisiana, the couple decided to stay through the autumn and winter on her estate in Chambly while he gathered provisions and made arrangements for their move to Louisiana. This gave her more time to select the personal items she wished to transfer to her new home, some of which he had to reject as too heavy and awkward for transport by canoe and portage.

"The only way we could deliver these larger pieces to Louisiana would be to ship them to France, then to Biloxi, then up the Mississippi river."

"How long would that take?"

"I'd guess close to a year."

"Has it ever been done?"

"I vaguely remember that a group of twenty young *Canadiennes* had traveled that route to Mobile when my family first arrived at the plantation."

She decided against risking the loss of her furniture.

Jean agreed to voyage with Michel and his new wife but sought advice from Laurent Barette on how to prepare for this much longer voyage. Barette's sons, Laurent *fils* and Baptiste, had already signed on as part of the crew, so Laurent shared his experiences with all three of them.

Louis regarded this as a very special opportunity for Jean and was delighted that he was free to take advantage of it. He realized that Michel's spring departure would allow his party to avoid winter travel, but he knew that if Jean were ever to return through northern territory, he might one day need such skills. His own father's descriptions of a winter spent in the northern forest had impressed upon him how dangerous that could be.

Although he felt confident that his oldest son could handle this new experience, he decided to teach him some of the additional native survival skills he had learned from Red Dawn and his sons. These included fashioning raquettes, hunting and fishing gear from raw materials that could be found in the natural environment, tracking and hunting with bow and arrow, preserving meat and fish in the wild, and recognizing natural food sources in the forest. They worked on the development of these skills throughout the fall and early winter.

Simonne was more hesitant. Although she had always understood and accepted her husband's attraction to traveling through the wilderness, her own family had never engaged in the fur trade and therefore had never ventured far from home. Jean was the first to leave the family on such a long journey; she grew increasingly concerned that she might never see him again.

Louis *fils* listened with interest and without envy, but all this talk and preparation regarding Jean's voyage fascinated nine-year old François.

That December, Madeleine Dionet announced her first pregnancy. Her husband and father-in-law both agreed that the overland journey to Louisiana must be postponed until after the baby's birth.

LOUISIANA

Eight

1719

Michel's descriptions of travel down the length of the Mississippi River valley were a constant source of wonder for Madeleine.

"Whatever prompted you to take that first voyage?" she asked.

"Papa's parents arrived from France and married in Québec in late autumn of 1665. *Pépère* immediately signed a three-year lease for a farm in Cap-de-la-Madeleine—he considered himself lucky to find shelter so quickly. They reached the cape just as the river began to freeze.

"A few days before Christmas of the following year, *Mémère* died when Papa was born. Their neighbors took care of him during his infancy while *Pépère* continued to work Monsieur Joliet's land. At about that time, the Jesuits granted him a concession in Batiscan with the understanding that it could not be developed until he fulfilled his lease obligation at the cape.

"*Pépère* died a few months after he and Papa had moved to Batiscan. He had begun to build his house which left a debt that his only son was legally obliged to repay. Papa was orphaned at the age of three with no relatives to raise him, so local authorities placed him under the guardianship of the local notary. When he was old enough, he served as an engagé to a local master-carpenter who had no children of his own.

"Word of his situation eventually reached his *pépère* in Paris who died in 1704, having transferred to Papa ownership title to land in Louisiana that King Louis XIV had granted him. It measured 500 square arpents and bordered the Mississippi River near the southern sea. Papa learned of this through our local notary. He was about my age then, had paid off his father's debt, and had married *Maman*."

"How old were you?" she asked.

"Three years old. My older sister Marie-Josephte was five."

"Then it must have been a while before you saw the plantation."

He nodded. "There was no colonial government in Louisiana when Papa received the land title; travel on the Mississippi River was very dangerous. I was six years old by the time *Sieur* de Bienville and his brother sailed into the southern gulf and discovered the river's outlet. It remained a military fort manned by soldiers rather than an official settlement until a year before the last peace treaty."

"When did you first see the concession?"

"In 1704, when Papa and *Maman* moved the entire family to Louisiana."

"What was that like?"

"The voyage was long and difficult for *Maman*, especially after we learned that she was pregnant. She died when my youngest brother was born, shortly after we reached the land grant. Conditions were harsh. We camped out until Papa was able to build a shelter."

Madeleine felt tears well up in her eyes. She covered his hand with hers. "That must have been awful for her and your father," she said softly.

He nodded. "For all of us—Papa hired a local Canadian couple to help improve our situation. I was eleven by then, old enough to be of help to him and to realize how deeply he mourned her death. He seemed to blame himself and he hated to bury her in that wilderness so far away from home. My twin brothers and I worked with him to build a more permanent shelter, to clear, drain, till some of the land, and raise barely enough food to feed ourselves and the engagés. Marie-Josephte managed to take care of the baby and the younger children, and helped with the cooking, baking, and the laundry.

"Three years passed before Papa finally worked through his grief. There were still very few settlers there, only about two hundred in all of Louisiana. Native warriors from the east attacked and massacred some of the French habitants. Then Papa learned that a ship had arrived from Havana with typhus aboard. He quickly leased the concession to the hired couple and we managed to leave within a matter of days.

"Papa gave me title to the land when he remarried and decided that he would never go back to Bonnet Carré."

Madeleine realized now how difficult his life had been, how different from hers. She thanked God that their paths had crossed. She knew him to be a good man, strong of character, unassuming, and darkly handsome.

That winter, word got around Montréal that Michel planned to return to Louisiana with his wife in early summer, soon after the birth of their child. News had reached Nouvelle France that a new company was greatly improving conditions in the southern colony. He received an invitation to join a brigade of Canadian settlers who intended to return to Louisiana at that time.

Several men approached him to apply as engagés for the one-way trip. Michel saw this as an opportunity to transport more of Madeleine's belongings. He hired five of the applicants and ordered delivery of two of the newer and larger five-man canoes from Trois Rivières. These were to be equipped with collapsible single mast and sail, and a generous supply of repair materials.

Michel longed to spend some time with his family and introduce Madeleine to his lifelong friends. She readily agreed, having never seen much of the Saint Lawrence River valley beyond the Montréal area. They left shortly after the spring débâcle and traveled leisurely by chaloupe, stopping to eat and sleep in small auberges along the way.

Michel *père* and his second wife Catherine Laraire greeted them warmly, as did his brothers and sisters. Marie-Josephte introduced her husband and several children. She and Madeleine became close friends as they eagerly discussed the coming trip to the southern plantation. Josephte and her stepmother answered all of Madeleine's questions about childbirth.

Michel worked with his father at the sawmill and on the farm while Madeleine thoroughly enjoyed the slow-paced rural setting, especially the long, leisurely walks along the river.

Their baby was born in Batiscan in mid-May, four weeks earlier than expected. The local doctor examined Michel III and declared him to be a healthy infant although underweight. Catherine and Josephte helped her nurture the child.

Michel and his father felt certain that if the couple left Montréal by mid-July, they would avoid the snow and the need to winter in Michillimackinac. Although Michel planned to set up a small canvas tent at each *campément* for his wife and infant son, and would provide additional amenities for the young woman, Madeleine was well aware of the hardships this long overland voyage would entail and she was determined to face up to them. Louis and Simonne provided a native-style carrying cloak for the baby to ease the young mother's burden and keep the baby warm and close to her breast.

He informed the couple that once an infant could maintain its own normal body temperature and was strong enough to be swaddled, traveling native women placed a bundle of moss on his bottom to keep him from spoiling his clothes and used a padded baby board on which the child was securely but comfortably bound. The board and baby were then strapped upon his mother's back. They traveled back to back so that the mother's hands remained free and she could maintain a better sense of balance during the voyage. The infant's head was kept lightly covered to protect him from the sun and the weather, and his legs hanged free yet were also protected. If she needed to unburden herself, the mother hung up the carrying board on whatever was strong enough to safely support the baby's weight. At the end of the travel day, the baby was released from the board and encouraged to stretch and exercise. Louis offered to provide such a board for her and would show her how to use it.

Michel and Madeleine left Montréal by the end of the second week of July. The brigade of eight canoes started out at dawn and headed up the Ottawa River toward the Strait of Mackinac, following the route Jean had already traveled with his father. Pesky mosquitoes and black flies were not as troublesome in mid-summer as they had been on earlier trips. The terrain was familiar to Michel, but seeing it now through his wife's eyes, he found himself appreciating the countryside as he once had as a child during his first voyage south with his family.

They followed Champlain's original route to Georgian Bay, then Marquette and Joliet's course across northern Lake Huron, and traveled west to Fort Michillimackinac

This was Madeleine's most uncomfortable part of the trip. The midday sun provided comfortable temperatures, but nights were definitely cooler by the time they reached Michillimackinac. She felt the late September chill and worried about the baby as nightly offshore winds and rain blew in over their *campéments*. Michel crowded inside the tent to provide extra warmth for his new family.

He added several woolen blankets and warmer clothes to their provisions and replenished their food supplies at the trading post before starting off on the second leg of their journey. They merged with a larger fleet of birch-bark canoes that headed south toward the Illinois posts and beyond.

After more than a month's descent along the western shore of Lake Michigan, they arrived at the outlet of the Checagou River. Michel led them briefly up that river, through a swampy portage and over a height of land, the subcontinental divide that many voyageurs considered to be midway between Montréal and southern sea. They reloaded their canoes and embarked on the Des Plaines River then headed southwest and downriver into the headwaters of the Illinois River. Although the weather continued to be cold, they saw no sign of snow.

The river's current carried them through fifty leagues of a forested lowland area until they sighted a series of sandstone bluffs reaching high above them on the southern shore.

"This is where we'll set up camp," Michel announced. The sun reached low in the sky as they set up their campfire near the riverbank.

Michel explained that this was where La Salle and Tonti had built their first trading post and palisades during their return trip from the southern gulf.

The following morning, they explored a native trail that led them through a mixture of oak, cedar and pine trees that grew in the dry, sandy soil. Jean spotted a rabbit scurrying through the underbrush and reached for his bow and arrows. They found a flat area at the summit of the trail that showed the remains of palisade-postholes on three sides and another open side atop the sheer sandstone cliff. The Canadians stood 125 feet above the water and enjoyed a magnificent view of the Illinois River and a prairie that extended far beyond both of its banks. They could see great buffalo herds grazing on the distant flood plains.

The men investigated the strange beauty that surrounded them, and explored the nearest part of the broad flatland that extended as far as they could see. They began by searching the base of their perch and discovered moss-lined canyons that sliced dramatically through the tree-covered, sandstone bluffs for several miles around.

Madeleine remained tired after her night's sleep and was relieved to learn that Michel and his crew would spend the following week hunting on the prairies to provide a change in diet. Michel promised wild turkeys for feasting, and deer whose meat they would dry for their continuing voyage. Jean pointed to signs of beavers and muskrats during their walks along the riverbank and shot a few wood ducks as they paddled along the water's edge.

Michel saw to it that his wife and son were never left alone. Away from the bluffs, red oaks and hickories thrived in deeper soils; their leaves were gradually turning color. She and her assigned escort saw raccoons and flying squirrels in search of nuts and dried berries; this led her to collect her own. Bright blue indigo buntings drew her attention to the wild crab apple and plum trees that grew along the edge of the prairie; she gathered some of this fruit in the basket she always carried during her walks. She spotted her first white-tailed deer munching on nearby sumac, and red-tailed hawks soaring gracefully overhead in search of small rodents. She collected moss whenever she saw it, all the while remembering Michel's warning to avoid contact with the poison ivy plant whose greenish-white berries provided an important food source for the birds.

They resumed their journey with a generous variety of fresh and dried foods. Five days later, they reached another French fort on the west bank of the Illinois River, at a widening of the waterway known as *Lac Pimitoui* (Peoria). Michel told his wife that this was where Tonti had rebuilt Fort Saint-Louis after abandoning the sandy bluff that they had just left.

French farmer-traders in this thriving settlement offered to share a meal with them in exchange for news from Nouvelle France. They warned the *Canadiens* that this section of the

Mississippi River had fish large enough to overturn their canoes. Michel assured them that they would navigate the more shallow waters.

The brigade reached the Mississippi in mid-December, and Michel announced that since they would likely reach the Arsonneau plantation in mid-February, they would have to celebrate Christmas along the way.

The great river carried them east, then around a southwesterly bend to where they encountered the muddy waters of the Missouri River which entered from the west. A strong turbulence jostled their canoes. Michel reassured Madeleine that it would not last.

They rode the swift-flowing current for a distance of about eight miles until they arrived at the northern portion of a large fertile floodplain and the prehistoric terraced mounds of Cahokia.

Michel stopped for the night and introduced his crew to the old trading post and twenty-year old Mission of the Holy Family. Canadians had built several homes around the mission, European immigrants who spoke a foreign language had recently settled nearby, and French soldiers were building a new fort.

This was the first of a half-dozen French settlements along the Mississippi where pockets of French-Canadian settlement were surrounded in all directions by miles of Indian country. In Cahokia as in the other frontier villages along the river, French and Amerindian communities existed peacefully side-by-side, traded goods, worshiped together, and often intermarried.

The Illinois natives had concluded their summer council-meetings and prepared to leave for their winter hunt on the prairies. Michel inquired about the apparent decline in the native presence. The Jesuit missionary explained that a three-year epidemic had taken its toll among the older chieftains, that a younger generation of warriors had assumed control of tribal leadership and were less friendly toward the Canadian voyageurs.

Cahokia had long been recognized as the regional center for the Illinois fur trade; its pelts had always been shipped to France through Montréal. Michel learned that day that these pelts would now be exported through the southern port of Nouvelle Orléans. He knew how this would affect the Montréal economy.

Madeleine told him that night that she felt the weather growing warmer as they moved farther downriver.

They resumed their southward progress after Mass the following morning. The terrain progressively changed to fertile bottomland that extended far beyond both riverbanks and spanned the fifty-mile distance between Cahokia and Kaskaskia, allowing white settlers to grow abundant crops of wheat, corn, and meat. Farmers delivered their surplus south to Kaskaskia for shipment to Nouvelle Orléans.

More than halfway between these two French settlements, the Canadian travelers heard, then saw soldiers and laborers building a major wooden garrison-fort by order of the *Compagnie des Indes*. The laborers told them that Fort Chartres would extend the military and governmental authority of the new Louisiana Company into the Illinois territory which had not been part of Crozat's monopoly. It would serve as the main link in the chain of French trading posts extending through both territories. Such news fully explained this fort's impressive size and the need for its four solidly constructed stone bastions.

Eighteen miles farther south they landed on the east bank where another fort neared completion. Sixteen years earlier, the Kaskaskia tribes had left their cousins in Cahokia and had moved to the southern portion of the bottomland. Jesuit missionaries and many of the French settlers had followed them. Seventy to eighty houses now lined the banks of the Kaskaskia River above where it merged with the Mississippi.

This colonial settlement was well-known for its exports of wheat, corn, and buffalo meat. Its merchants sent two shipments a year of excess farm products to Nouvelle Orléans, loading these on row galleys of eighteen–twenty oars. The return trip upriver usually required ten weeks.

Shortly before reaching the Ohio river mouth, the Mississippi entered its lower alluvial valley and began to meander erratically to the east and to the west, bending its flow first to the southwest, then southwest by south. This flat floodplain covered an area 600 miles long and 25–125 miles wide.

Approximately 200 miles beyond its encounter with the Missouri River's enormous contributions of water and sediment, the Mississippi channel remained muddy and swift-flowing. Its second major tributary now poured in from the east, doubling the great river's volume and forming a blue stream that flowed through the brown Mississippi current but did not merge with it. The Canadians were fascinated by the persistent difference in color of the two waterflows.

They passed Chickasaw Bluffs (Memphis) on the east bank where La Salle had set up the temporary palisades of Fort Prud'homme on his return trip north from the southern sea in 1682. Barely a trace of his effort remained.

They encountered another strong current from the west-bank confluence of the Arkansas and Mississippi rivers where Tonti had established the French settlement of Fort Arkansea on relatively high ground, on the edge of *la Grande Prairie*. The fort had been abandoned at the turn of the century, yet new settlers continued to harvest logs from the great cypress groves of that area for the construction of French houses, trading posts and stockades.

Michel pointed out the remains of an original trading house built on this site to serve the Quapaw Indians who lived nearby. Jean was amazed to see that this structure had been built of horizontal squared logs. Most of the settlements he had seen during the voyage consisted of houses constructed in a palisade-style that the Canadians called *poteaux-en-terre* (posts in the ground), as distinct a technique of eighteenth-century Louisiana architecture as was *pièces-sur-pièces* in Nouvelle France.

Farther south, the travelers sighted newly-built palisades on the east bank, high on a bluff overlooking the river. Michel explained that three years earlier, Bienville had completed Fort Rosalie to protect French river traffic from the Natchez warriors. He did not stop because he knew how close they were to their final destination.

Another sixty miles farther, the Red River merged from the west and copiously delivered its clay-colored water into a swampy, snake-infested semi-tropical area that bordered the Mississippi. On either side of the mighty river, Michel's crew saw miles of marshland and bayous—the "trembling prairies" of Louisiana.

They passed Baton Rouge high up on an eastern escarpment. Michel identified this as the first high ground north of the southern sea. *Sieur* d'Iberville had named it after a large red pole he had clearly seen from the river. He related how two native nations had set that post to mark the common boundary of their hunting grounds, and had colored it with the blood of animals they had killed.

Jean asked: "Why are the houses built so far back from the river?

Michel replied: "To protect them from the yearly spring floods; we've also learned to build our homes on stilts and open foundations. We're entering a lowland area which is very fertile, its soil is enriched by yearly spring-flooding. Once we've drained the land, we can manage two planting seasons a year."

They reached a developed area on the west bank that was neatly outlined with rows of oak trees. "Oh, look at that!" Madeleine called out. "Isn't that beautiful?"

"Papa and I planted those trees when we first came to Louisiana." Michel said joyfully as he prepared to disembark. "My brother Louis should be here!"

Nine

1720

Louis Arsonneau let out a jubilant whoop when he spotted his brother's arrival. He dropped his tools and ran to greet them at the landing. His sudden outburst startled the field workers who were quick to follow him down the slope to help with the disembarkation. Two native women were particularly solicitous of their *patron*'s wife and baby.

Louis picked up Madeleine, hugged her, and exuberantly twirled her around. "At long last! Michel has found himself a wife—a lovely one at that!"

His brother sought to restrain him. "We're certainly happy to see you too, *p'tit frère*, but please be gentle with Madeleine and young Michel."

Madeleine chuckled after she caught her breath. "Are you always this enthusiastic?" she asked.

"Only when big brother's arrival is long overdue." He noticed just then that she showed the first signs of pregnancy. "Are you all right?"

"Of course I am! But it's been a long voyage and I'm very happy to reach the end of it."

Louis spoke earnestly: "I'm so relieved that you've arrived safely and that you had the courage to travel such a long distance!"

He turned to his longtime friends from the cape and welcomed each of them in turn.

"What do you think of the Mississippi?" he asked them.

"That's one magnificent river!" Jean replied.

More than once, Louis caught Madeleine staring at him. "Is there anything wrong?" he asked.

"You look so much like your brother…"

"Oh that, of course! Then you've met my twin, François—It's been a while since anyone has reminded me of that."

Michel scanned the property and the old cabin that he and his father had built so many years ago. Time to build a new one, he thought. He directed his crewmen to grab the long poles and anchor both canoes to a tree that stood close to the riverbank. "So we can avoid a *décharge*, and leave early tomorrow morning to continue downriver to the main house," he explained.

The men prepared to set up camp nearby and keep watch over their cargo throughout the night. Louis approved of the arrangement. "Once you've finished here, you must all come up to the house and make yourselves comfortable while our servants prepare a meal in honor of your arrival!" He turned to the other Canadian crewmen to tell them that there would be enough food for all of them and that if they needed anything at all, not to hesitate to let him know.

L'Allée-des-Chênes consisted of 250 square arpents located on the west bank of the Mississippi delta, just north of *La Vacherie*, a natural pasture where local settlers left their cattle to graze.

Michel transferred his son from Madeleine's back to his own and satisfied her curiosity by leading her right up to the nearest row of oak trees. She saw that they were tall, lanky, and spaced so that they would interlace with each other as they continued to grow into full maturity.

"You planted these with your father when you were only eleven years old?"

"Yes. He told me then that they'd be a welcome sight to anyone passing by on the river. They certainly were for me today."

"And for me…" She leaned against him and tried to imagine how they would look when fully leafed out.

They continued up the slope to the cabin which was built of *poteaux-en-terre*. A *bousillage* of mud and moss filled the joints between the uprights, making the walls weather-tight. Michel explained to Jean and the Barette brothers that this was the easiest and earliest mode of construction in the Illinois and Louisiana territories, that it was based on a technique that the local natives had used to shelter and protect their families for countless generations. The entire structure had been built of cypress, a local wood that was especially resistant to ground rot.

Jean compared the small cabin with the house his father had recently built and learned that this building's frame was confined to the unshaven plates, roof trusses, window- and door-frames.

"Where's the kitchen?" Madeleine asked.

"Our servants prepare and cook our food in a separate building to avoid adding extra heat in the house during our long hot summers," Louis replied. "Right now, the men are gathering fresh shellfish and meat for us. I hope you'll enjoy the meal."

Madeleine released the baby from the carrier-board, saw to his needs, and made him comfortable. Then she laid him down to exercise freely on a folded blanket that Michel had spread out on the wooden floor. While he enjoyed this newfound freedom, the adults caught up on local news.

Louis smiled as he told them that the workers were obviously happy to see Michel again and were fascinated by his lovely wife. He assured his brother that things had gone well on this property, that their slaves had been healthy, cooperative and productive.

"While you were away, the company ordered us to produce indigo in this part of the valley. The results didn't meet their expectations nor ours because there are far better varieties available elsewhere. So we concentrated on the traditional native crops of corn, sweet potatoes, and tobacco. They produced a good profit.

"Governor Bienville recently decided that sugar, cotton and rice would thrive in this area. Because the blacks can work more easily in this summer heat and humidity than we can, the company is delivering them directly from French Africa. Those who arrived last year were much healthier and stronger than those we received from Saint-Domingue and they already understood and spoke our language."

Michel voiced his approval. "Do you remember the condition our black people were in when they first arrived from the island?"

"Yes, but with proper food and care they've certainly regained their health and become good workers," Louis replied.

He turned to Madeleine and asked: "How was your voyage?"

She hesitated, still overwhelmed by the journey.

Michel replied: "We've traveled with a brigade of former Canadian settlers who chose to return to Louisiana as soon as they learned that conditions had improved. Traffic has definitely increased on the river."

Louis agreed. "Messieurs Crozat and Law both promised that great mineral wealth could be found in the Mississippi valley. Several boatloads of European settlers arrived from France during the past two years—gentlemen, former military officers, craftsmen, and farmers who looked forward to getting rich by finding the promised treasure farther upriver. They had sold everything they owned to buy up company shares and come in search of gold and pearls.

"Many died during the crossing, others from fevers when they arrived during the mid-summer heat. Most who survived and stayed were soon disillusioned by our living conditions. They had arrived without enough provisions to meet their own needs. Our own limited supplies and resources were stretched thin by our attempts to feed and house them as quickly as the men landed, often with their families.

"They learned quickly enough that there were no easy riches to be had and insisted that the company release them from their indenture contracts. The company finally offered each man the choice of free passage back to France or a new land concession. Most accepted the land and stayed."

Michel frowned at the deception. "We saw quite a few foreign settlers along the river. France seems to have opened up immigration to other countries and religions. That's quite a change in policy."

"This colony can certainly use the extra manpower—Have you heard about France joining England, Austria and the Netherlands in an alliance against Spain?"

"Vaguely, there wasn't much fuss about it back home—It seems that France is forever at war in Europe, perhaps that's why it can't offer much help to us here in the colonies..."

Jean, Laurent and Baptiste had rarely been exposed to such a lively political discussion in Nouvelle France. People apparently spoke more openly in Louisiana.

Louis continued: "The Spaniards are closer to us here—they've been trying to turn some of the native tribes against us. Last May,

Sieur Sérigny arrived from France with a shipload of African blacks, and orders to seize the Spanish port of Pensacola. He and Governor Bienville sailed out of Mobile on five ships with several hundred men and natives. They did seize Pensacola, left their brother Monsieur de Châteauguay in command of the fort, and sent two of their ships to deliver their Spanish prisoners to Havana. Their governor seized the ships and crews, then sailed with a larger force to recover Pensacola. They won the battle, captured Châteauguay and his fifty men. They've been imprisoned in Havana since August."

The Canadians recognized the names of the Le Moyne brothers of Montréal.

"Why have France and Spain turned against each other?" Michel asked.

"The Spanish envoy in Versailles was plotting to gain support for his king's claim to the French throne."

"On what grounds?"

"The Spanish king is Louis XIV's grandson, so he's a generation closer to the throne than is Louis XV, but he gave up his right to assume power in both countries by signing the Treaty of Utrecht."

Michel shook his head in disbelief. "Are they still fighting?"

Louis nodded. "Naval skirmishes, mostly in the gulf. At the end of July, Spanish forces tried to capture our port in Mobile Bay. Bienville and Sérigny boarded two French battleships and returned to Pensacola last August. Four days later, the Spanish surrendered the fort and 1500 of their men."

Michel noticed that Madeleine's eyes had grown heavy and realized how tired she was. "You could sleep in the other room while Louis and I continue to catch up on our news," he suggested. "I'll keep watch over baby Michel."

She welcomed his offer and fell asleep as soon as she lay down on the bed.

When she awoke fully refreshed three hours later, two black women had set up a buffet table laden with corn bread, sweet potatoes, root vegetables, roast beef, shrimp, crayfish, and fruit pies. The Canadian travelers savored their first complete meal since leaving Montréal; most of them returned for second helpings.

That night, Michel's small family slept in a bed for the first time in eight months.

They reached the Arsonneau Plantation by late afternoon of the following day, having traveled farther south and to the east riverbank where Michel's family and friends enjoyed another joyous reunion with his younger brother Alexis. This slightly larger house built of *poteaux-sur-soles* (posts on sills) stood farther back from the river, and was elevated above ground on piers of cypress blocks. Cypress shakes covered its steeply hipped roof that extended in lean-to fashion over the *galerie* that encircled the structure. Other buildings such as the kitchen, barn, stable, and slave quarters stood nearby on this elevation of the Bonnet Carré river bend. Neatly tilled fields surrounded the complex and stretched beyond it toward Lac Ponchartrain to the northeast.

Jean asked Michel about the advantages of this unusual building style and learned that the raised sill protected the structure from rising spring floods, and that air flowing under the house kept it cooler and less humid during the summer. The surrounding *galerie* sheltered the occupants from heavy rain and the heat of the sun but it also served as an external connector to all of the rooms. Michel explained that during the summer heat, the residents usually left their doors and windows wide open at the end of the day to provide a cooling cross-ventilation.

Once they reached the front porch, Jean examined the upright *pièces* and saw that they were trimmed flat only on their abutting sides. The vertical spaces between them were filled in with a *bousillage* of clay and retted Spanish moss. When they entered the house, he saw three rooms built end to end and separated by boarded partitions. Each room had doorways opening to the front and back *galeries*. The middle room had a fireplace and direct access to both end rooms. Casement windows were located in all outside walls. The house was built entirely of cypress wood.

Michel had quickly scanned the fields and told Alexis: "You must have had a good year."

"It worked out well for us," his brother replied with a hint of pride in his voice. "We experimented with indigo and everyone was disappointed with the results, but our corn, sweet potatoes, and tobacco turned a good profit."

"What are your plans for this year's crops?" Michel asked.

"I'd like to try growing rice on the back arpents, but we'd need some of the new African blacks."

"Have you seen them?"

"Our neighbor downriver has three."

"Then I'll visit with him tomorrow and see how they compare with those of Saint-Domingue."

Jean, Laurent and Baptiste offered to stay and work for Michel during the following year in order to fully evaluate what life would be like in this semitropical region. Michel welcomed their help and began to build a cabin to house them.

Madeleine settled comfortably into her new home with the small furnishings and personal items she had brought from Chambly.

Michel visited his neighbor and evaluated the condition of his new slaves. Although their bodies were strong and healthy, their dark eyes revealed a depth of despair and suspicion that startled him. He had never seen this before, but he recalled his father's years of involuntary servitude and recognized the human vulnerability he saw in the eyes of these men who were so far removed from their normal environment. He frowned and stifled his outrage when he noticed that one of them had angry red welts across his back.

Michel took Madeleine and his guests on a sightseeing and shopping excursion to Nouvelle Orléans. The couple traveled one full day by horse and carriage down the winding river road to the Louisiana delta area, while Jean and the Barettes followed them in a horse-drawn wagon.

Until about halfway to their destination, a heavily settled area of immaculately maintained fields and farms graced the opposite shore. Michel told them that the concessions on this *Côte des Allemands* extended forty arpents inland, and added that over the past few years, *La Compagnie* had organized an immigration of thousands of Swiss, German, Belgian and Austrians to Louisiana. As a result of poor planning and overcrowding, five thousand of them had died before the ships reached Louisiana. Many of the recruits had given up and gone elsewhere in France or nearer Biloxi, but those who had reached the Mississippi established the first German colony in Louisiana. He added that on this section of the river, rich alluvial soil extended over one league inland from both riverbanks, and that the land beyond that inclined into cypress-filled wetlands and bayous.

Nouvelle Orléans occupied the shortest distance between the Mississippi River and Lac Pontchartrain, an area which had long been used by the natives of the delta as a depot and market for goods carried between the two waterways.

This narrow strip of land was located on a crescent-shaped section of the riverside about 100 miles north of the gulf. Bienville had judged it to be a highly valuable location for the rapid deployment of troops, and the river's curve could slow the arrival of enemy ships coming up from the gulf, making them easy targets for the fort's defensive artillery. It proved to be more convenient and secure than the ports of Mobile and Biloxi.

The newcomers were given a tour of the governor's new settlement where residential housing and shops were rapidly filling in a neatly defined city plan. Masons worked on the foundation of the first church in Louisiana, the future Saint Louis Cathedral. The governor's residence was still under construction; Madeleine considered it to be as fine as any in Montréal.

The streets buzzed with activity, many homes and offices were already occupied. An informal census had counted more than 370 people, including 147 male colonists, 65 female colonists, 38 children, 28 servants, 73 slaves and 21 Amerindians.

While Michel accompanied his wife during her shopping tour through all the shops, their trio of friends went sight-seeing. Jean saw a great mixture of building styles. Most of these new structures were set on high brick foundations with front staircases leading straight up to their second-level living and business areas.

Michel arranged to spend that night at a local auberge and the group rejoined for dinner that evening. They shared stories of their day's activities, and Michel announced that since Madeleine expected their second child in May, their present home would be too small for their growing family. They had already decided to build a larger house of *pièces-sur-pièces* above a brick foundation.

He asked Jean about the construction of his family's home, and asked Laurent and Baptiste about their experiences while working with the mason during the church construction.

Jean described what it was like to build such a house. He cautioned Michel that he was not qualified to plan and design a home for them but was experienced in hewing the timbers for such a square-logged house. He advised his friend to find a reputable architect or master-carpenter who could prepare a sketch according to his needs, and he agreed to supervise and assist in the preparation of the lumber. He and the Barettes volunteered to help raise the structure, but Jean warned that a local carpenter must advise them on local construction practices and assume responsibility for working out the measurements and joining the frame.

The wagon was filled with Madeleine's purchases on their ride back home.

Ten

J ean and Baptiste Barette asked Alexis how much farther than Nouvelle Orléans did the river flow before reaching the southern sea. Alexis replied that he did not know but that they could explore that section of the river with the Canadian canoes.

During their absence, Michel and Madeleine refined their house plans and met with French master-carpenter André Pénicault who agreed to take on the project.

Michel described a house two rooms deep by three rooms wide, supported on a solid masonry base by a first-floor storage "basement" with walls and floor constructed entirely of bricks to a height of eight feet above the ground, and with four cast-iron doors that could be opened during the summer heat. This structure would protect the house and its occupants from yearly spring floods and allow additional cooling and ventilation during the summer.

The second-floor living area would be built of *pièces-sur-pièces* with windows and doors in each room that opened onto a wooden *galerie* that would encircle the entire house. Inside doorways would allow direct access between rooms. There would be no hallway.

The double-pitched pavilion roof would extend over the *galeries*, and be covered with split cypress shingles to allow further cross-ventilation of the house during the summer. All outside walls were to be stuccoed and inside walls to be plastered.

Pénicault assured them that their plan was feasible. He advised Louis that the local mason would require a large supply of bricks that his slaves could form with local red clay. He explained that the mason would furnish the wooden molds for the bricks and would fire them in his own kiln.

Michel agreed to provide the bricks and also dig the shallow foundation base once its boundaries were accurately laid out and marked. He stipulated that the entire second-story structure above the brick foundation must be built of cypress.

"When you consider that the roof would be taller than the walls of the living space, that's a lot of cypress, Monsieur!"

"I know," Michel agreed, "but we plan to raise our family in that house and we expect it to last our lifetime. We recently returned from Nouvelle France where this style of construction has proven to be much warmer during the winter, so we expect that it will prove to be much cooler during a Louisiana summer."

"That may be so, Monsieur, but we've developed a shortage of hand-hewn lumber with all the construction that's going on in this area, especially in Nouvelle Orléans."

"Surely, there must be several working sawmills by now. There's certainly no shortage of cypress trees in this part of the Mississippi valley."

"The present sawmills can't keep up with the demand, Monsieur."

"Then we should build one," Michel suggested. "I worked my father's sawmill for several years."

Pénicault's eyes brightened at this revelation. "Perhaps you and I could build and operate one to meet our local needs?"

Michel laughed jovially in agreement and shook the hand of his new friend and business partner.

During their excursion to the Mississippi river mouth, Jean and the Barettes described the sites they had seen and visited during their journey south. Alexis was surprised to learn that so many changes had occurred since he had last traveled that way.

His thoughts turned to his home and family in Batiscan. He could see that the birch-bark canoes were still in good condition but he knew that they would quickly deteriorate in this southern environment as the weather grew warmer and more humid.

Upon their return to the plantation, Alexis had a long talk with Michel, and his brother agreed that it was time for him to return to Canada. When their other brother Louis also expressed his desire to head north, Michel assured him that he could replace him at *Allée-des-Chênes* by hiring one of the Canadian engagés who had recently voyaged south with him. When they learned that the two Arsonneau brothers planned to return to Canada as soon as they could find others to join them, Laurent and Baptiste decided that they were ready for the homeward journey and volunteered to accompany them.

Madeleine asked that they delay their departure until after the birth of their second child so that the baptism could be recorded in Montréal. There was no such registry in Louisiana at that time.

Jean remained enthusiastic about Louisiana's semitropical climate, lush vegetation and available land. He decided to stay and help Michel build his new home and sawmill.

The others agreed to postpone their journey and joined in the construction effort by overseeing the production of bricks for Michel's house. The master-mason invited them to observe this process which was underway at another construction site a few miles downriver. Jean accompanied them even though he would be primarily involved in assisting the carpenter to mark, fell, and collect the cypress timber.

Laurent and Baptiste Barette trained the plantation workers in the production of bricks. They dug a shallow treading pit, lined it with a wooden retaining wall, then hauled and dumped muddy clay into it. The two white foremen and several black men vigorously stomped and mixed this wet clay with their feet until it reached a smooth consistency.

The workers pulled batches of the processed clay and piled these onto sturdy tables that stood in a nearby shaded area. Several men pounded and kneaded these by hand to clear the substance of air bubbles and organic debris. They divided and shaped it into brick-sized loaves each of which they sprinkled with fine sand before throwing it into a section of the sand-dusted wooden molds. Laurent and Baptiste then drew a straight wooden screed across the top of the compartmented forms to remove any excess clay and smooth the brick surface. Once a form had been completely and properly filled, a worker carried it to a raised bed of sand where he carefully dropped the moist bricks out of the mold and left them to dry.

A week later, they transferred the partially hardened bricks into a drying shed to protect them from the weather and allow them to finish drying slowly over a period of six more weeks. Meanwhile, the mason's helpers collected firewood and built a kiln to heat the bricks continually up to a temperature of 1850 degrees Fahrenheit over a period of six days. They would remain in the oven to cool slowly; their quality could not be evaluated until a week later.

Kennebec River valley

Since the signing of the Treaty of Utrecht in 1713, *les bostonnais* had rapidly expanded their settlements northeastward into what they had long claimed as their frontier territory of Maine. The Canadians had always regarded it as a traditional Abenaki homeland that offered a natural buffer between New England and the Saint Lawrence River settlements. The language of the treaty concerning the cession of *Acadie* and the recorded history of this land remained so ambiguous that this boundary dispute would not be settled until well over a century later.

The Jesuits had several missions among the Abenakis, but the French had never attempted to settle on their land. In 1646, native emissaries from the Kennebec tribes had petitioned the Jesuits of Québec to send a missionary to live among them. Father Druillettes had returned with them to their homeland to create the first Catholic mission on the Kennebec River.

In 1695, Father Sébastien Râle had founded a more permanent missionary village at Norridgewock, across from the Sandy River outlet into the Kennebec, a fifteen-day overland journey from Québec. Ever since then, this missionary had lived among the Abenakis and had mastered their Algonquin dialect. The natives continued to trade with the English Puritans of Boston who were a few days journey away, but they remained loyal to the French through the bonds of the Roman Catholic religion.

Cap-de-la-Madeleine, April 1720

Soon after the swift spring current of the Saint Lawrence River subsided, pastor Paul Vachon approached Louis after Sunday Mass and asked: "Can you still speak the Algonquin language?"

"Yes, *Père*, I managed to communicate with the Ottawas during our last voyage."

"The Jesuit missionaries in Bécancour could use your help. They've had a major migration of Norridgewock refugees and need extra interpreters to help them understand how best to meet their needs."

"Their language is a bit different from what I learned so many years ago, but I can give it a try." Louis recalled that Nicolas Perrot had often served in that capacity.

"They will surely appreciate your efforts. There are so few people now who understand the native languages."

His son Louis offered to help him cross the great river by canoe. Upon their arrival at the mission, they found the Norridgewocks to be confused and despondent, but relieved to have the opportunity to relate their story in their own dialect.

The group's spokesman explained to Louis that his people were tired of war. He acknowledged that the French had traditionally respected their territorial integrity, but the English continued to claim that the Abenaki homeland was given to them by France through their last treaty. A delegation of his people had traveled to Québec and had been reassured by the French governor that this was not so, that the French understood that the Abenaki land was not theirs to give away and the Abenaki people believed him.

Shortly after the signing of that treaty, the English governor had promised to build honest trading houses closer to their village, and provide a blacksmith who could repair their guns for the hunt so that his people would not have to travel all the way to Boston.

Once the English had gained permission to do this on tribal land, they had rapidly divided and occupied the rich soils of the native homeland in the Kennebec River valley. They had built stone forts and farm houses, had cleared the forest, tilled the soil, and set up wooden fences that deprived his people of their traditional hunting and fishing grounds and blocked their way to the sea. The promised trading posts and the blacksmith had not been provided.

The Abenaki chiefs had negotiated other treaties in good faith with the English governors through which both parties had promised to live in peace with each other. Their chiefs had repeatedly reminded the English that some Abenaki land had been sold to them west of the Kennebec River but none on the east side. The English soldiers had continued to build a series of stone forts at key points along the Kennebec, moving ever closer to the village of Norridgewock. Because of this, his people suffered from food shortages, displacement, and drastic changes in their traditional lifestyle.

The spokesman related that although both parties had agreed that each side would render justice unto its own law breakers, his people repeatedly complained to the English authorities about specific traders who cheated and defrauded them, yet they were never punished for their crimes. On separate occasions and during peacetime, the English had seized and held hostage two Abenaki chiefs and four of their Abenaki traders in Boston.

His people had grown fearful about their future. English construction of Fort Richmond was the final and most intimidating insult that forced the Abenakis to undertake the two-week journey to Nouvelle France to trade with the French. Some now sought refuge in Canada for their families.

Their highly respected priest and counselor Father Râle had written a letter to Captain Moody that winter, claiming that English ownership of Abenaki land had been gained through trickery and fraud, that the Indians had the right to defend their homeland and the duty to protect it for their future generations, that he would not forbid them to do so. The priest further stated that he would write about these things to the King of France and that it would be published so that the world would know how the English treated the native Americans.

Louis gave a full report to the Jesuits before visiting his and Simonne's relatives who lived on the south shore. His youngest brother François still occupied the first land he had bought in 1698. Its three arpents fronted the Saint Lawrence River and faced directly across from their boyhood home.

They caught up on family news, and François asked him if he had seen Sébastien's new land.

Louis was surprised and curious. "I haven't heard from him since last autumn. When did this happen?"

"About a month ago. He tells me that this is where he wants to spend the rest of his life."

"Where is it located?"

"On the Nicolet River, on the northern point of land that divides a fork in the river."

"I'd really like to see it."

"Then it might be best to travel there by canoe; we can ask him to show us around," François suggested.

Sébastien and his sons Joseph, Jean-Baptiste, Simon and Alexis were working together in the fields of his original concession. They all looked forward to showing Louis the new land concession. They decided to join them and picked up Louis Massé along the way.

Sébastien and François shared Louis' canoe. Each had his own personal characteristics, some of which they had either inherited or adopted from their father. Louis, the experienced woodsman and voyageur, had always bought developed land and hired people to manage his farms. Sébastien enjoyed farming above all else and had acquired several parcels of good arable land that he had developed into thriving properties. François, the thoughtful one, the helpful one, who could be hot-tempered if he felt badly treated, was a good farmer and a devoted family man whose greatest pleasure was to carve and shape wood with his father's hand tools.

They reminisced about their years together as a family after Bastien and Catherine, both widowed, had merged their thirteen children together in a new and larger house that Bastien had built with their help.

"What courage they both had!" Louis exclaimed.

"What love for their families!" Sébastien interjected.

"What patience!" François added, initiating a round of laughter.

They could appreciate those qualities so much more now that they had families of their own, having come to recognize their parents' sacrifices at a time when supporting such a large family must have been a constant, major endeavor. And they all agreed that it had turned out well.

Isle-de-la-Fourche-en-bas was located on the Nicolet River, a short distance upstream from its outlet into the Saint Lawrence. Sébastien's densely forested land overlooked the water to the north, east, and west. Louis and his son enjoyed the quiet beauty of the site.

Sébastien told them: "I was reminded of our family history in France when I first set foot on it."

"I remember Papa telling us about that when we worked on the second house," François recalled. "Louis was away then, on his first trading voyage out west."

"I'd like to hear those stories," Their older brother prompted them.

Sébastien asked: "Did you know that he and I were named after his own father Sébastien Provenchère?"

Louis nodded. "Papa was so disappointed years later when he learned that his name had been misspelled when he arrived in Nouvelle France."

His brothers shrugged their shoulders. They and their father had never learned to write their own names.

Sébastien continued: "He told us that his *pépère* was a notary in Artenay and that he had a beautiful signature."

"I wish I could have seen it," said Louis.

"Strangely enough, he had signed as witness to church registries relating to *Maman*'s family. *Pépère* had shared with him many stories about our ancestry that dated back to a time when England was ruled by the Normans, and well before France became the kingdom of provinces that it is now."

"How did he know all this?"

"The oral history was passed down through the generations from father to son," François replied.

Sébastien continued, "There was a château in Franche-Comté that belonged to our ancestors. It overlooked a river and sat high above it. He told us of a family tradition where a father taught each son early on to recite '*Je suis* (first name) *de Provenchère de Belleville de la Rosière*'."

Louis was amazed and saddened."I've never heard any of this until now."

His brother continued: "I've followed that custom with my sons and I encourage them to carry it forward to their grandchildren."

"What else did he tell you about the past?"

"He told us that he hadn't followed that family tradition because it probably meant nothing now that we lived across the sea."

"Do you know what it meant?" Louis asked.

"He said it was like a map that could lead each generation back to the family château."

"Is it still standing?"

"He didn't know because he had never traveled there. Franche-Comté was quite far from Pithiviers where he grew up."

Although Joseph, Jean-Baptiste, Simon and Alexis had heard this story before, they never tired of it.

Louis looked over Sébastien's new land. "Where will you build your house?" he asked.

"Right here, where we stand."

This was indeed an ideal spot with adequate elevation against spring flooding and a magnificent view in all directions.

They walked the boundaries together; there was only one adjoining lot on the southern, inland border of the property and it was unoccupied. The rest of the surrounding land remained undeveloped.

"I plan to build *pièces-sur-pièces* as you have," he told Louis.

His brother was happy to hear it. "I'd highly recommend it if you can find an experienced carpenter. Your boys would learn to hew lumber to measure as we did, and could help to raise the framing."

His nephews welcomed the idea. François and Louis Massé offered to help with the project. They started that same day by laying stones to mark the proposed placement and rough outline of the building, then identified the closest trees with bark that showed signs of straight growth and grain.

"You still have time to girdle those trees to dry up their sap and make them easier to cut down. You might be able to prepare the lumber and join the shell before next winter sets in," Louis advised them.

"Sébastien looked at him quizzically. "Are you sure of that?"

Louis and his son nodded. "We found it to be true."

"That would allow us to finish the inside during the winter..."

"I believe so."

Everyone agreed it was worth a try and Sébastien had a lot of volunteers who were willing to help.

On their way back to Bécancour, Sébastien showed them his other most recent concession in Roctaillade which bordered the *seigneurie de Nicolet*. Louis *fils* saw the piece of land he had been looking for, and it was located right alongside his uncle's northeast border.

A few days later, Sébastien signed a contract with a local carpenter who agreed that the lumber was likely to be ready by late summer and the house enclosed by November. Sébastien and his sons immediately began to girdle the marked trees to interrupt their flow of sap. They soon started digging and gathering stones for the cellar foundation and planned to do so whenever their chores allowed. They felled and stripped the timber on site until they had collected enough to ship by shallop to Batiscan where it would be sawed into squared *pièces* by the Arsonneau sawmill.

Nouvelle Orléans, May 1720

Several company ships arrived in Louisiana with news that a peace treaty had been signed that winter by Spain and France. Spain had thus given up its European territorial gains and the two colonial powers exchanged all of their continental and colonial prisoners. Governor Bienville released the port of Pensacola to the Spanish after his brother Châteauguay returned safely from his imprisonment in Havana.

La Compagnie des Indes announced the reorganization of the *Conseil supérieur* of Louisiana, placing it mostly under the leadership of Canadian officers and settlers who governed the colony from Biloxi.

Jean-Baptiste Arseneau was born on the family plantation on May 26th. Alexis and Louis Arsonneau prepared to leave soon after the baptism. Michel advised them to travel the more direct route by way of the Mississippi, Ohio, Wabash and Maumee rivers, lakes Erie and Ontario to avoid wintering in Michillimackinac and arrive in Montréal before the northern rivers iced up. Although they knew this to be a more difficult route, they accepted his advice and planned to travel lightly to ease the tasks of unloading and portaging the canoes.

Boston

An English translation of Father Râle's letter to Captain Moody was delivered to Governor Samuel Shute and the governing council of Massachusetts. In mid-July, the general court offered a reward of 100 English pounds for the capture of any Jesuit missionary found in the frontier territory of Maine.

The following November, an Abenaki delegation arrived for a second conference in Georgetown to protest the continued imprisonment of four of their kinsmen and the rapid increase of English settlement along Merrymeeting Bay that threatened to completely cut them off from access to their traditional winter camping and fishing grounds. Father Râle was not with them.

Kennebec River valley

The English restated their "rights to lands on the Kennebec River by Deeds and Conveyances from Indians seventy years ago."

Effectively intimidated by the English representatives, the native delegates left that meeting after pledging to pay a ransom of 200 beaver skins for damages to cattle claimed by the English, in order to gain the release of their kinsmen.

The Norridgewock spokesman had told Louis that his people feared for their missionary's life, but that Father Râle refused to abandon them and urged them to unite with the other Abenaki tribes to present a united front against further English encroachment upon their lands.

Neither the Abenakis nor the Canadians knew at that time that although Nouvelle France had recently counted 24,951 habitants, the English provincial population had risen to 475,000. There were now nineteen English provincials to every French colonist in North America. The English settlements were crowded between the Appalachian Mountain range and the eastern seaboard and the thirteen provinces had not yet united.

Montréal

The Barette and Arsonneau brothers arrived in Montréal before the rivers froze but winter was definitely on its way. The owners of a local auberge told them that the fur trade had greatly declined in the area. Fewer native flotillas had arrived for the annual trade fair due to the Fox Wars and the diversion of Illinois furs to Louisiana.

Madame Dionet gratefully received the news that her daughter and grandson had safely reached the Arsonneau Plantation. She was surprised but happy to have the privilege of registering another grandson's birth and baptism at the local church.

The travelers awoke the following morning to light snow flurries and the presence of thin ice formed overnight along the edges of the Saint Lawrence River. Nevertheless, they set off to reach Batiscan by canoe.

Eleven

Cap-de-la-Madeleine

Darkness had already fallen that late November afternoon. Louis and the boys played a game of piquet by the firelight while Simonne and the girls prepared a light supper. They heard a loud knock at the door. Angélique peeked out the window and saw the dark shadows of four young men standing in the dooryard.

Joseph opened the door and was greeted by the Barette and Arsonneau brothers. Louis and Simonne quickly invited them in out of the cold. They rejoiced at seeing the Barettes again, but wondered why Jean was not with them.

"You two must not have stayed long," Louis addressed Laurent and Baptiste who now stood nearer the fire, welcoming the cups of wine Simonne offered them.

Laurent reassured them that they had all safely reached the Arsonneau plantation. "Jean liked Louisiana so much that he volunteered to stay on a while longer."

The family breathed a sigh of relief.

Baptiste Barette explained Jean's reasons: "Shortly after we reached Bonnet Carré Bend, Michel decided to build a larger house for his family and offered construction work to all three of us. Laurent and I would make brick for the foundation while Jean would work with the master-carpenter to construct the house and a sawmill with squared timber."

Laurent added: "But when Louis and Alexis decided to return home, Baptiste and I were ready to travel back with them."

Simonne asked Alexis: "How did Madeleine and the baby manage during the journey?"

"Would you believe that Michel has a second son already?"

Louis and his family laughed at the thought. "It must have been a good voyage!" he remarked, and his daughters blushed.

Baptiste added: "Your son and I felt honored that they chose to name the baby 'Jean-Baptiste'."

Louis had many questions to ask but he and Simonne realized how tired these young men were and so he thanked them for sharing the welcome news. "I'm sure your families will be very happy to see you!" he said as they prepared to continue on their way.

Louis wondered what kind of house Michel would build for his family. Simonne hoped with all her heart that Jean would not settle so far away from Champlain. If so, she doubted that he would ever marry because Louisiana had developed a reputation as an outlet for the street people of Paris. Little did she know that the continental French held the same impression of Nouvelle France.

They met again after Sunday Mass and the four voyageurs accepted Simonne's invitation to join the family for dinner.

"We've heard that southern tobacco is now being grown in Canada," said Baptiste.

"My father always grew his own native tobacco," Louis replied, "but it was never as good as this new crop." He offered some and they enjoyed a smoke together.

"Mail service has been the greatest improvement between Québec and Montréal," he told them. "It's already increased commerce between Trois Rivières and the two other districts. It's much easier now to keep in touch with my sisters who live near Sorel."

"Did you say that Jean helped Michel build a new house?" Simonne asked.

Alexis nodded. "A *pièces-sur-pièces* and also a sawmill."

Louis smiled. His oldest son had learned more from his own construction project than he had thought.

"Along most of the lower Mississippi River, houses are usually framed and built of cypress wood which is as durable as our cedar and well-adapted to that climate," Alexis added. "Large swampy areas support great forests of cypress trees that extend inland for several leagues both east and west of the southern Mississippi."

He and his brother talked about the surge in construction that was underway all along the Mississippi but particularly in the delta area where their family properties were located, that most of it was meant to accommodate the waves of new immigrants who arrived on company ships.

Baptiste told them: "We've heard that hundreds of those new arrivals were hired to work in lead mines along the Upper Mississippi and Missouri rivers."

"Alexis and I are really impressed by the progress you've made in the new church construction," said Louis Arsonneau. "The bishop had just recently announced the project when we left for our journey south."

"Once we reached an agreement with the residents of Bécancour and Dutort, everyone got into the spirit of it. We're very pleased with the results. Monsieur Dufaux completed the permanent roof and steeple early last summer. Since then, he's been working on the arched doorway, the windows, and the floor of the chancel. Even though we can use the new church with the old benches, there's still much more to be done inside the building."

"The *croix fleurdelisée* and *coq-gaulois* are very special," Baptiste noted to everyone's agreement.

"Those two chefs d'oeuvre were produced by Antoine Bouton of Trois Rivières; the cross is of iron and the rooster is of lead. Both will be mounted once the roof and steeple are completed. We're all very happy with his work.

"How were things in Montréal?" Louis asked.

"They've started raising the stone wall around the town," Alexis replied. "The farmers appear to be more prosperous. The merchants complain about the French company's decision to ship the Illinois furs through Louisiana rather than Québec. We noticed more horses on the streets and in the countryside."

This was all news to Louis. "The horses can pull five times their weight and provide better transportation but they require more feed than the oxen. We've been growing extra grain to accommodate that and ship much of our surplus to Louisbourg and the West Indies. In spite of the growing migration of Canadians to Illinois and Louisiana, our own communities continue to grow as more land is cleared and cultivated. Our sheep continue to multiply so that wool is plentiful. More pork and dairy products are now available. We don't need to hunt as much anymore, which is just as well since the edge of the forest moves farther back every year." He added pensively: "My Papa once told me that farm production thrives during times of peace—He was so right."

They pondered his statement. Seven peaceful years since the Treaty of Utrecht had certainly made a difference in their lives.

The Barettes described the remarkable sights they had seen during their trip south, all of which impressed Louis and his family.

Louis Arsonneau told them: "We took a more direct route north to reach home before winter. We avoided the northern lakes altogether and crossed through the Illinois and Miami territories to enter Lake Erie. While heading north on the Illinois River, we met a group of Canadian canoes and *Père* Charlevoix who was exploring and reporting on our settlements to the king. He had planned to travel west past Lake Superior but after we described Louisiana and the southern gulf, he changed his mind and headed south on the Mississippi to visit Louisiana and Saint-Domingue."

Alexis added: "We talked to several Métis settlers in Illinois. They told us that they'd seen Spaniards travel that far north on horseback to attack the French and natives of that area, so the Métis taught their allies to defend themselves by shooting down the horses."

Louis asked why, because horses were highly valued in Nouvelle France.

"The Spaniards wear heavy armor and become helpless when they're forced to stand and fight."

The children giggled as they pictured this. Simonne scolded them.

"When we reached the Niagara Portage, we were told that Governor Vaudreuil had sent a trader named Joncaire who had befriended the Senecas. They granted him permission to build a trading post on their tribal land. He and others had recently finished the construction of a small loopholed storehouse at the foot of the Niagara Escarpment. He called it *Le Magasin Royal* and it flies the king's colors.

"The Iroquois offered to help us with our portage in exchange for shirts, bullets, gunpowder or other trade items but we had nothing to barter since we traveled so light—We were really pressed for time."

Louisiana, 1721

Eighty-one young *filles à la cassette* arrived in Biloxi aboard the French ship *Baleine* on January 5th. Port authorities advised the group's chaperone that since the ship would soon leave to deliver supplies to Nouvelle Orléans, she should remain on board to deliver her charges where Governor Bienville could surely provide more appropriate accommodations for them.

Michel, Madeleine and Jean were in the new capital when they learned that a reception was being held in the governor's mansion to introduce this group of young French women. Since Michel had occasionally met and consulted with the governor, they did not hesitate to attend.

Michel paid his respects to the governor and introduced his wife and friend. Jean's eyes scanned the crowded room and came to rest on one particular young woman who stood alone in a corner, casually observing the activity around her. Her dark hair was neatly and softly groomed and she wore a dress that was slightly different in style from the rest of her group. Her demeanor seemed calm and self-confident, her expression broke into a sympathetic smile whenever she spotted a friendly pairing across the room.

He was impressed, yet noticed that her poise seemed to have discouraged others from approaching her. Their eyes met and she did not turn away, so he moved toward her.

Jean welcomed her to Nouvelle Orléans and introduced himself.

She replied with a lilting voice: *"Je suis enchantée, Monsieur Provencher,"* and identified herself as Mademoiselle Thérèse Dalberni.

He was intrigued by her unusual accent. She told him that she was from southern France. Her hair and eyes were the darkest he had ever seen in a land whose French-speaking population was originally derived from the northwestern-most part of France.

"I must tell you that I'm also a recent immigrant to Louisiana."

She looked at him inquisitively.

"I arrived from Nouvelle France about a year ago."

"By ship?" she asked.

"No, by canoe on the great Mississippi River from Nouvelle France, a northern region where winters are much colder and more isolating than they are here. Ice covers its rivers five months of the year and prevents any communication with France from November through April."

She smiled and said: "Then I'm happy to have come to Louisiana." Michel and his wife approached just then, and introduced themselves. Madeleine explained that her own purpose for attending the reception was to find a governess for their two young sons.

"How old are they?" Thérèse asked.

"The older boy is two and the younger is less than a year old."

The young woman's face glowed with pleasure. "They must be very active!"

Madeleine appreciated her enthusiasm. "That's why I need some help—my husband requires my assistance in managing the plantation."

She was indeed very interested as they described their location and available accommodations.

Madeleine took her aside and explained that such an arrangement offered room, board, income, and extra time to adjust to her new environment. She also admitted that she and her husband would prefer to hire a governess who spoke fluent European French.

Thérèse accepted the offer. It relieved her of the need to rush into a lifelong commitment.

The chaperone approached them and agreed that this would be an ideal arrangement for the time being. Her greatest and most immediate problem was to find safe shelter for all the young women.

Once the official documents had been signed and notarized, Thérèse gathered her few belongings and left with them. She and Jean became better acquainted while on their way upriver to the Arsonneau Plantation. Thérèse told him that she was of mixed French and Spanish descent, that she had been orphaned at a young age and had been educated by the Ursulines as an *enfant-du-roi*. Jean told her that his grandmother had had a similar experience and told of watching her for hours at a time while she worked at the spinning wheel and loom. Thérèse learned that Jean was a lifelong friend of Michel, that he lived in the old plantation house, had trained under a master-carpenter and occasionally worked as a sawyer in Michel's mill which was located on the outskirts of the plantation.

They both looked forward to getting to know each other better.

Twelve

Nouvelle France, 1721

In late afternoon of February 15ᵗʰ, government representatives Collet and Boucault arrived in Cap-de-la-Madeleine to assess its parish boundaries. They were greeted in the rectory by *curé* Paul Vachon and *Sieur* Jean-François Boullanger de Saint-Pierre, and were joined later that evening by militia captain Jean Joliet, representatives of the Jesuits of Québec, and churchwardens: Louis *père*, Michel Arsonneau *père*, Adrien Barette Descormiers, Michel Rochereau Duvivier, and Joseph Barette.

Boucault recorded that the Jesuit *Seigneurie du Cap-de-la-Madeleine* measured 1.5 *lieues* (3.75 miles) along the Saint Lawrence River by 3 *lieues* (7.5 miles) deep, and was located between fief Marsolet to the northeast and the first canal of the Saint-Maurice River to the southwest. Its land remained mostly uninhabited except for a row of concessions that fronted the northern riverbank of the Saint-Lawrence and extended 40 arpents inland. Collet also noted that the population of Cap-de-la-Madeleine had dropped to sixteen heads of household and that the parishioners were mainly inconvenienced by the quality of the roads and the distance they must travel to attend the nearest house of worship, Sainte Marie-Madeleine church. However, the residents claimed they were happy to belong to that parish.

Curé Vachon reported that although the new stone church was near completion, it had limited financial support because of the decreasing number of habitants on the north shore where the soil had gradually become more sandy and less fertile. He recommended an expansion of the parish population on the more productive south shore of the river directly opposite Cap-de-la-Madeleine.

The two officials crossed the Saint Maurice River the following morning to meet in Trois Rivières with regional government officials and parish representatives.

Their discussions provided an assessment of the dependent seigneuries on the south as well as the north shore. That parish census revealed that eight families resided along the northern riverbank in the rural area of Trois Rivières, and seven families lived along the southern riverbank. It listed Sébastien as the only habitant residing in the *Seigneurie de Nicolet* which extended 50 arpents along the southern shore, west of Bécancour.

The following month, Louis *fils* was granted a land concession that measured 6 arpents frontage by 40 deep in *Seigneurie de Roctaillade* adjacent to his uncle Sébastien's 10 arpents frontage by 20 deep. The seignorial estate maintained its rights to the property's oak, cedar, and pine timber, and required him to deliver yearly payments of *cens et rentes* in the form of six live capons and 5 livres, 10 sols to the seignorial manor on Saint-Martin's Day.

Louis had recently received 80 livres for the sale of his first concession which was located just east of his parents' home in Champlain. He would now join his uncles and cousins on the south shore.

Sunday civil announcements reported in May that a smallpox vaccine had been successfully developed and used in England. The militia captain also reported that John Law's *Compagnie des Indes* had declared bankruptcy, thus creating a deep financial crisis in France.

Louis and Michel were shocked to hear this. How would this affect French support for its North American colonies?

They knew that John Law's financial schemes for the rapid development of Louisiana had shown early promise of raising France out of the heavy public debt left by Louis XIV, but now they learned that this had quickly led to frantic over-speculation that finally collapsed the development fund. Prodded by the French regent, Law had issued over four times as much paper money as could be backed by the available coinage.

Greed and corruption among the British, French and other European investors had already driven the eleven-year old British South Seas Company's bubble to collapse earlier that year.

John Law's company had aggressively promoted Louisiana as a sound investment for those who looked for quick profits. Frenzied bidding had rapidly inflated stock prices while the new company's expenses had soared, due in part to the Natchez War and the ever-increasing subsidies for the surge in immigration to the southern colony. During the summer of 1720, the plague had arrived in the Mediterranean port of Marseilles, had quickly moved northward, and killed thousands, thus deepening the sense of gloom in all of France.

Stock-holders who had managed to cash in their banknotes for hard currency before the company's collapse had reinvested in gold, silverplate and jewelry which they had easily smuggled out of the country. Funded by the Royal Bank of France, the *Compagnie des Indes* could no longer pay dividends which had led to a rapid loss of public confidence. This panic set off a run on the bank and a rapid deflation of the value of its shares, sending the company and many of its investors into bankruptcy and John Law into exile.

Once they became aware of all this, Louis and Michel understood the full implications for the French colonies.

"The bishop and Québec officials have repeatedly complained about the declining quality of immigration. So many of last year's émigrés never settled down to work the land," Louis pointed out.

Michel *père* had deeper concerns. "Louisiana is even more dependent on French financial support than we are. I wonder if Michel will be able to provide for his family's needs. The colony has already suffered serious food shortages while trying to feed last year's flood of immigrants."

"Didn't your sons say that they'd been trading with the French of Saint-Domingue, the local natives, and the Spaniards?"

"They have in the past, during times of crisis, but there are so many more people to feed and house right now—there's very little if any surplus to trade."

"We've been shipping surplus grain to the islands; wouldn't that help to meet their needs?"

"Only if they have something of equal value to trade for that wheat and corn."

"What about their ability to hunt for meat and furs?"

"They've told me that there's a great demand in France right now for deerskins. The tanners of Niort process these into chamois clothing for the king's horsemen. Deer and wild cattle (buffalo) also provide much of the meat for northern settlers who live along the Mississippi and the Missouri. They dry their surplus and ship it downriver from Kaskaskia."

"I'm confident that they'll manage. Jean's an excellent hunter, and I'm sure your son will be able to provide enough vegetables and rice for his own family and workers."

Montréal

A few weeks later, Intendant Bégon issued an ordinance forbidding people to fire guns in any of the towns. He established a fine of 50 livres for each offense, citing that trigger-happy citizens were causing too many fires. Yet in mid-July, word reached Trois Rivières that a great fire had swept through the city of Montréal, destroying *l'Hôtel-Dieu* and over one hundred twenty homes and businesses.

Louis paddled his canoe to *Isle-de-la-Fourche* and arrived just as Sébastien and his twenty-year old son Joseph prepared to leave. They were both surprised to see him in voyageur traveling clothes.

"Is Jean Guillon in Montréal?" Louis asked them.

His brother nodded and replied tensely: "He's been working in his office and overseeing construction of their new home."

"Is Marguerite with him?"

"She and baby Joseph are here with us. She's very concerned about Jean's safety—She's had no direct news from him."

"Do you want me to come with you?"

Sébastien thought this through. "We'd probably get there faster if you did—What about your family?"

"Simonne knows that I plan to go with you. She packed these supplies of pemmican, corn and peas, extra clothing and blankets."

Tears spilled from Sébastien's eyes but he managed to maintain his control. "I really appreciate that, Louis. You know, our young

Marguerite and Jean were married little more than a year ago and they have an infant son. They looked forward to moving into their new home and place of business. His present office is—was close to *l'Hôtel-Dieu*. I pray to God that he's all right."

Louis could see the fear in his brother's eyes. He said: "Let's go!"

What they saw upon their approach to the walled city did not reassure them. Even now, nearly a week after the fire, the scene was one of confusion and despair. Families were encamped outside the city walls in makeshift tents and huts set up in the great oval prairie where Louis and his father had witnessed the signing of the Iroquois peace treaty in 1701.

Louis set up camp and watched over their supplies while Sébastien and Joseph immediately began their search for Guillon. They found the fur trader inside the city walls, rummaging through what was left of his office. Half the town had been destroyed. Jean was relieved to learn that they had brought extra provisions. Sébastien and Joseph helped him search through the ruins for business records or trade goods that might have survived.

Louis had prepared a hearty meal by the time they returned to the campsite with Jean. That evening, as they sat around the campfire, Guillon described how the terrible event had unfolded.

"It happened during the Corpus Christi celebration which had been postponed a week because of heavy rains. Crowds of people lined the route. During the traditional procession from convent chapel to church, a local *arquebusier* celebrated the occasion by firing his gun in the air; this accidentally set fire to the cedar roof shingles of the chapel. The church roof was completely engulfed in flames before the Holy Sacrament reached its destination.

"The fire spread quickly from roof to roof throughout the town. People ran into their burning homes, trying to salvage what they could. Some were luckier than others, depending on how far they were from the original fire. It spread so quickly, most of us were lucky to escape the flames."

"Were there any deaths?" Sébastien asked.

"None that we know of," Jean replied, "and that was a miracle in itself because there was so much confusion and panic at the time. It became so hot within the city's stone fortifications that everyone was forced to flee. Several days went by before we could safely search through the ashes and ruins.

"Most of the inhabitants lost everything they had except for the clothes they were wearing at the time. Most of my records and inventories were burned."

Sébastien placed his hand on his shoulder and told him: "We thank God that your family escaped unharmed."

"How can we help you?" Louis asked.

Jean quickly replied: "Please take care of my family while I clean up this site and rebuild our home and office."

In response to this enormous loss in Montréal, Intendant Bégon issued an order that from then on, all houses must be built of stone. Jean Guillon had already decided to clear the debris and rebuild in stone on the same lot. Since this type of construction was beyond the means of the majority of the local population, new wooden houses would be built outside the city walls.

Royal Engineer Chaussegros de Léry reported to the French Ministry of Marine that cedar shingles were highly inflammable and frequently required replacement. He recommended that slate be installed on all of the king's buildings. Since importation of this heavy construction material was too expensive at this time, he wrote that slate-quarries did exist near Lake Champlain, and near Grand-Étang which was located about 100 leagues downriver from Québec. He judged the second site to be the more practical because its location near a natural port would offer easier delivery of the slate to Québec and Montréal. Since no one in the colony had the expertise to split the stone, Léry formally requested that two expert slate-tradesmen be sent to Nouvelle France to evaluate and assist in collecting that material.

Georgetown on the Kennebec River

On July 28, 1721, ninety birch-bark canoes approached Arrowsic Island in the Kennebec river mouth. These carried two hundred fifty representatives from various Abenaki tribes and the Canadian missions of Bécancour and Saint-François, Iroquois from Caughnawaga, and Hurons from Jeune-Lorette. The lead canoe flew a French flag and carried three white men: Ensign Charles Legardeur de Croisille from Québec and Jesuit priests Râle and

La Chasse. Close behind them, another canoe carried Penobscot Chief Anselm de Saint-Castin, son of the baron and an Abenaki chieftain's daughter. Everyone was dressed in full regalia befitting his official rank to meet with the English at the invitation of Boston Governor Shute.

The Kennebec tribes had recently sent a letter to the English governor asking for a cessation of hostilities. Three weeks of peace had preceded this meeting.

Captain Penhallow represented Governor Shute and accepted the delivery of two hundred beaver skins as promised ransom for the release of the four Norridgewock tribesmen held captive in Boston over the past several years. Penhallow accepted the furs in payment of past damages inflicted on the settlers by the Abenaki, but announced that he was not authorized to deliver the prisoners.

Massachusetts officials intended to hold the warriors as security for the future good behavior of the native tribes. This further angered the sagamores who had expected to meet with the governor at this gathering. The chief delegates dictated a letter to Governor Shute written in Abenaki, English, and Latin by Father La Chasse. They asked by what right the English continued to hold their fellow tribesmen after the ransom had been paid. They stated that if the English settlers did not quit the Abenaki homeland within two months, their houses would be burned and their cattle killed. The chiefs of all allied tribes in the disputed areas and Canadian missions signed the letter by marking it with their totem signs.

Their joint message reached Boston a few days later. Its mode of delivery and its English translation infuriated the Massachusetts officials and roused the Puritan population against the influential Jesuit missionaries. Râle was already considered an outlaw by the Boston authorities.

On August 23, 1721, the General Court of Massachusetts held a special meeting during which they decided to punish the Indians for their crime of rebellion. It authorized the establishment of a force of three hundred soldiers to carry out English retribution. The court declared that the Indians must deliver Father Râle and all other missionaries to the English authorities. Furthermore, the Abenakis were ordered to pay for all past damages or else they would be captured and held in prison in Boston.

Many among the Massachusetts colonists argued that there was no moral or civil basis for this proclamation.

The following December, Governor Shute reported to the Lord Commissioners of England that Governor Vaudreuil, the Jesuits, officers Croisille and Castin openly incited Indian rebellion throughout the northern frontier territory of Massachusetts.

Before the end of the month, an English provincial captain anchored his ship off the coastal village of Pentagouet (Castine, Maine) and cordially invited Anselm de Saint-Castin to share refreshments with him aboard his ship. Castin accepted his invitation but once he reached the ship's deck, the entire crew emerged to seize and take him captive to Boston where he would remain imprisoned and questioned during the following five months.

The Abenaki tribes of Maine and Canada thus received their final insult. Governor Vaudreuil of Québec could no longer restrain their fury.

Thirteen

1722

Early that year, the General Court of Massachusetts dispatched 300 provincial troops to destroy the Penobscot mission, another four hundred to raid and lay waste the rest of the Abenaki villages, and directed Colonel Westbrook to journey up the Kennebec with a company of soldiers to seize Father Râle and bring him to Boston to face English justice.

Most of the Norridgewock warriors were away from their village during their winter hunt, but Father Râle had stayed behind with several women, young children, and elderly people. Fifteen years earlier, the Jesuit missionary had broken both his legs in a fall from the chapel steeple which was then under construction at the Bécancour mission. His compound fractures had never healed properly. As he approached age seventy, he increasingly suffered from those injuries so that he could no longer leave the mission.

At noontime of that cold January day, two young hunters came running into the village to warn the priest and the fifty remaining villagers that a large group of English soldiers and several Mohawk guides were approaching overland from the south. The priest quickly swallowed the consecrated hosts, gathered the altar's sacred objects, and followed the Abenakis into the winter forest where he crouched behind a tree. The English soldiers passed within eight steps of his hiding place but somehow failed to see him.

Westbrook's men destroyed the village and its winter food caches; replacement of these vital provisions from Québec would require one month's travel time. They ransacked the church, and the priest's cabin where they found his strongbox. In it were Father Râle's letters from Governor Vaudreuil and Intendant Bégon, along with the Abenaki-language dictionary that the Jesuit had painstakingly compiled during his three decades of living among his converts. Colonel Westbrook carried these away to Boston.

The English translation of the original French correspondence convinced Massachusetts authorities that Father Râle had been ordered to encourage an alliance of the various Abenaki tribes against the northern English settlements. It also supported what the English had long suspected, that the French governor of Québec had freely provided arms and ammunition in support of the native rebellion.

Governor Shute sent a letter to Governor Vaudreuil stating that since he so adamantly claimed that the Abenaki tribes were under the protection of the French Crown, the Indians should move to Canada and away from British territory. He warned that Father Râle's presence in Norridgewock was illegal.

Bécancour, 1722

Bishop Saint-Vallier arrived in early March to dedicate and bless the new church, *La Nativité-de-Notre-Dame-de-Bécancour*. He opened the parish registry beginning with the sacramental recordings that had been entered in the chapel registry since 1716, and he officially set the parish boundaries of Bécancour and Nicolet.

François, his lifelong friend René Leblanc, and their families jointly celebrated the fulfillment of the agreement they had stubbornly negotiated with their pastor, the bishop, the intendant, and the habitants of Cap-de-la-Madeleine. However, their joy was tempered by the growing possibility of war in the Abenaki territory to the east of the Saint Lawrence River valley.

The Bécancour mission mostly sheltered women and children; the Norridgewock warriors had joined their allies to retaliate against the English winter raids. French missionaries and parish priests led their native converts and Canadian Christians in organized prayer sessions in support of the Abenaki efforts to defend and regain control over their ancestral land. The quality of their traditional way of life had been gradually and inevitably eroded during the previous nine years of expanding English settlement.

The Abenaki warriors resumed their raids along the lower Kennebec River in mid-July. They captured and burned the village of Brunswick after allowing its forty families and garrison to flee to Boston. They captured nine families in the northern end of Merrymeeting Bay but freed their captives except for five Englishmen whom they intended to hold against the release of their four fellow tribesmen still held hostage in Boston. They attacked Fort Saint George where they burned a sloop and took prisoners. They seized a fishing boat near Damariscove and a sloop in Passamaquoddy Bay.

The governing council of Massachusetts officially proclaimed its fourth Indian War against the Eastern Abenakis On July 25, 1722.

In a letter to his French nephew in mid-October of that year, Father Râle related that the Norridgewocks feared for his safety and urged him to move to Québec. He wrote: "Only death can separate me from them. I say to them: '...do not be anxious about that which concerns me...I do not fear the threats of those who hate me when I have not deserved their hatred; and I do not consider my life more precious than myself, so that I may finish my course, and the ministry of the word which has been intrusted to me by the Lord Jesus.'"

Cap-de-la-Madeleine

Michel Arsonneau *fils* arrived in Montréal that October to record the birth and baptism of his third son Joseph. On his way to visit with his father and family in Batiscan, he stopped at Louis and Simonne's house to bring them news of their son.

"Jean's met a lovely young woman by the name of Thérèse Dalberni who has been our children's governess these past two years. They've recently married and live downriver from us, near Nouvelle Orléans."

"What is she like?" Simonne asked warily.

"She was among a group of *filles-à-marier* who arrived from France early last year. Thérèse was raised and taught by the Ursuline nuns in southern France."

"Just like my mother!" Louis recalled.

Simonne took a deep breath and relaxed.

"The three of us met her at the governor's reception soon after the group's arrival in Nouvelle Orléans. Madeleine liked her right away and they've become close friends. Our children love her and were very disappointed when they moved away.

"Jean has already developed a reputation as a reliable building-contractor and plans to construct a sawmill of his own."

"So he's become a carpenter," Louis murmured.

"And a good one at that. Shortly after we arrived at the plantation, Madeleine and I hired a French master-carpenter to build a new house of *pièces-sur-pièces*. There were very few of those in Louisiana at that time. Since Jean seemed to know a lot about the building technique, he worked closely with our contractor and learned to draw up standard plans and measurements."

"Did you also build a sawmill?"

"Yes, in partnership with my building-contractor. Jean also helped us with that project. As a matter of fact, he's running the sawmill while I'm away."

"He's always enjoyed working with wood, like my father and François."

Simonne reached for Louis' hand in quiet communication. He added that her father had also been a carpenter.

"How was the voyage this time?" Louis asked.

"I chose to travel the shorter route and was surprised by the changes I saw at the Niagara Passage. We stopped at the new Canadian trading post and the clerks told us that English traders were already building their own log-palisaded store 150 miles to the east at Oswego. The Albany merchants apparently hope to draw the western fur trade away from Niagara by setting up their dealers closer to the source. The natives seem to prefer English goods and red blankets over our blue—their trading goods are less expensive than ours."

Both men realized that the opposing frontiers were drawing closer to each other in the Great Lakes area.

Late January 1724

Louis and Simonne's relatives and friends crossed the ice from Bécancour to attend another wedding celebration at their house, that of their daughter Marguerite's marriage to local mason François Rochereau.

During the reception, Louis joined his two brothers who seemed intensely involved in serious discussion.

Sébastien welcomed his presence: "Big brother, we need your advice."

François explained: "Now that Sébastien and his family have permanently settled down in Nicolet, he plans to sell his land in Bécancour. I'd like to buy his and Antoine's original concessions, but that would involve several separate transactions. We'd appreciate your counsel because right now, it all seems very complicated to both of us."

Louis considered the implications of such a series of agreements. "Those two lots have been connected with this family for quite some time and they're both well-developed, but Antoine's land reverted back to the seigneurie some time after he and Marguerite moved to Sorel." He considered the value of both concessions. "How do you plan to pay for them, Francois?"

"If this works out, I'd own three adjoining lots along *le fleuve Saint-Laurent* that extend inland all the way to Lac Saint-Paul. I'd be willing to give up my land in Dutort and Nicolet."

"Do you have buyers for both of those concessions?"

"Sébastien has offered to accept the one in Nicolet in exchange for his old homestead and a promissory note. My brother-in-law in Dutort is interested in the other lot."

"Since Sébastien's homestead and your land in Nicolet are original concessions, you'll need to seek approval from the seigneurs before the transfers," Louis explained. "You might want to sell in Dutort before you buy anything else. As for Antoine's original concession, the seigneurie continues to have a vested interest in its value and sale price, so I believe you'll have to buy it directly from *Sieur* Robineau.

"All this sounds like an unusual opportunity for both of you. I can see that counting your present home lot, Francois, this would give you a land holding that extends eleven arpents along the river. Congratulations! That's quite a property!" He tapped them both on the back and told them: "Papa would highly approve and be proud of both of you."

Louis recommended a series of agreements with Seigneur Pierre Robineau of Bécancour, and advised François to sell his land in Dutort for 150 livres which he could use as a down payment for the other transactions.

He looked around the room and suddenly realized that the majority of the guests who lived across the river were second- and third-generation descendants of family and friends he and Simonne had grown up with on the cape. Their own son Louis was currently negotiating the purchase of a concession in Bécancour.

One month later, Louis *fils* bought that land from Joseph Normandin. He immediately began to clear a building site and collect the timber to build his house. His aunt Catherine lived nearby and invited him to stay with her family until he completed the project.

The following week, his uncles François and Sébastien signed their land exchange agreement through which Sébastien ceded his Bécancour homestead of 4 arpents frontage on the Saint Lawrence River, extending inland to within one arpent from Lac Saint-Paul. In return, François traded undeveloped land of 6 arpents frontage on the Saint Lawrence by 30 deep in Nicolet. He also signed a promissory note for 450 livres in currency with down payment of 186 livres.

Young Louis hired a contractor to design and supervise construction of a smaller version of his father's house. Several relatives had already volunteered to help him with the project, among them were two masons: his uncle Michel Crevier-Bellerive and brother-in-law François Rochereau who both lived near the site.

Other uncles, François Ducharme and Louis Massé also offered their help, as did their sons who lived nearby. Together, they succeeded in clearing, hewing, and moving the lumber throughout that spring and early summer whenever farming chores allowed. His aunts and their daughters provided food and beverages as did several nearby widows and their daughters. Through this community effort, the house was raised and enclosed before the autumn harvest.

Among the several young ladies Louis *fils* enjoyed meeting that summer was a young woman of twenty-two who had grown up in Trois Rivières. Marie-Anne Leclerc dit Fleurant was the youngest of nine children whose voyageur father had died during her infancy.

Anne had recently moved to Bécancour with her mother and sister to live with a bachelor brother whose farm was located near Louis' new concession. When Jeanne Aubuchon began to send her two daughters to serve refreshments at the construction site, Louis welcomed their visits and soon found himself looking forward to the next.

New York Province

During the summer of 1724, Governor Burnet upgraded the wooden trading post at the mouth of the Oswego River by building a wooden blockhouse to counter the French *Magasin Royal* on the Niagara Portage.

Bécancour

That September, a flood of emotionally and physically traumatized Norridgewock refugees arrived at the Bécancour mission with reports that their beloved missionary priest *Père* Râle had been martyred, their people massacred, and their village totally destroyed by *les bostonnais*.

Louis *père* offered to interpret and help construct additional shelters for them. His sons, brothers and nephews helped in any way they could. They found the grieving village overwhelmed by the continuing arrival of weeping and wailing survivors. Priests, doctors and nuns struggled to treat the festering wounds of the men, women and children.

Louis learned through patient interviews that during the afternoon of August 24th, an armed force of over two hundred Englishmen and several Mohawk guides had surprised fifty Norridgewocks in their village by firing unexpectedly into their tents, killing and injuring many with their initial volley.

The remaining warriors had sprung into action with the Abenaki war cry *"We are dead men! Let us sell our lives dearly!"* But in their effort to cover the flight of their women, children and elderly, they had rushed out of their tents with unloaded weapons, directly into a second volley of English musket fire.

The grieving refugees reported that Father Râle had rushed to the center of their village to distract the raiders and protect his converts. In so doing, he had run into a third simultaneous round of musket fire. Many of their people had either drowned or been shot in their desperate attempts to cross the river and reach safety in the forest.

After the English had left, a few escapees had returned to their smoldering mission and found the priest's body lying under the heavy wooden cross that stood in the center of the village. The

Norridgewocks wept and wailed as they reported that he had been scalped, his skull crushed, and his body hacked. They had moved his remains from among the smoldering embers and buried him where his thirty-year-old wooden altar had once stood.

One hundred fifty physically exhausted and emotionally traumatized refugees from Norridgewock eventually managed to reach safety in Nouvelle France. They arrived in desperate need of shelter, clothing, cooking utensils and food, too weak to forage and hunt through the nearby forest to feed themselves or to prepare their winter stores and shelters. While many had found refuge in the Saint-François-de-Sales mission on the Chaudière River, these people had chosen to travel farther in order to reunite with their families and friends in Bécancour.

Word spread quickly throughout Canada that the English had finally driven the Eastern Abenakis off their land. Québec officials faced the realization that the English settlements were fast approaching the Saint Lawrence River valley from the east.

The habitants were shocked to hear that *les bostonnais* had killed a priest and mutilated his body—no Jesuit missionary had been martyred since the earliest days of the colony and then only by the Iroquois and Hurons, never before by white men. The reported circumstances of Father Râle's death nearly provoked an open rebellion among the French population of Nova Scotia.

Upon their return to Massachusetts, the English raiders collected a total bounty of 505 English pounds for twenty-eight scalps, including Father Râle's. Boston celebrated upon hearing that their militia had finally and permanently driven the Abenakis away from the Maine frontier.

Jesuit Superior *Père* de La Chasse eulogized *Père* Râle in Québec in October 1724: *"Puisse-t-il plaire le Seigneur que son sang, répandu pour une cause si juste, fertilise les terres de l'incroyance. Ils lui ont procuré une mort glorieuse ce qui fut toujours l'objet de ses désirs..."*

In January 1725, Boston Reverend Benjamin Colman proclaimed from the pulpit: "He who was the father of the war, the ghostly priest of these perfidious savages, like Balaam the son of Beor, was slain with them, after his vain endeavours to curse us. May these singular favours of God have their saving effects on us!"

Fourteen

1725

The threat of armed conflict began to grow on the western frontier as New York Governor William Burnet encouraged and protected the expansion of English fur trade into the northern Great Lakes area.

Upon learning that the English had built a new garrisoned blockhouse on the south shore of Lake Ontario, King Louis XV ordered that *Le Magasin Royal* in Niagara be rebuilt of stone.

The Senecas had recently expressed their concerns to both French and English colonial officials about the increasing traffic of western native traders who delivered their furs to Albany through Iroquois territory. Governor Vaudreuil sent Joncaire to persuade the western-most Iroquois chiefs that a larger trading house at the Niagara location might divert some of that undesirable traffic since Niagara was 150 miles west of the Oswego trading post.

In dealing with his native friends, Joncaire proposed to build a larger post, not a formal military fort but a house in which they could more comfortably barter their furs for provisions and meet with the French king's representatives. Early that year, the Senecas granted permission for such a building on their land.

Governor Vaudreuil and Engineer Chaussegros de Léry planned to construct a large stone house and surround it with a simple wooden stockade so that it would not appear to threaten its neighbors.

Bécancour

Louis *fils* had built his house within one year with the help of his brothers and other relatives who lived nearby. His home was now completely furnished, his land under cultivation, and he continued to farm and hunt on his land in Roctaillade. At age thirty, he had savings left over from his voyageur earnings and from the sale of his concession in Champlain. He proposed marriage to Marie-Anne Leclerc and she accepted.

Dated June 30, 1725, the couple's marriage agreement stated that Louis *fils* pledged to his bride a *douaire préfix* of 600 livres and a *douaire préciput* of 200 livres. The official signing took place in the Trois-Rivières office of merchant Maurice Cardin, a relative of the bride. It was witnessed and signed by Marguerite-Renée Robineau, Seigneur de la Baronie de Portneuf *Sieur* Charles Legardeur de Croisille, and members of both immediate families. "*Sieur* Sébastien Provencher, uncle of the groom" was listed as present but did not sign as witness to the contract.

A few days later, the local priest blessed their union in the bride's parish church of l'Immaculée-Conception in Trois Rivières where her grandparents, parents and all of her sisters had been married.

Both spouses were members of large and well-established families. During the crowded reception held that beautiful summer day, their guests drifted in and out of the spacious Leclerc home.

The couple settled comfortably in Bécancour, next-door to his Aunt Catherine and uncle Pierre Bourbeau-Verville.

Île Royale, August 27, 1725

The pride of the royal navy *Le Chameau*, was driven by hurricane-swept seas onto a rocky shore as it attempted to enter Louisbourg Harbor to deliver its new colonial governor. One of France's fastest and best equipped warships, a 600-ton vessel armed with 48 guns, broke into two sections and completely disappeared into the foaming surf.

The ship had sailed from France in July, heading for Louisbourg and Canada fully loaded with civil and church dignitaries, new French colonists and garrison recruits. All 316 persons on board perished; only 180 bodies were recovered along the shore and were buried in a mass grave. Among them were Guillaume Chazel who was to replace Intendant Bégon in Québec, the new lieutenant-governor of Trois Rivières Louis de La Porte de Louvigny, military engineer Jacques L'Hermite who had planned to retire in Trois Rivières, and Charles-Hector de Ramesay, son of the governor of Montréal.

All civic, military, and ecclesiastical dispatches were also lost, thus delaying the resolution of several important colonial matters in Louisbourg and Québec until the following year.

Among this powerful ship's most important cargo was France's full annual expenditure for its Canadian colony amounting to 289,696 livres in silver and gold. It was stored in the after-part of the ship that disappeared with its guns and treasure and could not be recovered.

Marquis Philippe Rigaud de Vaudreuil died in Québec on October 10th, having governed the colony since 1703.

On October 21st, Louisbourg officials dispatched an urgent message to Paris advising French officials to equip and send another fluyt, *L'Éléphant*, to replace all of the officials and cargo lost with the sinking of *Le Chameau*. They had given up any hope of recovering its treasure and supplies.

Champlain

The pace of Louis and Simonne's lives had moderated. Half of their children had married by now and had moved away to start their own families, but sixteen-year old François usually managed to liven things up with his constant activity and good humor. He never tired of hearing his father talk about his youth among the mission Algonquins on the cape, how he had learned their native language and survival skills, and later applied them during his voyages to the Great Lakes. The boy had talked his father into teaching him some of these skills and had convinced Louis that he would also become a voyageur one day.

Their third son Joseph was in his late twenties. His management skills seemed to improve every year. Louis' land-holdings thrived under his supervision. There he was, sitting at the desk, soberly working on the accounts. Time for him to get married, Louis thought as he quietly smoked his pipe.

Twenty-five-year old Angélique worked the spinning wheel by the firelight. This daughter would surely make some man a good wife, yet she seemed in no hurry to move away from home, had already turned down several suitors. He hoped she would meet someone who was worthy of her fine qualities. Oh well, he thought, all in good time.

Catherine helped her mother set up linen warp on the loom with thread they had spun on *Mémère* Massé's wheel. The most gentle of their daughters, this twenty-two year old had always seemed more frail than the others. He wondered if she would ever have the strength and energy to raise a family of her own.

Simonne turned to him just then and smiled. "Such deep thoughts, Louis. You seem unusually pensive this evening…"

He had never been able to hide his moods from her. Throughout their three decades of marriage, he had never tried to do so.

"The house seems unusually quiet. Where's our François?" he asked.

Angélique replied: "He's out hunting with Baptiste Barette. He should be back soon."

Louis yawned. It was so peaceful in the house, and he was unusually tired.

The weather had turned bitterly cold toward the end of November and the boys were busy with their farm chores, so Louis took it upon himself to bring in an extra supply of firewood. He enjoyed the fresh, crisp winter air.

During his second trip out, he felt some discomfort in his chest and upper left arm but thought nothing of it; after all, it had been a while since he had done this kind of work. On his third trip out, he found it difficult to breathe and the discomfort suddenly turned into a sharp, stabbing chest pain. His knees buckled and it suddenly turned dark. He called out weakly as his body slipped to the ground.

No one heard him, but Simonne was working at the loom and happened to look out the window at that time. She ran to him and found him motionless. She screamed to her sons to help their father and they came running, but he did not respond.

Louis had been overwhelmed by an acute heart attack, had died suddenly and unexpectedly at the age of fifty-seven.

Simonne was in a state of shock; there had been no warning, no time to say goodby. Her dearest and most intimate lifelong friend and companion was suddenly gone, without warning. She had never expected to see it end like this.

The women wept as the boys brought Louis' lifeless body into the house.

Joseph consulted with the priest and the doctor. He hired a *chaloupe* to inform and fetch his uncles Bastien and François from the south shore. They arrived to pay their respects and help with the funeral arrangements. François brought one of the *pervenche* plaques he had carved out of wood as his father Bastien had taught him.

Although they attempted to send a message to Sorel, the roads remained muddy from the November rains and thin ice had started to form on the river. Madeleine, Marguerite and Antoine could not be informed until a month later.

Most of Louis and Simonne's married children and siblings had migrated to the south shore. They and their spouses managed to travel to the funeral on a sailing shallop: Louis *fils* and Anne Leclerc, François Rochereau and Marguerite, Catherine Massé and Nicolas Gailloux, Louis Massé and Catherine, Sébastien and Anne Massé, François Ducharme and Marguerite Moreau. Pierre Picard and Madeleine attended from Trois Rivières, as did Jean-Baptiste Massé, his wife, and youngest sister from Bastien's original homestead in Cap-de-la-Madeleine, and their neighbors Michel Crevier dit Bellerive and Angélique Massé.

Simonne, her children, and the rest of the family grieved through that winter, especially during the holidays of Christmas, New Year, Epiphany, but they gradually learned to cope with their loss. Joseph took over as the man of the house and continued to manage the family properties. Baptiste Barette helped in any way he could.

Eventually, there were many discussions as to how they should proceed with the estate; should they divide it or maintain it as a whole for everyone's benefit? Joseph and Simonne finally consulted with Pierre Désy de Montplaisir who served as commandant of the Trois-Rivières militia and as judge in Champlain. He volunteered to inventory Louis' estate as a close friend of the family.

Lake Ontario, early June 1726

Engineer Léry arrived at the mouth of the Niagara River with a company of soldiers, masons and carpenters to begin construction of a larger and stronger trading post. Rather than rebuild on the site of *Magasin Royal*, he chose the point of land on which Governor Denonville had built his wooden fort in 1687. This new fortification would not appear to threaten its neighbors and would face east to guard against any English attack by river or lake.

Léry always referred to this fort as *une maison à machicoulis* because of its openings in the floor of its overhanging dormers from which its defenders could fire down upon an attacking enemy. The Canadians called it *la Maison de Paix* when dealing with the Iroquois. The English knew it as the "French castle".

Champlain

Later that month, Joseph accompanied his mother to Notary Pierre Petit's office in Trois Rivières where they met with Judge Pierre Désy for the official presentation of the inventory and assessment of Louis' estate.

Simonne submitted the report in turn to the royal notary and swore to its accuracy as trustee under the guidance of Louis Massé, the court-appointed deputy-guardian and maternal uncle of her children. Among its items were the couple's original marriage contract and fourteen other legal documents, mostly property deeds transmitted by concession or purchase.

Two days later, the entire family gathered in Simonne's home with the notary, the two assessors, and Louis Massé to divide the estate's inventory among the widow and children.

Simonne represented the interests of three of her children: Catherine and François who had not yet reached their majority, and Jean who was absent.

Pierre Picard and François Rochereau were expected to act on behalf of their wives Madeleine and Marguerite, but both men were absent and were represented by Jean-Baptiste Massé.

The total inventory had been evaluated at 1261 livres, 5 sols. The widow was permitted to withdraw her 100-livre *douaire préciput* as specified in the marriage contract, and three minots of wheat to offer Masses for the repose of Louis' soul.

They all agreed that in order to fairly divide the remainder among the nine heirs, they should first divide it into two lots. This resulted in one valued at 600#, 15 sols, the other at 576#, 10 sols. The children then unanimously agreed that their mother should first choose her half of the estate, since she would continue to live in the family home. Simonne carefully considered the individual items included in each of the two lots and chose that of 600 livres, 15 sols.

The other half was then subdivided into six smaller shares, each worth 75#, 10 sols. All of these basically included livestock, grain, and household tools.

The children drew lots from numbered slips of identical paper mixed in François' hat. Starting with the oldest, Simonne drew a share for Jean who was absent, then the other children drew their own in order of seniority: Louis *fils*, Joseph, Angélique, Catherine, and François. Those of Jean, Catherine, and François would be held on their behalf by their mother until they reached their legal majority at age twenty-five and Jean came home to claim his.

Pierre Picard's lot on behalf of Madeleine was drawn and would be held by Jean-Baptiste Massé-Beaumier until Pierre was ready to claim it; the same rule applied to François Rochereau's drawing on behalf of Marguerite.

There remained a mixture of odds and ends: Louis' clothing, household linen, odd pieces of furniture, farm and house tools. These were divided into eight shares, each valued at 14 livres.

They drew lots again, following the same procedure.

The entire process was recorded by Pierre Petit, witnessed and signed by Louis Massé, Montplaisir (Désy), Angélique, and the royal notary.

Louis *fils* of Bécancour and Joseph met again with notary Petit the following day to record the sale of Louis' seniority rights of inheritance to his younger brother for 300 livres in currency. Joseph had already paid him 115 livres. The remaining balance would come due in two payments, half to be paid the following November, and the rest by November of the following year. Louis' wife Marie-Anne Cler was present and signed as witness to the agreement.

Although Jean-Baptiste and Louis were both older than Joseph, neither one of them had ever expressed any interest in managing the family property.

Albany

New York officials realized that by strengthening their post on the Niagara Passage in addition to their forts in Cataracoui and Detroit, the French could block English access to the northern

Great Lakes and draw the northern Indian fur trade away from Oswego and Albany. Governor Burnet's immediate response was to build at his own expense a strongly fortified trading station on the Oswego River.

English merchants and traders encouraged the Senecas to travel farther west in order to draw the western tribes into trading at Oswego for English goods. The Iroquois were thus introduced to the role of middleman in the western fur trade and soon recruited the Fox and their allies to disrupt French trade along the Missouri River, further frustrating Québec officials.

The period of peace that had followed the first Fox War rapidly deteriorated, forcing the French to strengthen and rebuild their old western forts.

GUERRE DE COURSE

Fifteen

Nouvelle France, August 1726

Québec officials reported to the Minister of Marine their increasing concerns over the movement of English colonists and traders westward into territory that French explorers had long claimed as their own through early exploration and native trade alliances.

French officials had already decided that in Canada as well as at sea, their strategy would become essentially defensive. They judged forest warfare to be similar to the naval *guerre de course* since both required small, quick, surprise attacks against the enemy's weak points.

Newly appointed Charles de la Boische marquis de Beauharnois arrived in Québec as the first French naval officer to serve as governor-general of Nouvelle France. His cousin Jean-Frédéric Phélipeaux comte de Maurepas served as Minister of Marine.

Soon after his arrival, the new governor considered Nouvelle France to be challenged on three fronts.

On the eastern frontier, the Penobscots had already concluded an agreement with Governor William Dummer of Massachusetts Bay. The English could soon pose a serious military threat from the east in the event of war. Beauharnois persuaded the colonial minister to create and maintain a yearly war fund of 6,000 livres to support the Abenakis. He recruited their warriors to join the Canadian war parties against the Foxes in order to maintain their alliances, and he encouraged their migration to the missions of Saint-François and Bécancour to discourage the re-establishment of their villages near the English settlements.

The strategic value of Lake Ontario had now gained military as well as commercial significance. The French governor was particularly concerned about the lake's outlet into the upper Saint Lawrence River. He understood that whoever controlled the lake also controlled a traditional invasion route between Montréal, Albany and Manhattan. His predecessor had ordered the commandant of Fort Frontenac to construct two sailing vessels for the efficient transport of trade goods to and from Fort Niagara, and to prevent English access to the upper lakes. Beauharnois now armed and assigned these two ships to also guard and protect French interests on Lake Ontario.

Beauharnois studied the primary southern invasion route through Lake Champlain and the Richelieu River that had traditionally been used by the Mohawks and the English of New York. His officers informed him that the French had tried earlier that year to establish themselves on the east side of the southern entry to the lake but had been opposed by the Massachusetts and New Hampshire governors who both claimed the site as part of their provincial territory. Beauharnois referred the matter to the French colonial minister.

Early in September, Intendant Claude-Thomas Dupuy, another French political appointee, arrived in Québec following a three-month ocean crossing. Intendant Bégon had served since 1712 and had long awaited his replacement; his two successively designated successors had never reached Québec.

Champlain

Two weeks later, Louis *père*'s estate disbursement was officially declared complete, valid, and legal by René Godefroy, seigneur de Tonnancour, Royal Counselor, and Lieutenant-General in the Jurisdiction of Trois Rivières.

Since Simonne, Joseph, Angélique, Catherine, and Jean-François would continue to live at home, Louis' remaining heirs agreed not to withdraw their inheritance and to wait for Joseph's cash payment of their shares. Until then, he was to pay them a lease from the annual profits of the estate.

Québec

Two months after his arrival, Intendant Dupuy proclaimed: "The fruit of the forest, wood, must replace the declining fur trade as chief export. Wheat and timber are of greater commercial value; they must be valued and husbanded."

He considered potential uses for the unexploited virgin forests. Oak, pine, spruce, maple, wild cherry, walnut, cedar, fir, ash, hemlock, and elm were valuable resources for naval construction, the production of furniture, and charcoal for the glass and pottery industries.

An excellent grove of seventy giant pine trees covering half a square league had been recently discovered near Chicoutimi. Their trunks were of 22–30-inch diameter extending up to 15 feet above the ground, without branches up to 40–50 feet in height, then with minor branching beyond that point. The grove consisted entirely of white and red pine and was located near convenient access to the river. However, the ship-builders of Rochefort, France rejected Canadian masts even though they had been well-accepted in Canada ever since Intendant Talon had built the first shipyard in Québec.

Dupuy tried unsuccessfully to persuade French officials to build naval ships in Nouvelle France; Versailles had no desire to invest heavily in the colony while France continued to struggle with its own financial difficulties. Minister Maurepas refused to acknowledge that administrative costs naturally increased with colonial growth. The French Court reiterated that the Canadian colony must become a self-sustaining source of wealth for France.

Meanwhile, the intendant's every attempt to develop the Canadian economy ran into seemingly insurmountable obstacles of limited outlets for the produce, and chronic shortages of specialized workmen and working capital.

Champlain

On November 11th, nearly a year after her husband's death, Simonne ceded to her son Joseph 1 arpent x 12 on the Bécancour River, and three non-adjoining riverside lots in Cap-de-la-Madeleine, totaling 3° arpents x 40. Two of the smaller lots were located on either side of Jean-Baptiste Massé-Beaumier's farm.

She also ceded half of all buildings, furnishings and animals she had inherited on these lands; the other half was to be distributed as part of her own estate.

This *donation viagère* would allow her to continue living in her own home with the assurance that Joseph would provide for her needs through health, sickness and proper Christian burial, and that he would have thirty Masses sung for the repose of her soul after death. It also required that he provide shelter and sustenance for his minor brothers and sisters as long as they continued to live at home.

Joseph thus gained majority control over his father's and grandfather's properties.

Lake Ontario

Construction of the new stone fort on the Niagara River was near completion by the end of the year. The French governor and intendant now focused their attention on reversing the gradual weakening of their western alliances as the English pushed steadily into the area.

1727

Governor William Burnet of New York kept himself informed regarding French activities at the new Niagara fort. The French had not only quickly achieved control over the great lake, but appeared to have established a growing military challenge to the New York colony. Oswego stood at one end of the waterway that led directly to Albany and Manhattan.

Burnet sought permission from his Iroquoian allies to build up English fortifications at the Oswego trading station. The Senecas gave their consent.

Threatened by the increasing commercial rivalry between the French and English colonies, the Five Nations insisted that no blood be spilled on their land and that they be guaranteed unrestricted trade both in Niagara and in Oswego. By negotiating a strict balance of French and English presence, they assured unchallenged French control of Niagara and English control of the Oswego river mouth.

Beauharnois received a steady stream of reports that the English were rapidly building a new stone fortress at the mouth of the

Oswego River. Construction of its four-foot thick stone walls were already close to completion.

Upon learning of this development, France adjusted as best it could. The French Court renewed the sale of fur-trading licenses to most of the Great Lakes posts. Minister Maurepas authorized a limited brandy trade to offset the attraction of unrestricted rum at Oswego, and instructed Beauharnois to renew the practice of selling western trading permits. He was empowered to issue twenty-five of these at 250 livres apiece to needy seignorial and merchant families.

Beauharnois later gained the Minister's approval to sell these at his discretion to the highest-bidding traders for as much as 500 livres, at times issuing as many as fifty. This enabled him to deposit 6,250 livres in the Marine account, and distribute 10,000 livres of pensions among widows of notable colonial families. This practice further benefitted the colony by strengthening the traditional western alliances.

The governor forbade the French traders to go to Oswego and Albany, and strongly advised the colonial minister to subsidize and stock more trade goods at the king's posts on Lake Ontario so that they could successfully compete with the English traders across the lake. Although the Minister rejected his counsel, French trade at those locations was maintained at a loss to further strengthen Canada's native alliances.

By the end of May, the French government had decided to encourage westward expansion and exploration farther to the north. The governor received orders from the minister to bypass Fox territory and establish a post and mission among the Sioux on the upper Mississippi River.

On June 6th, Beauharnois and fifteen leading merchants in Montréal, including two of Pierre Boucher's grandsons, formed the First Sioux Trading Company and hired six traders for the *Poste des Sioux*, among them was a native son of Trois Rivières, François Poulin de Francheville.

Ten days later, another of Pierre Boucher's grandsons René Boucher de La Perrière led his nephew Pierre Boucher La Jemeraye, the six traders and two Jesuit missionaries on an expedition to the proposed area. They ascended the upper Mississippi and reached the western shore of Lac Pepin on

September 4th to begin construction of Fort Beauharnois (near what would later become Frontenac, Minnesota).

René Boucher later reported to the governor that conditions had seriously deteriorated in the west. The Fox had renewed their war against the Illinois and had killed several Frenchmen. The voyageurs had sighted English traders on the *Ouabache* River, and had learned that English efforts were underway through Iroquois intermediaries to persuade the Fox and other tribes to drive the French from the west.

Québec, Summer 1727

Upon hearing that an English garrison had been assigned to Oswego, Governor Beauharnois sent Claude-Michel Bégon with an ultimatum ordering the English to withdraw their forces within fifteen days. The English ignored the message. The governor mustered the militia with the intention of enforcing his ultimatum but then canceled the call-up when he realized that for such an act of war, he must first consult with the Minister.

Dupuy's concern about the increasing Anglo-Saxon threat to the Canadian economy led him to write to the colonial minister: "The colony is on the verge of ruin unless we are assisted with men and money." He explained prophetically: "Moderate efforts will do more at present than great projects that would be implemented too late." He requested that France encourage immigration to increase the Canadian population. His appeals were again denied.

August ship arrivals brought news that on June 11, 1727, British King George I had died in Osnabruck; that George II of Hanover had succeeded his father as king of Great Britain.

Québec, Winter 1727–1728

Bishop Jean-Baptiste de la Croix de Chevrières de Saint-Vallier died in Québec during the night following Christmas day, having appointed Louis-Eustache Chartier de Lotbinière as archdeacon of the diocese, and Intendant Dupuy as the executor of his estate. He had also left instructions that he be buried in the chapel of *l'Hôpital général* which he had founded as a home for the poor in 1689.

Saint-Vallier's coadjutor automatically succeeded him, but he could not leave France because of his poor health.

In early morning of December 26th, Intendant Dupuy affixed seals to the bishop's possessions, and transmitted the seals of the diocese to the canons. As executor of Saint-Vallier's legacy, he carried out the bishop's wishes according to his last testament by appointing Lotbinière as the next episcopal administrator of the diocese in conflict with common church procedure. Meanwhile, the canons of the cathedral had also met, and had selected Étienne Boullard as the capitular vicar to administer church affairs.

A dispute broke out in the chapter on December 31st as to who would preside at the funeral which was to be held on January 4th. Lotbinière maintained that this honor belonged to him as archdeacon. Boullard claimed it for himself as capitular vicar.

Lotbinière appealed to the intendant, who summoned the canons to meet on January 2nd. Boullard questioned the Intendant's authority in matters of ecclesiastical discipline, and refused to appear. Dupuy became extremely annoyed.

The Intendant advanced the date of the funeral when he heard that the canons planned to remove the bishop's body and transport it to the cathedral for burial, contrary to the bishop's own expressed wishes. Without warning anyone, he ordered Lotbinière to proceed with the funeral and burial of Bishop Saint-Vallier during early afternoon of January 2nd.

The nuns and residents of *l'Hôpital général* were shocked to witness the archdeacon carry out these instructions. The capitular vicar Boullard immediately placed its chapel under interdict and deposed the mother superior.

Dupuy then summoned the canons to appear before the *Conseil supérieur* on the following Monday, January 5th.

A battle of wills ensued between the chapter led by Boullard issuing interdicts and threats of excommunication, and Dupuy issuing ordinances and fines through the colonial council.

The people of Québec were astonished by this series of bizarre events. Nouvelle France had not witnessed such disarray in government-church relations since Frontenac's legendary dispute with the religious authorities of Montréal.

Champlain, 1728

Saint-Lawrence River ice was thick enough by mid-January to support crossings by horse and sled. Relatives and friends arrived from Bécancour and Nicolet to join Simonne's family celebration of Angélique's marriage to Jean-Baptiste Barette.

The gaily decorated family home was filled to capacity for the wedding celebration, with little room left for dancing. The majority of the guests were of a younger generation whose own homes now extended on both sides of the river. The women brought the traditional foods. The men carried in their gifts for the bridal couple. Someone began to play the fiddle, another accompanied him with a wooden flute, both contributing to the festive occasion.

Sébastien and Anne offered their congratulations to the bride and groom. "Your papa would be so happy to see you two starting your life together," he told them.

Anne moved over to her sister Simonne and told her how delighted they were that these two childhood playmates had finally decided to marry. "You're so lucky to have them living practically next door to you. I know how close you are to Angélique."

Simonne nodded in agreement. "I'm blessed because we've always worked so well together—and Baptiste has been like a son to us, particularly since Louis died."

"He's certainly built a beautiful house."

"Yes, he has. He's done well with his voyages west and into the Illinois country, but I think he's tired of that now and looks forward to settling down and farming. He'll be a good husband for her."

The bride's uncles discussed the scandalous events unfolding in Québec and agreed that the situation worsened by the week.

François Ducharme observed: "It takes a while for French officials to adjust to our colonial way of doing things."

Sébastien's sons clustered around the groom. "What's it like on a trading voyage?" Simon asked. Joseph, Jean-Baptiste, Alexis, and René listened intently to their new cousin's reply.

Baptiste Barette smiled at his enthusiastic audience. "It's a hard life, *mes gars*—but it pays well and traveling the rivers and lakes of the wilderness is generally a quiet experience. The air and water are cleaner than you can imagine. The stars seem brighter at night than you've ever experienced. The food is always the same and workdays are long and hard—so is the ground that you lie on at night. During late spring and early summer, the black flies and mosquitoes are so hungry for your blood that you get very little sleep."

Sébastien overheard this and was reminded of the stories his father told of his own voyage to Hudson Bay in 1672.

Sixteen

Québec, late January 1728

Governor Beauharnois quietly arranged passage from Boston to France so that a church messenger could present Étienne Boullard's case before the royal court.

Fiery speeches by the intendant against the canons and particularly against Boullard dominated the colonial council meetings during the month of February. Such public confrontations continued to create unrest among the people of Nouvelle France as they began to take sides on the debate.

Since Dupuy showed no sign of relenting despite the scandal of public disorder, Beauharnois personally appeared before the *Conseil supérieur* on March 8th and ordered an end to all the ecclesiastical disputes of that winter. He announced that the king would render the final decision, and left for Montréal.

Dupuy refused to admit that the governor had any authority in matters of justice. He pressed the council to continue, but he failed.

Champlain

In March, Simonne's thirty-one-year old son Joseph signed a marriage contract with Claire Rouault in the home of *Sieur* Pierre Désy and his wife Thérèse Rouault, the bride's aunt.

Joseph's uncles Michel Crevier-Bellerive and François Ducharme, aunt Catherine, sister Madeleine, brothers-in-law François Rochereau and Pierre Picard attended the ceremony.

Claire would retain complete control over all her worldly goods and any future inheritance. Joseph pledged the bride a *douaire préfix* of 500 livres and a *douaire préciput* of 250 livres in money or worldly goods should she survive him.

Their religious wedding took place the following day in the church of Notre Dame de la Visitation in Champlain. The ice bridge held firm over the Saint Lawrence River so that the groom's extended family and friends were all able to attend and celebrate the occasion.

A royal decree arrived in Québec in late June, settling the dispute between the Intendant and the diocesan representatives.

Oswego

New York Governor Burnet had successfully completed the fort of Oswego with his own personal funds and without the support of his assembly. He garrisoned the loop-holed house of stone with four independent companies that were maintained in New York at the expense of the British crown.

Québec Governor Beauharnois was alarmed by Canada's increasing vulnerability. French financial retrenchment had obviously lowered Versailles' priorities in the maintenance of its colonial defenses.

The governor argued for a strengthening of Québec's fortifications and the addition of at least 1500 regular troops in Nouvelle France. He wrote to the Minister: "Who could have led the court to believe that Île Royale was the rampart of this country; the entire English army could travel overland to Québec and nothing be known of it in Louisbourg. Even if it were known there, what could they do about it?"

An uneasy alliance existed among Detroit's traditionally hostile tribes whose conspiracies constantly threatened the fort.

Within one year of the construction of the English fort at Oswego, 80% of western beaver traded by traditional French native allies was collected by the Fox and the Iroquois on behalf of the English. The Fox successfully disrupted French western trade to the north and west. Governor Beauharnois attempted to isolate them diplomatically from their new allies.

The Fox nation controlled the Wisconsin River west of Green Bay which was the traditional trade route to the Sioux and other upper Mississippi tribes. They constantly raided the Ojibwas who traded with the Canadians on Lake Superior, and the Illinois who traded on the Mississippi River with the Louisianans, thus further disrupting and threatening the delicate system of alliances which provided Québec's and Louisiana's main exports to France. Several French traders had already been killed in those areas.

The French governor organized a major campaign against the Fox home villages in 1728 and chose Constant Le Marchand de Lignery to head this mission. This military officer and Chevalier de Saint-Louis had successfully chastened this tribe in 1717, and had later negotiated a peace treaty in Green Bay with the Fox, Sauk and Winnebago chiefs in 1726.

On June 27th, Monsieur de Lignery and his associates hired Sébastien's son Simon to transport military supplies and equipment to *les pays d'en haut*. They left Montréal with six five-man canoes on July 3rd and traveled the Ottawa River route from Montréal to Georgian Bay, then continued west to the Strait of Mackinac in midsummer. Lignery led a flotilla of birch canoes carrying a force of 400 Canadians and 900 native warriors to the southern end of Green Bay, from where they paddled their canoes up the Fox River to reach a Winnebago village on August 24th. They followed a slow-flowing stream through a broad marsh to reach the main Fox village, an unfortified cluster of bark wigwams in an open area surrounded by cultivated fields. The village and its surroundings were completely deserted.

Lignery continued to lead his force up the Fox River to the Wisconsin River portage, and found nothing but more abandoned villages. On their way back downriver, his forces destroyed all of the abandoned wigwams and native crops of maize, peas, beans and squashes.

Beauharnois was frustrated by the expedition's lack of success. He knew that the failure of this campaign could only lead to a further loss of French prestige among the western tribes.

Early in October, Intendant Claude Dupuy was recalled to France and ordered to settle his debts before leaving Québec. This unexpected development led to his humiliation and bankruptcy.

Cap-de-la-Madeleine, 1729

Smallpox spread among the Abenaki populations that winter but few cases were reported among the Canadians.

In March of that year, Abbé Paul Vachon was returning to the cape from his ministry among the sick of the Bécancour mission when his horse and sled broke through the ice and plunged him into the river. He nearly drowned but was rescued. However, he developed pneumonia, willed his estate to the parish, died and was buried under the communion rail of the church of Sainte-Madeleine.

Two generations of habitants mourned his passing. He had served and guided the parish of Cap-de-la-Madeleine over a period of forty-four years.

Due to the population decline at the cape and a shortage of priests, the parish became a secondary mission served by Récollets of Trois Rivières, secular priests of Champlain, and Jesuit missionaries of Bécancour.

Coadjutor Pierre-Herman Dosquet arrived in Québec that spring, having been fully empowered to administer diocesan affairs while Bishop Mornay remained in France due to his failing health.

Three French tradesmen also arrived at Grand-Étang on the Gaspé peninsula to develop slate mining as requested seven years earlier by Intendant Bégon and Royal Engineer Chaussegros de Léry immediately after the great fire in Montréal.

In mid-May, news reached Champlain that Michel Arsonneau *fils* had died in Montréal at age thirty-six. His sixty-three-year old father was shocked to hear this since he had not yet heard of his arrival from Louisiana. When Baptiste Barette learned about it, he immediately approached his neighbor to offer his condolences.

"It must have been quite sudden," Michel told him. "He usually let me know of his travel plans. I wonder if Madeleine was with him..."

"Would you like me to take you there?" Baptiste asked.

"Louis and Alexis are already preparing to travel with me to Montréal. As a close friend of Michel, you're most welcome to join us, but I must warn you that if Madeleine was with him, we might stay a while."

Baptiste told Angélique what he was about to do. She understood the need for it, helped him prepare for the four-day journey, and sent notes of sympathy to Michel *père* and Madeleine Dionet in which she promised to keep them in her prayers.

They stopped at Madame Dionet's home as soon as they arrived in Montréal.

Madeleine's brother-in-law Joseph welcomed them at the door. "We're glad you've come, but so sorry that you couldn't be here for the funeral Mass and burial, Monsieur Arsonneau."

"Did he come alone?" Michel asked.

"Madeleine was with him and she's been staying here with her mother."

This news elicited a sense of relief yet of concern, for they knew that she would likely have to return alone to their home in Louisiana.

"May we see her?"

"Of course, Monsieur." Joseph led them into the parlor and they saw that Madeleine was near full pregnancy. She rose awkwardly and came forward to hug each of them in shared grief. "I'm so glad you've come, Monsieur Arsonneau."

"This must be a very difficult time for you," he told her. "I lost Michel's mother under similar circumstances."

"Michel told me about that shortly after we were married."

"How did he die?" he asked.

"He had not been well for some time. We decided that he'd get better care from the physicians in Montréal."

"Forgive me, but I would not have expected him to travel that far with you considering your condition."

"I was concerned enough about him and unsure enough about my pregnancy at the time to insist on accompanying him north."

"Do you know what was wrong with him?"

"No, I don't. I'm so sorry."

Michel and his sons fought to control their grief.

Baptiste Barette asked: "Did this sickness affect anyone else in your family—any of the children?"

"No it did not."

"Where are the boys now."

"We left them in the care of their governess. Jean Provencher and his wife Thérèse promised to check in on them every few days or so. They're in good hands, but they'll greatly miss their father." She paused as tears began to flow.

"And who is overseeing the plantations and the sawmill?" Louis asked.

"We have reliable men in charge and Jean is also looking after them."

"Have you had time to think about the future?" Michel asked gently.

She hesitated. "Much of that depends on you."

The boys looked at each other and silently agreed. Louis spoke for both of them. "Alexis and I decided upon our return to Batiscan that we have no interest in settling permanently in Louisiana. You and Michel have established your family roots there and we both agree that the property should belong to Michel's descendants if that is acceptable to you."

Their father listened quietly as Alexis continued: "We want to assure you that once your baby is born and is old enough to travel, we'll accompany you back to *Bonnet Carré*. We'll help you resettle there, then return to Canada and live quite happily along *le fleuve Saint-Laurent*."

Their sister-in-law immediately and visibly relaxed. "That's most generous of you!"

Michel was particularly proud of his boys that day. He spoke of his plans to stay in Montréal just long enough to visit his son's grave site and to legally transfer titles of the Louisiana properties to his grandson Michel III. Madeleine was to remain his legal guardian until he reached his majority at age twenty-five.

She promised to provide him with formal education and training until then and assured her father-in-law that all of her sons would be educated.

Simon-Joseph Arsonneau was born one month later in Montréal.

Saint-Maurice

Late August marked the arrival of the new *commissaire-ordonnnateur,* Gilles Hocquart, who was to serve as Intendant Dupuy's replacement.

A few days later, Hocquart conducted an official tour of Trois Rivières to judge the value of the bog-iron in that area. He was greeted by local dignitaries, and met with brothers Pierre and François Poulin on their seigneurie. He found the mineral resource to be extensive and readily accessible, therefore, he promised to examine the assay reports upon his arrival in Québec.

Several of these tests had already been done, starting with *Sieur* de la Portardière's results sent to Intendant Talon in 1670, and reaffirmed in 1687 by French Iron-Master Hameau. Monsieur Bégon had sought French support for the exploitation of this resource in 1717 but the regent had rejected the idea, stating that France had more than enough iron to supply Canadian needs.

Hocquart wrote a highly favorable report to the colonial minister which strongly supported the development of an iron industry in the district of Trois Rivières. He and Governor Beauharnois highly valued the possible development of such a commercial and industrial project. They lent their support and assisted the Poulin family with their application for a monopoly.

Pierre Poulin was too busy as a merchant, notary and clerk of court to become involved in the development of the valuable iron mines on the family seigneurie de Saint-Maurice. His next younger brother Michel had become a priest, but the youngest, Montréal merchant François Poulin de Francheville had no children, and was willing to take on the project on behalf of the entire family.

The brothers planned not only to mine the ore, but also to develop the capacity to turn the melted iron into useful tools and military hardware. They agreed that if they were to finance this project on their own, they must have the authority to extend their search into adjoining properties if necessary. They devised an equitable method of paying their neighbors for any damage done to their developed land, and also worked out the means by which they could protect their own interests once they invested in the development of the enterprise.

Québec

On September 2, 1729, the royal fluyt *l'Éléphant*, was shipwrecked in the north channel of the Saint Lawrence River, opposite the sandbank at Cap Brûlé, 29 nautical miles downriver from the port of Québec. Although fishing boats of all sizes soon converged on the site of the sinking, hundreds of passengers had already lost their lives.

This disaster convinced the colonial authorities that professional pilotage services must be provided to prevent any further maritime disasters in the river's estuary. Due to obstacles such as shallow and narrow channels, reefs, shoals, currents and ice, ships took from 10–12 days to sail from Newfoundland's Grand Banks and work their way upriver to Québec. Accurate hydrographic maps had not yet been drawn. These tasks were to be undertaken by King's Pilot La Richardière.

Severe shortages of coins and credit facilities in Nouvelle France had finally forced the creation of a paper currency which was quite different from that of the earlier playing cards. France authorized the issue of 400,000 livres in new Canadian card money in its effort to control the illicit colonial trade with the English for hard currency.

This new issue was on plain white cardboard, in various denominations, with each value having its own size and distinctive shape. The notes were embossed with two official seals and were handwritten like the original "playing card money". Each card was signed at the top by the Clerk of the Treasury Board, in the center by the Governor of Nouvelle France, and at the bottom by the Intendant. The two oval seals of France and Navarre were set at the top right.

Saint-Maurice, October

Backed by Governor Beauharnois and Commissaire Gilles Hocquart, François Poulin dit Francheville formally petitioned Minister Maurepas for the grant of a twenty-year monopoly to exploit bog-iron mining on his family's seigneurie and the surrounding area along the Saint Maurice River. The proposal included the construction of a forge at his own expense.

Sébastien remembered François as the nineteen-year old witness who had signed his land-purchase agreement in *Seigneurie de Godefroy* in 1711. He also knew him as the nephew of Jean-Baptiste Poulin, *Sieur* de Courval, Seigneur of Nicolet and Royal Procurator in the district of Trois Rivières.

Seventeen

Champlain, January 6, 1730

Simonne's children and grandchildren gathered together in the family home for the feast day of the Epiphany. Such reunions had been traditionally held by Simonne's paternal grandparents in Saintonge, France and dated back many generations. She had carried that custom forward by exchanging small gifts with each of the children. She expressed the hope that they too would carry it on into the future because it offered a joyous family celebration in the depth of the Canadian winter.

Her daughter Madeleine and Pierre Picard attended with their six daughters aged 18 months to fifteen years old. Angélique and Baptiste Barette brought their infant son Joseph. Marguerite and François Rochereau came with their two sons and two daughters. Eight-year old Madeleine Picard, five-year old Joseph Rochereau and his four-year old sister Marie-Josephte were the most enthusiastic and curious about the ceremony and its relationship to the Christmas celebration.

Simonne had baked a large *Galette des Rois* to honor the arrival of the Three Wise Men in Bethlehem. She added three hand-carved wooden figures of the oriental kings to her crêche and explained the significance of that event to her grandchildren.

The household furnishings had changed very little since Louis' death. Except for the livestock, perishables and other items that Simonne and Joseph had not needed, her sons and daughters had claimed very little of their inheritance from their father's estate.

They had postponed the option of claiming the rest in deference to their mother's mourning, but now she asked them what was to be done with the distribution of their legal inheritance.

They discussed this among themselves and decided that they had no wish to withdraw it from the estate. Simonne seemed relieved to learn that her home would remain intact during her lifetime. She thanked them for their consideration and remarked that Joseph had always managed to maintain the property much as it had always been. She was grateful for that.

Angélique, who lived nearby, asked her siblings if they would consider giving up their inheritance. She herself wished to do so.

Simonne was surprised by this suggestion because such a decision would also cede their rights to shares of her estate following her death. "Think this over very carefully now. Some of you haven't married or set up your own home yet."

They agreed to sell their shares to Joseph who accepted the proposal. He promised to discuss it with the notary and have papers drawn up to legalize the process.

On February 14, 1730, Simonne's heirs met with Pierre Petit to sign the official agreement. Simonne represented Jean, who still lived in Louisiana, and her minor children who continued to live at home. Sons-in-law Pierre Picard, François Rochereau, and Baptiste Barette represented their wives' interests as was required by law, and Louis *fils* acted on his own behalf. They ceded all their rights to a future combined inheritance valued at 315 livres. Joseph promised to make these payments within the following year.

After that signing, young François talked privately to his brother Louis: "Now that I'm old enough to travel, I keep thinking back to the stories I heard as a child about the voyages *Pépère* and Papa made to the north sea and to *les pays d'en haut*. Why is it that you've never talked about your voyaging with Papa?"

Louis was surprised by the question and the realization that at age twenty-one, his youngest brother was indeed old enough now to follow what had somehow become a family tradition. "I went along to please Papa, but I didn't really enjoy it," he confessed.

"Why not?"

"Men take part in the fur trade for various reasons. Some need to make money to build their homes and start a family. Others get restless and want to see the world beyond their village. *Pépère* talked about exploring the beauty of God's unspoiled wilderness.

"An Algonquin chief and his sons taught Papa how to live safely and comfortably in the forest—He developed a great love for it and was successful enough to be able to buy a great deal of land after he married *Maman*. As a result of that, life was much easier for us than it was for *Mémère* and *Pépère*.

"I've always enjoyed farming and would rather sleep in my own bed. If you think that the black flies and mosquitoes are bad here, clouds of them pester you day and night deep in the forest. The loads you carry during the portages really wear you out from sunrise to sunset.

"I never wished to go back, but I must admit that it paid well and I did enjoy the camaraderie of our group. If you're looking for more encouraging advice, Étienne Cottenoire and François Maudoux have continued to voyage since Papa took us to Michillimackinac. Jean and they enjoyed it the most."

Forges Saint-Maurice

On March 25, 1730, three days after adding fief Préville to the *Seigneurie de Saint-Maurice*, King Louis XV officially granted François Poulin de Francheville the right to exploit iron deposits on his family's land at his own expense. He granted him a twenty-year monopoly on all iron mining in the area, beginning along the west bank of the Saint Maurice River, west and north of Trois Rivières, extending into the areas of Yamachiche and Cap-de-la-Madeleine. The document stipulated that Poulin must achieve progress within two years, and granted him permission to build forges, blast furnaces and other required buildings to set up the first and only heavy industry ever sanctioned and encouraged in Nouvelle France. The king's only financial support was to excuse the monopoly from paying the customary 10% royal tax on any profit their enterprise would achieve.

Soon after the spring débâcle, Francheville was summoned to meet with Governor Beauharnois and Commissaire-ordonnateur Hocquart in Québec to ceremoniously receive the title of *Seigneur de Saint-Maurice* and swear fealty to King Louis XV.

In consideration of the breadth of this project, Beauharnois advised Francheville to enlist the financial support of his fellow merchants in Montréal. He offered to help him find the right people and to formalize the partnerships for all concerned.

Hocquart recommended that Francheville import two skilled foundry men from France who could study the New England method of casting iron.

The king had granted requests by Québec officials to provide additional manpower for the colony. The first pardoned *faux sauniers* released from Paris jails and exiled to Canada had recently arrived at the port of Québec. These men had been convicted of poaching, smuggling, and selling the king's salt while avoiding payment of *la gabelle*, the most onerous tax levied on the French population. This *impôt* had grown to be the second largest source of royal revenue, unevenly levied upon the provinces and at too high a price for such an essential food staple. Only the nobility, the clergy and other privileged citizens were exempt from paying it. Approximately 2300 men, 1800 women, and 6600 children a year had been arrested for this crime, 1100 horses and 50 horse carriages had been confiscated, and 300 men had been sentenced to work on the king's Mediterranean galleys.

These prisoners had chosen to spend the rest of their lives in Canadian exile where they could either join the colonial army or accept a three-year indenture as farm laborers, expert tradesmen, apprentices, or domestic servants. Most of them found employment with the local habitants in the hope of eventually earning their own concessions. Hocquart fully expected that many of them would prove to be excellent workers in the shipyards that he was nurturing in Québec and Montréal, or in Francheville's new industrial enterprise.

These developments stirred a great deal of interest and excitement along both shores of the Trois Rivières area since they were bound to increase economic opportunities within the region.

In late spring 1730, the new *Grand Voyer* launched an ambitious public works project with the strong backing of Gilles Hocquart. He and Hocquart both agreed that the growing colonial economy required that the road between Québec and Montréal be improved.

Lanouiller de Boisclerc began to survey and map the old road sections that existed within the limits of the various seignorial lands. He planned to widen these and join them together as *le*

Chemin du Roi which would be more consistently maintained. The new road would extend between parishes and across rivers and streams with the addition of ferries and bridges along the entire length of the inhabited north shore.

Lake Champlain, Summer 1730

Rumors spread throughout Canada that the English of New York planned to seize and fortify the southern opening of Lake Champlain and thus gain control over the traditional invasion route between Montréal and Albany.

Beauharnois consulted with the King's Lieutenant of Montréal de La Corne who knew and understood the geography and military significance of the area extending from the Saint-Lawrence River to the southern end of Lake Champlain. The lieutenant told him that the English planned to rebuild an old stone trading fort on *Pointe-à-la-Chevelure* (Crown Point NY), and related the history of French claims to the sixth largest continental lake.

"Samuel de Champlain first visited that site in the summer of 1609. He named it and claimed the lake and its surrounding area as part of Nouvelle France. Marquis de Tracy reclaimed the lake and its drainage area in the name of France in 1666 when he led French troops through Lac Champlain during his summer campaign against the Mohawk homeland.

"However, in 1690, the year after the Lachine massacre, a group of Dutch-British traders from Albany established that small stone fort on *Pointe-à-la-Chevelure* and this was not challenged by the French. That fort is still used by Dutch traders although it's now in disrepair. It's located halfway between forts Chambly and Albany, on a *détroit* just a quarter-mile wide which connects Lac Champlain to a great swamp that drains into a small river where the English encamped to build their bateaux in preparation of their attack on Montréal in 1709. Lac Saint-Sacrement (Lake George) lies 3–4 miles southwest of *Pointe-à-la-Chevelure*, a short portage away from the Albany River and the Mohawks.

"The English know as well as we do that whoever occupies that strait controls the invasion route between Montréal and Albany. We've tried to seize it these last four years but our attempts have been opposed by New Hampshire and Massachusetts who both claim the area—Now we've been told by our native allies that the

English are preparing to import Scottish Highlanders to settle along the shores of Lac Champlain."

Governor Beauharnois ordered La Corne to reclaim *Pointe-à-la-Chevelure* in the name of France. The lieutenant in turn assigned the task to officer Michel Dagneau and 30 soldiers who seized the site on August 19th while the two New England colonies continued to argue over their own territorial boundaries.

That summer, a small wooden fort was established with a limited garrison of French guards who changed monthly under the pretext of controlling the illicit French trade with Albany, a goal that was shared by both sides.

Acadia

The English once again demanded that the *Acadiens* pledge the unqualified oath of allegiance to the new British King, but they refused to do so on the grounds that they were neutral and had no intention of taking up arms against the English, the French, or the local natives.

Lieutenant-Governor Lawrence Armstrong began to distribute lands in the Annapolis-Royal area to Massachusetts settlers but none to the fast-growing French-Acadian population.

He wrote to London: "The French that I have to deal with are a perfidious, head strong, obstinate and as conceited a crew as any in the world."

Les pays d'en haut

That summer, French soldiers intercepted and seized foreign trade goods held by Canadian merchants and voyageurs who were forbidden to trade with natives for any blankets or other merchandise of foreign-make.

The Mississauga allies of the French drove the Seneca traders south of Lake Erie.

The Albany merchants incited the Iroquois to drive out the French traders from the west and encouraged them to become the middlemen between the western tribes and Oswego. The Iroquois soon allied with the Fox so that they could reach farther south and west of the southern tip of Green Bay.

Étienne Maudoux signed up in mid-June as an engagé to *les pays d'en haut.*

Twelve days later, Simonne's son François was hired as an engagé by *Sieurs* Marin and Alexis Lemoine-Monières for a voyage to *les pays d'en haut*.

The two cousins traveled with Paul Marin to the southern end of Green Bay. The Fox Wars had already greatly reduced the Sioux populations in that region.

Lately, many of the Foxes' tribal neighbors had convinced Jean Guillon Dubuisson, the French military commander in La Baye that the Fox must be exterminated. Dubuisson was a relative of Marin's wife.

Étienne Maudoux was eight years older than François, was serious and perceptive in his demeanor; these were qualities that François appreciated during his first voyaging experience.

While they sat smoking their pipes one night by the campfire near Lake Nipissing, François asked him: "How did you get started in the fur trade?"

"My older brother trained me. He was only nineteen years old when he first voyaged with your papa—Did you know that your papa was a skilled woodsman trained by an Algonquian chief?"

"I know that he spoke the native languages, that he had learned to hunt with a bow and arrows like *les sauvages*. We still have an Iroquoian peace-pipe hanging over our mantelpiece and sea shells that *Pépère* gave him when he was a child. They're both very special to our family."

"I hope you'll show those to me one day. I don't think I've ever seen anything that belonged to our *pépère*. I was told that he had voyaged all the way to the northern sea."

"It must be in our blood," François observed thoughtfully.

"You might say that, but it's also a heritage that we've been told to pass on to our children and grandchildren—and cousins," he reminded him.

"Life in the forest is so different from anything I've ever known," François admitted.

"I think it changes a man and makes him realize how big and beautiful the world is."

François nodded in agreement as he listened to the subtle sounds of his surroundings, smelled the pervasive scent of evergreen, and looked up that moonless night to see the brightest stars he had ever seen. Soon after, he emptied his pipe, curled up in his blanket and fell asleep by the fire.

Upon their arrival in La Baye, Étienne and François learned that in March of that year, a mixed force of six hundred French and allied warriors had ascended the Fox River by canoe and overland to surprise and dislodge the Fox warriors from *Butte des Morts*, an ancient Indian burial mound. They had killed many and scattered the rest of the tribe.

Fox refugees had since migrated east into the Illinois country where they had recently attacked French-allied Cahokia villages and set up a large village of their own just one league away from *Le Rocher* on the Illinois River.

French and allied forces from as far as Fort Chartres and Rivière Saint-Joseph now set up to besiege them in August and September of 1730.

The Fox held out for twenty-three days until an hour after sunset of September 8th when a terrible storm of wind and rain blew in and lasted until nightfall. A dark fog set in that night. The native allies refused to stand guard, thus enabling the Fox to sneak away from their fort and seek refuge among the sympathetic Senecas.

At daybreak, a reinforced French and allied army of 1400 men followed and routed them, killing more than two hundred enemy warriors.

Québec

In a letter and map to the colonial minister dated October 11, 1730, Royal Lieutenant de La Corne of Montréal pointed out the urgent need to build a stronger garrisoned fort on *Pointe-à-la-Chevelure*. He reported that the English had already granted the lake to a prominent Albany merchant's family and had promised lands along Wood Creek to immigrant Scottish Highlanders without previous consultation with the Mohawks. He emphasized the danger these developments posed to the safety of Nouvelle France.

Two days later, Beauharnois also wrote to the minister, adding further urgency to that of La Corne's message. "Dutch traders are already active among natives of that area. I have sent one officer and thirty soldiers to chase them away. We have been successful so far and will continue our efforts while awaiting your orders."

Eighteen

Nicolet, 1731

In mid-January, Québec merchant Claude Poulin *Sieur* de Cressé granted a land concession in Nicolet to Sébastien's thirty-two-year old son Jean-Baptiste. The lot measured 4 arpents frontage on Baie-du-Febvre x 40 deep, and extended two arpents into the bay. It was located near the seigneurial manor and between concessions held by his two brothers Charles and Alexis. The grantor reserved the right to harvest lumber for construction of a church, gristmill, and manor. The contract required that Jean-Baptiste build his home and reside on that land within one-and-a-half years of this date of concession or he would lose title to the land.

Québec

At the opening of the navigation season on the Saint Lawrence River, Québec Superintendent of Pilotage Richard Testu de La Richardière and his aides established a second location where the King's ships could pick up experienced river pilots. Île Verte was located 50 miles upriver from Île du Bic and across the river from Tadoussac.

The first ship to arrive in Québec that May delivered Gilles Hocquart's promotion from commissaire-ordonnateur to intendant of Nouvelle France, thus placing him in a stronger position from which to administer the civil affairs of the colony. His domestic policies had already resulted in a steady improvement of the colonial economy.

Governor Beauharnois learned that La Corne's proposal to quickly build a strongly palisaded wooden fort and garrison on *Pointe-à-la-Chevelure* had been approved by the French court. He was also ordered to develop plans for the more permanent construction of a large stone fortress that could accommodate a garrison of one hundred twenty men, and to offer land concessions to any French habitant who was willing to settle in the area of Lake Champlain.

Île Dupas, May

Antoine Cottenoire died at his son Étienne's home in early May. Sébastien and his brother François Ducharme left immediately to offer their condolences and support to their sister Marguerite. Simonne encouraged her sons Joseph and François to join them and represent their family.

Once having paid his respects to his aunt Marguerite, the younger François approached his cousin Étienne who was several years older than he.

"I've heard that you've spent some time out west. Was this your first voyage?" Étienne asked.

"Yes it was, and I thoroughly enjoyed it."

"Did you take part in any of the military actions against *les Renards*?"

"We arrived after the first campaign and left as *Sieur* Marin was planning the second. They told us that our native allies had destroyed the enemy villages and scattered their warriors throughout the Illinois territory."

"I've just heard from friends in Montréal that Marin's winter campaign was quite successful. *Les Renards* who survived this last attack were either enslaved by their enemies or fled west of the Mississippi to seek sanctuary among the Sioux.

"It's just as well that you missed the campaigns. I've heard that *les Renards* eat their captives. It's best to stay away from them," Étienne added with a twinkle in his eye.

François felt a prickling sensation on the back of his scalp and neck and changed the subject. "Have you ever traveled through the Illinois country?"

"Yes I have," Étienne replied. "I saw fertile flat land and natural prairies extending as far as I could see on both sides of the Illinois

River. It looks like ideal farmland because their summers are longer than ours, but since it's become part of Louisiana, most *Canadiens* travel that way only if they're heading farther south."

François finally broached the subject that most intrigued him: "Have you heard anything new about a proposed exploration farther west than the largest lake?"

Étienne gained new respect for his young cousin and nodded. "Now that's a very ambitious project. It seems that *Sieur* de La Vérendrye is preparing to search for the overland trade route to the western sea. He's been stationed at Kaministiquia for several years now and has gathered promising information from the far western natives."

"Where is Kaministiquia in relation to Mackinac?"

"I've never been there, but I know that you must enter the largest and westernmost lake through Sault Sainte-Marie which is north of Mackinac, then you must travel west to the far shore of that lake. I've heard that it's a longer crossing than from Mackinac south to La Baye."

Étienne grew quiet as he considered François' curiosity, then he resumed the conversation. "Your father introduced my older brother to voyaging you know, and when I was old enough my brother taught me. If you should decide to apply for Vérendrye's exploration, be sure to let me know. It's my turn to help you."

François' face brightened.

Étienne smiled at the young man's enthusiasm. "I know a few of the Montréal merchants. I'd be happy to recommend you."

Across the room, Joseph learned that his aunt Marguerite would continue to live with Étienne on Île Dupas where she was surrounded by the rest of her family.

Montréal

On May 24, 1731, François was hired by Monsieur de La Vérendrye to serve as engagé during his voyage to *les pays d'en-haut*.

The forty-year old son of the former lieutenant-governor of Trois Rivières had asked Governor Beauharnois to provide financial support for this western exploration. During the five years he had spent at his brother's trading post on Thunder Bay, La Vérendrye's native contacts had convinced him that the western sea was much closer to Kamanistiquia than it actually was.

French officials had previously ordered Beauharnois to bypass the Fox nation by establishing a post and mission on the upper Mississippi to trade with the Sioux. In lieu of financial support for the exploration, the king granted Vérendrye a three-year monopoly over the far western fur trade to finance the project.

The governor encouraged the explorer to form partnerships with Montréal merchants Louis Hamelin, Laurent-Eustache Gamelin Chateauvieux, and Ignace Gamelin *fils*. Their agreement granted Vérendrye credit for tools, supplies and trading items upon receipt of his written promise that he would set up forts along his route to develop the fur trade to pay off his debts to them.

La Vérendrye left Montréal on June 8th with his sons Jean-Baptiste, Pierre, and François, his nephew Christophe Dufrost de La Jemerais, Jesuit missionary Charles-Michel Mésaiger, and fifty voyageur paddlers he had engaged to transport the tools and extra provisions required for setting up the chain of forts.

Pointe-à-la-Chevelure

That June, Governor Beauharnois ordered Chaussegros de Léry to design a strong stone fortress for *Pointe-à-la-Chevelure*. He had already sent *Sieur* de la Fresnière with troops and workmen to clear the site and harvest the lumber for the strong palisaded fort they would build and garrison before winter at the headwaters of Lake Champlain.

Meanwhile, the governor successfully negotiated with the Mohawks to secure their neutrality so that the English could only protest diplomatically.

Nouvelle France

Bastien's oldest daughter Madeleine died in Saint-Michel-de-Yamaska in mid-June at the age of 70. Her sister Marguerite thus suffered through a second great loss within one month after her husband Antoine Cottenoire's death; she and Madeleine had remained close companions throughout their lives.

Two experienced French miners arrived in Trois Rivières that August to help François Poulin identify the richest sites and develop an effective system for the exploitation of bog iron on his seigneurie.

Pointe-à-la-Chevelure, August 16, 1731

Construction began on a wooden stockade 100 feet square with corner bastions that could accommodate a garrison of two officers and thirty soldiers.

Military engineer Morandière had selected the site, drawn up plans, and traced the orientation for the palisade and the buildings within its enclosure. The small fort would be built by La Fresnière's soldiers and laborers working under the supervision of officer Hertel de Montcour. This temporary military outpost would serve as a vital control point for the area while Chaussegros de Léry drew up plans for a more permanent stone fortress.

The English protested, arguing that this sudden French seizure had breached the Treaty of Utrecht's declaration that the Iroquois were subjects of the British Crown, thus placing their lands under English protection.

Beauharnois had thwarted the New York governor's plans to populate the area with Scottish Highlanders whose concessions would have extended along both shores of Lake Champlain.

London

That summer, English mathematician John Hadley presented a paper to fellow members of the Royal Society in London describing the advantages of the double reflecting "octant" he had invented. The improvements of the Hadley octant over previous navigational instruments enabled naval captains to establish their position at sea more precisely and more easily with rapid, multiple sightings. Although navigators had been finding their latitude for many centuries with the older instruments, ships, crews and valuable cargo had been lost at sea because it was impossible to determine longitude accurately.

The British Admiralty quickly recognized the merits of this instrument which they renamed the "quadrant", and ordered its commercial production, thus providing a major thrust forward for British sea power and imperial potential.

La Vérendrye

Most of the explorer's engagés refused to go any farther when they reached Grand Portage on the western extremity of Lake

Superior in late August. They were exhausted by the physical demands of the ten-month journey, and were discouraged by Vérendrye's description of the greater difficulties that lay ahead: a long series of lakes connected by portages and rapids which they must ascend, and the prospect of the approaching winter.

Nevertheless, Father Messaiger and La Vérendrye persuaded the stronger and more experienced paddlers to push on to Rainy Lake with Vérendrye's son Jean-Baptiste and nephew Jemerais. They would construct Fort Saint-Pierre, the first of eight posts to be established in the northwest.

Vérendrye and the majority of his men returned to Kaministiquia to recuperate through the winter. Following a week of rest, François was among a group of engagés who started back to Montréal to report on the progress of the expedition. Their return voyage was mostly downriver all the way to Montréal. They traveled light with minimal provisions.

Pointe-à-la-Chevelure

La Fresnière completed the project at the southern end of Lake Champlain by the end of September. He returned to Montréal in time to witness the launching of the first battleship to be built in Terrebonne, its masts having been harvested near *Pointe-à-la-Chevelure*.

Beauharnois ordered that a winter garrison of twenty soldiers be maintained under the command of officers de Moncourt and de Rouville, and he promised to send ten more soldiers in the spring. Once he had temporarily secured one of the most strategically important locations on the colonial frontier, Morandière also returned to Montréal.

On behalf of the king, the Québec governor had granted seigneuries on both sides of the lake to officials of the French Crown and officers in *Troupes de Marine*. Although the concessions were not immediately settled but kept for future generations, their presence clearly declared that France claimed the territory surrounding all rivers and lakes flowing into the Saint Lawrence River as hers, much as England had claimed Rupert's Land for the Hudson Bay Company in 1670 and La Salle had claimed the Mississippi River watershed for France in 1682.

Québec

The last ship to sail from Québec to France before the onset of winter carried letters from Engineer Chaussegros de Léry, Governor Beauharnois, and Hocquart. These reported on the completion of the *Fort de Pieux* on *Pointe-à-la-Chevelure*, and reiterated that the English settlements were only twelve leagues away from the new outpost which could only offer minimal and temporary protection from English incursions or attacks.

The two Québec officials wrote that Léry had already submitted various proposals for the future construction of a stronger and more permanent fortification. Of these, they both strongly supported that of a stonewalled *redoute à machicoulis* which could be built to withstand cannon fire, protect its own cannon and men from winter ice and snow, shelter and provision one hundred soldiers, yet was estimated to be the most economical choice to build and garrison.

Hocquart also reported to the colonial minister that 20,000 slates had been collected. He requested financial support so that his workers could replace cedar roofing with the new fireproof material on all of the king's colonial buildings.

Lake of the Woods, 1732

Soon after the western spring *débâcle*, Vérendrye reunited his two groups and added fifty canoes of Crees and Assinibouins before moving on to Lake of the Woods. The explorer had been told that the river of the west sprang from this lake, so he ordered his men to begin construction of Fort Saint-Charles in Cree territory.

This location had been considered since 1716 for the second major supply base westward after Kaministiquia. Based on his preliminary voyages to update French information about the western route, Charlevoix had reported to the French ministry in 1723 that the Pacific Ocean probably formed the western boundary of the country of the Sioux. Some western natives had told him that they had traveled to its shores and had met white men who spoke a language other than French.

Nouvelle France

Hocquart received King Louis XV's agreement to subsidize the colonial mining of slate to protect the roofs of the king's buildings, thus introducing a new light industry in Nouvelle France.

On May 26, 1732, François and his older cousin Alexis Beaulorier of Nicolet were hired as engagés by Pierre Gamelin of Saint-François-du-Lac to deliver supplies to Michillimackinac in support of Vérendrye's western explorations.

François Poulin de Francheville sent Canadian blacksmith Jean-Baptiste Labrèche to Boston that summer to study the New England methods of smelting iron ore.

He also hired several workers from among the second group of *faux-sauniers* who arrived from France. These men would live in the new barracks at Forges Saint-Maurice and earn wages to provide their own basic necessities.

Corvées were called to refine and extend *Le Chemin du Roi* beyond seignorial limits, to build wooden bridges or provide ferries across the various tributaries all along the northern bank of the Saint Lawrence River. The road would be up to seven meters wide and allow uninterrupted traffic between Québec and Montréal.

Champlain

Louis received payment of 94 livres from his brother Joseph on June 4th, and declared that the sale of his rights of succession to their father's estate had been paid in full.

Ten days later, Joseph payed his debts to his three oldest local siblings: Madeleine, Louis, and Angélique for their remaining future shares of the family inheritance.

That summer proved to be exceptionally hot and dry, ruining the harvests and slowing down all commercial activity in the colony.

Province of New York

French and English pressure had continued to increase on the eastern Iroquois lands. The Mohawks protested Philip Livingston's claims to a large section of land bordering both sides of the Mohawk River but to no avail. This tract had been granted to him by the king of England.

La Compagnie des Indes ceded its Louisiana monopoly to the crown in 1732, Governor Beauharnois and many among the Canadians argued that the Illinois territory should be returned to Québec control. Even though France refused, the governor continued to license Canadians for the Illinois fur trade, claiming that Louisiana could not supply the needs of the natives.

Upon his return to Saint-Maurice, Jean-Baptiste Labrèche convinced Francheville and his brother that the company should use New England's direct reduction method to process the iron ore. They knew that this would allow them to postpone the greater expense and effort of constructing the smelting furnace called *le haut fourneau*. Francheville sent Labrèche and two iron workers back to New England to master the direct method.

Montréal, September 16, 1732

The city was badly shaken by a 5.8-magnitude earthquake.

L'Hôtel-Dieu and most of the stone houses were particularly vulnerable because they had been rebuilt or patched up with building stones the masons had salvaged from the ruins of the great fires of 1695 and 1721.

Isle-de-la-Fourche

Sébastien and Anne were both relieved three days later when their daughter Marguerite arrived by shallop with her four children aged three to twelve. Her husband Jean had stayed in Montréal to salvage and protect what was left of their home and office. He had to deal with receiving the furs from his returning voyageurs and engagés, and planned to rebuild with *pièces-sur-pièces*.

Their children: Joseph, Marguerite, Jean-Baptiste, and Henri were also relieved to be back with their grandparents.

Anne noticed that despite her outward calm, her daughter's hands were shaking as she settled in with the children. Marguerite was obviously still under stress from the past few days. Anne quietly helped her and signaled Bastien to bring in everything left behind at the landing. Twelve-year old Joseph rushed out to help him.

They set up Joseph and Jean in one of the empty bedrooms, young Marguerite, Henri and their mother would share the other extra room. Then Anne sat at the table with her daughter and gave her a glass of wine to calm her just as Sébastien walked in and lit his pipe. Marguerite took a few sips and began to tell her parents about the ordeal the people of Montréal had lived through.

"Three days ago, a frightening roar filled the air at midday and the ground shook violently. The stone houses that we had been required to build after the fire of 1721 began to fall apart—even *L'Hôtel-Dieu!*" Her eyes filled with tears.

"Our beautiful home—hundreds of stone houses became undone, chimneys tumbled. Rocks flew through the air, injuring those who ran from their houses—one young girl that I know was killed. Outside the city walls, the wooden houses shifted off their foundations. Church bells tolled wildly. Towers and houses bent and swayed as the ground repeatedly trembled. People fled in panic. Cattle and wild beasts called out in terror.

"We've continued to feel the earth shake every day since then— Have you felt it here?"

"We did feel the earth tremble, Marguerite, but nothing like what you describe," her father reassured her. "You and your children will be safe and comfortable here. Jean was wise to send you to us. How will he manage?"

"He told me not to worry, that he planned to camp outside the walls and salvage as much as he could of the ruins of our house and office. Papa, so many of the stones were breaking apart even before they fell."

Her parents were surprised to hear this.

Once Marguerite and the children had settled down for the night, Bastien called his sons together and told them what had happened to their sister in Montréal. Although four of them were already deeply involved in developing their own concessions and building their houses, they discussed the situation among themselves and all agreed to travel to Montréal with tools and provisions to assist their brother-in-law in setting up a temporary office and shelter before the cold weather set in. The youngest son, René would remain at home to do the chores for his father. His brothers left the following day.

Aftershocks continued for over a month. More people fled from Montréal to find shelter downriver in Trois Rivières and Québec. Another violent earthquake as strong as the first shook Montréal on the night of October 25-26.

Forges Saint-Maurice

By the end of the shipping season, Francheville's company had successfully produced iron nails for the local farriers. Hocquart sent samples of these to France on the maiden voyage of the first man-of-war ship to be built in Terrebonne.

Nineteen

1733

Illness, food shortages, and poverty plagued the communities of the Saint Lawrence River valley that winter. Smallpox reached epidemic proportions in Montréal and the missions, then swept eastward to Québec where the hospital's census averaged 2,000 patients that winter.

In mid-January, Intendant Hocquart assisted François Poulin de Francheville in his efforts to raise additional financial support and enlist the essential metallurgical expertise required for the rapid development of Forges Saint-Maurice. They successfully recruited Montréal merchant Ignace Gamelin *fils,* François-Étienne Cugnet who was director of *le Domaine Occident* and member of *le Conseil supérieur,* and Intendant Hocquart's secretary Bricault de Valmur who would report directly to his superior.

Francheville retained 50% of the shares, Cugnet 20%, and the rest was divided evenly among the others. They would all share in the investments and profits of the new company and were determined to begin producing knives, axes, and other hand tools by the end of the year. The local blacksmiths could no longer keep up with the growing demand for those items.

Nicolet

Sébastien's son Jean-Baptiste completed the construction of his house and barn in Baie-du-Febvre by mid-February, thus fulfilling the terms of his concession agreement and officially securing the land *en censive*.

The family celebrated together in his new house with several members of the seigneur's family.

Sieur René Lefebvre congratulated Jean-Baptiste, Alexis, and Charles on their mutual accomplishments, and cordially welcomed them into his seigneurie.

Sébastien and Anne admired the view of the bay and walked through all three houses on their sons' adjoining properties. Each of their concessions measured 4 arpents frontage by 40 deep, extended two arpents into the bay, and allowed hunting and fishing rights. Their other brother Simon had already settled nearby after his voyage with Lignery in 1728.

Their parents embraced each of the new landholders. Sébastien told them with obvious joy: "We're very proud of you three—you've worked so well together to accomplish all of this."

Dusk settled early that mid-winter afternoon, prompting Jean-Baptiste to light his whale-oil lamps. They were all grateful that Canadian-built ships could now conduct whale-fishing in the Gulf of Saint Lawrence and provide this remarkably clean oil for the lamps of Nouvelle France.

Now that his house was built and the land was his, thirty-year old Jean-Baptiste sought to raise enough funds so that he could properly furnish his home and establish his own family. Most of his male relatives advised him to sign up for a voyage to *les pays d'en haut*. René Lefebvre mentioned that his merchant cousin was looking for engagés who were willing to travel to the Strait of Mackinac, and he offered to recommend him.

Trois Rivières, March 1733

Francheville hired Canadian master-blacksmith and edge-tool maker, Christophe Janson dit Lapalme of Montréal for three years as the new ironmaster at Forges Saint-Maurice, and sent him with Jean-Baptiste La Brèche to spend two months in New England to study the English colonial method of producing wrought iron.

Soon after the spring débâcle, Sunday civil announcements informed the populace that Monseigneur Pierre-Herman Dosquet had been named Bishop of Canada, and that Pierre Rigaud marquis de Vaudreuil de Cavagnal, fifth child of the former governor-general, had been appointed lieutenant-governor of the district of Trois Rivières.

News quickly spread that the king had granted a loan to initiate the smelting of iron ore by Forges Saint-Maurice. Francheville's new partnerships had gained royal approval.

Nouvelle France

By the end of April, new ferries and bridges carried traffic across all of the Saint Lawrence River's northern tributaries.

Because of the rising competition between the French, English, and Mohawks over control of the land surrounding Lake Champlain, Governor Beauharnois ordered that repairs be made to the stone-walled fort of Saint Louis-de-Chambly on the Richelieu River.

On June 2nd, Montréal merchants François Lefebvre-Duplessis, Fabert and Jean Paré hired Sébastien's thirty-year old son Jean-Baptiste as voyageur to Michillimackinac.

Fox Wars

Hostilities had ended in the Wisconsin territory beyond Lake Michigan. When the principal Fox chief Kiala appeared before the French governor in Québec to beg for mercy, Beauharnois sentenced him to slavery in Martinique and sent a warning to the remaining warriors that they would all be killed if they did not disperse themselves among the colonial missions.

In response to the severity of these French measures, many native allies began to sympathize with the surviving Fox warriors. That September, Nicolas-Antoine Coulon de Villiers demanded the surrender of those who had found refuge among the Sauks in Green Bay, thus inciting the killing of his son and several other Frenchmen. The remaining warriors of the vanquished nation found refuge among the Sioux.

Trois Rivières

A strong earthquake and forty days of aftershocks jolted and shook Nouvelle France that autumn, and were felt in the district of Trois Rivières.

By mid-November, Forges Saint-Maurice had produced knives, axes, hatchets and other tools for the local market. The quality of its iron products compared well to the best in Europe, but the use of the *bas-fourneau* limited the emerging production rate to one quarter of that achieved in France.

François Poulin de Francheville died at the age of forty-one on November 30th, just as his enormous efforts in building up the iron industry had begun to succeed.

A smallpox epidemic flared up in the Trois Rivières area. During the longest night of the year, as a full moon lighted the district of Trois Rivières, the highly infectious disease struck down its first victim in François Ducharme's family when his oldest daughter Charlotte died at the age of thirty. She had never married and had continued to live at home with her parents.

Bécancour, 1734

Bastien's youngest son Jean-François Ducharme died at age sixty on February 2nd and was buried the following day.

His twenty-five-year old daughter Marie-Josephte died twelve days later.

Marguerite Moreau was left with the following children at home: Marguerite who was the oldest at age twenty-nine, Jean-Baptiste, Charles, Antoine, Anne, Joseph, and Monique who was the youngest at age seven.

That spring, her son Antoine completed his apprenticeship with Louis Lemaître and was employed by the canoe-maker. He continued to live at home and contributed a share of his earnings toward the financial support of the rest of the family.

Montréal, April 10th

Fire raged through Madame Poulin de Francheville's home in Montréal and spread from roof to roof to consume forty-six houses, the hospital, an historic church, and the convent of *l'Hôtel-Dieu* before it was brought under control later that night.

Witnesses angrily assumed that the woman's black slave Marie-Josephte-Angélique had set the fire in a bid to escape slavery with her white lover, voyageur Claude Thibault. It was well-known in the community that her mistress Thérèse de Couagne had refused to pay Thibault the voyageur wages she had long owed him, and had denied Angélique's request to be freed from slavery. Her mistress had announced her intention to sell Angélique back to the slave brokers in the Antilles.

Thérèse Couagne had suffered financial distress ever since her husband's untimely death. François Poulin de Francheville had paid 900 livres for Angélique in the Manhattan slave market when she was barely eighteen years old. She had always bitterly resented her bondage and had always held a grudge against the French.

The slave and the voyageur were later arrested and imprisoned, but Thibault was soon released and she was not. Angélique repeatedly denied that she or Thibault had set the fire, yet witnesses testified that she had threatened to burn down her mistress' house in protest against her slavery and pending sale.

The French magistrate applied torture to force her to admit that both she and Thibault had set the fire. Angélique finally acknowledged her own guilt but refused to implicate her lover who had fled by then. She was taken by boat, with both knees broken and unbound, from Montréal to Québec where she was paraded through angry mobs, forced to publicly admit her crime, and finally hanged by the black executioner. The baptized slave's hands were then chopped off, her remains incinerated and scattered to the winds while the crowd rejoiced.

That spring, Pierre and Michel Gamelin hired Simonne's youngest son François for a voyage to the fur trading post on the Saint Joseph River, his first venture south of the Great Lakes, toward the Ohio valley. François had reached his majority which allowed him to sign a promissory note to merchant Jean Guillon for the purchase of trading goods valued at 339#, 5 sols, 3 deniers.

Québec

Early that summer, Bishop Dosquet and Father Nau arrived in Nouvelle France with twelve young uneducated abbots whom they had collected at the church doors in Paris. The passenger list also included one hundred soldier-recruits who had been cleared from the streets of Paris and sent as additional manpower for the garrisons of Nouvelle France. They were infested with lice, poorly dressed, covered with sores, and worm-infested. Twenty of them died during the passage; those who arrived in Québec were housed in Québec's *Hôpital général*.

Pointe-à-la-Chevelure

Royal Engineer Chaussegros de Léry completed his design of the new stone fort to be built on the western shore of Crown Point. It consisted of a four-story masonry tower with stone walls twelve feet thick at the base, and vaulted ceilings designed to withstand cannon fire. The two lowest levels would be constructed underground, the upper levels built *à machicoulis*, and each of the four floors would be divided into four rooms.

This structure would accommodate a one-hundred-man garrison with separate quarters for commander, officers and soldiers, a bakery, an armory, and an ammunition depot surrounded by masonry walls. Twenty cannon would be mounted in the stone tower and its entrance would be protected by a second drawbridge that was to be controlled from within. The outer limestone walls surrounding the tower would be built up to 18 feet high with a cylindrical sentry box in each corner bastion. Its entrance would face north, would be accessed by way of an outer drawbridge that crossed over a dry ditch, and by passage through a two-storied guard house that would house the winding gear for the bridge and an iron grating that could be lowered to further block the entrance. A chapel would share the guardhouse bastion and serve the needs of soldiers and settlers alike.

The French government had already promoted settlement of the land that surrounded Lake Champlain in order to provide food for the construction workers and garrison soldiers. Land grants, farming equipment, and tax remissions over several years had been offered to soldiers and civilians who were willing to clear and farm the area.

Louis XV declared that French soldiers who were stationed in Canada must first serve three years before they married. Governor Beauharnois praised their value as settlers and farmers, particularly around Lake Champlain.

Trois Rivières

On May 13, 1734, twenty-eight-year old French-born François Thomas dit Tranchemontagne, former sergeant of the garrison in Trois Rivières, married thirty-year-old Madeleine-Catherine Maudoux who had recently moved in with relatives in the area. He found employment at Forges Saint-Maurice and they settled in Trois Rivières.

Montréal

Governmental authorities organized the community's first fire brigade that summer, and passed new ordinances setting up police protocols and protections against structural fires. A month later, Intendant Gilles Hocquart ordered the manufacture of buckets, axes, ladders and other tools to be used in firefighting. All house-owners were now required to have a roof-ladder for each chimney, and all new buildings inside the city walls were to be built of fresh-cut stone.

La Verendrye returned to pay off his creditors and hoped for news of financial support from Maurepas. Although he received no additional backing from France or from his existing partners, Governor Beauharnois helped him set up a new partnership with two other leading Montréal merchants.

Québec officials discovered that the slate mined at Grand-Étang was not true slate after all, but a close imitation that would have to be replaced wherever it had been installed. The monopolist of that mining project died soon after hearing the news. Hope of finding another domestic source faded when further searches for quality slate at Île Verte and at *Pointe-à-la-Chevelure* revealed the same poor quality.

An early blizzard blanketed the Saint Lawrence River valley settlements that September. It isolated and caused much hardship among its inhabitants, restricted commerce, harvesting, fishing and hunting. Bastien's descendants were grateful for their traditional emergency storage of pemmican, corn, and peas, and family recipes for *banique* and *sagamité* to stretch their food supplies.

On October 3rd, the last of Bastien and Catherine's daughters, thirty-six-year old Madeleine signed a marriage contract with twenty-nine-year old François Didier who owned a farm near Sébastien's sons in Baie-du-Febvre.

Her step-brother Louis Massé, her nephew Alexis Provencher, and *Sieur* Tranchemontagne signed as witnesses to the agreement. Her niece Catherine Maudoux, and her older siblings Sébastien, Jean-Baptiste and Catherine Massé also attended the signing.

Six weeks later, Sébastien's thirty-one-year old son Simon married the seigneur's daughter, twenty-three-year old Madeleine Lefebvre. The entire family attended the reception in the seignorial manor.

Twenty

1735

Sébastien and his family's grief over the recent death of Anne
Massé was partially tempered by two family wedding alliances
with long-time friends.

On January 15th, his son Alexis signed a marriage contract with
Marie-Angélique Leblanc dit Labrie, daughter of Nicolas and
Geneviève Petit of Cap-de-la-Madeleine. He pledged her a *douaire
préfix* of 500 livres and a *douaire préciput* of 300 livres from wages
earned during his voyage for Gamelin in 1732, and he promised
to share all his wealth and property with her. If they were both to
die childless, his estate would revert to his family.

Both spouses signed, as did witnesses for the groom: brother-
in-law Jean-Baptiste Guillon, uncle Louis Massé, and his sister
Madeleine.

Witnesses on behalf of the bride included her parents, her
brother Nicolas, uncle René Leblanc and his wife Jeanne Bourbeau,
uncle Jean-Baptiste Beaumier and his wife Geneviève Leblanc.

Witnesses on behalf of the groom were his widowed father
Sébastien, his siblings Jean-Baptiste, Simon, Charles, Madeleine,
Marguerite and her husband Jean-Baptiste Guillon; uncles Louis
and Jean-Baptiste Massé, Michel-Crevier Bellerive; aunts
Catherine Massé and widow Marguerite Moreau; and his cousin
Jean-Baptiste Ducharme.

The following day, Sébastien's daughter Madeleine signed her
own marriage contract in Nicolet with Nicolas Leblanc-Labrie *fils*.

The same guests attended this ceremony and both church weddings which were held in the bride's parish church.

Sébastien's oldest daughter Marguerite and her merchant husband Jean Guillon stayed with him on *Isle-de-la-Fourche* during the week of contract signings, church weddings and receptions. The couple relieved him of all the related arrangements that he and Anne would have routinely taken care of together.

At age sixty-five, Sébastien had lost much of his stamina and recognized this as a natural part of the grieving process, but he was determined to make these days as memorable for his son and daughter as his own wedding had been for him.

He had been widowed less than a year and all of his children were either married or living on their own concessions except for twenty-one-year old René who remained with him to work and manage the family farm.

Sébastien grew pensive. There will be just the two of us now after these two weddings, he thought. This house had been so full of life and energy for so many years. It will seem unbearably quiet, he sadly acknowledged.

Marguerite sensed and interrupted his melancholy. "Papa, we've had a lot of good, happy years with you and *Maman* in this house but now that there's no one left here to cook or do the laundry for you, Jean and I would love to have you and René join our family in Montréal—when and if you feel ready for it."

Her offer stunned him. It had never occurred to him that he might not spend the rest of his days on *Isle-de-la-Fourche*. "That's very generous of both of you, *ma fille*, but you already have a house full of children."

"Maybe so, but Jean spends a good part of his time away from Montréal these days and I often miss having another adult to talk to during his absence. We and the children would enjoy having you and René live with us. Besides, you were so generous to us after the fire and the earthquake, let us do the same for you."

Her husband had been quietly smoking his pipe near the fire and joined in. "René strikes me as a young man who would enjoy living in Montréal…"

René blushed; Jean had read his thoughts! Although he never complained about having to do the farm chores, he had often envied the voyaging opportunities his older brothers had experienced.

"...and this might be the perfect opportunity for him to learn the fur trade."

Sébastien could see that his son was intrigued by the possibility.

"And of course, Joseph lives nearby, there's lots of family for you in Montréal," Marguerite added.

"I'm certainly grateful for your kind invitation but I'll need time to think it over. You know, this house holds so many good memories and this land is very dear to me. I've been a farmer all my life, and I'm not sure that I could bear to live in the city." He saw the disappointment in René's face and added: "I will think about it."

Sébastien had worked through enough of the grieving process by early March to realize that the house was less of a home without his wife's presence. He seriously considered his youngest son's future and understood that René was not a farmer at heart, but had a strong desire to either travel or learn a trade in the city. He had no wish to deprive him of either opportunity.

He sighed. In spite of his own strong attachment to the land, his oldest daughter had married a fur merchant, his oldest son had become a successful Montréal merchant, three other sons had voyaged and his fourth was looking to follow in their footsteps.

Faced with the prospect of living alone in an empty house, he donated his concession on *Isle-de-la-Fourche* to his eight surviving children and accepted Marguerite and Jean's invitation. Sébastien and René moved to Montréal a few months later.

Nouvelle France

French settlement expanded beyond the shores of the Saint Lawrence River as many of the retired *Troupes de Marine* married in Canada, and accepted concessions along the Richelieu River and the shores of Lake Champlain. Others migrated south to settle on the east bank of Wabash River, just north of its junction with the White River, in an eighteen-year old community called Vincennes.

An immigrant tile-maker produced four thousand clay roof-tiles which Hocquart and Beauharnois judged to be of French quality. The intendant bought thirty-five hundred of these to be tested as fireproof roofing on one of the king's warehouses.

Canadian officials officially inaugurated *le Chemin du Roi* on August 5, 1735. This four-year project had connected all the seigneuries from Québec to Montréal on the northern bank of the Saint Lawrence River. This uninterrupted roadway, up to seven meters wide of ploughed dirt and 250 kilometers in length, had thirteen small wooden bridges and ferries spanning the northern tributaries of that great river. Travel on horseback from Trois Rivières to either Québec or Montréal could be accomplished in two days, thus speeding up communications and transport of goods between the major communities.

Jean Guillon transferred François' promissory note to Joseph Rochereau dit Duvuvier on September 4th in settlement of his debt to the Bécancour farmer. Since François' farm had been used as collateral for the loan, Rochereau harvested its hay for his cattle and horses during the voyageur's absence.

Trois Rivières

The agricultural economy of the Trois-Rivières area had been greatly affected by the lack of activity at Forges Saint-Maurice since Francheville's death. The board of directors and Intendant Hocquart had carefully inspected the entire complex and concluded that its true potential could only be achieved through the infusion of new investment and French expertise.

French metallurgist Pierre-François Olivier de Vézin arrived in Québec early in September 1735 and met with the intendant. Hocquart directed him to completely reevaluate and inspect the existing industrial complex at Saint-Maurice, and the sources of iron located between Batiscan and Trois Rivières.

Vézin spent five weeks studying the availability of resources in Batiscan, Champlain, Cap-de-la-Madeleine, Trois Rivières and Saint-Maurice before presenting his report to the intendant. He praised both the quality and quantity of the local ore and the easy access of all essential raw materials near Saint-Maurice, but he advised that the direct-reduction method practiced by Francheville was inadequate to maintain the growth of the industry.

The new ironmaster announced that the project must be completely redesigned and based around a *haut fourneau* with all its supporting structures and services. He estimated the cost of such an enterprise at 36,000 livres, annual expenses at 61,000, and predicted an initial annual income of 19,000 livres which could soon rise to 60,000 livres annually and ultimately to 116,000 livres at full capacity.

His level of expertise and enthusiasm convinced Intendant Hocquart that the industrial project could finally succeed. However, Francheville's partners had realized no return on their five-year investment of 22,000 livres in the direct-reduction method and were now overwhelmed by the projected costs of the proposed conversion. By late October, they annulled their partnership and ceded the monopoly to the crown.

A new partnership was formed by ironmaster Vézin, Cugnet and Ignace Gamelin who announced to the Québec officials that they would seek financial support from private French investors. Governor Beauharnois and Intendant Hocquart disapproved of their plans and insisted that the partners must rely on Canadian backing and a royal loan of 100,000 livres in card money to restart the industry.

During the two years since their father's death, François Ducharme's sons had gradually paid off the promissory note of 264 livres their father owed to their uncle Sébastien as a result of the land-exchange agreement dated March 8, 1724. That December, Sébastien legally acknowledged that his brother's debt to him had been paid in full, thus reassuring Marguerite Moreau that her husband's estate would remain intact.

Spring 1736

Winter 1735–1736 had been exceptionally long. Tilling, sowing and planting was delayed by the late spring. The prospect of summer and autumn grain shortages threatened the farmers of Nouvelle France.

Cugnet bought the *Seigneurie de Saint-Maurice* from Francheville's heirs in early spring. His new partnership with Ignace Gamelin and ironmaster Vézin applied to the king for a loan of 100,000 livres.

La Verendrye

The explorer began to face a series of critical problems out west. His nephew Jemerais had taken ill at Fort Maurepas and had died May 10th on his way to Fort Saint-Charles. La Verendrye's new partners in Montréal had failed to deliver provisions to the western forts.

Desperately in need of fresh supplies, Vérendrye sent his eldest son Jean-Baptiste on an emergency expedition to Kaministiquia and Michillimackinac in early June.

A week later, his son, a young Jesuit priest, and nineteen Canadian voyageurs were slain on an island in Lake of the Woods, while on their way east for those provisions. The explorer's native allies pressured him to avenge their deaths, but he was in too vulnerable a position to take on the Sioux.

Forges Saint-Maurice

News arrived from France in early summer that the king had approved the new partnership and its plans for Forges Saint-Maurice. He had granted the loan and sent Jacques Simonet as second ironmaster with four more specialists to direct the forges.

Louis XV agreed to provide the advance and stipulated that it must be repaid within the following three years, either in iron deliveries or currency.

Thus reassured, the intendant provided teams of workmen who worked feverishly through the summer and autumn to build roads to the industrial site from Trois Rivières and the mining areas of Pointe-du-Lac to deliver supplies and equipment, and from the forges to the base of the rapids to enable the transportation of products and merchandise. Workmen also began to construct stone foundations for the forge, the waterpower channels, and walls of the complex.

Within the next few days, Francheville's brothers, widow and heirs sold their monopoly of Forges Saint-Maurice to Cugnet who then founded Cugnet and Compagnie to manage the enterprise. Member of the *Conseil supérieur* Thomas-Jacques Taschereau and second ironmaster Jacques Simonet joined Cugnet, Gamelin and Vézin on the governing board. Gamelin was the only native-born Canadian. The two French-born ironmasters had been in Nouvelle France less than a year when they began to redesign and reconstruct the new industrial complex.

One hundred workers were already employed to mine the ore, harvest hardwood and process it into charcoal to fuel *le haut fourneau*. François Thomas dit Tranchemontagne was now in charge of overseeing these last two operations.

Nicolet, winter 1736–1737

Shortly before Christmas, Sébastien's sons Alexis and his brother Charles began one-year terms as *marguilliers* of the Nicolet parish.

Alexis and his brother Jean-Baptiste now owned *Isle-de-la-Fourche*, having bought up all other shares of their father's estate from their siblings during the previous two years.

Thirty-eight-year old Jean-Baptiste married the daughter of the *seigneur de la Baie-du-Febvre* on March 5th. Marie-Jeanne Lefebvre's parents hosted the reception in their spacious seigneurial manor that overlooked the bay.

Soon after the wedding, Jean-Baptiste adopted the additional surname "Belleville", derived from the legendary location of the Provencher family's ancestral château in Franche-Comté of eastern France.

Forges Saint-Maurice

At their annual board meeting, the directors of *Cugnet et Compagnie* voted to build a *Grand'Maison* of stone at Forges Saint-Maurice. Vézin objected to such an extravagant expense for a commercial building that would dwarf the existing industrial complex, but he lacked the necessary support to prevail because Hocquart and Simonet could not attend that meeting. Cugnet and his supporters argued that this structure would provide living quarters for the ironmasters and supervisors, space for the farriers and stables, and protection for a large store of merchandise that the merchant-directors planned to sell on credit to anyone who worked for the company. Two hundred workers were now employed at *le haut fourneau* and the two forges.

Cugnet estimated construction costs would amount to 15,000 livres; other directors predicted 30,000 livres. Vézin suspected that these estimates were unrealistic and knew that funding for such a building would be drawn from the king's loan fund.

Québec

The previous annual report to Minister Maurepas on the production and installation of clay roof tiles had claimed that of the thirty-five hundred tiles used in replacing the defective slate roofing on one of the king's stores, only thirty-five had been damaged by the cold. A minor problem in firing had been explained as the cause of the damage and assurance offered that this could be avoided in the future. They continued to test the rest of the tiles through a second winter.

Soon after the spring thaw, Hocquart learned that two hundred more clay roof tiles had been damaged by severe winter conditions, that the problem was due to the quality of the mortar used in installation, that it had not dried properly. Thus the clay had absorbed the remaining moisture which froze and cracked the tiles during the frigid winter conditions. The roofers advised that they should be installed with nails rather than mortar if they were to be retested over the next two winters.

The investor did not renew the contract and the project was abandoned. The king's warehouses were once again left without fireproof roofing.

Bécancour

On May 2nd, Jean-Baptiste Ducharme married Josephte Duchaîne, daughter of *Seigneur* Julien Lesieur-Duchaîne *fils* of Saint-Anne's parish in Yamachiche.

Witnesses to the signing of the marriage contract were the groom's mother, his brothers Charles and Antoine, sister Marguerite, and uncle François Moreau; the bride's mother Simone Blanchet, brother Pierre Lesieur, uncle Charles Lesieur, and merchant Étienne Gélinas. The couple planned to settle in the new parish of Yamachiche where Jean-Baptiste had already cleared the virgin forest, built a home and barn, and tilled enough land to provide his own food supply.

A week later, the people of the trifluvian area heard reports of food shortages in Québec. Excessive rains had delayed the spring sowing of grain crops, further threatening famine in Nouvelle France.

Simonne, Sébastien's and François' wives had always maintained emergency food caches in their *greniers* and cellars, and had taught the native pemmican recipe to their children. It was under such threatening conditions that this generation particularly appreciated what they had learned from their parents.

After checking their food storage areas, the men and boys concentrated on preserving extra meat gathered by trapping, fishing and hunting. The women combined what surplus they had to produce the survival food that had often proven to be an excellent trail food for the voyageurs.

In mid-June, Simonne's youngest son François exchanged concessions in fief Gatineau with his brother-in-law François Rochereau. The new arrangement would benefit both parties since it added adjoining land to their existing farms.

Forges Saint-Maurice

The half-built *Grand'Maison* already loomed like a phantom castle over the ironwork complex.

Ironmaster Simonet returned from France with fifty-five new workmen raising Hocquart's hopes that the furnace might be lit by mid-October, a year earlier than previously expected.

In order to guarantee the reserve of hardwood required for the production of charcoal for the furnace, the company had been granted the concession of fief Saint-Étienne, which extended upriver from the forges to one league above the Saint Maurice River falls called *chutes de la Gabelle*. François Thomas dit Tranchemontage continued in his supervisory role over this part of the operation.

Construction of the new forges was finally completed that October. Its new blast furnace and its auxiliary structures were ready for testing. Everything seemed ready to light *le haut fourneau*, yet master-smelter Lardier failed in four attempts within a period of six weeks.

The company ran out of funds and suspended operations pending additional financial support from France to remedy this additional problem. The construction of the *Grand'Maison* had already absorbed a great deal of the previous funding.

French technicians were expensive to support on the payroll and impossible to discipline. Their unruliness soon spread through the local workforce.

Hocquart began to mistrust Vézin's judgement. To his dismay, he was forced again to request additional funding from France.

Twenty-one

Bécancour, 1738

L ouis' youngest son François was frustrated by the small return on his farming activities and his inability to pay off his debt which Guillon had transferred to Joseph Rochereau. He resolved to make one final effort on his double lot.

That spring, Hocquart forestalled the growing threat of malnutrition and starvation among the Canadian population by requisitioning the surplus grain held in storage by the colony's wealthiest merchants.

Soon after the spring débâcle, the governor received the minister's reply to his request for additional funds. The letter delivered a severe reprimand for what the king and Maurepas regarded as irresponsible management of the industrial project, a warning that this must be the last request for additional financial support, and that the requested amount was most reluctantly granted.

The intendant resolved to maintain a closer watch on the operation of Forges Saint-Maurice as efforts were renewed to correct the problems of *le haut-fourneau*. He learned that Cugnet and Vézin constantly bickered with each other. The ironmaster refused to be challenged in his direction of the works; Cugnet and his supporters repeatedly accused him of incompetence and mismanagement.

Hocquart decided to conduct a surprise inspection of the operation in July but Vézin learned of the official's upcoming visit and attempted to cover up his greatest mistake, that of having located the forges close to an insufficient source of waterpower.

During the demonstration of the works, Hocquart's specialist discovered the ironmaster's ruse and warned the intendant that the demonstration could potentially damage the great hammer of the forge. Hocquart immediately halted the operation.

Within days, the intendant assigned Engineer Chaussegros de Léry to conduct a full inspection of the entire ironworks and provide him with an honest, detailed report of its current state. Léry concluded that *la Grand'Maison* was unnecessarily ornate and expensive, and that the water source was insufficient to power the two water wheels although the facility had been built to accommodate six. He recommended that a second forge be added below the furnace since half of the high-salaried French workers had been idle during the recent problems with the existing forge.

Vézin and his assistant Delorme finally succeeded in relighting the blast furnace at Forges Saint-Maurice at noon of August 20th.

La Vérendrye

The explorer and his two remaining sons, Louis-Joseph and François, left Lake of the Woods and continued west to reach Lake Winnipeg. They ascended the Assiniboine River and built a sturdy log fort as their main base for a series of explorations into the Canadian Prairies. The location had traditionally served as a southern portage point for native and French traders traveling to Lake Manitoba and would enable Canadian contact with the Assiniboine traders heading north to Hudson Bay. This expedition promised to lift the Grand-Portage trade up to a competitive level with that of the Mississippi-Wisconsin-Fox river routes.

Forges Saint-Maurice

On October 7, 1738, the king's legal representative in the jurisdiction of Trois Rivières formally and ceremoniously declared the official lighting of the new blast-furnace.

Production levels were disappointing due to an insufficient supply of mined iron ore, and of water flow to power the great wheel that activated the works. However, the a steadying rate of production began to revive the area's economy.

Two weeks later, the company's directors acknowledged their debt of 192,642 livres to the royal treasury and promised to pay it off within four years of the official opening date of August 20, 1738.

Nouvelle France, 1739

Sébastien died in Montréal that February at the age of sixty-nine, surrounded by his daughter's family and two of his own sons, Joseph and René. He and his wife had raised seven boys and two girls. All of his sons served as *marguilliers* for the parish of Nicolet except Joseph and René who lived in Montréal and were involved in the fur trade.

Early that year, Chaussegros de Léry delivered his construction plans for the second forge at Saint-Maurice. He predicted that it would cost less to build than the first one.

La Vérendrye returned to Lake of the Woods with his two sons, one of whom headed north and discovered lakes Manitoba, Winnipegosis, Bourbon and Dauphin. Their father returned once more to Montréal to settle accounts with his creditors.

The latest census showed that the Canadian population had risen to 42,701 with 71.5% of that number living in the rural parishes. Beaver skins represented 70% of total exports; agricultural and fishing products another 27%; iron and forest products provided the rest. Two hundred sixteen thousand livres of tobacco had been harvested during the previous year.

One hundred thirty-seven settlements now extended over a distance of 350 miles along both shores of the Saint Lawrence River and its tributaries. These demographics compared well with those of the 1667 census which had reported 19 small communities from Québec to Montréal.

Bécancour

Simonne's François had become thoroughly discouraged by his inability to pay off his debt. His oldest brother Jean was very much in his thoughts because he seemed to be doing well for himself in Louisiana. Francois recalled the warmer climate and sights of his journey to *rivière Saint-Joseph*. He felt the need for a fresh start.

That spring, François seized the opportunity to return south of Lake Michigan where land and wildlife were free and plentiful.

Pierre Gamelin *fils* hired him as a voyageur into the Illinois country.

He bade farewell to his family. His mother hated to see him leave, sensing that she would never see him again. Yet she realized that he was a voyageur at heart and had to fulfill his own destiny.

Forges Saint-Maurice

Construction of the second forge was completed by the end of July, well within Engineer Léry's predicted time and cost guidelines.

The company produced 227,000 livres of iron by September 1, 1739, and expected to double that rate of output once the second blast furnace became fully operational.

Vézin returned to France to recruit another group of skilled technicians. During his absence, second-ironmaster Simonet refined the works, consolidated worker duties, and attempted to reestablish discipline among the workers. The directors fought him every step of the way, refused to accept his leadership and initiatives in such matters. They campaigned for his removal, but the intendant did not agree with them.

The company's funding ran out again before the full potential of the complex was achieved. Hocquart refused to renew his pleas to the king for an additional loan. The head of the *Conseil supérieur* of Québec, Cugnet, invested from his own personal wealth, and borrowed from the cash account of the *Domaine d'occident du Canada* which was accessible to him as its director.

Québec

Louis XV had expanded his shipyard and appointed an experienced director of naval construction to oversee its development and operations. On September 22nd, work began on *Le Canada*, the first royal naval vessel to be built in Nouvelle France. This fluyt would be of 500-ton capacity, armed with forty cannons, and require a crew of one hundred twenty men.

Europe

During the previous fifty years of unsettled colonial boundary disputes and growing commercial competition in North America, British trade had leveled off and been overtaken by France. While Britain, Spain and France restricted foreign trade with their own colonies, English merchants had been abusing the Assiento privilege granted them by the Treaty of Utrecht that allowed them to sell African slaves to the Spanish Caribbean islands.

English attempts to smuggle trade into the Spanish colonies, English logwooders operating on the coast of Honduras, the continuing boundary dispute between Georgia and Florida, and the growing number of English privateers operating in the Caribbean Ocean finally led to war between the English and Spanish colonies of North America. Governor Ogelthorpe's forces attacked Spanish Florida.

In Louisiana, Governor Bienville managed to preserve peace between the Choctaws and Chickasaws, thus keeping the English provincials at bay despite efforts by the Carolinians to erode French support in the west. The Cherokees, Choctaws, Alibamous began to join forces to resist the English, Spanish and French colonial competition for control over their native lands. Their strength in numbers would grow to more than twelve thousand warriors by mid-century.

Nouvelle France

In spring 1740, La Vérendrye's creditors served him with papers to seize his forts, goods and properties. The explorer returned to Montréal to straighten out this new problem with the hope of finding a new source of support for his exploration further into the Missouri River country. He and his sons had finally realized that this was the most direct route available to the western sea.

Upon his arrival home, the explorer learned that his wife Marie-Anne had died the previous September and was buried in Sainte-Anne's Chapel of Notre Dame Church. The Québec governor accommodated him as his guest for the winter and helped resolve his financial problems by granting him a fur trading monopoly over all the western posts he would establish after June 1741.

Beauharnois resented Hocquart's growing resistance against providing financial support for the maintenance of the western forts and military defenses. The intendant preferred to direct French funds toward the development of the colonial economy. The governor implied collusion between Intendant Hocquart and Cugnet, farmer of the Tadoussac fur trade and leading partner in the Saint-Maurice ironworks.

Forges Saint-Maurice

Vézin returned from France in early May with his brother and 13 additional iron workers. Three weeks later, they relit *le haut fourneau* but the company's profits remained unsteady. Hocquart paid close attention to the 396,000-livres operation and asked endless questions. The partners quarreled with each other and repeatedly accused Vézin of incompetence.

Québec

Bishop Dosquet's replacement arrived on *Le Rubris* one year after the elderly cleric had returned to France. Monseigneur François-Louis Pourroy de Lauberivière died on August 20th at the age of twenty-nine, one year after his consecration as the new bishop of Québec and merely twelve days after his arrival in Nouvelle France.

The first case of *fièvres pourprées* (contagious fever) had been diagnosed when the ship was 400 miles from Québec. The infection had spread quickly among the four hundred or so passengers who were crowded together in its darkened hold. Officers and some able-bodied passengers had replaced many of the disabled crewmen while the new bishop ministered among the sick.

Towards the end of its two-month crossing, the vessel flew a distress flag as it made its way up the Saint Lawrence River. No other ship captain dared to approach it. Upon hearing of the sickness of the passengers and sailors, Hocquart dispatched two vessels with experienced river pilots and a fresh replacement crew.

One of these rescue ships escorted *Le Rubris* to port while the other sped toward Québec with one hundred ten of the feverish passengers. Ninety-one of them were hospitalized immediately at *l'Hôtel-Dieu* and *l'Hôpital général*.

One hundred sixty patients were ultimately admitted to hospital where more than sixty of them died within days.

Nicolet

The diocesan vicar-general sang high Mass and dedicated the stone church in Nicolet on July 15, 1740. This second house of worship was built on a high point of land that jutted from the riverbank. It was visible from the Nicolet and Saint Lawrence rivers, and *Isle-de-la-Fourche*. Its small cove could accommodate the landing of one hundred canoes.

Europe

Charles VI of Austria died the following October, leaving no male heir to inherit his throne. France, Prussia, and Bavaria all laid conflicting claims to the kingdom, while England supported Charles' daughter Marie-Thérèse as the country's presumptive heiress. Although war was not declared, French and British ships attacked each other in the Channel and on the high seas.

French aristocratic attempts to maintain the courtly reign first established by Louis XIV in Versailles had become a constant drain on the royal treasury. The possibility of war over the Austrian succession now drew France toward another potentially expensive military contest in Europe.

Nova Scotia

The *Acadiens* of Nova Scotia had finally taken the British oath, with the oral assurance that they would not be required to bear arms against either the French or the British, thus clinging firmly to their neutrality.

Their population had greatly increased since France had ceded their colony to Great Britain. They had outgrown their ancestral lands in Port Royal, Beaubassin, and the Minas Basin. All arable land within the old boundaries had been fully reclaimed from the marshes and forests, divided and subdivided within families, so that their crops could no longer support and feed their families. They sought new concessions across the isthmus of Chignectou and north of Shediak.

Previous governors and their allied councillors had conveyed a very negative impression of the Acadians through their agents and friends in London. They had also divided 100,000 acres amongst themselves in Grand'Pré and Beaubassin, the most fertile farming areas on the peninsula which four to five generations of *Acadiens* had reclaimed from the salty marshes by laboriously building and maintaining their dike-systems.

On December 6, 1740, the newly appointed French Huguenot governor and administrator Paul Mascarène, wrote to the British Secretary of State: "...previous governors have denied new land concessions to the French habitants; the king's instructions reserved granting these to Protestants only. Several of the French colonists have nevertheless established themselves on such land. If we should hold them back by force, in case of war between England and France, they would represent a potent force against us and outnumber us ten to one, could easily destroy our garrison and capture Fort Anne which is near ruin."

Twenty-two

1741

During the previous ten years, France had gradually increased spending to support its commerce with Nouvelle France, Louisiana, Louisbourg, and the West Indies. Its Atlantic fisheries and sugar islands had dramatically expanded their exchange of fish, sugar and coffee. Since 1710, trade between the mother country and its colonies had risen from 25 million to 140 million livres per year. French commerce with Spain and its colonies had increased and had helped bring up the total French overseas trade to 300 million livres a year.

King Louis XV had heavily invested to develop Louisbourg into a major fishing port and key trading market for ships sailing from the West Indies, New England, France, and Québec. It had become a massive stone fortress, the strongest armed citadel in North America. Its growth and strength troubled those who governed the province of Nova Scotia where French *Acadiens* far outnumbered the British presence. New England fishermen and merchants considered Louisbourg to be a threat to their freedom of access to the rich Atlantic fisheries and West Indies commerce.

Confirmation of British trading rights in North America by the Treaty of Utrecht had initiated growing competition between the British and French colonial empires deep in the western interior of the North American continent. English ships delivered great quantities of merchandise to the Hudson Bay posts and to Albany; these goods were available year round for their Indian trade.

French trading goods could only reach Québec and Montréal during the ice-free months, and still faced a long, expensive canoe-haul westward, adding to the price of such items. Native traders appreciated the more favorable values of goods offered at the English posts and willingly voyaged great distances to Hudson Bay, Oswego and Albany.

The fur trade continued to be the major export of Nouvelle France and the colony's viability depended on this income. Governor Beauharnois understood that the French had to reach the natives first, to use their own knowledge of the wilderness and its people in order to draw newly-discovered tribes into French trading patterns and away from English contacts. He tripled the original colonial allowance on gifts for the native allies to 65,000 livres in 1741, and continued his strong support of the explorations *Sieur* de La Vérendrye and his four sons conducted ever farther into the western lands.

By 1734, La Vérendrye and his sons had outflanked the Hudson Bay trade by setting up a chain of new trading posts from Rainy Lake to Lake of the Woods, on Lake Winnipeg and the Red River, and out on the open western prairie. Four years later, they had built a wooden fort at Portage La Prairie that could intercept parties of Assiniboine traders heading north to York Factory on the English bay.

Nouvelle France

Heavy southeasterly windstorms buffeted the Canadian villages in mid-May. Several days later, farmers along both sides of the Saint Lawrence River were awed and pestered by tens of thousands of brown moths swarming over the prairie grasses and greening fields after dusk.

Bécancour

Marguerite Moreau and her family celebrated Antoine's twenty-fifth birthday on May 21, 1741. He surprised them by declaring that he had seriously considered a major undertaking during the past year. Now that he had reached his majority, he announced: "I may establish my own canoe-building business in Trois Rivières."

"How can you afford to do that?" asked his older brother Charles.

"Monsieur Lemaître is receiving more orders for his larger canoe than he can possibly accept. Since his sons are not interested in the family business, he recommended that I set myself up to meet the extra demand. He's offered to help me get started. It would certainly be a great business opportunity for me."

His mother exclaimed: "He must have a great deal of confidence in you, *mon gars!*"

Charles agreed and asked: "Why do you hesitate?"

"I'd be indebted to him. Do you remember how long it took us to pay off Papa's promissory note? What if I fail?"

"Monsieur Lemaitre wouldn't offer to help you if he didn't believe in you," his mother reassured him. "He knows the quality of your work, and must be confident that you'll succeed."

Antoine cautioned them that he would have to spend longer days across the river and might not come home except on Sundays.

"That's fine," his older sister Louise said with a grin, "I'll have one less hungry mouth to feed during the week and Sunday dinner will be that much more special!"

"I may not be able to contribute as much to the family income," he added.

"Then we'll adjust as we must," his mother said.

Charles was genuinely happy for him and added: "Don't you pass up this opportunity!"

Nouvelle France

In the early summer heat of June, Canadian farmers faced armies of small brownish streaked caterpillars that infested their fields and gardens, and fed voraciously on all green plants. They grew to be as large as a man's finger during the next few weeks as they endlessly swarmed forward, covering the ground and all man-made structures in their path, devouring all grass and field crops along their way. They suddenly disappeared three weeks after their initial appearance, and the farmers struggled to save whatever was left.

More moths appeared in even greater numbers in early July, and a few weeks later as many "armyworms" returned to devastate the recovering crops.

Louis Lemaître and Antoine Ducharme halted work on their canoes so that their workers could help fight this onslaught against the Canadian food supply. Antoine joined his brothers in the fields. They struggled helplessly to the point of exhaustion while their mother and sisters constantly swept the caterpillars out of and off the family farmhouse and buildings.

Out of desperation, Marguerite's family dug foot-deep trenches in their effort to block the progress of these pests. They fought a losing battle except to protect enough corn stalks to provide seed for the following year. These infestations threatened food shortages that would last through the following winter and spring.

The family was surprised again by the sudden disappearance of the caterpillars. The fields lay dry and desolate by then, stripped of the grain and corn needed to provide bread for their meals, feed for their pigs, and fodder for their cattle and horses through the coming fall, winter and spring. Yet their pumpkin vines and fruit had survived the onslaught and had thrived beyond expectations to cover the cornfields.

On August 12, 1741, sixty-one-year old widow Marguerite Moreau signed over a *donation viagère* to her twenty-eight-year old son Charles by which he promised to provide for the needs of his mother and siblings. Three sisters and one brother continued to live in the family home: thirty-six-year old Louise, Anne, Joseph, and fourteen-year old Monique.

The family especially welcomed the dense flocks of *les pigeons de passage* (passenger pigeons) heading south during their yearly autumn migration. Their great numbers darkened the sky overhead for several days in mid-September. Thousands roosted on the virgin trees of their back woodland. The men set up their nets to capture these colorful, long-tailed birds and caught hundreds of them at a time. The family feasted on tourtières filled with the fresh delicate meat of the young squabs and saved their oil and fat as a substitute for butter. They plucked the adult birds and set aside their blue, gray, wine-red, and white feathers to serve as fresh filling for their mattresses and pillows. Marguerite and her daughters spent the week cleaning out, drying and preserving the meat from the adult birds to add to their winter meals.

Forges Saint-Maurice

Directors Cugnet, Gamelin, and Taschereau declared bankruptcy on behalf of the ironworks on October 4, 1741 and resigned their positions. They refused to to acknowledge any responsibility for the industry's financial failure and cast it all upon Ironmaster Vézin in their individual letters to the king.

Intendant Hocquart held all of them responsible for this catastrophe and pleaded to the king that the enterprise could not, should not be abandoned. He argued that Forges Saint-Maurice could succeed and recoup the king's investment many times over if placed under more competent management.

All of their messages left aboard the last ship that sailed out of Québec before winter set in. Hocquart did not expect replies from the king and his colonial minister before late spring but he strived to maintain the current industrial function and workforce by naming Simonet *fils* as master of the forges, and delegating its administration to *Sieur* Guillaume Estèbe with the technical assistance of *Sieur* Claude Poulin de Courval-Cressé.

Estèbe, a merchant-trader and seal-fisheries entrepreneur in Labrador, served as a member of the *Conseil superieur* and now as director of Forges Saint-Maurice. Courval-Cressé was a Québec merchant, the administrator of the *Seigneurie de Nicolet* and director of its shipyard in Trois Rivières.

The intendant gave them strict orders on October 28th to continually replenish supplies of all materials used in processing the iron to avoid any closure of operations. He further ordered them to restore discipline among the workforce and to restrict their free access to alcohol from company stores, under penalty of fine or imprisonment if necessary. Rather than be paid with an open line of credit at these stores, employees would now be paid in card money every two weeks. He cautioned that no family should suffer for the mistakes made by the previous administration, that any overdue pay should be delivered in hard currency.

Hocquart told Estèbe that he must first of all conduct a complete inventory of the works, then must submit weekly reports.

1742

On the last day of January, Simonne and her family attended a double wedding in Champlain, that of Michel Bigot-Dorval's two daughters Anne and Geneviève whose mother had died the previous year.

Louis and Simonne had been neighbors of the Bigot family since the early settlement of the community. Michel and Angélique had known each other since childhood and he had often worked with Baptiste Barette when they were both clearing their lands. Michel's wife and Angélique had been close friends and their children had grown up together.

Michel still grieved over his loss. He asked Angélique how she had managed to cope with the deep sadness and sorrow of widowhood.

She told him that it had been very painful for her until she began to focus on the good times she and Baptiste had shared together. "There isn't one day that passes without my thinking of him. Even now, so many things will bring back a flood of memories, many of them lighten my heart."

"I'm looking forward to that day," he confided.

"I miss Anne too, Michel. She and I shared so much together as friends." She observed his five sons, ages thirteen through twenty-one. "Your boys will soon grow into manhood, and your two daughters will now have their own homes and families. Will you hire a domestic to manage the housework?"

"I hadn't thought about it, but I suppose I should."

"I could drop by with my daughter once a week to do that for you, but you'll need a full-time cook for a houseful of young men and boys—and there's always laundry to be done."

"My sisters have offered to take turns providing us with the meals—Do you have anyone in mind?"

"Perhaps our pastor could help you with that."

Bécancour

Twenty-one-year old Marie-Anne Ducharme died at home in late February. She was the fourth of Marguerite Moreau's daughters to die before age thirty; the last had suffered a stroke at age nineteen when Marguerite's youngest daughter Monique was only four years old. Ten years later, the memory still haunted her. Marguerite retreated to her room, leaving her oldest daughter to comfort Monique.

Louise gently hugged the young girl. "Now, now, *ma petite*, you know that death is a natural part of life, that it happens when God calls us to him in paradise. Anne's spirit is in a happy place now and she'll always be with us in our memories."

Québec

On March 21, 1742, Simonne's son-in-law, François Rochereau of Bécancour, met in Québec with Jesuit Superior Messaiger to sign a contract for the construction of a new stone manor in Cap-de-la-Madeleine that would measure 32 feet x 26. François and his family would use it as their home during his lifetime, but would reserve and maintain one room for any Jesuit who might travel through the area. Upon Rochereau's death, the value of the property would be assessed and sold by the Jesuits of Québec, and half of the sale price would revert to the mason's estate. The original wooden manor on the cape had closed in 1680.

La Vérendrye

That spring, French Minister of Marine Maurepas signaled his intention of recalling the explorer through his attempts to hire suitable colonial officers to replace the father and one of his sons.

La Vérendrye sent Pierre *fils* to establish Fort Dauphin on Lake Manitoba, and Fort Bourbon on the northern tip of Lake Winnipeg. He assigned his remaining sons Chevalier Louis-Joseph and François to travel with two faithful engagés across the western plains in search of other nations who might lead them to the western sea.

They set out from Fort La Reine on April 29th to paddle up the Assiniboine and Mouse rivers, and reached a Mandan village three weeks later.

Meanwhile, Governor Beauharnois continued his attempts to pacify the northwestern tribes. His expenditures on gifts had originally been fixed at 22,000 livres a year; they now increased to 76,600 livres.

Québec

Late in May, news reached Trois Rivières that the French warship *Le Canada* was to be launched in Québec on June 4th, following three years of construction. Louis Lemaître invited Antoine to accompany him to witness the launching.

"What's so special about this vessel?" Antoine asked him.

"It's the largest naval ship ever built in Nouvelle France."

Louis showed him a drawing of the fluyt. "It will serve as an armed military transport vessel with a capacity of 500 naval tons. I've never seen one that large. Will you come with me?"

"Of course!" Antoine replied. His father had once told him that *Pépère* Bastien had arrived from France on a fluyt.

The Canadian capital teemed with people and its harbor with fishing vessels. Antoine was impressed by the city's buildings, its streets, shops, cathedral and government buildings. It was the largest city he had ever seen.

They shared a room in *l'Auberge Québécoise* which had an excellent view of the harbor and a stable to accommodate their horses. Lemaître led him on a walk through the lower town where they saw *Troupes de Marine* in their oyster-white uniforms faced with blue, natives in French clothing and buckskin, habitants and craftsmen in rough homespun, moccasins, toque, and pipe.

They took the winding road that *Pépère* Bastien and others of his ancestors had once walked to the upper town. It remained less crowded than the more commercial level where they were staying. Antoine saw many black-robed Jesuit and secular priests, Récollets in hooded brown cassocks, wealthy merchants, officials and gentlemen in lace-trimmed surcoats and wigs, and elegantly dressed ladies.

Both men enjoyed the view overlooking the harbor, l'Île d'Orléans to the south, and the impressive falls of Montmorency to the east.

They dined in the auberge after sundown.

"You're well-organized in your new business, Antoine. I must tell you that you've more than lived up to my expectations. It's such a relief for me to know that I can confidently refer to you those customers whose orders I can't possibly fill. Several have told me that they appreciate the quality of your canoes and your ability to deliver them on time as promised—both are very important in this business, you know."

"Thank you for your kind words, Monsieur Lemaître. I greatly appreciate your help and confidence in me. I believe whatever success I've had is due to the training I received under you, also to your generosity and that of my merchant cousins in referring customers to me.

"You have an excellent crew of workers."

"I was lucky enough to find several Abenaki families from Bécancour who wanted to work for me. They're true craftsmen at this type of work and take great pride in it."

"How did you manage that?"

"By word of mouth. The Abenakis of Bécancour had great respect for my uncle Louis and knew of my relationship to him. They came to me and offered to join the project. I'm lucky to have them."

They talked at length about the rising demand for the *canot de maître*, the eight-man canoe that Lemaître had developed. It was built 33-feet long by 5-feet wide by $2^1/_2$-feet high, was priced at 600 francs and intended for voyages out west by the military or the fur trade.

The two craftsmen watched the launching the following morning. The size and weight of the vessel that slipped into the water were greater than either of them had imagined, and they were amazed to see that forms had already been set up for the construction of an even larger vessel.

On their way home, they galloped their horses west on *le Chemin du Roi*, stirring up masses of brown moths that covered and hovered low over the prairies and greening fields. These strange insects were unusual in that each of their fore wings was marked with a white central spot and a row of small black dots along its edge. In contrast, their hind wings were simply a dull gray.

Late June marked the beginning of second armyworm infestation with mature larvae colored green to light brown with a variety of longitudinal white, black and pale-orange stripes. They fed on grasses, leaves and straw, then moved on to the corn fields. Tens of thousands of caterpillars moved endlessly forward from brown to green areas, covered houses and highways along their path, destroyed grain, corn and hay crops except for the most mature plants, then suddenly disappeared in early August.

Autumn harvests were even smaller than those of the previous year, resulting in serious food shortages. Pumpkin vines were again left untouched.

Crime increased in the cities and countryside due to widespread unemployment and a desperate foraging for food.

Champlain

In late September, Michel Bigot-Dorval left his boys at work in the fields and came directly to meet Angélique when she arrived with her daughter to clean the house for him. He and Angélique sat alone on the front porch while he fidgeted and she patiently waited to hear what he had to say.

"What's wrong, Michel?" she finally asked.

He answered softly. "It's as you told me. I now remember mostly the good times Anne and I shared."

"That's wonderful! I'm so happy for you."

"I also find myself thinking of you more and more every day…"

Her cheeks flushed.

"I worry about you and your children living alone on that farm."

"Joseph is nearby and within call—I've never been concerned about that."

"Please be patient with me. What I'm trying to say is that neither of us should have to raise our children and manage a property alone."

"Are you considering marriage?" she asked.

Her frankness startled him. "Yes—Would you? I realize that I have a houseful of growing boys while you have only two younger children..."

She was quiet for a while, then smiled and admitted: "I've also been thinking and worrying about you, Michel. I think it's a wonderful idea."

They agreed to live in Michel's home with the understanding that he and his sons would maintain the Barette property as her children's heritage.

Family and friends witnessed their exchange of marriage vows in the church rectory in late October and attended a small reception that was held in Simonne and Joseph's home. Michel's sons were delighted with the new arrangement. Angélique, having been widowed eleven years, added her two children to the family: thirteen-year old Joseph-Marie and twelve-year old Marie-Josephte.

Twenty-three

1743

Vérendrye's two younger sons, Chevalier Louis-Joseph and François had followed several leads since leaving the Mandan villages, had encountered and befriended members of nations called *Les Beaux Hommes*, Little Foxes, Horses, and Bows. These last had never seen a white man nor heard musket fire until the arrival of the Canadian explorers, but they spoke of having heard of the western sea from their Shoshone captives.

The Bows were still at war with the Shoshone and planned to travel west toward their enemy's territory by following the Missouri River. They provided horses and led their new friends across the great prairie to explore the western wilderness through more rugged country up to 120 miles east of Yellowstone. The Vérendrye brothers reached within sight of the Big Horn mountain range of South Dakota and Wyoming on January 8th of the new year.

The natives set up winter camp for their women and children before proceeding any farther to engage the enemy. Chevalier Louis-Joseph offered advice during their war council, but declined to join their attack.

The Canadians followed the Bows twelve more days until they arrived within sight of the great Wind River Range and finally had the opportunity to climb a forested spur of the Rocky Mountains. More than 800 miles of mountains and forests still lay between them and the Pacific coast.

Their guides unexpectedly came upon a hurriedly abandoned Shoshone winter encampment in that area. Out of concern for the safety of their own women and children, the Bow warriors refused to go any farther and rushed back to their own encampment.

The French explorers regretfully began their long trek east to Fort La Reine. They reached the Saskatchewan River that led them back across the Great Plains, and built a trading post by its entry to draw the Plains Cree away from their annual trek north to York Factory on Hudson Bay.

France

Louis XV's life-long trusted counselor and prime minister of France, Cardinal de Fleury died in late January 1743 at the age of eighty-nine. The thirty-two-year old king finally took over the reins of government while Minister of Marine Maurepas continued to oversee the French colonial empire.

That spring, the Crown took over Forges Saint-Maurice and started producing anvils, ship's hardware, cannon, cannonballs, cooking pots, pans, cauldrons, bar iron, and stoves.

Nouvelle France

The first French ship to arrive in Québec that year introduced a typhus epidemic that swept rapidly throughout the colony. Its early symptoms of headache, general malaise, deep cough, chills and fever quickly debilitated the sick whose condition usually worsened and gave rise to an alarming rash on the torso that spread over the arms and legs. The following delirium and stupor usually lasted several days and often led to death unless the patient had access to traditional native herbal medicines. Blood-letting, the standard treatment at the time for all diseases of unknown origin, usually hastened death.

Governor Beauharnois' attempts to pacify the northwestern tribes finally restored an uneasy peace in the west.

Marquis de Vaudreuil-Cavagnal was transferred to the governorship of Louisiana. Claude-Michel Bégon, younger brother of former Intendant Bégon, replaced him as governor of Trois Rivières.

Madeleine, the youngest of Bastien and Catherine Guillet's children, died in mid-May in Baie-du-Febvre at age forty-five.

There were no surviving children. Her husband of nine years remarried within six months.

One month later in Montréal, Sébastien's oldest son Joseph hired two engagés for a voyage to Michillimackinac.

Jean-Baptiste Lemire-Marsollet acknowledged a personal debt of 3996 livres, 4 sols, 1 denier to Sébastien's youngest son René for provisions he had purchased on credit for his own voyage to the same post.

The Vérendrye brothers reached Fort La Reine on July 2nd to reunite with their father after more than a year's absence.

Nouvelle Orléans, late July 1743

Simonne's oldest son Jean directed the framing of another country house of *pièces-sur-pièces*. The work progressed slowly due to the midsummer heat and high humidity as his black laborers grew weary under the midday sun. He told them to rest in the shade of a nearby grove of old oak trees covered with Spanish moss, where he would have fresh water and food brought to them.

He valued his workers. They had proven to be conscientious and faithful at their work. Jean had followed Michel Arsonneau's practice of promising to free his slaves once they had repaid him their purchase price through their labor. He considered himself fortunate that many of them had stayed on with him as paid employees, relieving him of having to bid for replacements in the slave market, a practice that he abhorred.

A young stranger approached from the road and asked if he had any work available for an able-bodied man. Jean recognized the young man's Canadian accent and judged him to be healthy and strong. He glanced at his hands and saw that they were tanned and calloused, certainly those of an outdoor laborer. However, his clothing was of better quality than one would expect. He guessed that this stranger might be in his mid-thirties.

"Where are you from?" he asked.

"From Illinois," the stranger replied with a smile. "I've just recently arrived with a boatload of furs, wheat and flour for export."

"Well, you seem to have enjoyed the trip," Jean observed. "What brings you to this particular area?"

"I'm looking for my oldest brother—I was ten years old when I last saw him."

There was something about this man's voice and his eyes that suddenly registered in Jean's mind and he said very softly; "My youngest brother was that age when I left Champlain so many years ago..."

François broke out with a joyous laugh. *"Bonjour, Jean!"*

The brothers hugged each other for quite some time.

"This is unbelievable!" Jean confessed. François stood as tall and strong as he, and had a remarkable resemblance to their father. "How did you manage to find me?"

"I remembered Baptiste Barette's description of the Arsonneau plantation. I found it easy enough and they told me where you lived. I located your home and your beautiful wife directed me to this site."

Jean called off work for the rest of the day and headed home with his surprise guest.

"How's the rest of the family?" he asked.

François hesitated as he considered how much his brother did not know. He laid his hand on Jean's shoulder and told him gently: "Papa died unexpectedly in November of 1725. Since you had moved away and married in Louisiana, and Louis was well-established in Bécancour, the rest of us sold our shares of both parental estates to Joseph so that he could continue to manage the properties and *Maman* could live comfortably in her own home. She later signed half of her own estate to him by *donation viagère*."

Jean regretted that he had not been there to help her. "How is she?"

"She's doing well. Angélique and her children live nearby and you know how close she and *Maman* have always been."

"Whom did Angélique marry?"

"Your friend Baptiste Barette!"

"I'm delighted to hear that!"

"He negotiated several voyages after he returned to Champlain and built a comfortable home for his family, but he died a few years before I moved to the Illinois territory. The children were quite young but *Maman* and Joseph helped Angélique as much as they could."

Jean was deeply saddened by the news. He suddenly realized how much his family's life had changed since he had moved to Louisiana.

They continued to reminisce about their boyhood experiences that evening over and after dinner, as gentle cooling breezes flowed in through the open windows. François learned that Jean and Thérèse were childless, that she taught school to young girls.

"You and Papa were my heroes," François confessed to his older brother.

Jean was flattered but diverted the praise toward Louis. "He was a very special voyageur, you know. He understood the natives and had a natural instinct in the forest. His generation grew up under constant and murderous Mohawk raids, yet they managed to achieve peace with them."

"Our *pépères* must have lived in an even more challenging time."

"Why is that?" Thérèse asked him.

He explained: "From what I've been told, they were very poor when they first arrived from France. The land was entirely covered with a virgin forest up to the river's edge. They had no heavy tools or oxen to help them clear those giant trees to build their houses, cut their firewood, or till their soil. They provided all their needs from what was available in the forest, grew their own food on whatever land they managed to clear, and produced their own cloth from flax and hemp that they grew and processed. We're descended from peasant farmers who were forbidden to hunt and fish in France, yet during the first few years after their arrival in Canada, they learned to grow and gather their own grain, vegetables, fruit, meat, and preserve a good part of these for the following winter. It's difficult to imagine how they managed to survive their first few years in Nouvelle France."

"They had no winter crops?"

Jean told his brother that Thérèse had grown up in southern France where the year-round weather was much like that of Louisiana. "She's never experienced a snowfall or seen frozen rivers and streams."

"I envy you," François admitted.

"Is that why you left?" she asked him.

"I envied Jean when he left us to travel to Louisiana but I was just a child at the time. I guess I was never meant to be a farmer, although my mother prayed that I would become more like her side of the family."

Jean chuckled at the thought and added for his wife's benefit: "Her family was entirely tied to the land. She was very patient with Papa who often left for days at a time to hunt in the woods. We never lacked for fresh meat."

François continued: "I made several voyages *au pays d'en haut*. The farthest was with a group of explorers, beyond the largest of the western lakes. When we reached its far side and winter was near, I refused to go any farther. Later on, I traveled south for the first time to the Saint-Joseph River area. That journey seemed easier, the weather better, and the soil more fertile, less sandy than at home."

"Did you ever own land in Canada?" Jean asked.

"Yes, but I borrowed against it for a voyage and was never able to pay it back so I lost my concession." He shrugged his shoulders. "Voyaging always seemed easier and more enjoyable for me than farming in Bécancour.

"I finally had the opportunity to travel through the Illinois territory and felt very much at home when I first saw its plains, its fertile bottomland, and its wildlife."

"Did you ever marry?" Thérèse asked.

"I've had the means to because I've managed to develop a productive farm, and I hunt and trade, but there are very few available Canadian women of marriageable age in Illinois right now."

"So that's why you've come all this way to look me up!" Jean joshed.

"Do you have someone in mind?" François quipped.

Jean was fascinated by his brother's descriptions of what he had seen on both sides of the Mississippi as he traveled downriver. He mentally compared them with those of his own descent by canoe a quarter-century earlier and realized that thriving French and German farming settlements had multiplied; healthy crops of grain, cotton, and tobacco flourished on the fertile lowlands; large herds of *boeufs sauvages* (buffalo) roamed the tallgrass prairies of the Illinois territory. The large military forts that Jean had seen under construction between Louisiana and Illinois seemed to have been neglected over the years.

He and Thérèse introduced François to their friends and showed him what life was like in Nouvelle Orléans, but no young woman caught his eye or appeared interested in giving up her comfortable life in southern Louisiana. François learned that although houses in the countryside were of wood and covered with shingles, they were built entirely of brick in the city. In either type of construction, the main floor rested on a high brick foundation that reached above spring flood levels, a porch surrounded the second story and was accessed by way of a long staircase that extended from ground-level.

Despite their attempts to entice him into staying, François became restless during the sweltering heat of the late southern summer and grew anxious to return home to his life in Illinois. He awaited passage on a row-galley for the ten-week trip upriver to Kaskaskia.

They all realized that this would be their last reunion because Jean did not wish to subject Thérèse to that kind of travel and his business interests required that he remain in Louisiana.

The untimely death of his friend Baptiste and the apparent difficulty of Angélique's life remained very much on his mind. He and his wife agreed that he was not likely to claim his inheritance, that he had no need of it.

"Do you know how I can have a document delivered to Champlain?" he asked François as he prepared to leave them.

"I could carry it to Saint-Louis and arrange for direct delivery from there. I've already decided to send a letter to *Maman* to let her know that I've finally settled down in Illinois and that the three of us have managed to spend some time together.

On August 14, 1743, Louis and Simonne's oldest son Jean-Baptiste and his wife Thérèse Dalberni signed a notarized document by which they donated his share of his parents' estate to his sister Angélique, widow of his life-long friend Jean-Baptiste Barette, "out of affection and appreciation for her care of him in his youth". It clearly stated that this *donation* covered all of his legacy, including that of his mother's estate.

A few days later, François headed north on a row-galley of twenty oars loaded with cotton, oranges, sweet potatoes, winter cabbage, and pecans.

Louisbourg

While the great French fortress received inadequate provisions from France, its trade with Nova Scotia and New England had risen from 49 English merchant ships in 1739, to 78 four years later.

British merchants had grown impatient with what they regarded as illicit colonial trade with the French. Nova Scotian authorities resented the fact that the *Acadiens* who had migrated to Île Saint-Jean were provisioning Louisbourg at prices one-third less than what they charged the English who now occupied their native lands.

Early that autumn, a British man-of-war captured a French merchant vessel as it plied its usual shipping route from Île Saint-Jean to Louisbourg through the Strait of Canso. *Commissaire* Bigot and Commandant Duquesnel of Île Royale strongly objected to this incident and sent their representatives to Canso where they successfully negotiated the release of their ship and its crew.

Louisbourg, 1744

In mid-March 1744, France officially declared war against England in the European War of the Austrian Succession and allied himself with Austria two weeks later.

News of that declaration reached Louisbourg in May, several weeks earlier than in Québec or Boston. Commandant Duquesnel immediately ordered the capture and destruction of the British fort on the Strait of Canso.

Two small armed vessels transported Captain Duvivier and 600 men to the strait that separated Île Royale from British Acadia. The greatly outnumbered English garrison surrendered, the fort and its surrounding buildings were burnt to the ground, and the two French ships carried eighty English prisoners to the fortress of Louisbourg rather than to Boston as promised.

Encouraged by this easy victory, Duquesnel sent Duvivier to capture Annapolis Harbor, the last remaining British fort in old *Acadie*. Three to four hundred Mi'kmaq and Malécite warriors joined him along the way. This expedition failed because Boston vessels arrived with a reinforcement of fifty Indian rangers before the two promised French support ships reached Annapolis.

The French commandant's adventurism alarmed and aroused the Nova Scotians and the New Englanders.

By the 1740s, Louisbourg had grown to be the strongest citadel in North America, a bustling French colony with a population of two thousand French citizens, and a key entrepôt for ships sailing to and from the West Indies, New England, France and Québec. It also served as a major French fishing base.

Its financial *commissaire-ordonnateur*, François Bigot, was among many in Louisbourg who secretly provisioned French privateers who preyed on shipping and fishing vessels from Maine and Massachusetts. Bigot was a keen investor in the activities of the Dupont brothers whose vessels: *Succès, Cantabre, Saint-Charles,* and *Brador* were all fast moving schooners.

British officials in Acadia worried about the close presence of such a hostile fortress. New England merchants and fishermen regarded it as a constant threat to their own valuable Atlantic and West Indies commerce.

Québec, mid-May 1744

The naval shipyard launched an even larger fluyt, *Le Caribou* of 700-ton capacity, armed with 45 cannons, and handled by a 150-man crew. The king's naval shipyard immediately began to set up for the construction of a two smaller vessels: a frigate and a corvette.

News of the French declaration of war reached Nouvelle France in early June. Governor Beauharnois received orders to assure the defense of the colony, secure the native alliances and Iroquois neutrality, and take offensive action against the English North American possessions.

In his effort to maintain the loyalty of the native allies, the governor ordered a quick raid against English traders in the Ohio territory. He followed up by sending parties of militia and native warriors to conduct *la petite guerre* against the New England frontier outposts of New York, Massachusetts, and New Hampshire, laying waste the English forts and their surrounding countryside.

British and English corsairs prowled the Gulf of Saint Lawrence and intercepted many French cargo vessels heading for Québec, thus restricting the vital delivery of munitions, provisions, and trade goods.

The governor constructed earthworks and a palisade along the Saint-Charles River, restored the stockade forts in the seigneuries, set up signal stations down the Saint Lawrence, and prepared fire boats in strategic locations.

Minister Maurepas had rejected Beauharnois' request to strengthen the wall around Québec because he doubted that the English would make another attempt to capture the capital. But Beauharnois realized that if Québec fell, so would the rest of Nouvelle France. He had pleaded unsuccessfully for more troops to bolster the 600 colonial regulars who served in the several garrisons. The 12,000-man militia lacked discipline and training after three decades of peace. He reported that one third of this home force lacked firearms.

Meanwhile, the typhus epidemic continued to claim its victims, and three successive poor harvests had left the colony short of food provisions. Long years of experience in the navy had taught the governor not to rely upon French shipping in wartime; he had urged the stockpiling of supplies for more than a single year. Minister Maurepas had refused to acknowledge the need for such expenditures.

Canadian merchants and fur traders continued their trading activities as best they could. In June, Jean-Baptiste Belleville signed a promissory note to merchant Saint-Deschambault for three pieces of coarse cloth and 150 livres of gunpowder, then hired Jean-Baptiste Leduc as voyageur to *les pays d'en haut*.

Champlain

That summer, Simonne and Joseph received Jean's notarized document dated Aug 14, 1743, and a letter from François telling her of his recent visit with Jean in Nouvelle Orléans. He assured her that all was well with both her sons, that they missed the family and prayed that all was well in Champlain.

Simonne was deeply touched by the news of her sons' reunion and for Jean and his wife's generosity toward Angélique. She hurried over to her daughter's house with the message.

Angélique appreciated the *donation* and the letter but regretted that neither brother knew of her remarriage two years earlier to Michel Bigot-Dorval, a longtime friend and neighbor of their family.

Montréal

La Vérendrye and his sons arrived to settle accounts with their investors and were immediately confronted by jealous competitors and angry merchants. The explorers were deeply in debt and unable to find additional financial backing. Their furs had flowed east, but the promised supplies had often failed to arrive out west.

The merchants who had so eagerly invested in the explorer's enterprise took their cases before the courts. Their competitors accused Vérendrye of profiting from his monopoly of the western trade rather than searching for the route to the western sea.

Colonial Minister Maurepas judged La Verendrye to be incompetent due to his indebtedness and his repeated failures to discover the western route. French officials had no true concept of the distances these intrepid voyageurs had repeatedly traveled to establish new trading posts and alliances to subsidize their constant search for the west coast, which was much farther west than anyone had anticipated. There existed no accurate mapping of its location, and the North American continent was much larger than anyone had imagined.

Lack of support from French governmental authorities finally forced the explorer to give up the quest to which he had dedicated the best thirteen years of his life. He and his sons were the first white men to have traveled through the South Dakota, Montana and Wyoming territories, two thirds of the way across the North American continent.

Boston

The English prisoners taken at Canso and held by the French in Louisbourg were released at the end of the summer. Their reports of low morale among Louisbourg's garrison, of its deteriorating masonry fortifications and unmounted cannon meant to face inland toward the marshes convinced *les bostonnais* that the citadel might be vulnerable to attack after all.

By October 1744, Louisbourg privateers had taken twenty-eight English provincial vessels, mostly affecting Maine and Massachusetts fishermen and merchants. While England refused to offer any financial support, Governor Shirley and his colonial allies campaigned throughout the fall and winter of 1744-45 to convince Massachusetts and the other New England colonies that an attack on Louisbourg was practical.

His political advocates and recruiters stressed strong economic reasons for such a joint effort, reported the claims of weakness in the fortress walls, and promised all volunteers a wealth of spoils.

Puritan preachers railed against the "stronghold of Satan".

Champlain

Simonne Massé died in her home on November 5th at the age of seventy-seven. Her daughter Angélique and her family, Joseph and his family were present by her bedside.

Nouvelle France

Winter of 1744–1745 was unusually mild along the Saint Lawrence River. Typhus continued to claim its victims, especially in the crowded cities.

Twenty-four

1745

During the previous three decades of peace, the Canadian population had risen above 45,000, 4600 of whom lived in Québec and 3500 in Montréal. Since the turn of the century, such growth had developed through natural increase rather than by immigration and was mostly due to birth and survival rates that were higher in Nouvelle France than in the mother country. The colonial habitants continued to thrive under the colonial conditions of better nutrition and a healthier living environment than those experienced by their peasant cousins in France.

The majority of French Canadians lived in comfortable wooden houses while the seigneurs, officials, and the well-established merchants resided in their thick-walled stone buildings. Large fireplaces and the new cast-iron stoves produced by Forges Saint-Maurice heated their homes and workplaces with a plentiful supply of wood. A variety of furs and deerskin provided warm outer clothing for those who ventured outdoors during the winter. Farmers' wives processed homegrown flax and wool from their own sheep into homespun cloth for hardy everyday wear. Rivers and forest offered free access to fish and game. The large rural families continued to work in unison to provide most of their basic needs and those of the colony through their dedicated husbandry of fields, forest, and livestock.

Forges Saint-Maurice

Sieur Estèbe's weekly reports to Intendant Hocquart had shown consistent progress until that January, when he discovered that sizable amounts of card money and processed iron had disappeared from the company stores. The administrator conducted his own investigation and discovered an unofficial duplicate key in Simonet's closet. Hocquart confronted the ironmaster who admitted his guilt and returned the missing items.

Since Simonet had influential French connections, Hocquart reported the affair to the king and shipped the culprit back to France.

Boston

Governor Shirley's arguments prevailed when on February 5th, the Massachusetts House of Representatives narrowly approved a plan to move against Louisbourg but only in alliance with the other English colonies.

His supporters traveled as far south as Pennsylvania to persuade several of the other provinces to support the expedition. Their major argument to justify the English colonial attack was the need to end the destructive activity of French privateers against English merchant and fishing vessels, yet there had been ten times as much English piracy preying on French shipping in 1744.

The New Englanders raised a sizable land force, necessary transport and supplies. Massachusetts and its Maine district recruited seven regiments, New Hampshire and Connecticut each raised one. Rhode Island offered one warship and three companies of soldiers, and New York contributed some badly needed artillery.

Delegates from each of these colonies met together and chose merchant William Pepperrell to lead the joint forces. The new commandant was colonel of all Massachusetts militia in Maine and served as a member and president of the Massachusetts Council.

British Commodore Peter Warren, commander of the colonial fleet north of Virginia, received orders from the Duke of Newcastle to sail from the British island of Antigua to the port of Boston to provide naval support for the expedition.

Pepperrell thus assumed the first provincial command of a military campaign manned jointly by colonial and British troops.

Commander Pepperrell had not yet received confirmation of Warren's orders when on March 24th, his force of about 4,000 New England troops sailed from Boston on ninety fishing boats to reclaim Canso and seize Louisbourg. They were escorted by twelve armed provincial cruisers, the largest of which was armed with twenty-four guns; the fleet's entire naval armament amounted to one hundred seventy-six guns, the heaviest of which was of 22-pound caliber.

A northeaster snowstorm scattered the New England transports as they proceeded toward Canso, so that the majority of the vessels did not reach the strait until April 5th. Most of the recruits were tradesmen, merchants, and farmers who experienced travel at sea for the first time in their lives. Weakened by thirteen days of continuous seasickness, the troops needed time to recover their strength, rebuild the post's defenses, and participate in much-needed militia training while awaiting the arrival of the British fleet. They built a blockhouse, armed it with 8-pounders, and named it Fort Cumberland.

Pepperrell's primary concern was to deliver his troops to Louisbourg before the early spring arrival of French naval and supply vessels. His armed colonial ships cruised offshore, captured six French supply vessels, and reported that the entrance to Gabarus Bay remained blocked by ice, thus preventing his fleet from entering the harbor to land his forces.

On April 18th, Pepperrell received a report that the provincial fleet had engaged a French naval cruiser of thirty-six guns in a thirty-hour battle. It had finally outrun the New Englanders and returned to France to report the presence of a well-organized fleet of English privateers near Louisbourg.

Four British battleships arrived off Canso a week later: Commodore Warren's command ship the *Superbe* with 415 men and 60 guns, the 44-gun frigate *Eltham* with 250 men on board, the *Mermaid* and the *Launceston*, each with 250 men and 40 guns. Warren met briefly with Pepperrell to discuss their joint campaign plans, then sailed on to Louisbourg to set up a naval blockade and intercept any future French deliveries to the fortress.

The New England vessels left Canso with their 4,000-man force on April 29th, and headed up the coast toward Gabarus Bay, a single day's sail away.

France

The French Ministry of Marine had long considered the British colonies incapable of uniting their military forces. Maurepas also believed that a colonial siege would require the preparation and dispatch of British naval support from England which could be detected early and allow time for French reinforcements to arrive in Louisbourg from Québec and continental France. Maurepas had already received word of the planned British invasion, but had calculated that the fortress was strong enough to defend itself against the privateers without any help from France.

Louisbourg

Political connections and circumstance had placed Louis Du Pont Duchambon as interim commandant of Île-Royale, but he was ill-prepared by experience and temperament to deal with the major challenge he now faced. His predecessor Duquesnel and financial commissary François Bigot had on several occasions warned Minister Maurepas of Louisbourg's vulnerabilities to naval and land attack, but to no avail.

Duchambon faced major problems in planning his defense. Although its architects had anticipated any full-scale assault to come from the sea, its builders had allowed three of Louisbourg's four major seaward batteries to remain vulnerable to shelling from higher ground. They had used local sand to prepare their mortar for the fortress walls; this salty component produced weak binding material that needed constant repair. In fact, the fortress of Louisbourg had another serious defect: its base was of soft limestone and had gradually been eroded by seaside moisture.

The garrison consisted of eight companies of *Troupes de Marine* and a detachment of the Swiss Karrer Regiment, a mercenary unit that had mutinied in December 1744, barely two months after Duquesnel had died unexpectedly. Grievances built up under his command had been resolved under Duchambon, and the soldiers had returned to duty, but their officers remained concerned about their loyalty under fire.

Louisbourg officials remained unaware of the magnitude of the impending attack after they sighted the English colonial cruisers sailing past the mouth of the harbor on April 30th.

Spring came early that year so that the habitants along the Saint Lawrence River and the farmers of New England began tilling their fields three weeks ahead of schedule. They looked forward to a favorable farming season and prayed fervently that they would see neither the swarms of brown moths nor the armies of caterpillars.

This unseasonably warm weather also favored the sailing of English troops from Canso and their landing in Louisbourg. While Warren's fleet maintained its blockade against French shipping, the New England transports entered Gabarus Bay on the morning of April 30th and dropped their anchors within sight of the light house and steeples of the city.

The English recruits immediately clambered into their rowboats and landed about one mile west from the fortress to set up their cannon on its vulnerable landward side.

Duchambon had already called the militia, all French settlers and their vital provisions to safety inside the citadel and had closed its gates. He quietly kept watch from the ramparts, fascinated by the rapid but disorderly landing of the English militia. His officers persuaded him to send a detachment of trustworthy soldiers to oppose the landing. Their small party was rapidly outnumbered and retreated after a brief skirmish. Two thousand English troops continued to land unopposed until dark. Before the end of the day, great numbers of them emerged from the woods overlooking the town and cheered exultantly toward the fortress.

Louisbourg's architects had paid particular attention to guarding the harbor entrance with interlocking fields of fire from heavy artillery. Commodore Warren was frustrated by his inability to fire his heavy guns from inside the harbor, but he continued to patrol the offshore approaches to prevent French delivery of provisions and reinforcements to the fortress.

Meanwhile, Pepperrell determined that the fortifications had indeed fallen into a state of disrepair and identified several especially weak areas.

Two thousand more English colonials landed on the second day, while others established their camps and unloaded provisions. A large party of undisciplined New Englanders looted and burned storehouses at the northeast end of the harbor, laying to waste valuable supplies.

In order to establish a clear view of enemy troops who might approach the fortress' main landward entrance to the town, the

French burned a number of houses that lay just a short distance away from the walls, on the road leading to the Royal Battery.

The French officers believed that there were 13,000 Englishmen about to lay siege against the fortress. Their primary concern was for the quarter of Louisbourg's entire military force that was stationed in the Royal Battery. Their consensus was that although the mighty battery could easily fall to the enemy, it must not be destroyed, that its cannon must be disabled so that they could not be fired against the town. They agreed that the English colonial force would eventually give up the siege and abandon the bastion.

Duchambon finally ordered his men to spike the cannon, and withdraw into the walled city with their food supplies and military stores. In their haste to evacuate, the French soldiers quickly blocked the touchholes of the guns and left behind a quantity of mortar shells and cannonballs.

Two days later, about a dozen English provincials who were reconnoitering near the abandoned structure, entered it and claimed it for themselves by raising a red flag. They successfully defended it by firing their muskets down against several boatloads of French soldiers who had returned to remove the remaining military stores.

The easy capture of such a formidable structure provided the New Englanders with an ideal vantage point for their cannoneers and siege lines. Twenty of their men quickly drilled out the touchholes of the twenty-eight 42-pounders and two 18-pounders and began to fire these against the fortress the very next day. The French could only respond with an ineffectual bombardment from the town and the Island Battery.

The Connecticut general estimated that two hundred men could have held that battery against five thousand Englishmen without cannon, that it would have taken a week for the English to drag their own lighter guns to the site, which would have allowed time for the French to completely disable their own.

The New Englanders offloaded additional artillery at Freshwater Cove and prepared to move it across the rough and swampy ground to a rocky hill opposite the King's Bastion. A New Hampshire shipwright constructed large sledges upon which the heavy cannon could be loaded and dragged across the rough terrain by large teams of men.

Duchambon and his officers watched from the ramparts in disbelief. They were amazed by the English militiaman's ingenuity in dealing with military obstacles and his capacity to cope with such difficult environmental conditions.

Warren's written plan of attack was delivered to Pepperrell within three days of the English landing. Four days later, the naval commander went ashore to attend a council of war, after which he and Pepperrell jointly called upon the French officials to surrender the town.

Interim Commandant Duchambon quickly replied that in obedience to their king, his forces would answer from the mouths of their cannon.

Nouvelle France

Louis XV officially took over control of Forges Saint-Maurice in early May and canceled the former company's remaining debt of 192,642 livres owed to the crown.

He continued to subsidize the Canadian naval shipyards. Construction was currently underway in Québec on two naval vessels: the corvette *Le Carcajou* and the frigate *Le Castor*.

Louisbourg, May 19, 1745

The 64-gun French battleship *Vigilant* sailed directly toward the Louisbourg harbor mouth as it neared the end of its maiden voyage. During his final approach, Captain Marquis de La Maisonfort spotted the *Mermaid* and turned downwind to engage the 40-gun British man-of-war. Other armed vessels of the British and colonial fleets soon joined in the eight-hour naval battle during which the French ship was hit by three broadsides which eventually forced her captain to surrender his ship.

The British secured their prize the following day, towed it along the coast in full view of the fortress garrison, and set its anchor in Gabarus Bay. Five hundred sixty French sailors and soldiers were taken off as prisoners-of-war and replaced by British sailors who would refit the battleship for duty.

Within two days after its capture, three more British battleships arrived from Boston. The *Vigilant* was commissioned on June 4th as a British man-of-war, lending additional strength to Warren's fleet. Four more British battleships arrived directly from England on June 11th. Peter Warren then commanded the largest British squadron in North American waters since 1711, but he could not reach close enough to Louisbourg to employ his more than five hundred naval cannon.

In celebration of their king's accession day and the increased naval support, all English land batteries fired on the fortified city from noon until nightfall.

Had the *Vigilant* reached the harbor, Louisbourg's defenses would have been greatly strengthened by the one thousand barrels of gun powder, twenty bronze cannons, and three hundred additional French soldiers she was about to deliver. These might have extended French resistance beyond the summer season, until the first signs of the impending winter would have forced the invaders to quit their efforts and return home.

Nouvelle France

Québec and Versailles remained unaware of the crisis unfolding on Île Royale.

That June in Montréal, Sébastien's oldest son Joseph hired and outfitted men to voyage to Michillimackinac.

The first strawberry harvest in the Québec area occurred on June 22nd. There had been no further sign of brown moths or caterpillars.

Sunday civil announcements informed the population that in order to prevent excessive subdivision of the land due to the natural growth of the population, King Louis XV had published an ordinance forbidding house construction on lots smaller than $1^1/_2$ arpents by 40. The habitants were ordered to resume clearing the virgin forest to extend the existing tillable areas.

Louisbourg

Shortly after the arrival of British naval reinforcement, it became obvious to the French officers that preparations were underway for the final combined assault by New England land and British naval forces.

The town of Louisbourg was in ruins; the exhausted population had suffered through forty-seven days of continuous heavy bombardment by English colonial land batteries. Its wells were polluted. Its civilians were cowering in bomb shelters. Gun powder and food supplies had run dangerously low.

Enemy land forces stood ready to storm the breached walls of the town with a thousand scaling ladders. The British fleet was making final preparations to make its run into the harbor to position its guns.

The terrorized residents of Louisbourg petitioned their military to surrender the fortress knowing that this would mean a great loss for France but that it would save their lives.

The siege against the strongest fortification in North America ended on June 27, 1745.

As the official representative of Great Britain, Commodore Warren accepted the keys to the gates of Louisbourg and entered with his officers. He then opened the main portal to admit Commander Pepperrell and his colonial officers.

They found a complete village covering 57 square arpents within the great fortress walls. Built and developed over a period of twenty-five years and at the cost of 20 million livres, it housed the governor's apartments, chapel, officers' quarters, and soldiers' barracks in the 360-foot long Château-Saint-Louis. It also included a large hospital, bakery, laundry, school, convent, courtyard, many shops, and a population of 1000 French residents.

Its garrison of 700 soldiers had been armed with 116 cannon and mortars, but many had never been fixed in position to face inland.

Although most of the New England volunteers had enlisted due to the promised right to plunder, they were assigned to guard the French inhabitants and their possessions, to repair and strengthen the damaged stone walls against the possibility of a French counter-attack.

The British kept the French flags flying from the ramparts thus luring several unsuspecting East Indian cargo ships into the harbor. Their rich contents were divided among the British naval officers and crews as spoils of war.

The French deportees asked to be transported to Canada but commodore Warren refused to do so; he welcomed the opportunity to begin expelling the French from North America. On July 4th, all members and wives of the French military and civilian administration were transported to France.

More than 4,000 inhabitants of Île-Royale, including 2,000 immigrated *Acadiens*, were later deported to Boston, then to the port of Brest in Brittany, France.

That July, Warren also ordered the deportation of the 1,000 Acadian habitants from Île Saint-Jean, but his troops were driven back to their ships with heavy losses. He wrote to Colonial Minister Newcastle: "I hope they will be sent away next spring...it would be a good thing if those now at Annapolis could be removed."

In its report to Newcastle four months later, the Executive Council of Nova Scotia expressed its disapproval of Lieutenant-Governor Mascarene's benevolent policy toward the *Acadiens*. They recommended that the "French inhabitants...be transported out of the province of Nova Scotia and be replaced by good Protestant subjects."

Twenty-five

France, July 1745

James III's grandson, Charles Edward Stuart had been living in exile in Versailles as a guest of Louis XV. The French king supported his plans to rouse the Catholic highland clans of Scotland to regain their independence by marching to London.

French officials were in the midst of provisioning and preparing transportation in support of the third Jacobite Rebellion. They were shocked and outraged when they received the first reports of the loss of Louisbourg.

Upon their arrival in Versailles, Duchambon and Bigot were ordered to immediately prepare detailed accounts of their conduct and that of the British navy during the seven-week siege that led to their surrender of the French citadel.

Nouvelle France

The fall of Louisbourg greatly alarmed the Canadian population. Now that the British had seized that great fortress, what was left to protect the French settlements of the lower Saint Lawrence River or Québec from British naval assault? Rumors of invasion by land and sea rose throughout the countryside. Many younger Canadian men prepared to migrate southwest to Illinois and Louisiana.

Governor Beauharnois ordered the construction of stronger, more permanent stone walls around the city of Québec according to plans previously drawn up by Engineer Chaussegros de Léry.

His letters to King Louis XV and Minister of Marine Maurepas strongly urged that France wage a strong campaign to regain Louisbourg and Acadia, and reestablish naval security for French shipping in the north Atlantic.

French vessels had nearly ceased to arrive in Québec during the previous two shipping seasons. The colony suffered from a critical shortage of munitions, provisions and currency. The governor and the intendant reported to the king that the scarcity and high price of trade goods had already caused many of the colony's native allies to turn to the English traders for their goods and provisions, thus weakening the western alliances and the western colonial frontier.

Although lacking in mutual trust, French-English trade relationships had become advantageous to both sides. The French could produce sugar at lower cost than could the English in the West Indies. The northern French colonies had come to rely on New England goods and supplies that were shipped through Louisbourg and traded for sugar and molasses. New England turned these raw materials into rum to barter for western furs and African slaves, and shipped flour, meat, fish, and lumber to the West Indies.

The British royal navy preyed on French shipping which could be insured more cheaply in London than in France. London insurance agents often shared information concerning British naval plans in order to protect their French clients.

Bécancour

Eighteen-year old Monique Ducharme died at home that July. Her mother and siblings suffered grievously from having to bury a sixth member of their family. Monique was François and Marguerite Moreau's fifth and youngest daughter to die before reaching marriageable age.

Charles and his mother tried to reassure everyone that they had ample food reserves to cover any emergency, but a sense of gloom had descended upon the family. Much of it was due to the loss of Louisbourg and the pervasive rumors of impending English attacks against Québec and Montréal. None except Marguerite had ever experienced warfare. She described to her children how her parents had survived the worst of it and taught them how to prepare for the possibility of food shortages.

Trois Rivières

Milder weather continued and the caterpillars did not reappear to damage any of the crops. Farmers harvested their corn three weeks earlier than usual that August.

Two weeks later, Antoine Ducharme dit Boudor signed a marriage contract with Angélique Houle by which he agreed to pay off her outstanding debts rather than pledge a *douaire préfix*. *Sieurs* Louis Lemaître and Louis Parmentier signed as witnesses to the agreement.

Trois Rivières had become the major source of birch-bark canoes used by the military and fur trade, and Antoine produced more of them than any of the several other canoe-makers in the area.

"How can you afford to sell them for half as much as anyone else?" his merchant cousins asked during the wedding reception.

Antoine smiled broadly at Jean Guillon, Jean-Baptiste Belleville, Joseph and René. "An Algonquin friend helped me train several Abenaki families who work native-style. The men gather the heavier materials in the forest, set up the forms, cut and shape the birch bark and cedar sheathing. The children run errands, collect the fine roots of red spruce that the natives call *wattape* and prepare them for their mothers and sisters who use them to bind the bark sections together and lash them to the gunwales. The women then seal the bark seams with hot pine tar."

"How long do these people stay with you before moving on to other work?"

"They take pride in what they do and stay from year to year. I provide them with food and shelter while they work, and they share a part of my earnings. The wooden hangar allows us to work under cover year-round, in all kinds of weather."

"I've seen many of your *canots-de-maître* and *canots-du-nord* delivering furs and provisions between Michillimackinac and Grand Portage," René told him. "They certainly bear up well under heavy loads!"

"That's good to hear. I've been told that they've lasted as long as five years! My own greatest satisfaction is in carving a good paddle out of a single piece of cedar. That wood is a pleasure to work with because it's lightweight and strong, never becomes brittle."

"That's especially important in the longer ones we use at the bow and stern. Yours are easily recognized by your mark, but also by their shape and quality; I would never part with mine. Do you still use *Pépère*'s carving tools?"

Antoine nodded. "Oh yes, and others that Papa added to the collection. I treasure them as much as you value your paddle."

Louisbourg

The New England enlistees continued to occupy the city and repair the fortress walls against the possibility of French attack. Their promise of plunder was unfulfilled, their hopes of returning home before harvest-time frustrated. The weather turned cold and rainy, the city remained shattered and filthy, offering little shelter and no fresh water from its wells.

Pepperrell sent 700 of the most needy men home and begged for reinforcements but none arrived. He and Admiral Warren conducted courts martial to quell unrest among the remaining colonial troops. British and colonial speculators descended on the town. The New England volunteers came close to mutiny.

France

King Louis XV ordered the assembly of a powerful naval expedition to retake Île Royale, expel the British from Acadia, bombard Boston and New York, then sail down to the West Indies to seize the English plantations. He commissioned the thirty-year old French aristocrat Jean-Baptiste de Roye de la Rochefoucauld, duc d'Anville to lead a fleet that was to project the largest European military force in American waters up to that time. François Bigot was appointed *commissaire-général* to manage the enormous task of outfitting the invasion force.

Boston

The seizure of Louisbourg had emboldened Governor Shirley to consider laying siege to both Québec and Montréal. In October, he claimed in his letters to British Minister Newcastle that the English colonists stood ready to invade Canada at once, that he could raise 20,000 men to capture Nouvelle France. He argued that French and English colonists could not live peacefully together on the same continent, that expelling the Canadians would allow Britain to control all of America and make her first among nations.

Montréal

William Johnson of New York persuaded a few of the Iroquois chiefs to declare war upon the French for the first time since the peace treaty of 1701. Border conflict heated up as his Mohawk allies raided the outskirts of Montréal and the Canadians carried out a series of border raids with their own allied warriors against the outer settlements of the New York province.

In late November 1745, Governor Beauharnois dispatched Sieur Marin, with a military force and two hundred twenty Mohawk and Abenaki allies against the outermost stockade post of the New York colony. Upon reaching the small Dutch settlement of Saratoga, they discovered that the English garrison had recently burnt the neglected fort and withdrawn. The raiders killed thirty Dutch inhabitants and seized about one hundred prisoners in that attack, thus creating panic in Albany which was now left unprotected.

One of the Dutch prisoners reported to his French interrogators that over 13,000 English provincials were preparing to attack Montréal, that thirty-two British warships had arrived in Boston.

Also in late November, Catherine, one of Bastien and Catherine Guillet's daughters, died in Bécancour at age fifty-two. She and her husband Pierre Bourbeau-Verville had been close neighbors of Louis and Anne Leclerc's family ever since Louis had built his own home nearby.

Nouvelle France

France had spent over 640,000 livres on its Canadian and Louisianian defenses in 1745. The presence of military forces in both colonies produced a sizable market for the sale of surplus wheat, peas, and pork, enriching the local farmers who were not required to pay taxes and the merchants who profited from the sale of their goods.

French visitors tended to compare the habitants with the peasants of feudal France, to judge the rural Canadians to be too well off, and to suggest that they would work harder if they were taxed rather than be so generously subsidized by the French treasury.

Louisbourg, 1746

By the end of January, 1100 New England men were listed as unfit for duty due to sickness, and 561 had died from fevers and dysentery in the devastated fortress of Louisbourg. These epidemics had first flared up in late August and had worsened throughout the cold wet weather so that as many as twenty-seven men were dying in a single day.

The promised British regiments had failed to arrive from Gibraltar before the cold weather and were spending the winter off the coast of Virginia.

Boston

By early spring, Shirley's letters to the British minister motivated Newcastle to enlist Admiral Warren's assistance, and reimburse the Louisbourg expeditionary expenses that the New England provinces had incurred but could ill afford. In so doing, he encouraged the other provinces to join forces with Massachusetts in its effort to seize Nouvelle France.

Eighty-two hundred Englishmen from Maine to Virginia signed up as recruits for the new campaign. Newcastle promised to provide eight battalions of British troops under the command of Lieutenant-General Saint Clair; they were to join with the northern New Englanders in Louisbourg for transport up the Saint Lawrence River by Warren's fleet. Meanwhile, the southern colonists and their Iroquois allies planned to attack Montréal by way of Lake Champlain.

Québec

Governor Beauharnois received orders to provide colonial land forces in support of the proposed naval attack against Annapolis Royal. He appointed Jean-Baptiste Ramesay to command the expedition and lead 600 Canadians to the northern end of the Bay of Fundy to join with 300 Malicites under Lieutenant Saint-Pierre, and a large body of Mi'kmaqs under Marin.

The Canadian and native forces arrived in June to set up camp in Chignectou and awaited news of the French fleet's arrival. Their numbers gradually grew to 1600 men.

Culloden Moor, northern Scotland

The Scottish Jacobites had achieved major victories in September 1745 at Prestonpas, and in January 1746 at Falkirk which had caused British Earl Loudoun to retreat and sit out the rest of the uprising. On April 16th, the 7,000-man Highland army and its thirteen light field guns were positioned on the Culloden Moor about 500 yards away from British Duke of Cumberland's 9,000 army regulars, their ten 3-pounders and six mortars. The sky was overcast and a brisk east wind blew sleet across the rolling infertile land and into the faces of the rebels.

The British decimated this last Scottish rebellion within one hour. Cumberland's army spent the following months ruthlessly pacifying the highland population and wiping out the centuries-old clan system. The kilt was banned and all Highlanders disarmed.

Louisbourg

General Saint Clair's eight British battalions arrived from Virginia in April so that the remaining 1900 New Englanders could finally return home. Eight hundred ninety provincial militiamen were reported to have died from cold and disease on Cape Breton that winter.

Nouvelle France

The governor and intendant received orders from Minister Maurepas to cease their reconstruction of fortifications around Québec unless the Canadians wished to assume the costs. Much of the work had already been completed. *Le Conseil supérieur* discussed the king's ultimatum, did not reach a consensus, and postponed their decision.

Meanwhile, English privateers continued to destroy French fishing stations along the Gulf of Saint Lawrence.

That May, the Québec shipyard launched its fifth naval vessel, *la Martre*, a 26-gun frigate. Preparations were already underway to construct a much larger warship of 1100-ton capacity armed with sixty cannons.

That summer of 1746, Québec officials received reports from Acadian refugees that between 40,000 to 50,000 Englishmen were preparing to attack Nouvelle France. The governor ordered that fire ships be made ready to protect the capital, and fire rafts be prepared at Île-aux-Coudres. He dispatched reconnoitering parties to the Saint Lawrence river mouth and gulf, and recalled Ramesay, his Canadian troops and native allies from Acadia.

Boston

Governor Shirley was ready for battle within six weeks, but the promised British naval squadron and eight battalions of regulars had not arrived from England by mid-August. He wrote to British Minister Newcastle that it would now be too late to attack Québec.

The Massachusetts governor altered his invasion plans by merging his forces with those of Governor Clinton of New York.

Two months later, 1500 Massachusetts provincials were on their way to attack Crown Point, but were recalled to Boston when news arrived that a French Armada was on its way to retake Louisbourg, Acadia, and destroy the capitals of Massachusetts and New York.

Champlain, September 1746

Joseph's workers had recently completed the grain harvest. His records showed that the year's crops were as bountiful as those of the previous year, so he intended to set another sizable surplus of grain in storage against any future shortages. His wife Anne and their daughter were preparing dinner, their three sons were storing hay in the barn when Joseph answered a knock at the door.

He was startled to see his oldest brother. "Is this really you, Jean?" he exclaimed.

Both men hugged each other for the first time in twenty-six years as the rest of the family rushed toward them.

"We never expected to see you again. This is such an unexpected pleasure!"

Jean felt relieved and gratified by this welcome. He had often wondered what this moment would be like after such a long absence.

Joseph introduced him to Anne and their four adolescents. He opened a bottle of imported wine for this special occasion and asked Jean what had brought him back to Champlain. "We heard about your marriage. Did your wife travel with you?"

"Unfortunately, no—Thérèse died of epidemic fever a year ago last January."

"I'm so sorry to hear that," said Anne. "Were there any children?"

"None, I'm sorry to say."

He smiled at their four youngsters and added, "I see that you've been more fortunate!"

In a more sober tone, he explained: "Life in Nouvelle Orléans just wasn't the same after Thérèse died. I found myself greatly missing her presence, but also yearning to see my own family, my old friends—and experience a Canadian winter."

They all laughed at that.

"Strange as it seems, I grew to appreciate the four seasons of Nouvelle France, its culture and its people. So I sold everything and traveled to Illinois where I visited with François."

"How is he doing?"

"I found him in Cahokia, near East Saint Louis. He's enjoying the life of fur trader and farmer. The soil is very rich there, the weather is milder than in Canada, and game is plentiful. He keeps so busy that he's never found time to marry!"

"Will he ever come back?" Joseph asked.

"I doubt it. I tried to talk him into coming with me but he certainly wasn't ready to do so. He arranged for my transportation back to Montréal with a group of friends he's traded with over the years. He also advised me to dress as a voyageur and limit my visible possessions to a knife, a hatchet, bow and arrows, a knapsack and a flat leather pouch that I strapped to my chest under my shirt. I had sold everything I owned in Louisiana and had converted its value into the new French *billets de banque* which I carried inside that pouch. I kept only a few coins in my pocket."

"I thought you had gained a lot of weight," Joseph admitted.

"Was it dangerous for you to travel back?" Anne asked.

"We trusted the people I voyaged with, but there's a lot more traffic on the waterways now than when I last traveled through the rivers and Great Lakes. A surprising number of young Canadians are moving south, and many of our former native allies are switching their alliances over to the English traders.

"Canadians who arrived in Louisiana last winter reported that the British had seized control of the entry to the Saint Lawrence River, that Nouvelle France was threatened from the east, west, and south. It became clear to me that the men in our family will most certainly have to defend the colony and I realized how much I still cared about the future and safety of my family and old friends. It was time for me to come back.

"Settlement has greatly increased along the Mississippi, Illinois, and Saint Lawrence rivers. Houses are generally much better-built than when I traveled south. All along the way, settlers seemed to lead much more comfortable lives than they did so many years ago. It's sad to know that all of that may now be at risk."

The wine began to have its effect. He looked around and recognized many of the old household items, including his father's musket and his grandfather's Mohawk peace pipe that still hung over the fireplace mantel. He approached them and studied the small collection of Hudson Bay sea shells that remained on the shelf, then he noticed his father's smoking chair by the fire.

His sentimental reaction to these objects surprised Joseph; these family mementos had never meant much to him. He recalled that they had also been important to his mother who had kept them in place all those years since his father's death. Then he remembered that Jean had never signed his inheritance rights over to him, had instead signed them over to Angélique. He wondered if that might be a problem. No matter, he thought, he now owned the majority of their parents' estate.

"Is there anything in this house that you would like to keep as a souvenir?" he asked.

"Nothing right now," Jean replied, "but I'd greatly appreciate having these shells once I move into my own home."

Angélique happened to drop by just then. "Jean!" she almost screamed as they moved to hug each other.

"P'tite soeur!" he greeted her warmly.

"Are you back home to stay?"

"Definitely!"

Joseph interjected: "He'll be staying with us until he finds a place of his own."

"We hadn't discussed that, but thank you, Joseph and Anne. That's most gracious of you."

His Louisiana manners caught them all by surprise.

Jean repeated his reasons for moving back to the area.

"I'm truly sorry about your wife's death, Jean. I'm sorry that we never had the opportunity to meet each other, I'm sure we would have become good friends."

"I know you would have, Angélique."

Dinner was ready and they invited her to join them, but she declined because she was needed at home. Jean promised to come over later to meet and visit with her family after the meal.

Jean caught up on family news that evening and learned that except for their uncle Jean-Baptiste Massé and aunt Marguerite Moreau Ducharme, theirs had become the oldest generation of the family during his absence. He had looked forward to seeing his mother again and was saddened by her recent death.

He told Angélique that he planned to visit their parents' graves the following day.

She offered to accompany him. She explained that Baptiste Barette had returned from his last voyage with a lingering illness that eventually caused his death at age thirty-seven. She thanked Jean for the *donation pure, simple, irrévocable* she had received from him two years earlier.

Jean assured her that he and Thérèse had been happy to do that for her and her family. He had no regrets.

Twenty-six

D'Anville's Armada

Two advance scouting ships had set sail for Nova Scotia in early April 1746. D'Anville's fleet expected to follow within weeks but corrupt or inept French bureaucrats and merchants repeatedly short-changed the provisioning of the ships. The fleet finally left Brest on May 22nd and encountered strong head winds that forced d'Anville to seek refuge in the port of Rochelle.

The bureaucratic delays continued until the fleet finally headed out again on June 20th. Exhaustion and illness had already spread among the troops by the time its ships cleared the French coast. Passage through the Bay of Biscay was rough enough to damage and carry away some of the spars, sails, and bowsprits, slowing down some of the vessels and causing others to shorten sail in order to keep the ships together. Dead calm occasionally halted progress for days at a time, alternating with squalls and lightning storms. Turbulent weather continued to batter and scatter the French fleet during most of its three-month crossing.

Typhus, dysentery, and scurvy spread among the sailors and soldiers. Drinking water, ship's biscuits, and meat in brine barrels turned foul. Malnutrition and starvation inevitably developed on most of the vessels.

A mid-September storm disabled and dispersed the armada even as it approached the dangerous shoals of Sable Island near Nova Scotia. D'Anville's ships were caught in a dense fog, then a heavy lightning storm that reportedly generated waves as high as the ships' masts, causing some of the vessels to collide with each other and sink. These conditions scattered the fleet in the dark of night.

Only forty-two of the original seventy vessels managed to enter Chibouctou Bay where d'Anville had expected to rendezvous with Admiral Conflans and his four battleships from the West Indies. They had arrived earlier and had waited several weeks before finally sailing on to France just a few days before d'Anville's arrival.

The bay was empty, without the expected relief supplies from Nouvelle France. The advance scouting vessels had patrolled the bay and waited for d'Anville since June, but these two ships had also sailed for France one month earlier and reached Brest on the 22nd of September.

Duke d'Anville died of a massive stroke within a week after reaching safe harbor.

His council of officers opened Minister Maurepas' written instructions and learned that their primary mission was to recapture Louisbourg. They agreed that this had become impossible but argued in favor of seizing their secondary target, Annapolis Royal.

The new commander declared that this was also beyond their means to accomplish due to the weakened state of their fleet and army. He pointed out that vital provisions and munitions had not arrived, that 2000 men had already died of hunger and disease, that too many of their sailors and soldiers were now unfit for duty. He argued that their situation was hopeless, that they must return to France.

When his council of officers refused to support his decision, he retreated into his quarters and threw himself upon his sword. Although gravely wounded, he survived and chose to resign his position.

The only remaining senior officer, Jacques-Pierre de Taffanel, marquis de la Jonquière automatically assumed command of the expedition and regrouped his forces. He moved the ships deeper into the harbor where his troops could disembark for convalescence and recuperation. He designated several of the transport vessels to serve as hospital ships to isolate the contagion and the treatment of the sick, organized shore encampments for those who were fit, and purchased fresh food from Acadian farmers who insisted on payment in coin rather than paper.

The British presence in Nova Scotia at this time was limited to a 200-man garrison in Annapolis Royal.

Nouvelle France

Church bells rang jubilantly at the end of September, when the official report of the fleet's arrival in Chibouctou reached Québec. News spread throughout the Saint Lawrence River valley that France had provided the means to retake Louisbourg and Acadia.

Boston

The presence of the French flotilla in Acadian waters alarmed the people of New England. Since Governor Shirley had received no British support in answer to his previous warning that Canadian forces were encamped in Chignectou, he raised a 1000-man force from the colonies of Massachusetts, Rhode Island and New Hampshire.

Shirley wrote to the London Board of Trade: "The French will soon find a way to wrest Acadia from us if we do not remove the most dangerous French inhabitants and replace them with English families."

Although it was already late in the shipping season and the seas were stormy, the Massachusetts governor sent two English trading vessels with half of the new recruits to reinforce Annapolis Royal and ordered Colonel Arthur Noble to lead the remaining 500 men to construct a new English fort in Grand Pré.

Chibouctou

French sailors and soldiers continued to die from the epidemics, scurvy, and starvation. Six hospital ships left to carry the sickest soldiers and sailors back to France. Eighteen hundred men were buried at the campsite. Still, Jonquière hoped to seize Annapolis Royal with the help of several *Acadiens* who volunteered to guide them safely to Annapolis Royal. He sent word to Ramesay in Chignectou to position his force close to Annapolis Harbor to support the proposed naval attack.

A French man-of-war captured a New England ship just outside Chibouctou Harbor on October 22nd and intercepted a dispatch from Governor Shirley to British Admiral Lestock in Louisbourg.

It revealed the imminent arrival of eighteen British battleships along the Acadian coast. Jonquière received other reports that Louisbourg had been strengthened by British regulars and six British warships, that 1200 New England men were on their way to reinforce the garrison of Annapolis Royal.

The French commander and his officers finally abandoned their plans. They dismissed and landed their Acadian pilots, dispatched a message to Ramesay to withdraw his forces to Chignectou, and finally headed back to France with the remnants of d'Anville's Armada.

Annapolis Royal

While on their way to Annapolis, the Rhode Island transport vessels were shipwrecked by a storm off Martha's Vineyard and a New Hampshire transport sloop encountered a French ship, prompting it to return to Portsmouth Harbor.

Boston

Demands of the European war held top priority in England. British Lieutenant-General Saint Clair and his troops had not arrived as scheduled to assist the New England campaign against Nouvelle France because his fleet had been reassigned to a failed expedition against the coast of France. Minister Newcastle ordered Governor Shirley to remain on the defensive, and to disband the provincial recruits who were on British pay.

Shirley revised his plans and proposed to merge his colonial forces with the New York expedition against Fort Saint-Frédéric at Crown Point. This would concentrate all of the 8200 English provincial recruits against that French fortress.

He was forced to cancel this ambitious campaign on Lake Champlain upon receiving a report in mid-October that d'Anville's Armada was leaving Chibouctou Harbor and heading south, perhaps towards Boston. The governor recalled his troops to the capital and activated the militias in all the surrounding communities.

Annapolis

On November 4th, Ramesay learned of the fleet's departure for France and led his Canadian troops back to Chignectou where they set up winter camp near Beaubassin.

D'Anville's Fleet

That same day, another storm battered the remains of the armada as it reached halfway across the Atlantic. It left the command ship *Prince d'Orange* with only nine transport vessels carrying eleven companies of soldiers, all but ninety-nine of whom were disabled by the pestilence. Four or five corpses were buried at sea most days of that crossing.

On December 7th, Jonquière led the remaining fleet into Port Louis on the coast of Brittany and learned that several other vessels had reached safety ahead of him.

Bay of Fundy, January 1747

Four hundred seventy English provincial recruits reached Annapolis then sailed on to Grand Pré with a few additional reinforcements from the garrison.

Ocean storms, drifting ice, and the enormous tides of the bay compelled Colonel Noble to land his seasick troops on the southern shore of the bay and proceed overland to Grand Pré. Meanwhile, the lightened colonial vessels made their way up the bay and delivered their military supplies, provisions, and equipment by way of the Gaspareaux River.

Colonel Noble led his troops through rugged unfamiliar territory without a guide, in snowy weather without *raquettes* because these had been left on the supply ships. Each man carried fourteen days worth of provisions in his haversack and slept seven nights in the snowdrifts without shelter.

The English provincials suffered from cold and exposure by the time they reached their destination, and were unable to unload their supplies and building materials from the two vessels that lay firmly anchored in river ice. Noble took over twenty-three wooden Acadian homes and one large stone-walled building to house his troops, and promised future payment to the villagers for any food and supplies they could provide. The evicted *Acadiens* moved into their neighbors' homes for the duration of the winter.

Chignectou

Ramesay's evaluation of Acadian reports convinced him that the enemy force was slightly larger than his but more vulnerable now than it would be in the spring. Since he was disabled by a knee injury, he dispatched officers Coulon de Villiers, La Corne, and several lieutenants to lead a winter attack against the New England encampment. They left Beaubassin with two hundred Canadians, traveled overland on snowshoes and sledges to haul their equipment and provisions, and collected supplies from friendly *Acadiens* along the way.

The French force took the long route, detoured around tidal bays and rivers, sent scouts ahead to avoid alerting the English, and halted a few miles short of their objective on February 8th.

Acadiens who lived across the river from the English camp invited the French to warm and dry themselves around their hearths, and offered them meals of dark bread, cheese and hard cider. That night, the Canadians prepared their weapons for the coming battle and slept soundly under shelter.

Early the next day, Coulon de Villiers divided his men into ten parties, each to be guided by a local villager toward two of the many houses occupied by the English provincials. Coulon and second officer La Corne would lead two larger parties against the senior English officers who occupied the stone building and its closest neighboring house.

They launched simultaneous attacks in the middle of a blizzard, under cover of darkness at 2:30 in the morning.

The 240 Canadians, *Acadiens,* and their 20 Mi'kmaq allies overwhelmed an occupying force of five hundred New Englanders that night. English forces were permitted to march out of the village and head for Annapolis on February 14th.

Coulon de Villiers claimed possession of Grand Pré and counseled the inhabitants to remain faithful to the French king. He left with his forces nine days later and reached Beaubassin on March 8th.

One month later, Governor Shirley of Massachusetts sent another, larger garrison of Massachusetts soldiers to reoccupy Grand Pré and warn its villagers to remain faithful to the British king.

The *Acadiens* continued to be caught between the Québec governor's demands and British threats of expulsion, yet neither claimant had enough military force in Acadia to back up its claims of sovereignty.

Versailles, late April

French officials remained determined to regain Louisbourg and Acadia, and eliminate any future threat from Massachusetts.

Minister Maurepas had raised a second fleet at Île d'Aix, Charentes, and assigned Rear-Admiral Marquis de La Jonquière to command a division of three frigates and two ships of the line, one of 64 guns and the other of 50, during his second attempt to reach Québec as its new governor-general.

The fleet consisted of sixteen warships, six East India merchant vessels, and twenty-two transports, some of which were destined to deliver many of the recently deported French residents of Louisbourg to Québec.

British Admiral Anson and Rear-Admiral Peter Warren were well-informed of French naval activities when the flotilla set sail on May 10th. Once it cleared the French coast, the English Channel, and reached northwest of Spain, the British intercepted and attacked Jonquière's convoy near Cap Finisterre. Although the British had the same number of warships, their firepower was three times that of the French.

The battle lasted five hours. The merchant and transport vessels fled toward their destinations while five British battleships concentrated their heavy fire against Jonquière's 64-gun *Sérieux,* wounding the commander, and killing or wounding one hundred forty members of his crew. The marquis finally surrendered and was taken prisoner to London.

One month later, King Louis XV named Roland-Michel Barrin, Marquis de la Galissonnière to serve as interim governor-general of Nouvelle France pending Jonquière's release.

Montréal, May 1747

Nouvelle France could no longer rely on its western alliances. Three years of minimal imports from France had finally led to the collapse of its western fur trade and the disaffection of the natives who came to believe English tales of French weakness.

George Croghan played on native frustrations and incited the Hurons to kill Canadian traders in Détroit. Other tribes joined them and burned several settlements in that area. Violence soon spread northwest to Michillimackinac and the Illinois territory. Governor Beauharnois declared war against the Mohawks in retaliation for their several raids near Montréal.

That June, New York's agent for Indian affairs William Johnson and his close ally Chief Hendrick incited the Mohawks to target Montréal itself in spite of the Iroquois grand council's longstanding policy of neutrality. The Onondaga chiefs had managed to dissuade the other Iroquois nations from joining them.

The French and their mission allies ambushed and inflicted heavy losses on Hendrick's Mohawks near Châteauguay, just as they were about to cross the river to attack Montréal.

Bécancour

Jean bought a farm near his brother Louis' home in Bécancour and invited all of their relatives to an outdoor family reunion on the south shore. He looked forward to renewing relationships with cousins, aunts, uncles, nieces and nephews whose farms extended farther west into Nicolet, Baie-du-Febvre, Île Dupas, Yamaska, Yamachiche, and Montréal.

His sixty-six-year old aunt Marguerite Moreau answered his many questions about the family history. She had many tales to tell of what life was like on both sides of the Saint Lawrence River before he was born.

Marguerite was particularly pleased to see him again. "Simonne never gave up hope that you'd come home. It's such a pity that she wasn't here to greet you. She would have been so happy…"

"I'm sorry that I didn't get to see her again, *ma tante*, but life was good in Louisiana. I married a lovely woman, found work that I truly enjoyed, met some interesting people, and experienced an entirely different culture."

"And now you're back."

"Thérèse was all the family I had down there, and family has always been important to me."

"It's sad that you never had children."

"We were both greatly disappointed about that—I've often wondered what a son of mine would have looked like."

Antoine approached them just then.

"He looks so much like *mon oncle* François!"

She laughed. "Yes he certainly does."

The canoe-maker proudly introduced his wife Angélique and their nine-month old daughter whom he cradled in his arms. He asked what type of watercraft French habitants used in the south.

"*Les Canadiens* continue to travel by birchbark canoe all the way down to the gulf," Jean replied. "Michel Arsonneau's brothers and the Barettes were able to return home with one of the two canoes that had carried us to Louisiana because they traveled back that same year. Birch trees don't grow much beyond the southern edges of the Great Lakes, so travel on the lower Mississippi is mostly by wooden river bark or row galley. Both are built of cypress, a durable wood that is highly resistant to rot. The weight and bulk of the load, and the strength of the current determine which type of boat is chosen; both conditions vary with the season and the river location.

"I've mostly borrowed Louis' canoe since I've been back but I plan to visit you soon to purchase one of yours. I've heard good things about them."

"I'll be glad to show you around."

They shared fond memories of other family reunions they had attended every summer of their childhood and youth. Antoine confessed that they had not held one in quite a few years but suggested that this was likely to change now that everyone seemed to be enjoying the outing.

Louis arrived with his wife Anne and their seven surviving children. Jean noticed that Anne looked tired and frail.

Louis confided: "She's tired and sad so much of the time now. We've buried five baby boys during the past eight years. Our François-Xavier died this past March at the age of sixteen months and Anne is expecting another child late this summer."

Jean saw that of all his siblings, Louis had changed the most; his hair had thinned and turned white. He seemed haggard. "None of your children are married yet, Louis—They must be of great help to you and Anne since they're all living at home."

"Yes, everyone helps out, but you know the house seems to be getting smaller every year."

"Have you ever thought of adding to it?"

"Yes, I have, but I'm not much good at that kind of work and it's so expensive to hire someone."

"Do you remember how much we all enjoyed building that *pièces-sur-pièces* with Papa?"

Louis' older sons joined them. Twenty-two-year old Joseph asked: "You built *Pépère*'s house?"

Their father nodded. "Yes, but with the guidance and help of a master-carpenter."

Jean briefly took the measure of his nephews who appeared to be sturdy, bright young men.

He asked Louis. "Would you add to it or build a new one?"

His brother seemed puzzled by the question.

"You're now speaking to an experienced master-carpenter and saw-mill operator," Jean explained.

Louis was startled by the suggestion, yet they both knew that there was more than enough standing timber on both their lots to construct either choice.

The boys were excited by the proposition, and when they mentioned it to their mother, her eyes brightened and a weight seemed to lift off her shoulders.

That following week, Jean marked the best trees to cut for lumber and the boys began to clear and burn the undergrowth, saving the ashes for the production of lye their sisters would use for soap-making. Their cousins enthusiastically volunteered to help with the project and their fathers promised to help raise the house frame. Jean marked the outline of the foundation and the boys began to collect fieldstone.

Twenty-seven

Québec

Governor-General La Galissonnière arrived in mid-September 1747 and during the next two days, seventy-six-year old retiring Governor Beauharnois informed him of the dangers facing Nouvelle France. He warned that the steady encroachment of English fur traders into the Ohio valley had already seriously impacted the colony's defensive alliances, its major source of income, and its vital overland link with Louisiana.

When Galissonnière learned that the Québec garrison was limited to 169 soldiers, he asked Beauharnois to deliver his written plea to Minister Maurepas for the immediate military reinforcement of the capital of Nouvelle France. The former governor then sailed home to France after a two-year delay.

Their brief consultations led Galissonnière to revive, reorganize and retrain the colonial militia. He developed plans to strengthen the frontier outposts in the Ohio valley and on Lake Michigan, and to build new forts at Baie-Verte, and at La Présentation on the upper Saint Lawrence River. He continued Beauharnois' strong support of La Vérendrye's western explorations and ordered that an additional fort be built in Sioux territory.

Bécancour

Jean visited often with his aunt Marguerite and learned more about his family's activities during his twenty-eight-year absence. Cousins Marguerite Moreau and Simonne Massé had married brothers Jean-François and Louis and had remained close over the years.

During one of their long conversations, he asked: "How did my parents die, *Ma Tante?*"

She studied his face, saw deep concern in his eyes, and answered in a subdued tone: "Your father died quite suddenly and unexpectedly, and your mother grieved a long time. Your brothers and sisters took very good care of her and avoided any of the conflict we often witness in such situations. You were away, Louis had no interest in claiming his rights of seniority, everyone focused on maintaining your mother's peace of mind by keeping the family home much as it had always been. They sold all their shares to Joseph because your father had been relying on him to administer his several properties. Your *Maman* was well taken care of with Angélique living nearby. Her health had been failing for a little while before she passed away, but she did not suffer."

She smiled as she reminisced: "I remember how excited she was to receive the news that you and Jean-François had visited with each other in Nouvelle Orléans, that you were both in good health and doing well for yourselves. Then the *donation* to Angélique! That was very generous of you and your wife."

Jean shrugged his shoulders. "The voyage home would have been very difficult for Thérèse, and the construction projects just kept piling up so that I couldn't leave, nor did I want to leave her alone for a year."

She understood his reasoning. Jean had always had a strong sense of responsibility. "It's good to have you back with us now."

He thanked her for that and casually asked: "Do you remember the recipes for pemmican and *banique?*"

"*Mon doux!* That was such a long time ago, but I did make some of the pemmican during the droughts and caterpillar invasions. I would have to think about that— I'm sure it will come to me..."

"Didn't Angélique write down the recipes?"

"Yes, she did, but I can't read. Why do you ask?"

"I sense that the English are stirring up trouble with the Mohawks against Montréal, and if there's to be another war after the loss of Louisbourg, I think it would be wise to share that knowledge with the younger members of the family. We should start building up our reserves of food supplies."

She agreed and advised him to speak to his sister Angélique.

That winter, Louis and his sons cut timber to length and hauled it to the work site. Since they had decided to build the new house of *pièces-sur-pièces*, Jean arranged for delivery of the logs to the Arsonneau sawmill in Batiscan where they could be squared along their entire length. He taught his nephews to shape the ends and tenons according to his markings, while he cut the lengthwise grooves of the posts. They worked at these tasks in the barn throughout the winter.

Required ownership of a musket, drilling in its use and in martial arts were new experiences for these two generations of men.

Louis told his sons: "The Iroquois often raided our settlements when my *pépère* first arrived from France. My own papa and his both witnessed the signing of the great Treaty of Montréal that sealed the peace between all the native tribes and the settlers of the Saint Lawrence River valley. I was only six years old at the time but I can remember the celebrations that followed. Up until then, all men sixteen through sixty years of age could be called to militia duty at any time of the day or night, often to travel great distances to chase the Iroquois raiders through the wilderness, sometimes on two- or three-week journeys to their villages."

Sixteen-year old Claude asked: "Did they ever kill with their muskets?"

"No," Louis replied. "I was told that my *pépère* nearly did once, when he had wandered away from his neighbor to gather hickory in the forest. A young Mohawk came up from behind and threw his tomahawk at him, barely missing his head, then quickly attacked again with his knife. *Pépère* threw him over his shoulder as he had been trained to do, quickly managed to grab, cock and aim his loaded musket. He was ready to fire when they heard his neighbor's call. The Iroquois suddenly and quietly disappeared into the forest."

His four sons had listened intently as he related the details of this family legend. Although they often complained about having to undergo militia training, this helped them to understand its value. They recalled how vulnerable they had felt two years earlier when the English seized the fortress of Louisbourg, and grew to appreciate their growing ability to defend their homes and families if the need arose.

1748

Forges Saint-Maurice showed a modest profit. Small industries such as tanneries, sawmills, brick and tile works had multiplied. Apprenticeships in silversmithing and woodcarving became available in the three major population centers. Joseph had some of his coins melted down into silver goblets, platters, and bowls.

Bécancour

The weather warmed enough in early May so that local masons, Louis' brother-in-law François Rochereau and uncle Michel Crevier-Bellerive, could cross over from Cap-de-la-Madeleine to begin building his cellar walls and fireplace foundations. Jean, Louis and the boys roughened the surface of each stone in preparation for its first application of mortar.

When Louis left to get more water, Jean inquired about the new cast iron stoves that were now being produced by Forges Saint-Maurice.

"They're not perfect and cost 100 livres each, but they certainly give off more heat than our old fireplaces," his uncle replied.

François looked up from his work and asked him: "Are you thinking of buying one?"

"Maybe two—one for me and another for Louis and his family."

"Ours uses less firewood and spreads the heat more evenly into the other rooms after I set up metal ducts," Michel added. "We take the system down at the end of the heating season, before the women begin their *grand ménage*."

"I'll certainly look into it," Jean decided.

When all posts and beams were ready for joining, Louis' sons shifted to cutting and carving tenons at both ends of the horizontal wall members. Meanwhile, Jean shaped two doors, several shutters and windows with tools borrowed from a recently retired master carpenter who often visited their work site out of natural curiosity and interest.

Joseph arrived by canoe and congratulated them on their progress. He told Louis: "I'll provide a stone kitchen sink for your new house, just like the one Papa installed in our second home in Champlain."

Louis' face brightened. He thanked his brother while Anne and the girls rejoiced. It warmed his heart to see his wife smiling and laughing again.

That following Saturday, his neighbors gathered together to raise the house frame. This turned out to be a social and family gathering with the ladies providing a great variety of food for the outdoor tables and Jean donating several kegs of cider for the group.

Québec

Antoine Ducharme dit Boudor and his cousin Jean traveled to the capital in mid-June to witness the launching of the great battleship *le Saint-Laurent*. Preparations were already underway for the construction of its sister-ship *l'Orignal*. These two battleships of 1100-ton capacity and armed with 60 cannons would be the largest ever built in Canada up to that time.

Jean had never been to the capital before, nor had he ever been this close to such a large vessel. He was greatly impressed by both. Antoine told him that this was the biggest crowd he had ever seen at one of these events. They met and talked to people from as far downriver as Cacouna, Île du Bic, and Île Verte.

Marguerite Moreau's son Charles married Madeleine Desrosiers of Bécancour in late June. Jean and Louis attended the contract-signing which was witnessed and signed by the groom's brother Antoine, cousin François Moreau, and friend François Arsonneau.

The groom had been managing the family farm for his mother, his forty-three-year old sister Louise and twenty-six-year old brother Joseph who continued to live at home and share everyday chores.

Ohio valley

Although French claims to the area had been originally established by La Salle as a major watershed and tributary of the great Mississippi River, and had long been considered a major link between Canada and Louisiana, the Ohio valley remained relatively untouched by permanent Canadian development.

Government emissaries from Virginia and Pennsylvania accompanied the English fur traders into the Ohio country to treat with the Shawnees and Iroquois of that area. The natives subsequently appointed joint chiefs to protect their own interests while dealing with the English and the French.

Several prominent Virginia planters, including George Washington and his two brothers, joined together to form the Ohio Company of Virginia to seek a royal land grant west of the Alleghenies.

Nouvelle France

In mid-August, the grand-vicar of the diocese of Québec inspected the parish registries of Cap-de-la-Madeleine and found many to be torn and others missing. He ordered the pastor of Champlain to gather and arrange in sequence all previous parish records, so that he could provide exact copies to the local notaries who must judge their validity and officially update their civil records.

Intendant François Bigot arrived in Québec on August 26, 1748 and learned of Governor Galissonnière's strategy to expand Canadian control over the western landmass. Bigot did not share the governor's ambition, having experienced first-hand the loss of Louisbourg to an army of English provincials. His enormous effort to provision d'Anville's fleet had also been laid to waste by the powers of nature. These events had rendered him pessimistic about the future stability of French colonial expansion. He suspected that Nouvelle France lacked the financial resources, French military and naval support to justify such an expansion.

Before leaving Bordeaux, France, Intendant Bigot had privately contracted with the shipping firm David Gradis *et fils* to form a company to trade with Québec. Their agreement dated July 10, 1748 required Gradis to finance a ship of about 300 tons loaded with wine, brandy, and other goods, in return for half of the profits or losses realized by their contract. Bigot also held a 50 percent interest in the company but ceded a 20 percent share to the controller of the Marine in Québec, Jacques-Michel Bréard, and retained the balance.

Aix-la-Chapelle,

France and England ended the War of Austrian Succession by signing the Treaty of Aix-la-Chapelle on October 18, 1748. Both powers had exhausted their financial resources during the conflict but had gained little advantage in the European theater. Their territorial seizures on the continent and in the colonies reverted to their prewar status, including the fortress of Louisbourg.

Now that peace had been restored in Europe, Marquis de la Jonquière was finally freed from London imprisonment and reappointed governor-general of Nouvelle France.

The population of Nouvelle France rejoiced at having regained free maritime entry and exit through the Gulf of Saint Lawrence.

The New Englanders were infuriated to learn that Great Britain had given away so easily that which had cost them so dearly. The militiamen who had suffered through the winter of 1745–46 and had seen so many of their friends and neighbors die in Louisbourg would not soon forget.

Nouvelle France, 1749

Sébastien's oldest son, Montréal merchant Joseph married Louise Déjordy on February 11th in the nearby parish of Saint-Sulpice. The bride was twelve years younger than he and his godmother's niece. Marguerite and Jean Guillon hosted the reception in their home.

Louis and Jean traveled to Montréal with their cousin Antoine who had produced numerous canoes for his merchant-cousins Joseph, René and Jean Guillon. This proved to be a special occasion for Jean who had not yet had the opportunity to reacquaint himself with his relatives in Montréal: Joseph's older sister Marguerite and her husband Jean Guillon; his brothers Jean-Baptiste Belleville, Alexis Beaulorier, Simon Villebrun, Charles Villard, and René; his younger sister Madeleine and her husband Nicolas Leblanc-Labrie.

London

In mid-March, British King George II granted a royal charter that secured the rights of the Ohio Company of Virginia to 200,000 acres of land near the Forks of the Ohio River, at the junction of the Monongahela and Allegheny rivers. The grant required the Virginian shareholders to settle one hundred families on that land and erect a fort to protect them and British claims to the area.

Nouvelle France

Two weeks later, King's Lieutenant François-Pierre de Rigaud de Vaudreuil succeeded Claude-Michel Bégon as lieutenant-governor of Trois Rivières. François-Pierre was the younger brother of Pierre de Rigaud, marquis de Vaudreuil-Cavagnal who had governed Trois Rivières beginning in 1733, and was currently serving as governor of Louisiana. Both brothers had been born in Trois Rivières.

That April, Governor Galissonnière dispatched officer Portneuf of Bécancour with a garrison of soldiers to rebuild and defend old Fort Rouillé at Toronto on the northwestern shore of Lake Ontario. His main objective was to restore French alliances with the northern and western natives who now headed southeast to trade their prime furs at Oswego.

Such an expedition required a corps of militiamen to transport the skilled craftsmen who would guide the construction, and to portage the project's equipment and provisions. Portneuf called up the younger members of the Bécancour militia, local carpenters and blacksmiths for the expedition.

Jean and several of his nephews and cousins were on the duty roster: Louis' older sons Joseph, Jean-Baptiste, and Claude; Charles and Joseph Ducharme; Louis Massé's younger sons Joseph and Charles; and Pierre-Charles Bourbeau-Verville *fils*. Jean, as the most experienced voyageur in the family group, guided them through the experience.

The governor ordered Captain Céloron de Blainville and his colonial troops to reestablish French authority over the Ohio River valley and those of its tributaries.

Céloron left Lachine in mid-June, with twenty-three birch-bark canoes carrying fourteen officers and cadets, twenty colonial regulars, one hundred eighty Canadian militiamen, and a band of native warriors.

Ten days later, they stopped halfway up the southern bank of the upper Saint Lawrence River, where Abbé Piquet's was building his mission chapel at *La Présentation*.

The French expedition continued upriver to reach Fort Frontenac on the northeastern shore of Lake Ontario where Céloron saw firsthand how much this post's fur trade had declined.

Acadia

French troops reclaimed possession of Louisbourg on June 29th with orders and provisions to strengthen it into an even more powerful military and naval station.

In anticipation of this event, the British Ministry had ordered the development of an English fortress and major port in Chibouctou Bay, on the southern coast of the Acadian peninsula.

A fleet of British transports arrived that month to deliver 2500 naval and military men to build and garrison the new fort, and English, Irish and German immigrants of various trades and occupations to settle with their families on free royal land grants in the new community of Halifax.

Lord Edward Cornwallis arrived as the new governor-general of Nova Scotia, had new streets laid out in its new capital, planned and managed to get everyone under shelter before winter set in. His former Louisbourg garrison soldiers quickly set up wooden palisades and redoubts to surround and protect the new settlement.

The governor began to expand the British military presence on the peninsula and ordered the *Acadiens* to take an unconditional oath of allegiance. They refused to do so, stating that they wished to remain neutral on their own land as had been permitted since the Treaty of Utrecht.

Great Lakes area

On July 6th, Céloron and his men reached the small palisaded fort at Niagara on the southwestern shore of Lake Ontario. They portaged seven days past the falls and through the steep forest path to launch their canoes on Lake Erie, and landed nine days later to portage across eight more miles of rugged territory to Chautauqua Lake. When they eventually entered its outlet, the stream was so low that they had to drag their canoes for much of its length before reaching the Allegheny and Ohio rivers in late July.

Nouvelle France

In his sixties and in failing health, Governor-General marquis de la Jonquière arrived in mid-August to replace Galissonnière. Intendant Bigot welcomed him warmly, having shared with him the experience of the d'Anville fleet disaster three years earlier.

Jonquière had orders to discourage the growing presence of British settlers on the Acadian peninsula, and to safeguard French control over the mainland north and west of the Missaguash River. In a letter written October 9, 1749, the governor assured the French Minister of his continuing efforts through Intendant Bigot, Abbé Le Loutre and Father Germain to discreetly encourage and provision the native Mi'kmaqs in their efforts to protect their native lands.

Captain Céloron de Blainville returned to Québec in early November and reported to Governor Jonquière that English traders had already formed strong trading alliances with key native tribes in the Ohio country, that French influence and prestige in the area had greatly declined. The priest who had accompanied him estimated that the expedition had traveled 1200 leagues (3000 miles) to reclaim the Ohio country for France.

The arrival of these soldiers and militiamen initiated a fever epidemic that spread among the native and Canadian populations.

Montréal

Joseph and Louise Déjordy's son was born in Montréal on November 18, 1749 and was baptized in Notre Dame Parish the following day with his uncle René serving as godfather.

In spite of Marguerite Guillon's efforts to help Louise regain her strength following the delivery, Joseph *fils* was ten days old when his mother died at the age of thirty-six. Marguerite and her daughters assumed responsibility for the baby's care throughout his infancy.

Sixty-four-year old Pierre Gaultier de Varennes, *Sieur* de la Vérendrye died in Montréal on December 6, 1749, soon after he had purchased and sent a large supply of trading goods and provisions to his trading posts in preparation for the resumption of his western explorations.

His sons intended to fulfill his final goal of ascending the Saskatchawan River up to the Rocky Mountains, to build a fort there, then scale the continental divide, travel overland and downriver to reach the western sea. Jonquière and Bigot denied them the privilege by transferring Vérendrye's commission and its attendant privileges to Jacques Legardeur de Saint-Pierre, an officer of the *Troupes de Marine*.

Governor Jonquière, Intendant François Bigot, and Jacques Legardeur de Saint-Pierre profited from the years of personal expense and sacrifice the Verendryes had invested in their quest for the overland route. Bigot and Jonquière did not reimburse the sons for their preparatory expenses even though their supplies would be used by Saint-Pierre.

Bécancour

Having died peacefully in his sleep at the age of fifty-six, Louis and Simonne's oldest son Jean was buried in Bécancour on December 22, 1749, three years after his homecoming from Louisiana.

Twenty-eight

Nova Scotia, 1750

France and Great Britain appointed governors Galissonnière of Québec and Shirley of Boston as chief negotiators of the disputed colonial boundaries in North America. The most troublesome contention involved the border between Nouvelle France and Nova Scotia. In order to retain overland access to Île Saint-Jean and Louisbourg, the French insisted that the Isthmus of Chignectou was the dividing line between the two territories. The English claimed a large portion of the mainland (the future state of Maine and the province of New Brunswick) and they insisted that Acadia historically included the shores of *Baie-de-Chaleurs*.

Although the two European countries were officially at peace with each other, skirmishes continued to occur at sea and over the western frontier of Nova Scotia following the spring thaw.

Three hundred more German immigrants arrived in Halifax which was now armed with cannon.

The *Acadiens* sensed that British policy toward them was changing drastically as they strengthened their military presence and increased British settlement on the peninsula. Many began to migrate toward French-held areas, mainly north of Nova Scotia to Île Saint-Jean and east to Louisbourg. Others moved across the northern isthmus, into the mainland that French and Canadian officials insisted had never been ceded by treaty.

Rumors reached Halifax and Boston that the *Acadiens* were exporting hundreds of their cattle to Louisbourg rather than selling them to the Nova Scotians. Regardless of the rules delivered in English from a small, isolated garrison, the French habitants had continued to drive their cattle to ships anchored off Baie-Verte on the northern end of the isthmus, and along the shores of Northumberland Strait to French traders from Île Royale. French silver flowing into Louisbourg drew the *Acadiens* and their produce.

Several British governors had declared this to be illegal and subject to severe penalties, but such infractions had never been prosecuted.

That April, Governor Cornwallis declared in French to the *Acadiens* that they were forbidden to farm new lands, build boats, sell their lands or belongings. He dispatched Major Charles Lawrence with 400 men to dislodge Chevalier Louis de La Corne and his forces from the Isthmus of Chignectou and to occupy the village of Beaubassin.

News of the British troop movement reached Abbé Jean-Louis-Joseph Le Loutre who preached fire and brimstone and threatened to excommunicate any *Acadien* who gave in to English demands.

The priest's fiery harangues prompted Pierre Cormier's and Jean Cyr's sons and daughters to gather their families for a temporary escape. The men quickly packed their firearms, knives, hatchets, blankets, pots and kettles. The women collected a few days' supply of honey, bread, cheese, dried meat and fruit. They bundled the children and carried their rosaries into the wilderness, praying that the crisis would not last so that they could return to their homes within a few days at the most.

In anticipation of the arrival of English forces, Le Loutre entered the village of Beaubassin on April 25, 1750, chased away those *Acadiens* who had remained in their homes, personally set fire to the chapel, and ordered his Mi'kmaq allies to burn all 121 buildings including barns filled with grain and hay, the gristmill, and tannery in order to deny them to the English.

Major Lawrence landed his men and attempted to secure the smoldering site which Governor Jonquière had acknowledged was in British territory, but La Corne's forces greatly outnumbered those of the British and forced them to withdraw.

Forced by Le Loutre to flee to the French-occupied north side of the isthmus, shocked and heartbroken by the totally unexpected loss of their ancestral homes and of all their earthly possessions, 946 men, women and children wandered across the marshland and Missaguash River to seek refuge on the mainland, or cross over to Île Saint-Jean. This unexpected influx of poor, homeless refugees overwhelmed the limited resources of the rest of the Acadian population.

The Cormier and Cyr families had formed a tight-knit, compatible migratory group through two generations of intermarriages. The men discussed the several destinations that were open to them on the mainland and chose to move west toward the Petitcoudiac River. Their primary concerns were to provide safety, shelter, food, and warm clothing for their families before the arrival of winter.

The refugees spread out northwest of the Missaguash, along the banks of the Chipoudy, Petitcodiac and Memramcook rivers based on Abbé Le Loutre's promise that provisions would soon be delivered to those areas from Québec.

The district of Beaubassin consisted of several other smaller villages. Le Loutre and his faithful Mi'kmaqs returned that summer to carry out another scorched earth policy, torching every French structure and field crop on the southeastern side of the Missaguash as far as Rivière Hébert.

Twenty-five hundred more reluctant *Acadiens* moved from Cobequid, Minas and Piziquid to Île Saint-Jean, Île Royale, and villages along Rivière Saint-Jean on the southwest coast of the Bay of Fundy.

The French governor of Île Saint-Jean reported that the refugees had left their ancestral homes under duress and with great regret, that they were impoverished, exhausted, suffering from exposure, and close to starvation upon their arrival.

Lieutenant-Colonel Lawrence returned to Beaubassin in September with seventeen small vessels, a force of 800 British troops, and Gorham's Rangers. They succeeded in driving La Corne, Le Loutre and the rest of their followers across the isthmus, and quickly built a blockhouse and barracks on a low hill southeast of the Missaguash River. The palisades of Fort Lawrence were erected within two days of their landing; the rest of the construction proceeded at a rapid pace.

Québec

The royal shipyard launched its new battleship *l'Orignal* on September 2, 1750, two years after its sister-ship *le Saint-Laurent* had been set afloat. But this exact copy of that fluyt sank shortly after it slipped into the water.

In preparation for the launch, two great anchors had been released in the middle of the river, each with two strong cables extending to two corners of a flat-bottomed barge. Three strong hawsers moored to the barge were spliced together into one strong triple hawser that was connected to the ship and should have held it afloat in the middle of the river. According to Jonquière's report to Minister Maurepas, the system failed to anchor the ship. *L'Orignal* struck a reef below Cap Diamant, thus breaking its keel, resulting in its near total loss.

French officials and engineers drove the financing, design, and expertise for all of Québec's naval projects. They never considered nor adapted to Canada's particular environmental conditions and resources.

René-Nicolas Levasseur, the able and conscientious head of royal shipbuilding and inspector of woods and forests in Canada, had faced mounting problems in his efforts to maintain high standards for quality production. Chronic shortages of qualified manpower inflated the payrolls because skilled workers had to be recruited from France. The widening search for the larger logs that the shipyard now required proved to be more costly; poorer quality wood was occasionally used. Intendant Bigot and his allies within the Québec administration had begun to make personal use of the shipyard's manpower and lumber, all at the king's expense.

French authorities complained about the increasing costs, yet Maurepas was pressured to replace the royal battleships the navy had lost through the d'Anville and Cap Finisterre disasters.

In spite of all these problems, workers immediately set up for the construction of the next battleship. Whatever they could salvage from the ill-fated *Orignal* would be used in the construction of the 72-gun *Algonquin*.

Bécancour

Louis and Anne Leclerc's daughter Marie-Josephte married Alexis Leblanc on October 4th. The reception was held in their new family home.

Antoine Ducharme answered many questions regarding the disastrous ship-launching in Québec.

"I was shocked to see that grand vessel sink so quickly and unexpectedly," he admitted. "Jean and I were both impressed two years ago when *le Saint-Laurent* smoothly slipped into the water. I can't imagine what caused this to happen to *l'Orignal* because the two ships were identical.

"I've heard rumors about the quality of the wood that was used, and a growing shortage of qualified workers at the yard, but that's been true for some time now."

"Could it be due to defective materials?" Louis asked.

"It may be a combination of problems. I suspect that the Québec shipyard is now called upon to build vessels that are larger than our Canadian resources can support. These last two ships are the biggest ever built in Nouvelle France and the next one will be even larger."

Québec

In November of 1750, Governor Jonquière ordered Charles Deschamps de Boishébert to restore and strengthen the fort on Rivière Saint-Jean. He also ordered Chevalier de La Corne to build a French fort on the southern end of Beauséjour Ridge, a little over one mile from the western edge of the Missaguash River and three miles west of Beaubassin.

La Corne's men felled timbers for the project throughout that winter with the help of the Acadian refugees who worked to provide shelter, winter clothing and provisions for their families.

France

Since his return to Versailles, former governor Galissonnière had repeatedly warned the French Ministry that the survival of the French colonies in America required the preservation of loyal native alliances, and that France must protect the overland link between Canada and Louisiana from British interference.

His memoir of December 1750 warned: "…it is of the utmost importance and of absolute necessity not to omit any means, nor spare any expense to secure Canada, inasmuch as that is the only way to wrest America from the ambition of the English, and as the progress of their empire in that quarter of the globe is what is most capable of contributing to their superiority in Europe."

Louis XV did not follow his counsel; Marquise de Pompadour had gradually seduced him away from his royal responsibilities with her many theatrical performances, intimate parties and suppers. The king's official mistress had revitalized the sense of intimacy and extravagance to the court in Versailles with her varied cultural activities and patronage of the arts. He had become so captivated by the bourgeoise that she was now his major counselor in matters of state. The marquise was particularly influenced by Voltaire who condescendingly belittled the value of the North American colonies.

Nouvelle France, 1751

Another typhus epidemic spread throughout the colony. Intendant Bigot prohibited anyone from practicing surgery and medicine in Canada without the approval of the king's surgeon in Québec.

Joseph's seven-month old son and namesake died on June 8th in Montréal. His sister Marguerite was distraught, having taken care of the infant's needs since his birth and his mother's death.

Four days later, Governor Jonquière granted their youngest brother René a permit to travel to the Strait of Mackinac with one six-man canoe and forbade him to trade for furs anywhere else but at that post and its dependencies.

Seven thousand Canadians, Hurons, and Ottawas now lived in and around Fort Michillimackinac. It had grown to be a vital link between Montréal and most of the western trade, therefore its fortifications were currently being strengthened.

Forges Saint-Maurice listed four hundred employees on its January payroll. In addition to providing all iron fittings and joining pieces for naval shipyards, this industry also produced valuable tools and equipment for the Canadian population.

The domestic production of cast-iron stoves had improved and they were now more commonly available. They required less firewood and heated homes more efficiently during the bitter Canadian winters through direct radiation from a system of stove pipes that eventually exhausted the smoke to the outside. However, the Canadian women continued to rely on their traditional fireplace hearths for meal preparation because the new stoves lacked ovens and cook-tops.

Louis and Simonne's family learned that their youngest brother, François had died the previous year in the Illinois territory of Louisiana. On March 10th, notary Pillard of Trois Rivières drew up and notarized a document by which Joseph and his sister Marguerite (Dame François Rochereau) gave up their rights of inheritance to their brother's estate.

Marguerite's brother-in-law Joseph Rochereau-Duvivier had held François' old promissory note to Jean Guillon since September 4, 1735 when Guillon had transferred it to him in payment of his own debt. Duvivier had occupied François' double-lot and home in Bécancour since shortly after his move to Illinois. He would now seek a separate agreement with the other brothers and sisters of the deceased.

(In 1720, Jean Guillon had married another Marguerite Provencher whose father was Sébastien *fils*. As cousin of the deceased, she was not present at this signing.)

Acadia

Actual construction of Fort Beauséjour did not begin until April of 1751. By the end of August, La Corne and his garrison had set up their headquarters and garrison in full view of Fort Lawrence. He began to fulfill the second part of his assignment by developing the construction plan for Fort Gaspareaux which his men would build at the other end of the isthmus, near the village of Baie-Verte. One hundred forty-two Acadian refugees had settled there following their forced migration from Beaubassin.

Québec

Reports continued to stream into the capital informing Governor Jonquière that Canada's hold on the Ohio Valley was slipping. The town of Pickawillany was known to be the center of trade and incitement against the French by English and Dutch traders, and their allied Miami chief Old Britain (*la Demoiselle*). The governor's plans to destroy that post had repeatedly failed due to insufficient military manpower and a marked decline of allied support.

Bécancour

Marguerite Moreau's thirty-eight-year old son Charles died in late December, surrounded by his seventy-one-year old mother, his twenty-six-year old wife Madeleine Desrosiers, two-year old daughter Angélique, forty-six-year old sister Marguerite, and twenty-nine-year old brother Joseph.

Two weeks later, after the formal presentation of Charles' estate inventory, Marguerite legally transferred her *donation viagère* to her youngest son Joseph who promised to manage the family properties and provide for those family members who continued to share the family homestead. All agreed that Madeleine Desrosiers and her daughter should continue to live with the family until she remarried.

Nouvelle France

A French Jesuit missionary in Manchuria had studied the use and healing powers of Asian ginseng, and had written a detailed description of the plant's physical characteristics and of its normal growth environment. Jesuit Father Lafitau, who lived among the Iroquois, had reasoned that growth conditions in Nouvelle France were similar to those described in China. Following a months-long search, the priest had discovered a similar root near Montréal in 1716.

American ginseng had long been used by many native Americans, including the Cherokee, Iroquois, Delaware, Creek, Pawnee and Sioux nations. The priest was surprised to learn that the Mohawks called the plant *garantoquen*, which translated to "man's image". The native name and use of American ginseng were similar to those of the Chinese population.

American ginseng was increasingly dug up by the natives of North America, and bartered with French, English, and Dutch fur traders for export to China. The commercial value of this herb was so great that its trade nearly surpassed hunting and trapping as a source of revenue. Nouvelle France exported a total of 500,000 pounds of ginseng in 1751.

Twenty-nine

Québec

Governor Jacques-Pierre Taffenel de la Jonquière died in Québec on March 2, 1752 at the age of sixty-seven, and was buried three days later, next to Frontenac, Callières, and Vaudreuil in l'Église des Récollets.

Charles Le Moyne *fils,* baron de Longueuil became interim governor of Nouvelle France.

In mid-April, King Louis XV accepted Jonquière's earlier request to be recalled to France, and the court named Ange Duquesne de Menneville as his successor. Based on his many conversations with former governor Galissonnière whose advice he highly respected, the king gave Duquesne several specific goals to achieve by whatever means possible in Nouvelle France. The new governor-general was to ensure the territorial integrity of the French empire in America, drive the British merchants from the Ohio territory, and establish peace with the native tribes who had been hostile toward the French since 1747. He was to seize Oswego if the British gave him cause for reprisal, and help Intendant Bigot establish tighter control over Canadian expenses. Colonial Minister Rouillé also ordered him to rely on Abbé Le Loutre in dealing with the Acadian problem.

Montréal

In mid-May, Sébastien's son René hired several more engagés to travel with him to Fort Michillimackinac.

The following week, two fires in as many days devastated the city of Trois Rivières. A soldier eventually admitted having set them in retaliation for his unjust imprisonment on false charges.

Ohio Valley

Young Charles Langlade and his friend Chief Pontiac arrived from *Baie-Verte* (Green Bay) in early morning of June 21st, with 250 Chippewas and Ottawas to attack the village of Pickawillany in retaliation for its Miami chief's insolent behavior toward the French fur trader.

Most of the 8,000 natives were away during the summer hunt so that only fourteen Miamis and their chief *La Demoiselle* were killed and three English traders captured during the brief skirmish. The raiders destroyed George Croghan's warehouse and torched the town and its crops. Langlade planned to personally deliver his English captives to the Québec governor.

The English did not strike back against the Canadians. The Miamis abandoned the site and moved west into present-day Indiana. This event convinced other Ohio nations that friendship and alliance with the French offered them more security. They believed that the English were either incapable or unwilling to protect their allies.

Several Montréal traders, including Joseph, felt secure enough that summer to hire engagés for a voyage to *poste de la Belle Rivière* on the Ohio River.

Paris

Border Commission representatives Galissionnière and Silhouette of France, Shirley and Mildmay of England, gave up their diplomatic efforts to settle the North American boundary disputes. French, English, and Spanish representatives had never wavered from their conflicting claims during their three years of negotiations.

Governor Shirley returned to Boston with his young Roman Catholic wife, the daughter of his Parisian landlord and was scorned by his colleagues.

Nouvelle France

Governor-General Marquis Duquesne de Menneville reached Québec in September and was highly critical of Longueuil's accomplishments as interim governor. Once Duquesne had familiarized himself with the colony's military resources, he developed a plan to raise and equip an army that could seize and occupy the upper waters of the Ohio.

Early in February 1753, the new governor assigned 1,000 troops under the command of Canadian Lieutenant Joseph Marin to secure the upper waters of the Ohio for France by constructing three strongly garrisoned forts. The canoe-builders of Trois Rivières worked overtime during the following three months to provide the means of transportation for this military expedition.

Duquesne mustered the colonial regulars and militia soon after the spring débâcle. He was particularly impressed by the discipline shown by the Canadian men, but puzzled by the angry reaction of the general population. The habitant families knew of no immediate danger to Nouvelle France, so they deeply resented his arbitrary withdrawal of so much manpower from the farms at this time of year. Many tried to incite the citizen-soldiers to rebel against his orders.

Bigot complained about the governor's growing military expenses for supplies and equipment, yet by the time Marin reached the southeastern Lake Erie in late spring, the Canadians were exhausted from portaging heavy and awkward nonmilitary baggage. Bigot had purchased velvets, silks, and other costly and useless articles at the King's expense, under the guise of providing essential trading goods and native gifts for the expedition.

Marin discovered a new and better route than the one Céloron de Blainville had followed. He and his men constructed their first fort on the shore of the protected harbor of Presqu'île (Erie, PA), and cut a road through the forest to Rivière-aux-Boeufs (French Creek) where they built Fort Le-Boeuf.

The expedition's size and coordination of activity awed the western natives who saw their lakes and rivers covered with bateaux and canoes. This generated several reports to Oswego that a French army of 6,000 was heading toward the Ohio country to drive off the English traders.

The Miami chief Half-King ordered the French to leave the area. Marin's haughty response humiliated him, thus winning the respect of the Miamis, Sacs, Ojibwas and Pottawattamies on the

Ohio River, and the Iroquois, Delawares, Shawanoes on the Allegheny.

Duquesne had designated the location of a third fort (Machault) at the junction of French Creek and the Allegheny River or closer to where the Allegheny River merged with the Ohio, but by September, Marin's officers were continuously grumbling about their work assignments. Sixty-three-year old Marin finally sent most of them back to Montréal and chose to remain at Fort Le-Boeuf to finish his assignment. He became gravely ill with dysentery.

Upon learning of his condition, Duquesne replaced him with Legardeur de Saint-Pierre who had recently returned from his three-year exploration of the far west where he had failed to reach beyond the route already established by the Vérendryes.

Marin's replacement arrived at Fort Le-Boeuf in late autumn with fresh food provisions and 500 troops. Saint-Pierre's instructions were to complete construction of all three forts, and once they were properly garrisoned, to send Marin's second-in-command down the Ohio River with the remaining troops to pacify the rest of the Ohio tribes

This last assignment failed because the epidemics of fever, lung disease and scurvy continued to spread among the French and Canadian troops. Three hundred of the healthiest men were left to garrison the two existing forts while the rest returned to Montréal. Governor Duquesne was shocked by their appearance.

London, August 1753

Lord Halifax revived Britain's claim to the Ohio country through the "right of conquest by subject Iroquois". He instructed Governor Dinwiddie to build English forts in the Ohio territory at colonial expense and to use force of arms if necessary to drive off the French incursion.

The Virginia Assembly refused to raise taxes to build, garrison, and support such forts.

Fort Le-Boeuf

Just after sunset of Dec 11th, twenty-one-year old George Washington, his Dutch interpreter, several Indians and five white men leading packhorses arrived on horseback to meet with fort

Commandant Saint-Pierre and deliver two letters from Governor Robert Dinwiddie. The first message introduced Washington as Adjutant-General of the provincial militia of Virginia. The second expressed the governor's written challenge against the French presence in the Ohio valley and called upon Saint-Pierre to withdraw his forces from British territory.

Fifty-two-year old Captain Saint-Pierre extended every courtesy to his English guests and invited the young officer to share an evening meal with him and his officers. He informed Washington that Dinwiddie's letters would be delivered to Governor-General Duquesne in Québec, but that he, Saint-Pierre, must await official instructions.

1754

Washington arrived in Williamsburg in mid-January to report the results of his mission to the British governor. Dinwiddie drafted a 200-man militia and placed George Washington in command with William Trent as his lieutenant. He ordered Trent to move quickly to build a fort on the Forks of the Ohio before the arrival of French reinforcements in the spring.

In mid-February, Trent and his fifty men reached the site where the Monongahela and the Allegheny rivers merged with the Ohio. They worked feverishly to establish the fort, hoping that Washington would arrive before the French with enough men to secure their position.

The Virginia governor tried to rouse the Indian tribes against the French. He reconvened the provincial assembly to obtain funding for 500 more men; the people's representatives granted less than he had asked and assigned its own committee to control its disbursement. Dinwiddie wrote to his London friend Hanbury, who served as agent for the Ohio Company, asking him to obtain more military support from the British government.

Dinwiddie asked the governors of New York and Massachusetts to wage a diversionary attack to lure the Canadian forces away from the Ohio. He requested direct aid from New Jersey and North Carolina. Pennsylvania refused to help. North Carolina provided enough funding to raise 400 recruits.

British officials believed that another North American war was imminent and urged provincial governors to prepare for the common defense. The king ordered his two independent companies of soldiers in New York and South Carolina to join the Virginia forces. The British Cabinet urged joint colonial action in negotiating treaties with the Indians to offset the growing French influence over the native tribes.

Forks of the Ohio

By early April, Captain Trent felt secure with the progress of the fort's construction. He left Ensign Ward in charge of supervising the remaining work while he traveled 140 miles to Will's Creek to replenish his supplies.

Two weeks later, a fleet of bateaux and canoes arrived by way of the Allegheny River and delivered over 500 French and native allies under the leadership of officer Pierre-Claude de Pégaudy de Contrecoeur. He aimed several cannon against the unfinished English fort and called for Ward's immediate surrender. The ensign complied. He and his fifty Virginians made their way back to Will's Creek.

Contrecoeur's men tore down the English structure and immediately began to replace it with a larger, stronger French fortification which would eventually grow to house a garrison of 1400 men and be called Fort Duquesne.

Cap-de-la-Madeleine

Jean-Baptiste Massé dit Beaumier, who had maintained, and raised his family on Bastien and Marguerite's original concession, died on April 17ᵗʰ at the age of sixty-seven.

Forks of the Ohio

The Virginia government considered the introduction of French cannon in this seizure as an act of war. Governor Dinwiddie sent twenty-two-year old Lieutenant-Colonel George Washington with 120 militiamen to expel the French from the Ohio valley.

Contrecoeur, who had replaced Legardeur de Saint-Pierre as commander of Fort Duquesne, sent young Ensign Coulon de Jumonville with an escort of 34 men to remind the Virginians that they were on French territory. The ensign was to deliver a written directive to the provincial officer, ordering him to withdraw his troops from the domain of the King of France, and threaten the use of force if he failed to comply.

Without warning on May 27th, Washington and his Virginians attacked "a French scouting party" that had raised his suspicions in the Ohio Valley. Jumonville and ten Canadians were killed, twenty-two captured, and one escaped to Fort Duquesne to report the incident. Washington withdrew quickly to build up his defenses in Great Meadows.

The escapee's report to Contrecoeur led the French to believe that Washington had ordered his men to open fire while Jumonville was reading the diplomatic declaration, that Jumonville had been assassinated.

French outrage fomented plans to retaliate. The Québec governor asked Langlade to raise an army of Indian warriors to help defend Fort Duquesne at the Forks of the Ohio River.

Although war had not been officially declared by France or Great Britain, it had already broken out in North America over the issue of their undefined colonial boundaries.

Europe

Both European powers lacked strong political and military leadership. British Duke of Newcastle was generally regarded as more of a politician than an able administrator. No French king had ever taken a bourgeoise as his official mistress until Jeanne-Antoinette Poisson entered Louis XV's life. He granted her the title of Madame de Pompadour and she ultimately became his closest advisor in Versailles, inordinately influenced government appointments and decisions, and monitored military activity to the extent of sending scoldings and directives to generals on the battlefield. This did not bode well for France in the coming years.

While England had built up its navy to more than 200 warships; France had little more than 100. England had reduced its army to 18,000 soldiers; France had nearly ten times as many.

France needed time to increase its navy, reinforce its garrisons in America, and strengthen its colonial defenses. England's policy was to block its adversary's ability to defend its colonial empire and its mercantile efforts to compete globally in Europe, India and Africa, as well as in the western hemisphere.

Albany Congress

Representatives from seven of the British colonies met in Albany with forty leaders of the Iroquois Confederation on a daily basis from June 19 to July 11, 1754 to improve mutual relations and devise common defensive measures against the French threat.

Mohawk Chief Hendrick and William Johnson of New York managed to repair the Covenant Chain, an alliance between the Five Nations and the English provinces that had been seriously neglected during the previous three years.

Benjamin Franklin praised the Iroquois confederation as a union of strength and persuaded the provincial representatives to emulate it by approving his proposed Albany Plan of Union. It was unanimously approved by the twenty-one representatives of New York, Pennsylvania, Maryland, Massachusetts, Rhode Island, Connecticut, and New Hampshire.

The Crown rejected the plan because it transferred too much power to the colonies. The colonial legislatures opposed it because it required them to give up too much of their provincial power to a centralized Grand Council.

Discord continued unresolved between the British provincial governors, and between the British governors and their own provincial legislatures. Governor Dinwiddie of Virginia finally appealed to the home government to levy a tax by Act of Parliament so that he could properly develop and maintain proper colonial defenses. He begged the London government for arms, ammunition, and two infantry regiments to protect Virginia from French and Indian forces who terrorized its western frontier.

Cap-de-la-Madeleine

Two months after the death of his uncle Jean-Baptiste Massé-Beaumier, Louis and Simonne's son Joseph signed over his grandparents' original homestead to his niece Josephte Barette and her husband Alexis Bigot-Dorval who had married four years earlier.

Nearly a century after their immigration to Nouvelle France, Bastien and Marguerite's original concession and family home in Cap-de-la-Madeleine passed on to their great-granddaughter.

London

On June 26, 1754, Newcastle's inner cabinet resolved to defend Britain's North American colonies "from French invasion" in Nova Scotia and in the Ohio valley.

Fort Necessity

Coulon de Villiers marched to Washington's Fort Necessity in Great Meadows on July 3rd, to avenge his younger brother's death. He had already visited the place of ambush. The bodies of Jumonville and his men still lay unburied, exposed to animal scavengers.

Washington's provincial troops withstood twenty-four hours of exposure to heavy rain and a nine-hour siege against their makeshift defensive barrier before they finally succumbed to exhaustion. His Mingo allies informed him that they would leave early the following morning.

The young officer signed a French document of capitulation on July 4th that stated his guilt in the assassination of officer Jumonville. He learned later that his Dutch translator Captain Vanbraam had misinterpreted the term *l'assassinat du Sieur de Jumonville* as "the death of Sieur de Jumonville".

Washington and his force retreated from the Ohio valley, leaving captains Robert Stobo and Jacob Vanbraam hostage pending the return within two months of all captives taken during the surprise attack upon Jumonville's party.

Three weeks later, two Delaware chiefs smuggled Captain Stobo's map and full description of Fort Duquesne's defenses to Philadelphia.

Governor Dinwiddie did not release the French captives.

Nicolet

Jean-Baptiste Belleville died at his home on *Isle-de-la-Fourche* on September 8th at the age of fifty-one, having suffered from lung disease since his early-winter evacuation from Fort-aux-Boeufs.

Louis', Sébastien's and Francois Ducharme's sons and grandsons attended the funeral and family reception, and discussed events in the Ohio valley. Everyone expressed growing concern over the rising conflict with the English. Although militia duty had been revived and become more intense under Governor Duquesne, these young men had not yet been called to duty.

London

That same day, Newcastle received the news of Washington's surrender. The British Board of Trade and Ministry discussed the need for unified action by the American provinces and considered the appointment of a military commander-in-chief who would be financed by the colonies. The prime minister consulted with the Minister of War, the Duke of Cumberland who had led the British army during and following the Battle of Culloden. The duke recommended General Edward Braddock.

Acadia

Brigadier-General Charles Lawrence was appointed Lieutenant-Governor of Nova Scotia on October 21st. Upon learning of the French-English battle in the Ohio valley, Lawrence demanded that the "French Neutrals" accept the unconditional oath of allegiance to the British Crown. When they refused to do so, he prohibited them from shipping grain to Île Saint-Jean and the fortress of Louisbourg.

When the habitants of Piziquid refused to cut wood for nearby Fort Edward, its commandant Captain Alexander Murray ordered the arrest of their priest and his imprisonment in Halifax. He also enforced the grain embargo by seizing all Acadian bateaux and canoes in that district.

London

King George II of Great Britain made his opening speech to Parliament on November 14th, 1754. He congratulated the members on the prevailing peace, and recommended that measures be taken to improve it by protecting the colonial possessions that provided much of the country's wealth.

Parliament responded by greatly increasing that year's military budget, appointing Major-General Braddock as commander-in-chief of British expeditionary forces in North America. They also appointed Sir John Sinclair as quartermaster-general to prepare the way for a four-pronged campaign against Canadian incursions into British North America.

Two 500-man regiments of foot prepared to sail for Virginia where each would be strengthened by the addition of 200 provincial enlistees who would be armed and clothed at the king's expense.

Boston

Based on their successful expedition against Louisbourg in 1745, Governor William Shirley and Sir William Pepperrell received orders in December 1754 to raise two provincial regiments of a thousand men each from New England and the mid-Atlantic region, and rendezvous in Boston. These orders also dictated the establishment of a common fund by the provinces to pay for their defense needs, and appointed Governor Shirley of Massachusetts to lead all provincial military operations.

Thirty

1755

The 44th and 48th British regiments boarded their transport ships in Cork, Ireland and sailed to America in mid-January. General Braddock arrived in Hampton, Virginia at the end of February. His troops set up camp near Alexandria.

Fort Duquesne

In mid-March, Governor Duquesne ordered newly-commissioned Ensign Langlade to enlist his old friend Chief Pontiac and his warriors to reinforce the French garrison at the Forks of the Ohio. Langlade successfully rallied his western allies and led them to the fort.

Alexandria, Virginia

General Braddock joined his troops at the end of March and called a council of war to meet with representatives of all the English provinces.

On April 14th, governors Dinwiddie of Virginia, Shirley of Massachusetts, Dobbs of North Carolina, Morris of Pennsylvania, Sharpe of Maryland, and Delancey of New York met with the renowned British general and listened intently as Braddock outlined the British Secretary of War's strategic plans for eliminating the French colonial presence in North America.

The council agreed to launch simultaneous attacks on four separate fronts: General Braddock and his two British regiments against Fort Duquesne in the Ohio valley; Shirley, Pepperell and their two new provincial regiments against Fort Niagara on Lake Ontario; Colonel William Johnson, his faithful Mohawk allies, and other provincial troops from New England, New York and New Jersey against Fort Saint-Frédéric in the Lake Champlain area; British Lieutenant-Colonel Monckton and other New England troops to seize Fort Beauséjour and end the border dispute in old Acadia.

Although war had not yet been declared, London officials approved and justified these military objectives on the premise that they were all located on British soil that had been illegally invaded and occupied by the French.

Ohio Valley campaign

General Braddock assembled his troops on April 20th and marched them toward Will's Creek where the British quartermaster had ordered provisions and equipment to be delivered for the general's campaign.

His army consisted of 1400 regimental soldiers, 30 sailors, and 450 Virginians who were drilled by the British officers.

Braddock's military objectives were to free English access to lands beyond the Allegheny Mountains all the way to the Mississippi River, and sever overland communications between Nouvelle France and Louisiana. He was then expected to work his way north to destroy French forts all the way to Niagara.

Brest, France - spring 1755

French officials knew of the major British troop movement to America and prepared their colonial defense on a larger scale. Eighteen warships of Admiral Du Bois de la Motte's fleet awaited sea duty at Brest and Rochefort. On May 3rd, six battalions drawn from the metropolitan regiments of *La Reine, Bourgogne, Languedoc, Guyenne, Artois, and Béarn* embarked for Nouvelle France. Baron Jean-Armand Dieskau was to command these 3,752 *Troupes de Terre*.

Newly appointed Governor-General Pierre de Rigaud de Vaudreuil also embarked that day. He had been highly recommended by his fellow Canadians who believed that he could restore the security his French father had once provided the colony.

A squadron of nine ships under the command of Admiral MacNamara escorted the fleet to the open sea until it was presumably safe from British interception.

At sea

The British court kept well-informed of the French fleet's preparations from mid-April through May 9th. Its long series of delays gave Admiral Boscawen and his eleven battleships the opportunity to arrive near the southern coast of Newfoundland ahead of the French, and lie in wait for their fleet's approach into American waters. Rear-Admiral Holbourne joined Boscawen a few weeks later with seven more British warships.

Ohio Valley campaign

Braddock moved his forces up the Potomac and arrived at Will's Creek on May 10th. Sir John Sinclair had transformed the old Ohio Company trading post into Fort Cumberland. Braddock's provisions for his army, horses, wagons, and forage had not been delivered. Sinclair was as irate as the general for he had personally negotiated the procurement contracts that winter.

Braddock's first encounter with the provincial soldiers and Indian warriors gave him little confidence in their military capability because of their lack of martial discipline.

Rather than the 15 miles of mountainous terrain he had been told to expect, more than 50 miles of steep forested ridges loomed ahead of him.

The general's forces were to travel overland with the aid of 600 baggage and artillery horses but the Allegheny mountains offered no natural grass forage for the animals.

Boston

Colonel Robert Monckton assembled his 270 British regulars and 2000 New England recruits when British muskets arrived on May 20th. He informed his men that their mission was to seize Fort Beauséjour on the Isthmus of Chignectou.

Two days later, he and his troops boarded forty-one provincial sloops and schooners and sailed to Nova Scotia under escort by Captain John Rous' three small frigates. They arrived at Annapolis Royal another two days later to rendezvous with 300 British regulars on three transport ships, and a battle-sloop carrying an artillery detachment from Halifax. The combined fleet sailed toward the head of the Bay of Fundy that following week.

Ohio Valley campaign

George Washington had accepted General Braddock's invitation to join him as aide-de-camp on this campaign, but business and family matters had delayed his arrival at Fort Cumberland until May 30th.

Although speed and timing were vital for the simultaneous launching of all four military thrusts, Braddock waited through weeks of delays. Long-standing procurement contracts signed months earlier by British quartermaster-general John Sinclair for the delivery of wagons, horses, provisions of food and forage were only partially honored. Braddock complained bitterly about this series of setbacks until Benjamin Franklin managed to procure for him 150 wagons and a large number of horses from his fellow Pennsylvanians. Among the wagoners was young Daniel Boone.

General Braddock faced an enormous challenge in moving such a large army of men, equipment, provisions, and heavy cannon across the densely wooded and mountainous terrain of western Virginia.

Although he had often conducted such military campaigns in Europe, he had never encountered this difficult a route. Progress was painfully slow as John Sinclair's 300 axmen broadened the packhorse trail that Washington had used in October 1753. This new 12-foot-wide road through the virgin forest eased the movement of Braddock's four-mile-long train of packhorses and horse-drawn wagons that were heavily loaded with supplies and cannon.

Halifax, Nova Scotia

While Monckton and his provincial army sailed toward Beauséjour, Governor Lawrence dispatched Captain Alexander Murray with 200 British regulars and New England rangers to seize all Acadian arms and ammunition in the villages of Piziquid, Grand Pré, and Riviere-aux-Canards. They spread out under cover of darkness on June 2nd, and simultaneously surprised all of the inhabitants to seize 400 muskets and small arms at midnight.

Two days later, Lawrence publicly proclaimed that in the future, any French inhabitant caught carrying a firearm would be considered a rebel against the British crown. The *Acadiens* surrendered close to 3,000 additional weapons.

Fort Beauséjour

A protégé and close associate of Québec's Intendant François Bigot, Captain Louis Duchambon de Vergor commanded the district of Beauséjour and its palisaded fort housing a garrison of 165 French officers and regulars armed with twenty-six artillery pieces. Although it had been built to accommodate a garrison of 800, it presently held a force of 200 *Troupes de Marine* and Canadians.

Commissaire-Ordonnateur Thomas Pichon was a man of divided loyalties, a literate and ambitious man who lacked the French political connections necessary for further advancement in his professional life. He had maintained a secret correspondence with Lieutenant-Colonel George Scott of Beaubassin throughout his two years at Beauséjour, thus keeping the British well-informed of ongoing French military activities and Abbé Le Loutre's manipulation of the refugees from Beaubassin.

Before dawn of June 2nd, Commandant Vergor received a report that an English fleet loaded with English provincial soldiers and militiamen had stationed itself just five miles from Beauséjour, that it appeared to be waiting for the turn of the tide to enter the Bay of Chignectou.

Vergor dispatched emergency calls for aid to Québec, Rivière Saint-Jean, Louisbourg and Île Saint-Jean, and ordered all able-bodied habitants of the Beauséjour district to assist in the defense of the fort. Three hundred armed *Acadiens*, a small portion of the district's population, reluctantly responded to his call.

Most Beaubassin exiles, including the Cormier and Cyr families, had already abandoned their new farms and fled into the woods upon hearing of the English fleet's arrival.

They knew that provisions had been sent from Québec during the past five years to feed and assist them after their forced exodus from across the Missaguash, but very little had been distributed to the most needy. These *Acadiens* had learned not to trust Vergor nor Abbé Le Loutre who was known to be present in the fort. The priest had been driving them to build dikes to turn the surrounding marshes into rich farmland as their ancestors had done in Beaubassin, had drawn them away from strengthening the fort's defenses against English attack.

The priest's destruction of their fourth-generation farms had taught the refugees to maintain an emergency food supply regardless of the size of their harvests. In anticipation of the torching of their second village, the women and older children had quickly collected their food cache, blankets, extra clothing, and whatever cooking utensils they could comfortably carry. The men and boys had gathered their concealed weapons, powder, ammunition, and tools.

While most of the refugees headed towards the northeastern end of the isthmus to cross over to Île Saint-Jean, the Cormier and Cyr patriarchs led their clans deeper into the inland forest. They merged with a larger group of refugees who moved northwest along the Petitcoudiac River toward a village of that name.

Late that afternoon of June 2nd, the English fleet's provincial escort laid anchor at the entrance to the Bay of Chignectou and the transports were run aground close to Fort Lawrence, across the bay and within sight of Beauséjour. The New England volunteers and British soldiers disembarked about an hour later to set up camp.

Two days later, 2000 Massachusetts provincial soldiers struck their tents and lined up in marching order with four short six-pounder field guns and one 13-inch mortar trailing behind them. The Acadian dikes of Beaubassin had been neglected during the past five years; the marsh had recovered enough to slow down the English army's movement south of the Missaguash River. They reached a demolished bridge which Winslow ordered his men to restore for the crossing of the artillery.

Vergor watched their labored movement from inside his wooden fort with his 150 *Troupes de la Marine*, a dozen artillerymen, and the 300 local Acadian conscripts. He had repeatedly discounted his military engineer's counsel: had not heeded his warning that lack of merchant traffic at Beaubassin meant an impending attack against Beauséjour, had not built a series of redoubts on the nearby height of land as extra defense for the fort, and had disregarded Acadian warnings from the Annapolis district that a New England expedition was forming for such an attack.

Five years earlier, Acadian refugees from Beaubassin had built their new settlement on the north side of the river between the marsh they were now diking, and the French fort. Their sixty empty buildings and a church stood directly in the path of the English advance. Vergor ordered that all provisions and cattle left in the barns and dwellings be brought into the fort, and that all wooden structures be torched to deprive the enemy of shelter.

The Acadian refugees watched from the distance as heavy black smoke rose above their former settlement and gray ash settled over the district.

Ohio Valley campaign

Braddock left Fort Cumberland on June 10th and set out with his regulars and provincials on their journey to Fort Duquesne.

At sea

Admiral La Motte's fleet evaded the combined British armada so that most of them made their way safely to Louisbourg and Québec, however, a stormy sea and fog had isolated three of his ships near Cape Race. The British caught up with them when the weather cleared on June 10th.

The *Dunkirk* came abreast of *l'Alcide*. Captain Hocquart asked Captain Howe: "Are we at peace or at war?"

Later French reports quoted Howe's reply as: *"La paix! La paix!"*

Soon after, the British fired a broadside at the French vessel, killing or wounding seven French officers and eighty crewmen. Return fire killed seven Englishmen and wounded twenty-seven. Several more British cannonades disabled the French vessel and forced it to surrender.

A second French vessel, *le Lis* was also seized while *le Dauphin* managed to escape into the fog and reach Louisbourg.

French losses amounted to several officers and eight companies of the *La Reine* and *Languedoc* battalions. Governor Vaudreuil's younger brother François-Pierre de Rigaud, known by the Canadians as *Monsieur de Rigaud*, was taken prisoner to Halifax then to England.

Great Britain and France were now embroiled in an undeclared war in North American waters.

Fort Beauséjour

Monckton's engineers prepared to set up their siege cannons on a small hill north of the fort. The French engineer officer led 150 men against the enemy's attempt to seize the high ground; 500

Englishmen drove them back and began to dig their trenches that evening under repeated but ineffective French cannon fire.

On June 10th, British soldiers labored at opening a road through the marsh to ease the movement of their artillery closer to the target. Within the next forty-eight hours, they dug siege trenches after dark, slowly extending these to within 700 feet of the walls. They moved 13-inch mortars ever closer to the fort, began to lob fireballs over its palisades, and settled in to wage a long siege.

The reluctant *Acadiens* inside the fort knew what their fate would be if the English succeeded in their attack. Vergor assured them that reinforcements were on the way, but just as the siege began, French couriers arrived from Louisbourg to inform Vergor that their commander could not assist him because Gasparus Bay was under British naval blockade.

Word spread quickly through the ranks of soldiers and *Acadiens*. No one expected help to arrive in time from Québec. Since the English were approaching only one side of the fort, many slipped over the other three walls that night to join other refugees deep in the forest.

On June 16, 1755, Le Loutre, Vergor, and several other officers were dining in one of the two bomb-proof munition shelters when they heard and felt a powerful explosion. Seven French officers were killed when a British fireball happened to roll through the open doorway of the other shelter, exploded and ignited its stored powder and ammunition.

Vergor, son of the commandant of Louisbourg who had surrendered the fortress of Louisbourg to Great Britain in 1745, yielded Fort Beauséjour in 1755, thus forever settling the international dispute over the land boundaries of ancient Acadia. The English took possession of the fort that evening, four days after they had started digging their trenches.

Vergor swore that he had compelled the captured *Acadiens* to take up arms and defend the fort under threat of execution; they were pardoned and released with those of their families who had sought shelter with them. During the confusion, Abbé Le Loutre dressed as a woman and fled to Baie Verte with the released *Acadiens*, hoping to reach Québec by ship.

The entire garrison swore not to bear arms in America during the next six months and were permitted to march out with their guns and personal belongings, flags flying and drums beating.

Their commander retired with honor. Colonel Monckon planned to evacuate these troops to Louisbourg on provincial ships.

Colonel Monckton named his prize Fort Cumberland, and dispatched Lieutenant-Colonel Winslow with 500 men to seize Fort Gaspereaux which was located twelve miles to the northeast near Baie Verte. This was accomplished the following day.

Lieutenant-Governor Lawrence further tightened British control over the district of Chignectou. He ordered Monckton to immediately distribute a proclamation in French to all *Acadiens* of Chignectou and the rivers of Chipoudy Bay which declared that since most of them had not yet submitted to the British king, they must report immediately to the British camp to give up all their firearms, swords, sabers, pistols, and other weapons or else they would be executed.

When asked for his advice, Pichon encouraged the habitants to trust the British. Within one week, several hundred *Acadiens* voluntarily surrendered the weapons they had considered vital for the protection of their families and livestock. They were then ordered to clear away the rubble, repair the fort, and prepare to take the unconditional British oath.

Ohio Valley campaign

By June 18, 1755, General Braddock had traveled less than 30 miles from Fort Cumberland to reach Little Meadows. Fever and dysentery had spread among the men, lack of proper forage had already weakened the horses, and travel on the rugged road had slowed the progress of their wagons to three miles a day.

The commander-in-chief continued to struggle with the logistics of moving 2200 men, and a four-mile long train of over 600 packhorses and horse-drawn baggage- and artillery-wagons.

When they received news that 500 French regulars were en route to reinforce Fort Duquesne, George Washington recommended to the general that he move forward with a vanguard of their fittest soldiers, minimal artillery, provisions, wagons and packhorses, and leave the more cumbersome part of the caravan to follow at its own pace. Braddock accepted his advice and placed the rear supply division under the command of Colonel Dunbar.

Engineer John Sinclair directed the large group of axmen who continued to clear the road. Lieutenant-Colonel Thomas Gage led the advance column of well-armed metropolitan and provincial soldiers ahead of a train of thirty wagons and a large number of packhorses. Yet again, British preoccupation with smoothing the way and building bridges for the passage of troops and horses slowed down their progress to three miles a day.

Québec

Baron de Dieskau and his *Troupes de Terre* arrived in Nouvelle France on June 22, 1755, in time to greet Governor-General Vaudreuil upon his own arrival from France three days later. During their consultations with Governor Duquesne, the outgoing French official demonstrated little respect or patience toward his Canadian-born replacement.

Rivière Saint-Jean

Captain John Rous sailed from Chignectou on June 23rd to escort the transport of Beauséjour officers and garrison to Louisbourg. He was well-acquainted with the area, having been second-in-command of the provincial fleet at Louisbourg in 1745.

One week later, Rous sailed with three 20-gun ships and a sloop to seize the French fort at the outlet of Rivière Saint-Jean, on the western shore of the Bay of Fundy.

As soon as Boishébert and his small French garrison spotted the overpowering English naval presence, they burst their cannon, blew up their magazine, and led the French settlers and Acadian refugees upriver where English ships could not follow.

The British thus gained access to the mainland and seized control over all of "ancient Acadia".

Québec

Small fishing and merchant vessels loaded with despondent Acadian refugees began to arrive from Île Saint-Jean; among them was Abbé Le Loutre who was still dressed in women's clothing. Governor Vaudreuil received their tragic reports of the loss of Fort Beauséjour, the blockade of Louisbourg, and the increasing severity of their treatment by British authorities.

Thirty-one

Halifax - summer 1755

Several serious concerns confronted Lieutenant-Governor Lawrence: British authorities fully expected that the French would make a determined effort to recover Acadia; the Nova Scotian capital and port of Halifax was particularly vulnerable to naval attack; the *Acadiens* remained disaffected, had repeatedly refused to take the unqualified oath of allegiance even though most of them had been born under the British flag.

The governor called a meeting of his provincial councilors: Benjamin Green, son of a rector in Salem Massachusetts, who held commercial interests between Halifax and Boston; John Rous, former privateer out of Boston and chief naval officer of Nova Scotia; Jonathan Belcher, the first chief justice of Nova Scotia and son of a former Massachusetts governor; Charles Morris, born and raised in Boston, with military service in Minas, and one of the first settlers in Halifax; John Collier, a retired army officer, recently arrived from England; William Cotterell, also recently arrived from England and serving as secretary to Governor Lawrence. These men unanimously concluded that all Acadians must surrender their weapons and boats to the nearest fort commander.

The governor increasingly threatened the liberty and property of the French inhabitants in order to pressure them into signing the unabridged oath.

Conditioned as they had been through five generations of neutral isolation, the *Acadiens* persisted in their refusal to take up arms against Great Britain, France, or the Mi'kmaqs.

Monckton's early seizure of Beauséjour had empowered governors Lawrence and Shirley to carry out a plan they had mutually considered over a long period of time, one that had first been proposed by Samuel Vetch in 1709, and reiterated by Commodore Peter Warren in 1746. It had been further developed by Charles Morris, the official land surveyor and census taker of Nova Scotia who had drawn a complete map of the Acadian settlements in Nova Scotia in 1748 to determine what areas remained open for the settlement of Protestant immigrants.

Morris had argued in 1751 that the province would never be secure if the "French Neutrals" continued to hold its "chief granary and all the water communication". Three summers later, he had submitted to the governor and council a detailed comprehensive plan for the swift, efficient, and permanent deportation of all the French inhabitants from Nova Scotia.

In June 1755, Lawrence and Shirley finally had the manpower and resources to implement that project. Approximately 2500 well-armed British and New England soldiers under king's pay would remain under their joint command until the end of the year. New England sea captains and merchants could provide the transport ships. Nova Scotia's royal subsidy account would finance the deportation.

Fort Duquesne

Commandant Contrecoeur's health continued to deteriorate while he waited for his replacement. The garrison of this formidable wooden fortress consisted of a few companies of regular troops, and a considerable number of Canadian militiamen drawn from the districts of Montréal and Trois Rivières. Eight hundred native warriors were encamped nearby, including mission Iroquois and Hurons from the Saint Lawrence River valley, members of several tribes from the northern lakes area under Charles Langlade, others from the Ohio valley, and Chief Pontiac's Ottawa followers from Détroit.

An enemy deserter had recently informed Contrecoeur that British General Edward Braddock was moving towards Fort

Duquesne with a force of 3,000 soldiers and a dozen 18-pounder cannon to besiege the French.

The fort's newly-appointed commandant, Captain Daniel de Beaujeu arrived at the end of June with deliveries of wheat, fourteen dozen muskets, bullets and gunpowder. Beaujeu agreed that Contrecoeur should remain in command during the immediate crisis.

They decided to avoid the full brunt of a British siege by setting up an ambush at the second English crossing of the Monongahela River. Beaujeu and his captains Dumas and Lignery recruited 637 warriors to join their 246 French regulars and Canadian militia volunteers in setting up the ambuscade.

Albany - early July

William Johnson and William Shirley arrived in Albany to gather and provision their respective armies. Neither man had any previous professional military experience.

Johnson's mission was to gain control of the traditional invasion route between Albany and Montréal by seizing Fort Saint-Frédéric at Crown Point. He planned to ascend the Hudson River by bateaux with his 3,000 provincial soldiers and Mohawks to reach Wills Creek where Phineas Lyman and his English troops continued the conversion of the Ohio Company's old trading post into a fortified military supply base. Johnson contracted with a group of English merchants in Albany to supply and deliver his army's provisions to Fort Lyman at Wills Creek.

Shirley's first military mission was to destroy Fort Niagara in order to establish English control over Lake Ontario, sever Canadian communication links with French forts and settlements to the west and south, free English access to the upper Great Lakes, and gain control over the secondary invasion route down the upper Saint-Lawrence River to Montréal.

General Braddock's promotion of Sir William Pepperrell to Major-General in the British army prevented him from leading his 51st provincial regiment as its colonel in the field. Provincial Major-General Shirley then took command of both the 50th and the 51st, yet he doubted that this force would be strong enough for the Niagara expedition when reports came in of a French military buildup at Fort Frontenac. As commander of the provincial forces in North America, he transferred Colonel Peter Schuyler's New Jersey regiment from Johnson's campaign to his own.

Shirley planned to seize Fort Frontenac within a week after his arrival by transporting his army directly across 50 miles of Lake Ontario in row-galleys, whaleboats, and two English sloops: the 12-gun *Ontario* and the 5-gun *Oswego* that were currently based on the lake's southern shore. Once he had canceled the only French threat against his base, he planned to sail two captured French ships against Fort Niagara, another Canadian gateway to the Ohio valley and the West.

The Massachusetts governor and general awarded his army supply contract to the partnership of Peter Van Burgh Livingston and Lewis Morris, Jr. with whom he shared various political connections. He chose Livingston's other partner William Alexander as his secretary to handle purchases and disbursements of wages and provisions during the Niagara campaign.

In his capacity as Superintendent of Indian Affairs, Johnson disapproved of Shirley's choices; he had recently chastised these same Dutch merchants for their unfair dealings with the Mohawks. He was also understandably upset over his campaign's loss of the 500 "Jersey Blues".

The English traders, whose profitable smuggling trade between Albany and Montréal had been disrupted by Shirley, now found themselves excluded from Shirley's highly profitable army contracts. They joined together to retaliate against Shirley by frustrating Alexander's efforts at his supply base in Albany.

Lake Ontario campaign

Shirley reached the Great Carrying Place at the intersection of the Hudson and Mohawk rivers with 2,000 regulars of the 50th and 51st provincial regiments, 400 New Jersey provincials, 50 Albany scouts, and 100 Indians. He assigned a company of Pepperrell's regiment to garrison the portage site, and another 350 regulars in Schenectady to guard the expedition's supply lines.

Monongahela River

British Lieutenant-Colonel Gage and his advance guard had reached within 12 miles from Fort Duquesne as they approached their first crossing of the Monongahela River on July 7, 1755.

Braddock's main force marched in parade formation a few miles behind them, with fife and drum, flying banners, mounted officers, light cavalry, red-coats, blue-coats, wagons, cannon, howitzers, mortars, a train of packhorses, and a cattle drive. Their cacophony of sounds resonated through the virgin forest, set wild animals to flight, and cast a feeling of dread among its native inhabitants.

Captain Beaujeu failed to set up the ambush as scheduled because 300 of his more reluctant warriors had left his command and did not rejoin him until after Gage and his men had forded the second river crossing. The Canadian officer's smaller force reached within one mile short of the Monongahela and about 8 miles from Fort Duquesne when they had a surprise encounter with the British at midday of July 9th.

Beaujeu was killed by the third disciplined British volley. Captain Dumas immediately took command to rally the French and allied warriors. They followed Charles Langlade and his allies into the surrounding forest to escape the formal fusillades. The Canadians and their allies positioned themselves behind the trees, and encircled the uniformed British regulars in a deadly crossfire.

Shrill native war whoops echoed endlessly from the gloomy woods. British officers struggled to keep their lines of musketeers on the road. The metropolitan regulars could not see the enemy, were totally unprepared for this type of warfare; they shot back at puffs of smoke and sounds of gunfire while fellow soldiers died all around them.

Colonel Gage brought forward his two cannons and fired grapeshot toward the elusive snipers. Most of the hundred young Canadian militiamen retreated, but the warriors and the more experienced colonials continued their deadly fire against the redcoats who now huddled together in large compact groups and fired aimlessly in all directions.

At the first sound of gunfire, General Braddock had galloped forward and into the fray, leading his main force to support Gage's troops. He arrived just as the British artillerymen abandoned their cannons and began to retreat from their deadly entrapment.

Confusion and panic continued to rise on the British side. The Virginians broke formation and individually resorted to their more familiar forest warfare tactics. The British general was outraged.

He shouted orders, stubbornly beat the provincials and his soldiers with the flat of his sword, forcing them to line up and fire their muskets in disciplined European fashion.

Two horses were shot down from under George Washington, four from under Braddock who suffered a mortal wound through the upper arm and into his lungs. His officers evacuated him to safety across the river and propped him up in sitting position against a tree. He continued to direct his officers, and dispatched Washington to Dunbar's camp for additional manpower, wagons, provisions and medical support.

The three-hour Battle of Monongahela ended with a complete rout of the British metropolitan forces. They ran out of ammunition and fled towards Dunbar's camp, ahead of a wild Indian pursuit.

Officers Dumas and Lignery did not join the chase, but reassembled their remaining troops and rested amid a scene of desolation. Red and blue uniformed bodies covered the field of battle.

Later on, the French and Canadians rummaged through the British train of field artillery, munitions, baggage, and provisions that extended down the road. They found a cache of approximately 25,000 English-pounds worth of silver, and a campaign chest filled with General Braddock's official military correspondence.

The officers headed back to Fort Duquesne with their remaining troops, the hoard of silver, and the general's papers, having agreed to return later with fresh troops, horses and oxen to identify and bury their dead, and salvage the enemy's abandoned cannon and wagons.

British forces had lost 63 of their 86 officers; only 459 of their 1373 soldiers escaped unharmed. Washington wrote to Governor Dinwiddie: "Our poor Virginians behaved like men, and died like soldiers…I believe that out of three companies (150 men) who were there that day, scarce thirty (men) were left alive." He estimated that "two-thirds of those killed and wounded were shot by panicked British soldiers who gathered together ten to twelve deep and shot indiscriminately."

The French reported three officers and forty men killed or wounded.

Great Meadows

Colonel Dunbar shouted orders to his troops as soon as the first exhausted, terror-stricken fugitives streamed into his camp with reports of the military debacle. His drummers beat the call to arms, his soldiers prepared to evacuate the campsite, and the Dutch wagoners fled.

By the time Braddock arrived, wagons, stores, and ammunition had already been burnt or destroyed. Over one hundred wagons still smoldered. Soldiers frantically burst or buried cannons, mortars, and shells, scattered gunpowder and provisions throughout the woods and swamps.

Further retreat had already begun. Dunbar led the demoralized troops across 60 miles of rugged country toward Fort Cumberland at Will's Creek. Officers carried the dying general as gently as they could on an improvised litter. "Who would have thought?" were among General Braddock's last recorded words. He died near Great Meadows on the fourth day of the final march and was secretly buried in the middle of the night under what later became known as Braddock's Road. Evidence of the site was deliberately trampled beyond recognition by the doleful traffic of withdrawal.

Dunbar withdrew his own troops beyond Will's Creek and led them back to Philadelphia. The governors and frontier settlers of Virginia and Pennsylvania were outraged and fearful; rather than extend their western frontiers, the British campaign had rendered their provinces more vulnerable to enemy attack from the west. Their outer settlements were completely defenseless now that the western forts had been abandoned. Braddock's Road offered the French and Indians a cleared path east through the forest and over the mountains.

Fort Duquesne

Contrecoeur was finally able to relinquish his command to Captain Dumas who was now seconded by Lignery. The new commandant incited the western tribes against the English border settlements of Pennsylvania, Maryland, and Virginia. The Delawares, Shawanoes, Mingoes and other Iroquois turned against the English settlers with the intention of regaining their traditional native lands. Braddock's Road offered them easy access to and from the outer English settlements. Dumas tried to prevent the Indian torture of their prisoners, but the French had rarely been able to exert any control over this native practice.

George Washington was given command of a Virginia regiment consisting of 1500 undisciplined troops to protect a frontier that extended 350 miles through the ancient forest of the Alleghenies. The English had never felt the need to build and garrison forts to protect their western settlements.

Lake Ontario campaign

General Shirley began his first military venture into the wilderness on July 11th. Most of his troops were already rowing their bateaux 60 miles up the Mohawk River and dragging them on sledges through the swampy forest of northern New York.

He and the rest of his men followed the same route in ascent the Mohawk River, crossing the length of Lake Oneida, and then descend the Onondaga and Oswego rivers to Lake Ontario.

Nova Scotia, July 13, 1755

The *Acadiens* of Annapolis Royal were at Sunday Mass in Saint Jean-Baptiste church when the doors suddenly swung open to admit an English officer and a company of soldiers. The officer announced that the parishioners must deliver all their weapons to the fort, and nominate thirty deputies to represent them at a general meeting in Halifax.

The male parishioners delivered their several hundred muskets the following day, and a petition signed by 207 adult males through which they pledged their fidelity to the British government but stated that their deputies were charged not to contract a new oath. They claimed to have remained faithful for many years to the last one they had taken.

A few days later, English troops from Fort Anne seized and burned all Acadian seagoing vessels to enforce the grain embargo.

Heads of households in the Minas area were told to choose seventy deputies for a meeting in Halifax. They did so and charged them with the delivery of a petition, signed by 300 adult male inhabitants, which outlined their history with the oath of fidelity and stated that they could not take another which changed in any way the conditions and privileges their former sovereigns and ancestors had obtained for them.

Vice-Admiral Boscawen, who was close to the center of power in London, and Rear-Admiral Mostyn arrived in Halifax in mid-July to meet with Governor Lawrence. They warned him that a large French fleet had evaded them a month earlier to safely reach Louisbourg and Québec, and they supported the governor's assertion that it was "now the properest time to oblige the inhabitants to take the oath of allegiance to His Majesty, or to quit the country."

Lawrence wrote to the Board of Trade that he was determined to bring the "French Neutrals" into compliance "or rid the province of such perfidious subjects".

Five days later, news arrived from New York concerning General Braddock's disastrous defeat and his subsequent death in the Ohio valley. The fact that this loss had been credited to the Canadian militia and their allied native warriors further strengthened Governor Lawrence's resolve.

Québec

Governor Vaudreuil studied Braddock's captured military correspondence and learned the details of the multipronged British campaign. He was particularly concerned about the English threat to the Lake Champlain corridor leading directly to Montréal. His Mohawk scouts had recently returned from the Hudson River valley with news that 3,000 provincial militiamen had assembled near Albany and most had already moved toward Lac Saint-Sacrement.

Fort Frontenac

Baron Dieskau's primary mission focused on the seizure of three small English forts at the outlet of the Oswego River. He had already organized his 4,000-man army to accomplish this when he received Governor Vaudreuil's orders to reposition large portions of his troops to reinforce the garrisons in Frontenac and Niagara, then return to Montréal with 1500 of his metropolitan regulars to strengthen the defense of Fort Saint-Frédéric at Crown Point.

Thirty-two

Halifax, Nova Scotia, July 28, 1755

The one hundred Acadian representatives from Annapolis and Minas respectfully stood before the seated British Executive Council in Halifax at 10:00 a.m. on July 28, 1755, shortly after Governor Lawrence had received reports of General Braddock's defeat in the Ohio country. The governor reminded them that this was their third and last opportunity to take the unqualified oath of fealty to the British Crown and warned them that if they refused to do so again, they must give up their lands. He instructed them to reply with a simple "yes" or "no".

Upon receiving their negative response, the governor declared that everything they owned other than their money and household goods was forfeited to the British king, and he immediately ordered their imprisonment, thus depriving the *Acadiens* of their community leadership.

Governor Lawrence, the Executive Council of Nova Scotia, and their invited guests admirals Boscawen and Mostyn continued their meeting after the Acadians had been led away under guard.

According to the recorded minutes of the July meetings, Lawrence had warned the Acadian deputies that further refusal would lead the British government to regard them as "Subjects of the King of France" and that they would be transported to France as soon as English ships became available.

However, when the council meeting was resumed after their dismissal, the governor proposed the plan of deportation outlined by Charles Morris during the summer of 1754: "the Acadians should be dispersed in small groups throughout the American colonies or other parts of the British empire, as far from their homeland as possible, as expeditiously as possible."

The recorded minutes of that meeting read as follows: "After mature consideration, it was unanimously Agreed That to prevent as much as possible their Attempting to return and molest the Settlers that may be set down on their Lands, it would be most proper to send them to be distributed amongst the several Colonies on the Continent, and that a sufficient Number of Vessels should be hired with all possible Expedition for that purpose."

Lake Ontario campaign

Shirley reached Oswego by the end of July.

Since none of the provisions, equipment and supplies had arrived at the fort, he immediately ordered food rationing for the troops and garrison.

His officers informed him that approximately 800 of his men had defected during the journey, due to the extremely difficult terrain leading to the lake.

Shortly after his arrival, he ordered his remaining troops to clear the ground for the construction of Fort Ontario, two sixty-ton vessels, two row galleys, and eight whaleboats of twelve-men capacity.

Couriers arrived from Albany in early August to report General Braddock's defeat and death in the Ohio valley, the resultant desertion of Dutch boatmen and wagoners at the carrying places, and the death of his older son William Shirley.

William Shirley was officially notified that in his capacity as Major-General and commander of all provincial forces and highest-ranking active officer in America, he had automatically succeeded General Braddock as command-in-chief, pending the arrival of Braddock's British replacement.

His grief over the tragic loss of his son and namesake overshadowed this honor, and a series of unexpected problems further delayed his own ambitious campaign plans.

Many of his provincial troops were already sick, most began to weaken due to short rations and grumbled because of lack of pay.

He left it to his officers to deal with these problems while he supervised his many construction projects.

Nova Scotia

Governor Lawrence wrote to Monckton and the other fort commanders on August 3rd to inform them of the council's decision. "In the meantime, it will be necessary to keep this measure as secret as possible, as well to prevent their attempting to escape, as to carry off their cattle...the better to effect this you will endeavour to fall upon some stratagem to get the men, both young and old (especially the heads of families), into your power and detain them till the transports shall arrive, so as that they may be ready to be shipped off; for when this is done it is not much to be feared that the women and children will attempt to go away and carry off the cattle...it will be very proper to secure all their Shallops, Boats, Canoes and every other vessel you can lay your hands upon...their whole stock of Cattle and Corn is forfeited to the Crown by their rebellion, and must be secured & apply'd towards a reimbursement of the expense the government will be at in transporting them out of the Country...the inhabitants have now no property in them...they will not be allowed to carry away the least thing but their ready money and household furniture..."

Thomas Pichon's reports from Beauséjour had convinced the governor that the French Catholic priests of Nova Scotia had long acted as agents of the Québec governors to supply and incite the Micmacs against the Protestant settlements.

Lawrence ordered the arrest of the three Catholic priests remaining in the province, and that the Catholic churches be turned into military barracks.

British soldiers seized the priests in Minas and Annapolis Royal, along with all parish registers, parishioner contracts, records, deeds, and other legal documents.

One week later, the captive clerics were taken to Halifax where they were marched to the accompaniment of drumbeats in the market square, mocked by the townspeople for nearly an hour, then imprisoned on a warship to await deportation.

New England

In early August 1755, a Boston newspaper published a letter from a reporter in Halifax: "...We are now (engaged) upon a great and noble scheme of sending out of this province the neutral French who have always been secret enemies and have encouraged our savages to cut our throats. If we effect their expulsion, it will be one of the greatest things that ever the English did in America...By all accounts, that part of the country they possess, is as good land as any in the world...In case we could get some good English farmers in their room (place), this province would abound with all kinds of provisions..." This article also appeared in several other New England newspapers.

Nova Scotia

Lieutenant-Colonel Monckton ordered his officers and soldiers to summon all Acadian males aged sixteen years and older who lived in the Chignectou villages of Tantemar, Oueskak, Chipoudy, Aulac, Beauséjour, and Baie-Verte to meet with him in Fort Cumberland on Sunday, August 10th "to make arrangements for the return of their lands".

Four hundred Acadian men assembled on the fort's parade grounds at the appointed time. They were mostly earlier refugees from Beaubassin who represented one-third of all adult males living in the district of Chignectou. Colonel Monckton appeared with a military escort and read to them the council's proclamation that declared them to be rebels whose lands and all earthly goods were forfeited to the crown, and announced their immediate imprisonment pending deportation. The gates were shut tight and extra guards assigned to encircle the fort. They were shocked by Monckton's betrayal of their trust and the unexpected turn of events.

English soldiers scoured the countryside for those who had not answered the summons, but the other 800 Acadian men had already escaped deep into the woods.

Monckton later wrote: "We have undertaken to rid ourselves of one of the plagues of Egypt."

Fort Saint-Frédéric

By mid-August 1755, Baron Dieskau had descended the upper Saint Lawrence River to return to Montréal, had ascended rivière Richelieu and crossed the length of Lac Champlain to reach Fort Saint-Frédéric on Samuel de Champlain's *Pointe-à-la-Chevelure*, which the English called Crown Point. He arrived with a mixed force of 700 metropolitan regulars, 1600 Canadian militiamen who were mostly drawn from the districts of Montréal and Trois Rivières, and 700 allied Iroquois and Abenaki warriors.

The baron shared Braddock's attitude toward the colonials and native warriors; he considered them to be hopelessly lacking in military discipline. His reports to Vaudreuil and Bigot described the Iroquois as particularly unreliable, citing that they refused to serve as scouts and were a bad influence on the Abenakis who were otherwise cooperative and helpful.

Fort Lyman

The following week, Johnson ascended the Hudson River and reached Fort Lyman on the southern end of the Great Carrying Place. While he assembled and provisioned his 2200 provincials and 300 Mohawk warriors, four Iroquois scouts returned from Québec and reported that French preparations were underway to defend Crown Point with 8,000 men.

Johnson and his council of officers agreed to send for more provincial soldiers, move 2000 of their men to set up an encampment on the south shore of Lac Saint-Sacrement, and leave a 500-man garrison under Colonel Blanchard to defend and complete construction of Fort Lyman-Edward.

English axmen began to clear a road leading north through the forest.

On August 26th, Johnson moved most of his force to the southern shore of the lake which he renamed in honor of his British king. A train of Dutch wagons transported bateaux, provisions and equipment over the roughly cleared road while the three regiments followed closely at their leisure. They arrived the following afternoon to clear and set up the campsite. An additional 300 of Johnson's Mohawks joined them later.

Baron Dieskau's Canadian scout reported the next day that 3000 Englishmen were encamped at Lydius Place (Fort Lyman), and were converting the old Ohio Company trading post into a major military supply base. Dieskau moved his troops southward to Carillon (Ticonderoga) to challenge the enemy force before it reached Fort Saint-Frédéric.

Oswego

Shirley's campaign remained at a stalemate at the end of August. He continued to wait for the arrival of provisions; food supplies were becoming dangerously low. His troops grew weak, sickness greatly increased among them, progress slowed down on the construction projects. The rate of defection rose, those who escaped into the wilderness soon returned to relative safety; military justice increased in its severity. Morale among the officers and men declined.

Indian scouts reported that Fort Frontenac's garrison had increased to 1400 French regulars, Canadian militiamen and Indians, and that Fort Niagara's garrison had been strengthened by the arrival of 1200 Canadian militiamen and Indians from Fort Duquesne and the upper Great Lakes.

Nova Scotia

Governor Lawrence sent additional instructions to the military commanders in Annapolis, Chignectou, Piziquid, Minas, and Cobequid: "...you will give each of the masters their sailing orders in writing to proceed according to their assigned destination, and upon their arrival immediately to wait on the governor or commander-in-chief of the province to which they are bound with the said letters, and to make all possible dispatch in debarking their passengers, and obtaining certificates thereof agreeable to the form aforesaid; and you will in these orders make it a particular injunction to the said masters to be as careful and watchful as possible during the whole course of the passage, to prevent the passengers making any attempt to seize upon the vessels, by allowing only a small number to be upon the decks at one time, and all other necessary precautions to prevent the bad consequences of such attempts; and that they be particularly careful that the inhabitants carry no arms, nor other offensive weapons on board with them at their embarkation, and also that they see to it that the provisions be regularly issued to the allowance proportioned...

"You will use all the means necessary for collecting the people together, so as to get them on board. If you find that fair means will not do it with them, you must proceed by the most vigorous measures possible, not only in compelling them to embark, but in depriving those who escape of all means of shelter or support, by burning their houses and destroying everything that may afford them the means of subsistence in the country."

Ten New England transports arrived at Fort Cumberland at the end of August, providing Colonel Monckton with the capacity to ship out as many as 3,000 deportees. Upon sighting this fleet in the Annapolis Royal and Chignectou districts, local Acadian men and their sons fled into the woods, leaving their women and children behind to bring in the grain harvest.

Monckton in Chignectou and Major John Handfield who commanded the Annapolis district sent New England patrols to capture and prevent the fugitives from reaching îles Saint-Jean and Royale by destroying the village ports on the north shore. Monckton prescribed the use of terror tactics. His soldiers plundered and burned the homes of the abandoned families, causing hundreds of Acadian women and children to migrate inland into the area of Chipoudy and farther into the northwestern forest.

Their brutal campaign fomented the beginnings of an Acadian resistance movement. Canadian Lieutenant de Boishébert and his several dozen militiamen trained 300 of the Acadian fugitives and joined them with Mi'kmaq and Malécite warriors into a small but effective guerilla group.

On September 3rd, this mobile force unexpectedly ran out of the woods screaming and firing at the fifty New England raiders who terrorized and torched the small villages on the Petitcodiac River. After three hours of intense fighting, the English soldiers fled, allowing 200 Acadian families to escape deportation and emerge from the woods to harvest their winter food supply.

Boishébert advised these refugees to migrate westward along the upper Petitcodiac River, then travel overland to reach the upper section of rivière Saint-Jean which would eventually lead them to the Saint Lawrence River.

The Cormier family discussed this opportunity to seek refuge in Canada. Their 55-year old matriarch Marguerite Cyr listened quietly while her sons and sons-in law considered the possible dangers and considerable advantages this option offered them. Her husband Pierre had died in Beaubassin six years earlier. So much had happened since then, she thought, as she remembered the many unforeseen tragedies and challenges her family had survived together since his death.

The older men agreed that this option offered more security than they had so far enjoyed, but it would require a much longer trek than any they had ever undertaken.

"This may be our only chance to keep the family together," Marguerite reminded them.

The widow regretted that her oldest daughter Anne Cormier could not join them, but she and her new husband had a newborn daughter to care for and lived close to his family in Grand Pré. Marguerite sadly realized she might never meet this new grandchild.

The heads of families spoke more conservatively than did the younger, unmarried sons. The women listened quietly; Marguerite sensed and voiced their natural concerns. "We have the younger children to consider," she pointed out. "They must be kept warm and well-sheltered during the winter. Will we be able to provide for those needs during such a long journey?"

A younger woman suggested that they could convert their blankets into warm clothing and use animal furs for bedding. The men had their axe heads and knives with which to provide winter shelter and firewood.

"We can hunt and fish for meat," the young men and boys proposed.

"We have grain for bread, root vegetables and fruit," the daughters added.

Marguerite reassured them that they could pick enough from dry storage to meet their needs during the next few months, but would they be able to carry it with them?

"We should know by the time we reach rivière Saint-Jean," her son Jean suggested. "If it proves to be too much for us to bring the rest of the way, we can trade for whatever else we need."

They concluded that they must quickly take advantage of this opportunity and leave before the English returned with greater force.

A small group of Malécites volunteered to guide and protect them. Boishebert offered to provide from the king's stores the basic equipment and provisions they would need for the long journey and the coming winter. He made sure their weapons were reliable, that they had enough ammunition for hunting and self-defense, and he assured them that they could rely on their native guides to teach them how to survive in the wilderness.

They left two days later with thirty other families.

Carillon

Dieskau's troops had set up camp by September 4, 1755 when his scouts returned with an English prisoner they had captured near Fort Lyman. The provincial soldier claimed that the main body of the English army had moved back to Albany, that only 500 colonial soldiers had stayed to complete construction on the garrison-fort which was still indefensible.

On the basis of this information, the baron organized a *corps d'élite* of 216 regulars from the *La Reine* and *Languedoc* regiments, 684 Canadian militiamen, and more than 600 Abenaki and Mohawk warriors under the leadership of Legardeur de Saint-Pierre. Although Governor Vaudreuil had ordered him to keep his troops together, the baron left most of his men at his advanced base so that they could travel more quickly by canoe and overland to destroy Fort Lyman.

Québec

The Canadians rejoiced at the news of a rising Acadian resistance movement. Although French troops were tied down on three other war fronts and could not be spared, Governor Vaudreuil sent word to Boishébert that he would increase the delivery of supplies and provisions to his guerilla force.

Nova Scotia

Governor Lawrence ordered Lieutenant-Colonel John Winslow and Captain Alexander Murray to summon all Acadian males ten years of age and older in the Minas Basin district to assemble in the church of Saint Charles-des-Mines in Grand Pré and in Fort Edward in Piziquid.

The two officers coordinated their plans and agreed to wait until the autumn grain crops were harvested and safely stored to provision the transport vessels, then schedule the assemblies at 3:00 p.m., September 5th.

In Grand Pré, Winslow read the deportation order in English and arrested 418 Acadian men and young boys who feared they might never see their families again. The same fate awaited the 183 men and boys who answered Murray's call to gather together in Piziquid.

Two days later, Winslow and his 300 enlisted men received the startling news of an Acadian insurrection in the Petitcodiac River area. The fort commander had reason to be concerned: his New England troops were on edge and, according to his comprehensive list of Minas males, more than thirty-five of the *Acadiens* had not attended the assembly, having presumably disappeared into the forest.

He heightened security that night, and sent out some of his troops to search for the fugitives the following morning. In one particular village, his provincial soldiers terrorized the women and children by forcing them to kneel with their heads down to the ground and their backs toward their captors, while threatening to shoot them with grapeshot unless they renounced "papism" and adopted the Protestant faith. The victims refused to give up their faith and its salvation. The soldiers finally gave up, torched their homes and moved on to the next village.

The Acadian prisoners in Grand Pré grew angry and restless when they heard of the torment inflicted upon their families. Winslow ordered the transfer of 230 young males to five prison ships pending the arrival of the final transport fleet. In spite of their initial protest, they were marched one and a half miles under military escort to the embarkation point while their families watched and wept and feared that they might never see them again.

Winslow wrote to Major Handfield: "This affair is more grievous to me than any service I was ever employed in."

Thirty-three

Nouvelle France, autumn 1755

With war threatening on all four fronts, repeated militia call-ups kept the habitants on constant alert and often interrupted their seasonal farming chores. Food crops and animal husbandry suffered from their absences. Food shortages developed at a time when Acadian refugees began to arrive in Québec and additional troops had to be fed. Intendant Bigot set the distribution of bread rations at four ounces a day in the cities and villages.

The women, children, and elderly became exhausted from their attempts to provide for their own basic needs. Husbands and fathers were absent for long periods of time, all the while worrying about the welfare of their families while they served militia duty in far-off places.

Lake George

At sunset of September 7th, a Mohawk scout reported to Major-General Johnson that a French force was moving from South Bay toward Fort Lyman. Johnson dispatched a mounted volunteer to warn the provincial commander of that fort, and posted extra sentries before the men settled in for the night.

Fort Lyman

Dieskau's force reached Johnson's road the following morning, and met a warrior-scout who handed him a written dispatch he had taken from the English courier. Other scouts encountered a group of Dutch wagoners heading south on the forest road. Some were killed in a fire-fight, others ran away, but the few captives told Dieskau that 3,000 English troops were encamped on the lakeshore, that their provincial officers seemed confused about the strength of the French force.

Allied warriors refused to storm the English fort because they knew it to be armed with several cannon. They persuaded the baron to attack the unfortified English encampment on Lac Saint-Sacrement.

The baron redirected his forces northward. At about three miles from the lake, his scouts warned that 1000 armed Englishmen were marching south in his direction to reinforce Fort Lyman. Dieskau ordered his troops to withhold their fire until he signaled, and quickly set up an ambush. He kept his army regulars on the road, and directed the Canadians, Mohawks and Abenaki warriors to the front but hidden in the forest on both sides of the way.

Mohawk chief Hendrick and his 200 warriors preceded the English column. His horse was shot down from under him early in the battle, and he was killed by a bayonet thrust as he tried to get up.

The English force appeared on the road and advanced in disciplined formation with muskets raised against the lines of French regulars but were soon caught in a devastating crossfire. They panicked but were helped to retreat by the Virginians who rallied the regiment, and by the Mohawks who sniped at the pursuing French and Indians.

Dieskau halted the chase to gather his men together at about three-quarters of a mile from Johnson's camp, and learned that Legardeur de Saint-Pierre had been killed in the battle. Due to the loss of their leader, the native warriors and the Canadians hesitated, but French officers managed to rally them to follow their lead.

Johnson had heard the sounds of battle followed by those of retreat and had hurriedly set up an abatis of overturned bateaux, wagons, and tree trunks along the front and sides of his lakeside encampment. He had two cannons to sweep the road with grapeshot, and another on a nearby hill. His retreating men reached safety with many of their wounded, and positioned themselves to help repel the attack.

The Mohawk warriors and 1600 mostly untested provincial recruits faced ranks of gray-uniformed French regulars marching with fixed bayonets toward them. The English were tested by a series of disciplined French fusillades until their artillery fired its grapeshot.

Dieskau lost control over his Canadian militiamen and native warriors when the cannonade sent them scurrying for cover. While the general denounced their cowardice and lack of military discipline, he continued to march his regulars toward the abatis and was hit in the leg, then in the knee and thigh.

Johnson's men charged across the defensive barricade to counterattack with hatchets, knives, and musket-butts. A provincial soldier stood above the wounded baron, spoke to him in French, and shot him across the hips.

Dieskau's remaining army ran out of ammunition and was routed later that afternoon. His soldiers and militiamen tossed aside their weapons, dropped their knapsacks and fled ahead of the pursuing Mohawks through ten miles of forest. They reached their canoes and extra provisions late the following day, and although they were exhausted and famished they continued their retreat toward Carillon.

Baron Dieskau was carried into Johnson's tent for treatment of his wounds. The provincial commander protected him from several Mohawks who sought to avenge the death of their beloved Chief Hendrick.

Neither side had achieved its objective. Baron Dieskau could not claim victory against the English force; Johnson had failed to seize Fort Saint-Frédéric.

The English reported 262 casualties and the French counted 228. Most of the English deaths occurred as a result of the morning ambush. The French regulars bore the brunt of the battle and suffered the most casualties; nearly all of their officers were killed or wounded as they stubbornly led their men against the English camp.

Johnson ordered his own men to bury the dead, both English and French. He renamed the lake in honor of his king, and began construction of a solid English fort near his campsite which he named Fort George. It would later become Fort William-Henry and be renamed after another royal personage.

Grand Pré

Five transport ships arrived from Boston on September 10th. Winslow's greatly outnumbered soldiers quickly and brusquely forced the embarkation of their sullen and restless male prisoners: 141 adolescents and 89 young men who had been arrested in Sainte-Anne church of Beaubassin and Saint-Charles church of Grand-Pré. Another group arrived later from rivière Gaspareaux.

Oswego

One week later, Shirley called his officers to council and informed them that he now had 1376 men fit for duty. He declared that he expected the arrival of provisions and supplies at any time, that with these, he planned to move against Niagara with 600 soldiers and as many Indians as he could muster, leaving his remaining forces to defend Oswego against the possibility of French attack.

Although his troops had been on half-bread allowance and without rum during the previous three weeks, he presented a young bull to serve as a war feast for his Indian warriors and exhorted them to prepare for battle, to wait a while longer before returning to their villages.

Nights grew cooler; still there were no barracks for the troops.

Some provisions began to arrive another week later and General Shirley prepared to launch his attack against Fort Niagara the following morning.

During their third Council of War, held on September 27th, his officers argued that the prevailing stormy weather made it too dangerous to risk transporting his forces across the lake by bateaux, especially since there were too few of the clumsy river boats to accommodate the number of men he wished to take with him, and the two naval vessels were not ready to sail. They assured him that conditions would be more favorable in the spring if the fortifications were improved and strengthened through the autumn and winter, and if two additional naval vessels were built for troop transport.

Shirley reluctantly accepted their counsel and directed his soldiers to carry out the several projects. His provincial enlistees had grown weaker during the past month. They still lacked proper winter shelter and warm clothing. Indian raiders had taken their toll; the provincials complained about the quality of their muskets, that their locks and hammers were worn and useless.

Although Shirley's frequent, aggressive proposals and grand strategies to remove the French from North America had earned the respect of the Board of Trade, this was his first military command. He had never led an army into battle, nor had he any previous experience in organizing and supplying a campaign. The route from Schenectady to Oswego proved to be much more difficult than he had anticipated, and his political enemies in Albany managed to disrupt delivery of his army's provisions.

Shirley blamed it all on the desertion of the wagoners after Braddock's defeat, yet he and his contractors had consistently failed to pay and properly feed the soldiers. Shirley forced his men to labor deep in the wilderness without proper sustenance.

Although bateaux loaded with retail goods did arrive from the south, the soldiers never received their pay. When they applied directly to the contractor for their food allowance, he refused to provide it on credit and told them that he "could not make Provisions, and that if (they) were not Satisfied (they) might eat Stones."

Fort Lawrence

East of the Missaguash River, under cover of an intense lightning storm crackling through the predawn darkness of the first day of October, eighty-six Acadian prisoners slipped through a tunnel they had dug under the fort's wall, and escaped into the forest to join Boishébert's resistance force.

Monckton promptly ordered the embarkation of 1782 Acadian male prisoners, their wives and children into eight of the provisioned transport ships he had held back for two months. He sent the extra vessels to Winslow in Grand Pré.

Due to the sudden frenzied rush to accomplish the boardings, and the language barrier, grief and panic overcame the women and children. Families were ripped apart, their members assigned to different ships. Many would be delivered to different provincial destinations.

Twelve days later, the vessels sailed down the Bay of Fundy and waited two weeks in the Annapolis Basin for the arrival of the transports from Minas.

The holds of these ships had been divided into several levels four feet high, as in slave ships. The deportees were to be loaded at the rate of two persons per allotted space measuring six-feet long by four-feet wide. Half of the occupants were female; 60% were children.

The area below decks was damp, without light or heat, ventilation or sanitation. Food and water provisions proved to be inadequate as more people were forced to share the allotted spaces than had been specified; there simply were not enough ships to maintain the prescribed rate of occupancy.

Nova Scotia

In early morning of October 8th, Winslow's men moved throughout the district of Grand Pré to assemble and deliver all Acadian inhabitants to the village landing; several hundred had arrived by noontime. Attempts were made to have them embark by village group, then by family group, but the process proved to be too complicated over the following five days.

The scene quickly became chaotic due to the pressure exerted by the troops, the stress suffered by the *Acadiens*, and the language barrier between the two sides. Families panicked as they became separated. The soldiers grew impatient.

Oswego

Shirley assigned 700 of his men to complete his various construction projects, and left for Albany on October 19, 1755 with the rest of his soldiers, many of whom suffered from fever, scurvy, and dysentery.

He had ordered the construction of two 8-gun schooners and winter shelters, and the strengthening of the three decrepit palisaded buildings of Fort Oswego to guard the way from Lake Ontario to Schenectady and Albany. Dysentery continued to spread among the wintering troops; they became too weak to build their own military barracks. Most of the soldiers would sleep in makeshift bark huts and on the ground that winter.

Shirley headed southeast, leaving his soldiers as yet unpaid, without the means to purchase badly needed food, clothing, and blankets that were offered at highly inflated prices. His men remained underfed; their bread-baking ovens were falling apart.

The fort's commandant, Lieutenant-Colonel James Mercer reported that Shirley had left his men in Oswego with a forty-day supply of bread, two months of meat, and three weeks of spirits.

The colonel further asserted that Shirley and his secretary William Alexander repeatedly ignored his requests for provisions. Mercer's only option was to keep the garrison on short winter rations.

Grand Pré

The people from Piziquid suffered the most overcrowding at 30–50% over the prescribed occupancy. Captain Murray had managed to embark 920 deportees in four transports meant to carry 650. On October 20th, Winslow requisitioned a New England trading vessel and transferred 200 of these extra passengers to relieve some of the pressure.

In spite of the increased loading rate, Winslow reported to Monckton that he had a surplus of 600 deportees. Until the arrival of additional transports, extra women and children would have to live in the abandoned farmhouses of Grand Pré and the men would return to their imprisonment in the church building.

The day the vessels sailed away, the *Acadiens* of Minas Basin witnessed the English destruction of their dykes and the torching of their outer villages. Fires burned a full six days, forming clouds of thick black smoke and a gray ash that fell throughout the countryside, destroying any hope the refugees might have had of returning one day to their ancestral farms. Winslow recorded the destruction of over 250 houses, 270 barns, 10 mills, and a church.

Ten days later, Lieutenant-Governor Charles Lawrence wrote to the Board of Trade: "Fait accompli....One of the happy effects I proposed to myself from driving the French off, it furnishes us with a large quantity of good land ready for immediate cultivation."

Rivière Saint-Jean

The Cormier clan arrived at Boishébert's base in time to build their winter shelters beyond reach of the English forces. During the next three weeks, they felled trees, and trimmed timbers to construct four small cabins with clay chimneys to accommodate the entire extended family.

They moved their baggage under shelter just as the frigid northeast winds began to blow in from Hudson Bay. The men and boys hunted, stored their meat to freeze in outdoor caches and dried some by the fireplace to provision the next part of their journey in the spring. They had enough wheat grain, dried corn and peas that they had collected in Petitcoudiac. Their meals remained repetitious but nutritious.

Champlain valley, autumn 1755

Tension between the French and English camps continued to escalate during the autumn months. Governor Vaudreuil appointed Canadian engineer Michel Chartier de Lotbinière to design and oversee the construction of a sturdy fort at Carillon with labor provided by French regulars, Canadian militiamen, and local settlers who were already present in the area.

Construction began in October on what would become the southernmost French military post in that section of North America. It would be larger and stronger than Fort Saint-Frédéric, built to withstand artillery attack and block any British invasion force that might attempt to move northward toward Montréal.

Lake Ontario

Governor Vaudreuil assigned Captain Pouchot and the *Béarn* battalion to redesign and rebuild Fort Niagara to render it capable of resisting artillery fire. Two other French engineers were ordered to strengthen the defenses of Fort Frontenac.

Annapolis Royal, Nova Scotia

Twenty-two vessels carrying 1664 deportees formed the first convoy of deportation transports that sailed into the Bay of Fundy on October 27, 1755. The wind carried them into the leading edge of a powerful northeaster, a violent winter storm of hurricane force that generated enormous winds and waves that carried the *Pembroke* away from the rest of the fleet. One of its Acadian passengers from the Annapolis district, mariner Charles Belliveau, managed to lead an unarmed band of followers to successfully overpower the crew, seize control of the ship, and sail it safely into hiding in Saint Mary's Bay.

Fort Cumberland, early November 1755

Lieutenant-Colonel Monckton received a letter written over two months earlier by Colonial Minister Thomas Robinson. The British official questioned the wisdom of the deportation because of the "consequences that may arise...an additional number of useful subjects may be given by their flight to the French King."

New England

Due to continuing high seas, more than twenty deportation vessels sought safe harbor in Boston on November 5th. Port authorities warned the captains of all of the ships that food and water supplies were inadequate for the number of passengers aboard. Nevertheless, they sailed away to their various destinations as soon as the weather cleared.

At 9:15 p.m. on November 18, 1755, a violent earthquake shook northeastern North America from Halifax, Nova Scotia south to Maryland, and from Lake George east to a ship located 200 miles offshore of Cape Ann. The shock was felt so strongly on that vessel that passengers and crew believed they had run aground.

This event added to the panic of the *Acadiens* who were on the deportation ships and those who had fled into the winter forest to make their way to Nouvelle France. It caused considerable damage in Boston, knocking down or damaging as many as 1600 chimneys and collapsing several brick buildings. Stone fences fell apart throughout the countryside, particularly between Boston and Montréal. Cracks opened in the earth in parts of Massachusetts; water and sand gushed out of ground fissures in Pembroke. New springs reportedly formed and old springs dried up.

Grand Pré

Lieutenant-Colonel Winslow was relieved of his command and recalled to Halifax in mid-November after having shipped 1,510 *Acadiens* to Pennsylvania, Maryland, and other British colonies. His successor would complete the duty of rounding up escapees and shipping them off with the remaining 600 deportees who continued to wait for the last transports to arrive.

Meanwhile, Winslow returned to Massachusetts to spend the winter with his wife and sons.

Nouvelle France

Many of the militiamen and French regulars who could not be garrisoned in the outlying forts returned to the Saint Lawrence River settlements and were housed among the Canadian population for the duration of the winter.

Albany

On November 29, 1755, Governor Shirley received notification that another of his sons had died. Thirty-year old Captain John "Jack" Shirley had succumbed to fever and dysentery in Oswego.

Two weeks later, the governor held a two-day Council of War in New York to outline his comprehensive campaign plan against the French during the coming year. He planned to seize forts Niagara, Frontenac, and Toronto with his growing fleet of naval vessels on Lake Ontario. Other British and provincial forces would attack forts Carillon and Saint-Frédéric in the Lake Champlain area, and Fort Duquesne in the Ohio valley. Massachusetts provincials would approach the settlements near Québec by way of the Kennebec and Chaudière rivers in an effort to divide the response of enemy defenses.

Members of the council were impressed by the breadth of his overall scheme, but knew that they could not raise the 16,000 fighting men to support the entire proposed effort. They rejected the proposed thrust toward Québec.

Braddock's defeat at Monongahela and Dunbar's abandonment of the frontier defense were still very much on their minds. Virginia and Pennsylvania were too busy defending their western frontiers from French and Indian raids to consider a second attack on Fort Duquesne. Much criticism had been voiced by their fellow provincials about Shirley's military expertise and English failures to take Crown Point, Oswego and Fort Duquesne. Their provinces remained skeptical, and deeply in debt from the campaigns of 1755.

Grand Pré

The last transports arrived in mid-December for the final embarkation of the Minas deportees who had waited two months since their relatives had shipped out. Dozens of fugitives had surrendered and joined the evacuation. Captain Osgood recorded the departure of 732 deportees on four transports heading for Virginia, Connecticut and Massachusetts.

After the last ship sailed out of sight, the abandoned dogs reportedly howled for weeks as they mourned the loss of their human families.

By the end of December 1755, there remained no visible trace of the 150-year old French presence in the land of *Acadie*. Over 5,000 *Acadiens* had escaped into the Mi'kmaq country or northwest into

French-controlled Chipoudy, to the north shore, and to Île Saint-Jean. Nearly 7,000 had been methodically exiled from their ancestral farms. Their dikes, villages, homes and churches had been entirely destroyed.

A heavy blanket of snow covered the wasted land through the short quiet days and long dark nights of winter. The abandoned dogs eventually gathered in feral packs to hunt and roam the uninhabited countryside.

Thirty-four

Nouvelle France, winter 1755–1756

A deadly epidemic spread through the colony claiming among Bastien and Marguerite Manchon's descendants: twenty-six-year old Joseph *fils* on January 21, 1756, and his mother Claire Rheault five days later at age fifty-six, both in Champlain; Louis and Anne Leclerc's twenty-six-year old son Jean-Baptiste on January 25th in Bécancour; Marguerite Moreau's twelve-year old daughter Charlotte on February 7th in Bécancour; Jean-Baptiste Belleville's eleven-year old daughter Ursule on February 14th in Nicolet.

Rivière Saint-Jean

Abbé La Guerne reported on February 8th that a small English transport ship called the *Pembroke* had arrived from Port Royal with 226 Acadian exiles representing thirty-two families. Captain Belliveau had turned the vessel and its English crew over to Lieutenant Boishébert and his Canadian militia who had recently returned from Chipoudy Bay. The refugees were preparing to migrate to Québec.

Lake Ontario

The presence of Fort Oswego continued to challenge French control of the lake. Shirley had built Fort Bull on the banks of Wood Creek, at the western end of the Great Carrying Place to protect his route from Schenectady to Oswego. Its several storehouses were already filled with supplies and ammunition for Shirley's upcoming spring campaign against forts Frontenac, Niagara and Toronto.

Vaudreuil dispatched Canadian Lieutenant Joseph Chaussegros de Léry with a *corps d'élite* of 362 French soldiers, Canadians, and native warriors to destroy this major military resupply depot between Albany and the Great Lake.

Léry and his men left Montréal in late February, to ascend the frozen upper Saint Lawrence River on *raquettes,* then move south across the ice and snow of eastern Lake Ontario.

Albany

Commander-in-chief William Shirley learned in mid-March that the British government would partially reimburse the provinces for their military expenses of the previous year, making it easier for him to persuade their councils to recruit more fighting men. They did, but limited their assignments to specific campaigns.

He hired 2000 boatmen from all parts of New England, including twenty whalemen from the northern fishing ports, divided them into fifty-man companies and provided them with guns, hatchets and axes. He then placed them under the command of Captain John Bradstreet whom he appointed commissary-general.

Shirley chose John Winslow to lead the English troops against forts Carillon and Saint-Frédéric in the Lake Champlain area.

He chose to take command of the campaign against the French forts on Lake Ontario with the remnants of his and Pepperrell's regiments, Braddock's battalions, the "Jersey Blues", four provincial companies from North Carolina, and four from New York.

The general was confident that he could raise enough fresh recruits to strengthen all of these units to a total force of 4400 men, capable of seizing all three French forts. He planned to transport these troops across the lake on the four armed naval vessels and smaller boats that should be waiting for him in Oswego.

London

British officials became concerned about a rapidly increasing concentration of military force along the northern coast of France. They suspected that the French might be preparing to invade England.

There had developed a public outcry over the previous British military failures in North America and an uproar of political criticism in the House of Commons against Newcastle's government. London merchants applauded William Pitt's castigation of the Prime Minister's ineffective management of the North American conflict which threatened to spread globally to the Caribbean Islands, Europe, West Africa and India.

Colonial Minister Robinson had come to realize that the seizure of Beauséjour had been the only successful British campaign in North America in 1755. In reply to Governor Lawrence's defense of the Acadian deportation, he wrote back: "In the present critical situation of our affairs, We doubt not but that your conduct will meet with His Majesty's Approbation." He commended Lawrence for his performance and promoted him from lieutenant-governor to governor-general of Nova Scotia.

The British War Ministry had long procrastinated over General Braddock's British replacement. Shirley's growing number of political enemies and his failure to seize Lake Ontario persuaded the ministry to replace him as commander-in-chief in North America. They finally chose John Campbell Earl of Loudoun, but appointed Colonel Daniel Webb to fill in temporarily pending the arrival of Loudoun's deputy, Major-General Abercromby, who would assume command until the earl's arrival. British Secretary of War Henry Fox wrote to Shirley in mid-March to inform him of the change of command.

Nova Scotia

Governor Lawrence reported on March 30th: "Some (*Acadiens*) from the isthmus have joined the troops of the French officer (Boishébert) who withdrew last summer to his fort at the mouth of the Saint John...Reinforced by Micmacs and the Indians from this river (Malécites), there are according to the indications about 1500 men who employ great activity to harass our troops every time they make a sortie from forts Cumberland and Gaspereau. As they can receive help from Canada and from Louisberg by a little fort called Jediach (Shediac) there is no doubt but that they draw to themselves settlers who fled into the woods into the interior of the province."

Lake Ontario

Fort Bull was strategically located 50 miles south of Oswego. Léry's force arrived nearby at the end of March and captured twelve Dutch wagoners who described the fort as a collection of storehouses enclosed within a wooden palisade, weakly defended by a garrison of thirty English provincials. Léry immediately moved against it.

The English managed to close their gates against the French assault, but the Canadians and their allies were close enough to quickly take over the palisade's loopholes and fire into the compound. The English officer refused to yield in spite of his vulnerable position; his men maintained a heavy barrage of musket and grenade fire during the following hour.

The French beat down the gate. Léry called once more for the officer to yield. He refused a second time and his men continued to fire through the opening. On March 27th, the French charged in, setting off a heavy exchange of musket fire during which most of the Englishmen were killed.

The native allies rampaged through the compound while Léry's men tore down the palisades. Finally, they torched all the storehouses, setting off a mighty explosion of the ammunition stores that completely destroyed the fort. Léry then withdrew his troops to Montréal, having achieved a successful opening raid on the Oswego corridor.

Johnson's relief force arrived soon after the French had left. He realized that the loss of this major resupply depot would delay English movement toward the French bases on Lake Ontario, allowing time for Vaudreuil to further secure forts Frontenac, Niagara, and Toronto against English attack.

On April 6th, native scouts reported to Commandant Mercer the presence of 1,000 French and Indians in the area of Oswego and another five hundred on their way from Niagara. Mercer demanded the prompt delivery of reinforcements and supplies, but although the rivers were free if ice, transport by bateaux was under constant French and Indian attack.

Albany, spring 1756

Shirley had hoped to move his army to Lake Ontario while the southern waterways flowed freely and the Canadian rivers remained covered with ice, but he failed to recruit enough provincial forces by then.

He received his notification from the British Colonial Ministry that he must resign his command position upon the arrival of Colonel Daniel Webb.

Shirley continued to prepare his campaigns from his Albany headquarters. He stocked provisions, began to rebuild the fort at Wood Creek in May, and sent additional troops to guard the routes to Oswego. He also dispatched troops and supplies up the Hudson River to Fort Lyman-Edward, then 17 miles overland to Fort William-Henry in preparation for Winslow's siege against Carillon.

Rivière Saint-Jean

The Acadian refugees set off on their long journey to the Saint Lawrence River, knowing that this part of their migration would last through the summer. Marguerite Cyr had taken a deep breath when she heard this. She continually fingered her rosary, petitioning the Blessed Virgin to watch over her family, to give them all the strength to see this through.

The Malécite guides led the group of thirty Acadian families whom they managed to keep together by dividing themselves into two groups: half of the native warriors led the way and helped the refugees to hunt and fish; the rest of them followed to watch for stragglers.

The first two weeks proved to be the most difficult for the Acadian farming families, but their bodies gradually adjusted to the routine. Their diet of fresh meat or fish, ground wheat and corn *banique*, dried peas and corn had been developed over a century and a half of Canadian voyageurs and afforded them the energy to keep going.

The *Acadiens* had already learned a great deal from their guides. The natives were patient with the children and had already taught them a few words of their Malécite language. The women could now identify the edible plants of the forest and occasionally used them in their cooking. Everyone sat and ate together by their campfires for the evening meal. The women and children usually fell asleep early at the end of the day.

They made slow progress. The adults often had to carry the younger children over the rough or steep sections of the ancient native trail. The men took turns at pulling the several travois; they were grateful for these because they eliminated the need to carry loaded knapsacks, and enabled a quicker set-up of the nightly encampment.

Nouvelle France

After the breakup of river ice, Monsieur Coulon de Villiers left Montréal with a force of 900 men to harass the English garrison of Oswego, sever its link to Albany, and weaken its defense against French attack and seizure.

Brigadier-General Marquis de Montcalm-Gozon de Saint-Véran arrived aboard the frigate *Licorne* after thirty-eight difficult days at sea. He landed at Cap Tourmente, traveled overland to Québec, and arrived in the capital on May 13, 1756. Colonels Bougainville and Bourlamarque, and two battalions of regulars from the *La Sarre* and *Royal-Roussillon* regiments were there to greet him, but Governor-General Vaudreuil was in Montréal consulting with his younger brother, the lieutenant-governor of that frontier community.

London

Great Britain officially declared war against France on May 17, 1756. The imperial competition between the two countries had grown globally beyond Europe and North America. The British had a powerful navy of more than two hundred strongly-armed warships which enabled them to extend and protect their empire across the oceans. France had ten times Britain's military force, but only half its naval strength, which already limited its capacity to project its armies overseas.

Mediterranean Sea

The French invasion of the British island of Minorca prompted the Admiralty to quickly dispatch Admiral John Byng to relieve its garrison with a squadron of ten ships of the line, all of them undermanned and in a state of disrepair.

Several battleships had escaped the island port and joined Byng's small fleet before it arrived off the Mediterranean island on May 19th. Although Minorca was already overrun by French troops, the garrison of Fort Saint Philip in Port Mahon still held firm.

Twelve French battleships and five frigates under the command of Comte de la Galissonnière confronted the British that afternoon.

The two fleets positioned themselves and fought each other the following morning. The French ships were more heavily armed and better able to hold their line; they seriously damaged several of the British vessels. Byng's senior officers unanimously agreed in council that their ships could not prevail against the French naval force nor could they get close enough to relieve the garrison. The admiral therefore gave orders to return to Gibraltar.

The British Admiralty severely criticized Byng's decisions and charged him with having breached the Articles of War by failing to do all he could to fulfill his orders to support the garrison. The admiral was court-martialed, found guilty, and sentenced to be shot by firing squad.

Nouvelle France

Marquis de Montcalm remained one week in Québec where he met with various government officials, and inspected the city's defenses and shipyards before leaving for Montréal. He rode comfortably on the *Chemin du Roi* in a horse-drawn, enclosed chaise from which he could leisurely enjoy an unobstructed view of the countryside through front and side windows. Canadian women and children were struggling with horses and oxen to till the soil for their spring sowing. He saw very few men other than the elderly working alongside them; the militia had served garrison duty through the winter at the various French frontier posts and others had already left on other duty assignments.

The marquis surveyed the thriving seignorial farmland, its long narrow fields lined up along the river and extending deeply into the forest, the white-washed timbered and stone farmhouses that overlooked the Saint Lawrence. That river and the rural features of Canada were of a larger scale than any he had seen in France.

Montcalm stopped long enough in Trois Rivières to inspect its canoe works and Forges Saint-Maurice. He had been impressed by Engineer Franquet's four-year old assessment of the canoe industry in that community. Franquet's inspection had identified this area as the best source of reliable birch-bark canoes due its excellent workforce, its easy access to massive groves of large white birch trees, and the negligible tide in the area.

The general was reassured that the community could produce great quantities of these lightweight canoes to transport French soldiers, militiamen, native allies, and military provisions over the waterways that led to the threatened frontiers. He could see that they were light enough to be portaged overland.

Montcalm was also impressed by the quality of the cannons, and balls for both cannon and musket produced by the ironworks of Saint-Maurice.

Montréal

On May 22nd, the French commander arrived in the frontier community and had his first meeting with Governor-General Vaudreuil and his brother, *Monsieur de Rigaud* the following morning.

Both Canadians greeted him with cordial reserve. Baron Dieskau's failed performance against Johnson's Fort George had fostered Canadian mistrust of French military effectiveness in America. Due to Vaudreuil's insistence, the Minister of War had ordered Montcalm, an experienced continental regimental commander, to assume a subordinate role under the Canadian-born governor-general, who maintained overall command of military, naval, and colonial forces.

Governor Vaudreuil outlined the multiple British-provincial threat facing Nouvelle France and the strategy he had developed to meet it. He told the French general that he planned to keep the British on the defensive and as far away from the Canadian settlements as possible. He informed him of his decision to take the offensive against Fort Oswego to protect Montréal and ensure French control over Lake Ontario and the Great Lakes. He explained that seizure of that English fort would also secure overland communication between Canada, Louisiana and the western forts.

His brother described how Canadian and native war parties had been harassing the English frontiers of New York, Virginia and Pennsylvania ever since General Braddock's defeat in the Ohio valley, and added that the allied warriors intended to reclaim their lands from the English settlers.

Vaudreuil then informed the marquis that Canadian engineer Léry and his small force of handpicked men had already captured and destroyed the English military arsenal at Fort Bull in March, thus destroying the bombs, bullets, cannonballs, other munitions, and 45,000 pounds of gunpowder that the English had planned to use against forts Frontenac and Niagara.

Monsieur de Rigaud explained that although the English provincial population greatly outnumbered that of the Canadians (1.5 million to 75,000), the seven English provinces had so far failed to unite against the Canadian and native allied forces, and their provincials were mostly farmers and tradesmen who lacked experience in traveling through the wilderness.

Governor Vaudreuil had established a reputation for being particularly effective in managing native alliances. He was well-trained in guerilla-warfare tactics, but lacked battle-command experience. He acknowledged this when he informed the general that the role of his French *Troupes de Terre* was to protect the colony from British European-style assaults.

Although both parties addressed each other with great civility, there immediately developed a clash between their European and Canadian mind-sets. Montcalm's entire training and experience had prepared him to encounter the enemy face-to-face on the battlefield, to exchange highly disciplined musket- and cannon-fire against an opposing battle line, or to lay siege against enemy fortifications.

The marquis had no desire to lead his troops through the wilderness to fight along the distant colonial frontiers, but rather proposed meeting and decisively defeating the enemy European-style in pitched battle at key points of defense.

He later wrote to his superior, the French Minister of War, that he would prefer "to lose a battle rather than win it with the help of *les Canadiens*."

Québec

The French troopship *Le Léopard* arrived on May 30, 1756 and was immediately quarantined in port because of an unidentified epidemic among its passengers: six companies of French metropolitan soldiers and two of grenadiers.

Montcalm's second-in-command, François de-Léran Chevalier de Lévis arrived from Brest the following day after a two-month ocean voyage on the frigate *le Sauvage*. Two sailors had died and had been buried at sea during the crossing. Several officers were hospitalized upon arrival.

Albany

Shirley's men worked from May to August to restore the fort and munitions depot near Wood Creek. He established posts and garrisons along the way to Oswego to safeguard the route, and gathered provisions and stores at these posts in preparation for the renewal of his campaign to seize control of Lake Ontario.

He mustered 5,000 raw provincial recruits and placed most of them under Winslow's command to renew the English attack against Fort Saint-Frédéric at Crown Point. They were encamped a short distance up the Hudson River by the end of May.

Rivière Saint-Jean

The Cormier clan reached a major turn of the river and headed north. They encountered fewer tributaries, sparing them the need to build rafts for the transport of baggage and family members across the water. Their daily progress increased; they stopped only when the women and children became tired or when the sun reached low on the horizon.

Other refugees kept pace with them, heading in the same direction, always on foot. They began to meet native hunting parties on the trail, in which case their guides would stop to exchange information about what lay ahead.

The days grew longer as they approached mid-summer; they often lost track of time and walked farther during the pleasant weather.

They stopped for a week in Bécaguimec so that the men could hunt and dry meat for the next leg of their journey, the women could catch up on their laundry, and the children could bathe and frolic in the water with their older siblings. Marguerite enjoyed a much needed rest.

Thirty-five

New York - summer 1756

Colonel Daniel Webb arrived from England on June 7th to relieve
William Shirley as interim commander-in-chief. Rather than
move on to army command headquarters in Albany, Webb chose
to wait nine days in New York for the arrival of his own
replacement, General James Abercromby.

Nouvelle France

The second *La Sarre* battalion had been refitted and provisioned
in Québec by June 6th. A small fleet of vessels transporting these
Troupes de Terre sailed upriver, drawing the attention of the
Canadian farmers along both shores of the Saint Lawrence. The
ships crossed the length of Lac Saint-Pierre to enter Baie du Nord
and land the troops at Maskinongé, where they joined with the
local militia and began their 15-league march to Montréal.

This highly disciplined parade of uniformed soldiers followed
by their train of field artillery on the *Chemin du Roi* profoundly
impressed the Canadians, convincing them that this had indeed
become a very different kind of war.

The second *Royal-Roussillon* battalion left the capital on June
12th, three days after France officially declared war against
England. These French metropolitan regulars marched overland
to Trois Rivières and traveled by *canots-de-maître* to Montréal. A
different segment of the Canadian population watched in awe as

the martial parade of brightly uniformed soldiers marched by on *le Chemin du Roi*.

Antoine Ducharme dit Boudor struggled in Trois Rivières to keep up with the increasing military demand. Although his most reliable male workers were excused from militia duty, he had to hire more female employees, drawing even more farmers away from the fields.

June 16th was a very special day for Antoine. He and his workers had succeeded in having all the canoes ready for the arrival of the regiment; this was the largest order they had ever managed to fill. He was relieved to learn that the military command had hired experienced militiamen to properly handle and maintain the canoes. These Canadians would also do much of the portaging during the coming campaigns.

Antoine and his workers watched as the militiamen and troops loaded their equipment and provisions, embarked, and paddled awkwardly toward Montréal in their new *canots-de-maître*. The people of the district cheered them on. Antoine and his workers celebrated the occasion with a cup of wine before straightening out and setting up their empty work and storage areas for the next military requisition.

Food shortages had become even more common in Nouvelle France with the increasing calls to militia duty and the rapid arrival of metropolitan troops, native allies and Acadian refugees in Québec, Trois Rivières, and Montréal.

The Ursulines of Trois Rivières reported that prices of flour, beef, egg, butter, and wine had risen beyond the means of the general population. This became especially critical for city-dwellers and villagers who could not grow their own food.

Intendant Bigot ordered food rationing while he and his partners bought farm produce at lower prices and sold at higher than what he recorded in the king's account. They partied and gambled some of their profit away in the Intendant's palace and invested the rest in overseas properties through a French associate.

Québec

Frequent arrivals and movements of regular soldiers and militiamen had already set off a series of epidemics in Nouvelle France. Two hundred eighty of the soldiers who had arrived on *Le Léopard* were hospitalized in Québec by mid-June.

One week later, twenty soldiers, fifty sailors, the ship's captain, surgeon, chaplain, and one domestic died from the pestilence. It spread quickly throughout the Saint Lawrence River valley by the end of the month. Autopsies in Québec finally identified the arrival of typhus in the colony.

Montréal

Montcalm, Lévis, Bougainville, and Bigot monitored reports from all three war fronts as guests of Lieutenant-Governor *Monsieur de Rigaud*. They could quickly dispatch forces from Montréal to any of the southern and western frontiers.

Native scouts reported at the end of June that 10,000 English soldiers were moving towards Fort Carillon. Vaudreuil sent *Troupes de Marine* to reinforce the battalions of *La Reine* and *Languedoc* who were already stationed there.

Lake Ontario

The Irish *Béarn* battalion was garrisoned in Niagara by the end of June while those of *Guyenne* and *La Sarre* guarded Fort Frontenac with the aid of the Canadian militia.

Governor Vaudreuil and General Montcalm agreed that French movement against Oswego could draw off some of the English force directed against Carillon and might even lead to seizure of the English fort if they acted promptly and quickly.

The governor dispatched Montcalm and Lévis to inspect the southern approaches to Lake Champlain and Montréal. The French general reluctantly complied and led the *Royal Roussillon* battalion to provide additional reinforcements at Carillon.

The two officers assessed the Richelieu River forts of Chambly and Saint-Jean, then moved on to Fort Saint-Frédéric at the southern end of Lake Champlain. Upon reaching farther south at Fort Carillon on July 3rd, Lévis scouted the two southern approaches from Fort William-Henry to Carillon and verified that the English were rapidly increasing their forces at the southern end of Lac Saint-Sacrement.

Captain Louis Coulon de Villiers' war parties had harassed and interfered with Bradstreet's deliveries of provisions to Oswego throughout the spring and into early summer. Governor Vaudreuil now made final preparations to seize the fort.

While English scouts focused their attention on the French general's presence south of Lake Champlain, *Monsieur de Rigaud* gathered 3,000 men at Fort Frontenac. His brother, the governor-general, planned to assign these troops under Montcalm's command to attack and destroy Oswego.

Vaudreuil secretly recalled Montcalm from Carillon, leaving 3,000 men under Lévis' command to repel any northward movement by the English. The marquis arrived in Montréal on July 19th to assemble his troops from Québec, and native allies from the far west. He and Bougainville left with this combined force two days later.

Rivière Saint-Jean

The Acadian refugees passed through a hilly region farther upriver. They spent a full day admiring the power and grandeur of Grand Falls, then moved northwest into the greater Madawaska region.

The river turned sharply to the southwest, but their guides led them onto an alternate Indian trail and headed northwest away from Rivière Saint-Jean. They moved along the western edge of Lac Temiscouata which was surrounded by mound-shaped, forested mountains. Early that afternoon, everyone stopped to rest, enjoy the view, and set up camp for the night.

Albany

John Campbell, Earl of Loudoun was several months overdue when he arrived in New York on July 23rd with wine, silverware, dinner plate and other essentials such as two secretaries, a surgeon, seventeen personal servants, including a maître d'hôtel, a valet de chambre, a cook, a groom, a coachman, a postilion, a footman, helpers, and two women, one of them his mistress. He also brought his own nineteen horses with their harness housings of green velvet and of black and gold, his traveling coach, his chariot, and his street coach.

The new commander-in-chief of British troops in North America ignored George Washington's advice and did nothing to fortify the western frontiers. He canceled Shirley's well-laid plans to seize Lake Ontario, and decided to concentrate all his forces against Fort Carillon in the Champlain valley.

Cabano

The Cormiers and the Cyrs followed the ancient trail along the western shore of Lac Témiscouata until they reached the small

Malécite village of Cabano where their guides were welcomed by their friends and relatives. Marguerite had the impression that they were close to the end of their long journey.

The natives celebrated the occasion with a special feast that night. There was much dancing and storytelling. The Malécite and Acadian children played together and Marguerite was amazed by their ease of communication with each other.

Lake Ontario

Montcalm and Bougainville arrived in Cataracoui on July 29th but did not lead their army south until after Engineer Léry had cut a road through the wilderness to ease the transport of artillery and supplies.

They reached Oswego on August 6th with 3500 French regulars, militiamen, and native allies. *Monsieur de Rigaud* arrived two days later with an advance force of 500 militiamen and warrior scouts. They landed their artillery the following day, and lined up their cannon battery on the 12th while 300 men dug the trenches.

Albany

That same day, a courier arrived from Oswego to warn Loudoun that Oswego was in imminent danger of falling. The earl belatedly dispatched Webb with the 44th regiment and some of Bradstreet's boatmen to Oswego. Both officers had been ready and waiting for orders to move against Carillon.

Oswego

The French besiegers moved their cannons closer to the wooden Fort Ontario on August 13th, prompting its 370-man English garrison to evacuate across the river to Fort Oswego during the night, increasing that garrison to 1700 men. This older fort consisted of rough stone walls and outer enclosure laid in clay in 1728.

The French fired a barrage from their twenty heavy cannons, including some that Braddock's army had abandoned on the battlefield of Monongahela. The cannonade breached the walls and killed the fort commandant, Colonel Mercer.

Monsieur de Rigaud's and Bougainville's men completely surrounded the old fort.

The English council of war advised Lieutenant Littlehales to yield. This officer signed the capitulation agreement at 11:00 p.m. on August 14th, five days after the French artillery had landed.

The English surrendered 1780 English prisoners of war including sailors, laborers and more than 100 women. The fort's inventory consisted of a great number of boats, over 100 pieces of light artillery, 23,000 pounds of gunpowder, 8,000 cannonballs, 1800 muskets, 2950 bullets, 1476 grenades, 450 bombs, enough provisions to supply an army for a campaign against Montrèal, and three wooden chests holding 18,000 English pounds sterling.

While the marquis supervised the demolition of all three forts and destroyed whatever military supplies his troops could not carry away, the western warriors tapped into the rum barrels and ran wild, as was their custom. Montcalm was disgusted by their rampage, yet was honor-bound to rescue their English captives with 10,000 livres of the king's money. In doing so, he unknowingly taught the warriors that the French would ransom the release of their captives.

Montcalm's successful siege secured the western access route to Montréal, decisively drove the English out of the Great Lakes area, and opened up the western frontier of New York to French invasion and raiding parties.

This decisive French victory, the destruction of the fort, and Montcalm's decision not to occupy the site deeply impressed the Iroquois and relieved their concern over Oswego's growing military posture on their land.

The event led the Six Nations to believe that the British would lose the war. Within two weeks after the fall of Oswego, the Iroquois promised to remain neutral toward Montréal.

New York

British Colonel Daniel Webb had scarcely reached the Great Carrying Place with the 44th Regiment and some of Bradstreet's boatmen when he first heard the shocking news that Oswego had fallen. Allied Mohawk scouts reported that French forces were advancing toward the province of New York with an army of 6,000.

The English had recently cleared Wood Creek to ease delivery of military supplies and other provisions to Oswego; Webb immediately ordered his axmen to block it again to impede French movement toward Carillon, Schenectady, and Albany. He destroyed Fort Wood Creek which had been recently completed and provisioned, and retreated down the Mohawk River to Albany.

Albany

The British commander-in-chief was in Albany, haggling over the purchase of provisions, when the only English fort on Lake Ontario fell to the French.

Loudoun now turned his attention to the English militias and announced the royal proclamation that all colonial officers and militas must serve under British command regardless of their provincial rank or enlistment agreement. Then he sent his subordinate, Lieutenant-Colonel Burton, to assess the state of preparedness and the quality of living conditions in the camps of the provincial forces.

These directives set off a long period of protest and political wrangling during which the British and provincial forces remained inactive. Neither problem would be resolved until late August, when Loudoun forced Winslow to submit to his orders or declare mutiny. The provincial officers heeded Shirley's counsel and chose to submit.

Europe

The Seven Years War officially began in Europe on August 29, 1756 when Frederic II of Prussia invaded the German state of Saxony. Prussia and Hanover were allies of Great Britain against Austria, Russia, Saxony, Spain, Sweden, and France.

Albany

Earl Loudoun held Shirley responsible for the loss of Oswego. He wrote a letter to the Bostonian on September 6th, accusing him of being totally useless in America and ordering him to leave immediately for London.

The Acadian migration

In early September, the Malécite guides delivered the Acadian families to Rivière-du-Loup, just 38 miles north of Lac Témiscouata. The women wept for joy upon reaching the lower Saint Lawrence River.

The men debated whether they should attempt to reach Québec or stay in this village through the winter. They decided to explore both possibilities by walking to the port of Cacouna, in a small nearby harbor that teemed with river traffic.

Representatives of the Cormier and Cyr families entered the local auberge to inquire about the possibility of hiring passage upriver on a sailing vessel for twenty family members. They learned that several chaloupes regularly plied the trade route between Cacouna and Québec, but space was limited because much of it was reserved for the cargo. Although the Cormiers had little money, they had collected fur skins to trade for such a purpose.

They asked if there was free land available for farming in the Saint Lawrence River valley.

They were told that although many Acadians had chosen to settle in and around Québec, the capital was plagued by famine, epidemics, overcrowding, greedy merchants, and desperation among a population in search of any means to feed their families.

Many refugees had already moved and settled farther up the river near Trois Rivières where there was a better chance of gaining a land concession. Others had also settled on Île d'Orléans, across the water from Québec.

The new arrivals asked if they could build winter cabins nearby.

They learned that land was freely available for well-built structures to be occupied one winter, then left to the landowner to rent out to other Acadian refugees.

The Cormiers concluded that with winter fast approaching, they should not attempt to explore upriver. They decided to settle in Rivière-du-Loup until the spring thaw, to build four cabins with clay fireplaces as they had done in Saint-Jean, to accommodate their three young families, Marguerite Cyr with her unmarried children.

A building site was available near Rivière-du-Loup, close to the river and forest so that they could fish and hunt for meat. They traded furs for flour and vegetables, and settled into their temporary homes by late September.

On October 2nd, two Acadian ships loaded with refugees from Miramichi and Île Saint-Jean sailed up the Saint Lawrence River to Île d'Orléans.

London - early December 1756

Despite his dislike for the man, King George II responded to the British Parliament's vote and named William Pitt as First Minister of Great Britain.

Pitt's views and policies were more focused than those of Newcastle's. He had gained popular backing for the war effort by publicly identifying France as his country's primary opponent, a position that won the support of the leading merchants and British population.

The new prime minister saw North America, rather than Europe, as essential to the creation of a great British empire, and was convinced that Great Britain could win the war in America but not in Europe. He planned to liberally subsidize King Frederic II and his Prussian army to handle the bulk of the conflict on the continent, while he focused British sea and land power against the French colonies in America.

William Pitt recognized Louisbourg as the center of the triangular trade between the West Indies, Nouvelle France, and France. He understood that the keys to capturing Nouvelle France were Québec and Montréal. He was confident that British seizures of Louisbourg and Québec would completely cut off Nouvelle France from its mother country and weaken its chances of survival.

Pitt's first directives were to the Earl of Loudoun in Albany, ordering him to cancel all other military campaign plans and concentrate his forces in Halifax, Nova Scotia in preparation for the seizure of Louisbourg.

CAST OF CHARACTERS

Bastien and Marguerite Manchon's children and grandchildren who appear in this sequel:

MADELEINE m. AUBIN MAUDOUX, 1676; migrated to Saint François-du-Lac near Montréal. He d. 1715; she d. 1731/Yamaska.

MARGUERITE m. ANTOINE COTTENOIRE, 1682; migrated to Île Dupas near Sorel, west of Lac Saint-Pierre. He d. 1731; she d. 1739.

LOUIS m. SIMONNE Massé, 1691; settled in Champlain; he d. 1725; she d. 11/5/1744. He d. 1769/Bécancour.

    JEAN-BAPTISTE (Belleville) m. Thérèse Dalberni in LA, 1721; she d. in LA, 1745; he d. in Bécancour 12/23/1749; childless.

    LOUIS *fils* m. Anne Leclerc, 1725; settled in Bécancour.

    JOSEPH m. Claire Rheault in 1728; maintained the family home in Champlain. He d. 1763.

    ANGÉLIQUE m. Baptiste Barette in 1728; settled in Champlain; m. Michel Bigot-Dorval, 1742. She d. 1/1/1758.

SÉBASTIEN *fils* m. MARIE-ANNE MASSÉ, 1694; migrated to Nicolet and Isle-de-la-Fourche; he d. 2/17/1739. She d. before 1735.

    MARGUERITE m. Montréal merchant JEAN GUILLON, 1720 in TR. She d. 1761; he d. 1769.

    JOSEPH m. LOUISE DESJORDY of Saint-Sulpice, 1749. Montréal merchant. He d. 1763.

    JEAN-BAPTISTE (Belleville) m. JEANNE LEFEBVRE *(seigneur's daughter)*, 1737 in Baie-du-Febvre. Settled on Isle-de-la-Fourche; he d. 9/8/1754.

    ALEXIS (Beaulorier) m. ANGÉLIQUE LEBLANC-LABRIE, 1/17/1735 in Bécancour; settled on Isle-de-la-Fourche; he d. 1779/Nicolet.

    SIMON (Villebrun) m. MADELEINE LEFEBVRE, 1734; *(seigneur's daughter)*; he d. 1771.

    CHARLES François (Villard) m. MARIE-JOSEPHTE JUTRAS, Nicolet 1739; he d. 1775 in Nicolet.

    RENÉ: voyageur, *hivernant*; d. in Montréal in 1765; unmarried.

CHARLES François Villard) m. MARIE-JOSEPHTE JUTRAS 1739 in Nicolet. He d. 1775 in Nicolet.

MADELEINE m. NICOLAS LEBLANC-LABRIE, 1/18,1735 in Nicolet.

Jean-FRANÇOIS (DUCHARME) m. MARGUERITE MOREAU, 1701; migrated to Bécancour. He d. 1734; she d. 1764.

CHARLOTTE d. 12/26/1733; unmarried, age 30.

MARIE-MARGUERITE m. in 1753 at age 48 to J-B GATIEN (widower). Lived in Baie-du-Febvre.

JEAN-BAPTISTE m. *seigneur's daughter,* JOSEPHTE LESIEUR in 1737. Lived in Yamachiche; d. 1761.

JOSEPHTE d. 2/15/1734; unmarried, age 25.

MAGDELEINE d. 4/15/1731 of *apoplexie,* age 19.

CHARLES m. MADELEINE DESROSIERS, 1748; d. 1751.

ANTOINE-Alexis m. at age 31 to ANGÉLIQUE HOULE, 1745.

ANNE d. 2/23/1742 at age 22; unmarried.

François-JOSEPH m. PELAGIE BELLEFEUILLE, 1755; d. 1804.

MONIQUE d. 7/20/1745 at age 18.

M-CATHERINE m. LOUIS MASSÉ, 1702; migrated to Bécancour.

BASTIEN and CATHERINE GUILLET's daughters who appear in this sequel:

JEANNE m. MÉDARD CARPENTIER, 11/18/1715. She d. at age 60 of *apoplexie* in Champlain, 1750.

MARIE-CATHERINE m. PIERRE BOURBEAU-VERVILLE, 1717. She d. 11/23/1745 in Bécancour at age 52.

MARIE MADELEINE m. FRANCOIS DIGUE (Didier) in Bécancour, 1734. She d. 5/18/1743 in Baie-du-Febvre at age 46.

Glossary

abatis. Originally a French word. Defensive obstacle formed by felled trees with sharpened branches facing the attackers.

arquebusier. Gunsmith.

Baie-Verte. Green Bay, Wisconsin.

banique. Traditional flatbread of Algonquin origin baked by the campfire. Consisted of cornmeal or whole wheat flour, oil, sugar, salt, dried berries, and water. High-caloric trail food that kept well during travel.

bec-d'âne. Mortise-chisel. Twibill.

billets-de-banque. Paper banknotes.

bousillage. Packing and sealing material that seals between adjoining wooden *pièces*. Consists of mud, clay, and various natural fibers.

campément. Overnight voyageur encampment.

Carillon. Ticonderoga, New York.

chaise. Sturdy horse-drawn carriage with a raised seat on springs suitable for the transportation of two passengers on the King's Highway. Since its driver (postilion) rode one of the harnessed horses, it offered its occupants front and side views of the countryside.

château: Feudal castle or fortress in Old France.

Chemin du Roi. King's Highway.

Chibouctou. Present-day Halifax, Nova Scotia and its bay.

Chedabouctou. Present-day Canso strait.

Chignectou. Isthmus connecting present-day Nova Scotia and New Brunswick. Located at the northern end of the Bay of Fundy.

coiffe flottante. White linen and lace headdress.

commissaire-ordonnnateur. Overseer of colonial income and finances. Subordinate to the intendant.

coq-gaulois. French rooster.

cordelles. Towing of partially loaded canoes against the current, often while struggling forward on foot in chest-deep water.

corps d'élite. Small force of specially selected troops.

décharge. Unloading of cargo from a canoe. May be partial when followed by a *cordelle.*

détroit. Strait. Narrow passage of water between two larger bodies of water.

douaire préciput. Surviving spouse's share drawn before the family disbursement of the estate.

douaire préfix. Monetary gift granted immediately upon marriage.

donation viagère. Parental grant of legal title to the family property to a son who, in return, will provide shelter and support for his parent(s) and other family dependents.

en censive. Land rent due on a certain date each year, payable to the seigneur who continues to own the land.

fièvre pourprée. Epidemic fever.

filles à la cassette. Marriageable young ladies from France immigrating to Louisiana under royal subsidy. Similar to, but later than *filles du roi.*

galerie. Roofed porch.

grand ménage. Spring cleaning.

grapeshot. Cluster of small iron balls shot from a cannon or musket.

grenier. Attic, corn-loft, grain-storage area.

haut-fourneau. Blast-furnace.

hivernant. Trading clerk or trader in the far west who did not return to Montréal for the winter.

Hôpital-général. Hospital and poorhouse.

Hôtel-Dieu. Hospital run by nursing sisters.

Île Saint-Jean. Prince Edward Island.

Île Royale. Cape Breton, including Louisbourg.

interdict: Roman Catholic ecclesiastical censure withdrawing most sacraments from a person, group, or district.

Lac Saint-Sacrement. Lake George, New York.

La Présentation. Ogdensburg, New York. Indian name: *Oswegatchie.*

lieue. league; 2.5 miles; linear measure.

mâchicoulis: Openings in a second floor overhang through which defenders can fire down against their attackers.

marguillier. Churchwarden. Parish councillor.

maringouins. Mosquitoes.

ma tante: Affectionate title of address for an aunt.

mouches noires. Black flies.

pemmican. Traditional native concentrated trail food. Colonial emergency rations.

petit déjeuner. Breakfast.

petite guerre. Guerilla warfare

pipes. Voyageur smoking breaks taken from paddling the canoe. Also a smoking pipe.

planches chevauchées. Manually-split clapboards.

pays d'en haut. 'Upper country'. Initially a reference to the Great Lakes area which was accessed upriver from Montréal. Later referred to all of the western territory.

postillion. Horseman who rode the left rear horse pulling a coach or post-chaise especially without a coachman. Originally referred to the driver of the mailcoach.

poteaux-en-terre. Palisade-style posts anchored in the ground, used in early colonial house construction.

poteaux-sur-soles. Posts on sills, used in house construction.

Renards. Fox Amerindians; also called *Outagamis*.

rivière Saint-Jean. Saint John River in present-day New Brunswick.

Saint-Domingue. Present-day Haiti.

souper. Evening meal.

travois. Simple native carrying device for dragging heavy loads over the forest trails. Consists of two trailing poles spanned by a canvas or leather sling to carry the load.

Troupes de Marine. Colonial regulars dispatched overseas by the French Minister of Marine.

Troupes de Terre. Metropolitan regulars controlled by the French Minister of War.

trunnel. 'Treenail'. Wooden peg used to firmly join two heavy timbers together through tenon and mortice

wattape. Fine spruce roots used to sew edges of birch bark together and bind the bark shell to the gunwales in canoe-making.